URRAM

rekindled hope

ALSO BY CHEYENNE VAN LANGEVELDE

BETWEEN TWO WORLDS

PRINCESS OF THE HIGHLANDS TRILOGY
DÌLSEACHD - A STOLEN CROWN #1

ALSO FEATURED IN

SEA AMONG STARS
THE STARS WEEP TOO

URRAM

REKINDLED HOPE

PRINCESS OF THE HIGHLANDS TRILOGY
BOOK TWO

CHEYENNE VAN LANGEVELDE

"Cheyenne is a master of combining history with rich narrative. Her characters come to life between her words, dragging you into a vivid, startling story."
~ NATHANIEL LUSCOMBE, AUTHOR OF *MOON SOUL*

"An encouraging tale of holding on to hope, having courage even at the world's darkest times, wrapped in the beauty of Scottish vibes."
~ OLIVIA CORNWELL, AUTHOR OF THE *REBEL EMPIRE DUOLOGY*

"*Dìlseachd* is a tale you'll want to read by a fireplace with a cozy blanket and a cup of tea. Beautifully written, inspiring, and oftentimes poetic, this story will leave you wanting more. Filled with hope, Cheyenne weaves a wonderful mix of adventure amidst loss and hardship."
~ ANNE ELIZABETH; AUTHOR OF *A WORLD WITHIN ROOTS, THE ROOTS TRILOGY #1*

"Like a legend one is told before a grand adventure, *Dìlseachd - A Stolen Crown* invites us beside a warm hearth opposite a wise and ancient storyteller. By the smoking embers we hear a solemn tale of great heart and courage; of heroes and villains; of light breaching the lording walls of darkness; of a name whispered with both reference and awe: Fiona McCurragh, Princess of the Highlands.

"Akin to a folktale, *Dìlseachd* immerses the reader in Scotland's heritage and her people. In the author's artistry of the written word, we live the haunting stories she pens until those two little words, "The End", let us grip reality once more. And yet, *Dìlseachd* doesn't leave you quite the same as you were when you began."
~ GOODREADS REVIEWER

TABLE OF CONTENTS

AUTHOR'S NOTE

IT is a truth universally acknowledged among any writers who have tried to write a sequel, that the middle books of a series are the hardest and most difficult to write, let alone edit. There were many times, particularly in the editing stage, when I wondered whether this book would ever be completed and worthy of being read by others. In the words of my editor, the middle book of a trilogy is challenging because you cannot begin a story—it has already begun—and you cannot write the ending. Threads must be picked up and left unwoven. But this story, battered by many rewrites and edits, is finally ready for you, dear reader.

I will not bore you with notes on how much changed from the initial draft. Only know that it is very different, but in a good way. This book went from barely a novel size (44K words) to an epic fantasy length of nearly 120K words by the time line edits were finished. *Urram ~ Rekindled Hope* is much larger than its predecessor, *Dìlseachd ~ A Stolen Crown*, but I hope the journey is just as enjoyable.

But before we begin this new adventure together, I have a few comments to make.

Firstly, if you have not read the previous instalment of the *Princess of the Highlands Trilogy*, I suggest you do so. This book naturally contains spoilers and many things will not make as much sense without having read the first book.

Secondly, as a reminder to any who may have forgotten (or didn't read the author's note in *Dìlseachd ~ A Stolen Crown*), this book is *not* a work of historical fiction. It is, one might say, a non-magical historical fantasy inspired by real events and a real era, or alternative history, or...a mediaeval period drama. Though set roughly in the Dark Ages of Scotland (around 800 A.D.), when Vikings and Saxons encroached on the land, and the Scots and Picts warred with one another, later uniting to overthrow the enemy, there are some things I have taken liberty with. Castles and plate armour exist, for instance, though those were not as we know them to be until a few centuries later. And there are other, more minor details that are not accurate to history. But for the sake of this story, I have written it as such. And, of course, none of the characters or events or places exist as I have written them.

Which then brings me to accents. I use Scots' English (or variations of it) to represent Scottish Gàidhlig. For the Lowlanders, it is not as thick as the Highlanders much farther to the north. Naturally, for those for whom it is a second language, it is even lighter or nonexistent. The Danes and the Cymry do not speak in accents at all among themselves, and the occasional word in their own language is slipped in—because, after all, I am the author and can make such choices.

Dìlseachd ~ A Stolen Crown is dearest to my heart out of all the books I've written, as I've often said. But this book, *Urram ~ Rekindled Hope*, is perhaps my favourite out of the entire trilogy. This story begins in spring, and it's a tale of change, of new growth, and, as the title foretells, of hope. The characters are not quite the same people we have left them, but for a little while, we can journey with them and see for ourselves what they have become. As Angus says, not all change is evil, and I hope you enjoy this new adventure just as much as you did the first one.

But I will not hold you back any further.

This tale has been a long time in coming.

Spring is finally coming for Scotland, and I cannot wait for you all to read about it.

Come. A princess searching for identity, a lad yearning for love, and others fighting for freedom are waiting for us.

~ The Author

P.S.

Whatever happens, know this: I absolutely despise tragedy.

PRONUNCIATION GUIDE

Most names in this book are of Scottish or Welsh origin, with a few Danish exceptions.
The pronunciation of trickier words and names are below.
Tip: a common sound in both languages is a soft guttural sound in the throat, marked by a ch. A c is almost always pronounced like a k, and a g as a hard g sound as in "get."

Asbjørn — ahs-b-yorn (rolled "r")
Annag — ahn-nugk
Cymraeg — come-rige
Cymreig — come-rayg
Cymru/Cymry — come-ree
Cynfael — kuhn-vile
Dafydd — day-vidth
Daibhidh — day-vee
Eachann — ae-chahn
Fionnuala — finn-oo-la
MacClydno — mac-klid-no
McCurragh — mic-kur-rah
Merwyn — mair-win
Nuith — noo-ith
Sioned — shee-on-nid
Urram — oo-rum

MAPS

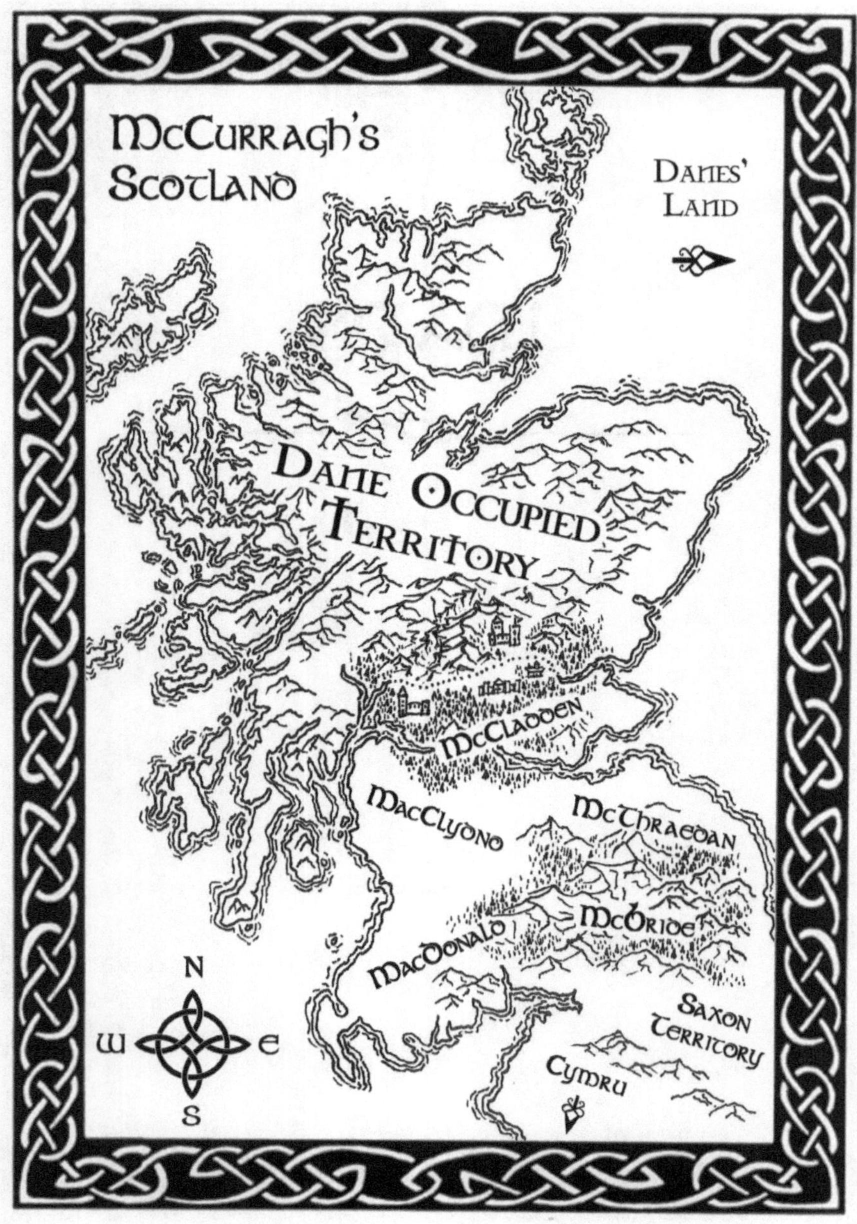

McCurragh's
Scotland
Danes'
Land
Dane Occupied
Territory
McCladden
MacClyono
McThraedan
MacDonald
McBride
Saxon
Territory
Cymru
N
W E
S

McCurragh's Scotland
Danes' Land
Danish Occupied Highlands
Caerloch
Glen of Tor-na-Cruithne
Drumdae Forest
An Dun
Caerdun
The Lowlands
Cymru
N

"A dream may be the best thing to die for."
~ Rosemary Sutcliff ~

~ PROLOGUE ~
A LOST BROTHERHOOD

VOICES rose and fell like the rolling waves of the ocean. But this surging boasted no sparkling waters beneath the sun. No, this sea was murky and grey, its depths dark and foreboding beneath a stormy sky.

Douglas McCurragh straightened in his hard-backed chair and blinked hard, resisting the urge to let his thoughts wander once again as a distraction from the dismal reports. As the heir to the Scottish throne, it was his rightful duty to be here and pay heed to what the High Chieftains had to say. One day, he might judge such matters himself. But it was none too thrilling to listen to gloomy reports of Danish attacks on the northern coasts.

For what youth liked to hear that his world was burning down around his ears?

The voices fell silent. The chieftains had finished their report, grim as it was, and now waited to hear what King Daibhidh had to say.

But the words never came.

The doors to the Great Hall of Caerloch Castle flew open, and in rushed a young lass with crimson curls that bounced with every step.

Douglas bit back a smile at seeing his little sister enter with no regard for the council. But his mirth quickly faded when he saw the grimace on his father's face, a shadow of pain and something far blacker.

Anger and bitterness was ever a stain marring what tenderness Daibhidh should have had towards his daughter. Even if she looked much like what his late wife, Fionnuala, might have as a wee lass, Douglas did not think it an excuse to show the coldness his father did. But he was not his father. And no one, not even the High Chieftains, dared to go against King Daibhidh, nor speak of his dead bride in his presence.

Not anymore.

"Father! Douglas! Ye should see—" Fiona McCurragh pulled up short, her freckled face blushing bright red upon realising she had interrupted an important council. The burning wave faded, leaving her creamy pale as she met her father's withering gaze.

Douglas winced as the light died in her green-gold eyes, her youthful spirit crushed once again.

The chieftains had greeted her with warm expressions, many of them having had young children of their own once upon a time, but at the king's stiff reaction, such amused looks dissolved into an uncomfortable silence.

"I am sorry, Father, I didnae realise—" the princess began, her voice painfully taut.

"Nae, ye never do," Daibhidh cut her off. Then he turned to Douglas. "Please take yer sister out and amuse her. I can finish this alone."

Douglas rose to his feet, swallowing the hurt and anger that stormed within him. He bowed his head towards the assembly before taking his sister's hand. Without a word, he led her gently out of the hall, down the corridors, and into the open courtyard.

The sweet spring air met their faces, warm and gusting, enlivening after the oppressive staleness of the Great Hall. Douglas inhaled deeply as he took his sister up to the battlements, where they could look out towards the moors from the confines of the castle. It was almost as good as being able to ride out towards freedom. But he dared not risk riding out today, not when his father might call him back at any time.

"I didnae ken Father was having a council," Fiona murmured, the first words spoken since she had attempted an apology to the king.

"'Tis all right. Ye werenae to ken. Father doesnae announce those things; the servants wouldnae hae kent, and if they had, they wouldnae hae told ye. Ye're too young to listen to them yet."

They came to a halt at the top of the wall. Fiona tucked a strand of hair behind her ear, her unruly curls staying put only a moment before the breeze tugged on it again.

"I donnae think Father would let me listen to the councils, even if I were old enough," she answered with a sigh.

Douglas had no reply to that. Finally, for lack of saying anything else, he said, "Well, ye are only eight. Perhaps when ye are my age, he might."

Fiona rolled her eyes, a smile spreading on her face. "Tha's seven years more!"

Douglas grinned.

"Wha' were they discussing anyway?" She flicked the hair out of her face, even though it kept blowing back, and looked at him intently.

"Danes hae been landing on our shores. No' jist sightings this time." He hesitated to go further. She was young yet. She did not need to know the ugliness of the world. Her innocence did not need to be destroyed before its time.

"Wha' does tha' mean? Are they trying to invade us then, like in the songs tha' harpers tell of other people? Will there be a war?"

Douglas blinked. "I donnae ken."

"How else will the Danes gae away? I donnae think they'll gae if we jist ask nicely, no' if they're anything like Guern." She shuddered involuntarily.

He stifled a chuckle at the thought of the kitchen boy who teased his sister unmercifully. Douglas naturally defended Fiona, but sometimes Guern's pranks really were quite funny. "Nae, they might try to make treaties first. I donnae ken if it will come to war." Except he did, considering the chieftains' words. If his father kept one thing from the days before Fionnuala's death, it was his passion for Scotland and her defence.

"If there is a war," Fiona continued, looking at the moorland beneath the fitful spring sun, "would ye gae to fight in it?"

"Aye, I would. 'Twould be an honour to defend my country." The words rolled easily off his tongue—it was the expected answer after all—but he did not feel them as strongly in his heart. What was Scotland anyway? A broken kingdom whose clans were drifting further and further apart? Was there anything left worth saving? And then he glanced down at his beloved sister and his doubt faded. *She* was worth saving, even if there was no Scotland left.

Fiona frowned, and not just from squinting against the sunlight that shone blindingly for a moment. "I donnae like war."

"Ye hae ne'er even lived through one! How would ye ken?" he sputtered, trying to make light of a matter that was not light at all.

"The harpers sing of them, like tha' harper last night, the one all the way from Cymru. Rhiada was his name, right?" At her brother's nod, she continued, "I think wars are awful things. They kill people."

Douglas bit his lip, thinking hard. "Wars donnae kill people. People kill people. War is jist another excuse fer them to do it."

"Aye, well, if ye went to war, ye might die." Her mournful expression destroyed any conviction he had to brush aside the sobriety of the situation with an easy laugh.

"No' everyone dies in war."

"Nae, but no' everyone lives either." The sun passed behind a silver cloud, and the castle was thrown into gloom. "If I were to lose ye, I wouldnae hae any friends left," she finished.

Douglas was silent. There was nothing to say to that. Both of them knew it to be true. For certain, there were a few servants who doted on her, but beyond that, most of them did not speak to her. And their father—oh, their father—he did not love her. Everyone could see that. No, if Douglas went away to war and did not come back, she would be left utterly alone.

But to choose between Scotland and his sister? Was it even a fair comparison? And yet, by defending Scotland, he was defending his sister. Perhaps the choice was not so vastly different, after all.

"We might no' e'en gae to war," he finally said. "Father might command it, but the chieftains might disagree."

"Why? Do they no' want to remain free?"

Douglas sighed heavily. Why did life have to be so complicated? Was nothing ever simple? "I donnae ken. I jist ken some of them disagree wi' how Father has become since Mother died. And other things tha' even I donnae understand. Scotland was once united, but wi' the way Father has become..." His voice trailed off.

"Are ye afraid we might hae civil war?" she prompted after a moment.

Douglas was silent. She surprised him, sometimes, with her swiftness in thought.

The wind sighed between them as he struggled for an answer to a question he feared to understand.

"I donnae ken. Scotland was once strong and thriving, but now? I fear tha' the dream fer such a brotherhood has faded, lost to our distant past. Even if we unite against the Danes, it may no' be enough. Wi' Mother's death and the way the clans hae become so distant and distrusting of Father's decrees, we may be beyond reconciliation. At least, as long as Father remains the way he is..." He forced a grin to his lips. His sister did not need to have the fears he did. "Then again, perhaps I am becoming too cautious. We may be all right in the end. We may reunite and be as we once were before. Father may yet change; nae one is beyond tha'." *Except in death*, said a voice in his mind, but he ignored it.

Fiona smiled back. "I hope so," she replied, her voice soft. But it was not the softness of the spring breeze. This softness was full of pain and fear, the likes of which she should not suffer so young. This softness was how she often spoke of their father, and the thought chilled him.

"Come," he said, offering her his hand. "Let's gae see the horses."

She grinned, the sparkle returning to her eyes, and followed him down to the stables with a lightness in her step that had not been there before.

Douglas buried his fears in the joy of her happiness. Perhaps hope yet lived.

∾ 1 ∾

TOMORROW'S DAWN

GREY and formless clouds hung like billowing shadows from the heavens. Bright bluebells, creamy snowdrops, and golden gorse dotted the verdant moorlands outside Caerdun Castle. The air blew cold about the towering stone walls, but not bitterly so, bringing with it a sweetened hint of the coming spring.

Fiona McCurragh stepped quickly through the arched entrance of Caerdun, ignoring the black murder holes and the sharpened tips of the portcullis above her, grim reminders of the castle's defences. But they did not frighten her like the ones she had been accustomed to at Caerloch.

These were meant for her protection, not her destruction.

Rolling her tense shoulders, Fiona sighed, glad that practice was finally over; the peace and quiet of her room, as simple as it was, had never seemed more inviting. She shifted her bow from one hand to the next as she passed the guardhouse, loosening her quiver strap. Her arm was sore from the bowstring snapping against it a few times during the archery drills, which everyone who was able had attended.

The treaty with Lord Erland and Lady Nuith signed two years ago had not made for an easy peace. The Lowlanders had heard reports of the Danes searching every village and castle for the High Chieftains and their princess last spring and into the autumn, but they had not yet come here. Fiona prayed they never would—there were so few hiding places left.

She stepped into the main courtyard, which, as usual in a place of this much importance and size, bustled with activity.

Men in chainmail and leather armour entered through the archway, and stable hands rushed to take their steeds. Fiona noted the mud streaking the mounts' flanks from the practice fields, where the men had ridden through obstacles such as fire and the clashing of swords while wielding their own weapons. For should the Scots ever go to war again, they would need every fighter they could get.

Upon the stone battlements, men-at-arms leaned on their spears as they watched the horizon for any coming stranger or host, whether it be the Danes or perhaps the Scottish embassy returning from Cymru, for whom they had waited a year with no news. Annag Mc-Cladden had sent a courier soon after they had arrived in An Dùn to let her husband know of their safety, and that the High Chieftain Jamie McBride's young widow was staying with them, but they never received a reply, even if not expected. Though the distance was too great to waste another messenger, Fiona often wondered whether the request for an alliance had been accepted. The Lowland Scots had too few men left after the last war to carry on the fight for freedom alone, and the Danes were merciless in their pursuit of total control over Scotland.

Fiona wove her way between the many people walking about the courtyard, returning greetings and waving in particular to Elspeth McBride, who gave a shy smile in return. To anyone else, it may have appeared like a mirror, two young women of similar likeness waving at their reflections. But Elspeth was the High Chieftain Jamie's widow with two young children, and the griefs of the past year made her appear far older than her one and twenty years.

A sudden gust of wind rushed through the place, ruffling the horses' manes and tossing about Fiona's flaming curls. She pulled the folds of her worn, pine-green cloak against the chill that lingered at the beginning of spring, and entered the keep inside the castle walls.

Fiona passed the Feast Hall, whose doors were open, a wave of warmth blowing into the corridor from the large hearth fire. The heat warmed her numb fingers for a moment before the draughty air took its place again as she passed on.

Though only a High Chieftain's residency and not the capital of Scotland, Caerdun was in many ways far grander than Caerloch in the Highlands, and she did not miss her old prison. What few good memories she had in that place had been lost with her brother's death in the first war against the Danes. She would be happy enough to never set foot within its walls again, even if she someday did indeed reclaim her throne. A bitter taste filled her mouth; any other place would feel strange to call home, but Caerloch had far too many painful memories.

Fiona thrust the thought away and continued down the hall, her footsteps ringing on cold stone. Turning a corner, she reached the southwest tower and opened the door, ascending the spiralling stairs to her own chambers on the second floor.

Closing the door behind her, she put away her bow and quiver and hung up her cloak. Then she collapsed onto her bed, her hands locked together over her eyes as she took steady breaths. At last, she could rest in peace.

But then the memories came rushing back.

Memories of this same spring breeze last year when she had bidden farewell to Angus and Malcolm—the only friends she had left; of the tense, humid summer in which the Danes almost found her; a message from Lady Nuith threatening war if they did not surrender the Lowlander chieftains and provide proof of the Scottish princess' death...proof that was given in the form of a much-worn McCurragh tartan. Whether the Danes believed her truly dead or not, war had not yet happened and Fiona was still safe. All the same, the danger remained, lurking in the hidden shadows, creeping in when the sun went down; and there were few friends to calm her fears. Those that had comforted her before were long gone, far beyond the mountains.

She exhaled sharply, her chest throbbing with bitter homesickness. Except she did not long for home; she longed for those that made any place so. She had not minded their presence being gone in the first few months because she knew their going was necessary, and besides—the sooner they left, the sooner they would return. But when months had gone by with no news, she began to worry if anything had happened to them, or whether she would see them again.

The window shutters banged against the wall, driving Fiona's unresolved thoughts back into the recesses of her mind.

She sat up, groaning. "Ye donnae seem to want me to rest either, do ye?" she complained to the wind as she rose, intending to shut the window. Yet she hesitated, gazing into the distance at the mist-en-shrouded and desolate moorlands, where she saw a horseman riding at full speed. He came from the southwest road that wound towards the village outside the castle walls. Rarely did Caerdun have a visitor—let alone from that direction—and her pulse raced faster for a moment in spite of herself.

A sense of fate weighed down upon her as she watched the rider draw closer. Even from this distance, she easily recognised the kilt and plaid that marked him as a Scot and not a Dane; none of them would have dared to dress so. Besides, the Danes would not come from the south.

The desire that she had kept inside her all this time surged upwards, and she left her room in great haste.

Messengers came so seldom. Perhaps they brought news of the Scottish embassy. And oh, what if it was Chieftain McCladden himself! Or Angus—

Her breath caught in her throat. Yet her mind said otherwise. The chieftain would be leading his men, not travelling alone. It could be Angus, perhaps, or even Malcolm, but the chances of that were very small. She tried to quench the joyful flame inside her with bitter desperation. It could not be them. After so long of silent waiting, it was impossible. It would be a mere messenger, perhaps from one of the other Lowland clans, not those that had gone south, not those she missed so dearly.

But oh, what if it was!

Fiona raced down the tower steps, returning the way she had come some minutes before, pausing now and then to look for Annag McCladden, who governed her husband's province in his absence. Though quiet in her own way, much like her son Angus, she was a great source of encouragement to Fiona. She greatly appreciated having her earnest and honest council since, in many ways, she had taken Rhiada's place when the harper had died and the Scots had departed for Cymru.

If a messenger had indeed come, Annag would know of it, as well as any news he might bring.

Fiona sighed in frustration as she passed several rooms and found no sign of the one she was searching for. She paused and then smacked her forehead. If a messenger had arrived, Annag would be in the Council Chamber to speak with him. *Why did I no' check there first?*

Gathering her skirts in her hands, she ran up the steps and turned left, entering the Hall while a man clothed in mud-bespattered garments passed her as he exited and headed, presumably, for the kitchens.

She did not recognise the man, and he gave her no greeting. It was none of the ones she had wished to see, after all. The lightness within Fiona's chest dissipated like a winter sunset.

Annag was the only one left in the Hall, standing with her back to the doorway. Light spilled in through the thin windows near the ceiling, any remaining shadows thrust into the corners by the peat fire on the hearth.

It was peacefully quiet, unlike the slowing hammering of Fiona's heartbeat. She stepped softly across the room, but her footsteps still echoed, far too loud in her own ears.

Annag turned around as Fiona drew near, a dimpled smile brightening her ageing face, light sparkling in her hazel eyes. "Princess, who do ye suppose tha' man was?"

"I hae nae idea," Fiona answered, attempting to sound light-hearted despite the bitter disappointment weighing down on her shoulders. She clenched and unclenched her fingers, waiting for Annag to continue, fear and longing racing through her veins.

Annag's eyes flashed with exuberant joy, the likes of which Fiona had rarely seen before. "He is one of the men who went wi' the escort a year ago."

Fiona's heart stopped for a moment. "Hae they returned, then?" she asked breathlessly, the blood rushing to her face in excitement.

"Aye, they are on their way." Annag's smile lit up her entire face, as if she too could scarcely believe the good news.

"When will they be here?" Fiona asked before another moment passed. Her throat tightened with intense emotion, and she struggled against the tears of joy that sprang to her eyes. They were coming home! At long last, they were coming home!

"My husband and sons will be here by tomorrow's dawn. The rest will arrive close behind them if the weather holds."

Fiona was about to answer when she remembered something, and her smile faded, cold dread taking the place of the warm elation that had filled her only seconds before. "Did he say how the treaties went?"

The light in Annag's eyes darkened. "Nae, he didnae. I suppose Donald wants to tell us himself tomorrow." Her tone was grave now. Grave and sad, as if she shared Fiona's fear that the worst had happened. If the alliance had failed, then there was little hope for freedom left. The Scots were not strong enough alone, and this had been their last chance.

Och, Rhiada, at least we tried....

Fiona glanced down at the floor beneath her feet, its stone thinly covered in herb-strewn rushes. She was afraid to lift her eyes and see her own fear reflected in Annag's gaze. Such a small flame of courage, and yet it had seen them through the loneliness of the last year. But for what? Had it all been for nothing?

Annag reached forward and gently lifted Fiona's chin with her hand, determination etched in her set mouth. "Donnae worry, princess, about things we donnae ken. Jist think about Angus and Malcolm and how soon ye'll see them," she added with a twinkle in her eyes.

Fiona's cheeks burned, but she could not stop the happiness that spread across her face. Nodding in agreement, she turned away and left the hall, a smile still playing on her lips as she ascended the stairs to the tower and walked onto the battlements.

The wind tousled her hair playfully, kissing her cheeks in warm welcome. She gazed south, looking out towards the hills, misty in the distance, and the road that wound between them, the road that they would soon be travelling on.

Tomorrow's dawn...and then they will be here. At long last, they will be here.

She could hardly believe it. After waiting for so long, it seemed so sudden now. Would Angus and Malcolm have changed much in the last year? Though surely they had grown in the year since she had last seen them, she could not picture them other than the two boys they had been. She knew *she* had changed, and that beyond simply growing taller. Would they remember her? Or had they made new friendships and brotherhoods, and left her far behind?

She thought of their parting last spring, of Malcolm's teasing kiss and Angus' reluctance to let her go. Surely bonds so strong would last a parting of this length, would they not?

She closed her eyes tightly for a moment against the emotions warring in her heart: the excitement of seeing them again and yet trepidation of how they might receive her. Annag was right. Thinking about such things would not change them, nor would it bring tomorrow any closer. She would have to wait to learn of what had become of them, as well as whether her dear, departed mentor Rhiada's last wishes had come true.

But she did not like to think of that, to think that such sacrifice might end in failure. So instead, she thrust aside the thoughts of fear and added to the songlike words singing in her mind, *Angus and Malcolm will come home.*

Fiona could not stop smiling.

The sun set over a land blooming to life. Scarlet and saffron melded in the skies, touching the clouds with pink and casting long shadows over the verdant moors. The evening breeze soughed softly among the grasses, a peaceful sound soon disturbed by the shouts and laughter of men and the neighing and stamping of many horses.

"I hae missed our sunsets," Malcolm McCladden announced grandly, watching the light fade behind the distant hills, his hands spread wide as if he had summoned the beautiful display all on his own.

"Aye, well, ye could watch it better if ye finished setting the picket lines first," his friend Merwyn retorted in broken Gàidhlig with a laugh. He muttered something else in his native Cymraeg tongue under his breath.

"My brother never works when he can enjoy himself and hae others do the work fer him," Angus McCladden added, driving home the last stake into the ground and tying the leather cord around it securely.

"Aye, I learned tha' much in the past year." Merwyn snorted and shook his head.

Malcolm turned around to face them, the sun behind him striking his copper hair into flames, his hands resting on his hips in defiance. "Donnae deny it, Angus, I ken ye're glad to be back home too."

Angus met his gaze, thinking of the past thirteen months' enduring loneliness despite new friends, and a wave of longing swept over him. "Aye, I am. But we're no' home jist yet." He walked back to the main encampment where fires were being kindled and food prepared for the evening meal.

"We will be tomorrow," Malcolm replied, Merwyn following them slowly. "And then we can see Mother and Fiona. I wonder if she's grown at all."

"Ye mean like ye hae?" Merwyn interjected.

Malcolm laughed loudly, causing a few heads to turn their way. "Och, she was taller than me then! If she still is, I'm gang to eat all the oatcakes and at least be fatter than her. She cannae outdo me in everything."

"Who said it was a competition?" his friend replied, confused.

Angus hitched a shoulder in a shrug. "Malcolm can make anything into a competition."

"Including the princess?" Merwyn continued.

Angus' face burned in something akin to embarrassment and he looked out over the growing twilight, seeing the beacons of firelight glowing brightly. "She is above mere competition," was all he said.

The three of them were handed some barley bannock from one of the men preparing the evening meal, and Malcolm ate half of it in one bite, making a face as he did so.

"I think I'm most looking forward to eating Mother's oatcakes," he said. "This stuff is awful."

"Her food had better be as good as ye say it is," Merwyn commented, "else I might hae to fight ye on this. I donnae think this sort is half as bad as ye claim."

Angus did not hear whatever Malcolm said in reply. His mind was elsewhere. Malcolm may have missed their mother's food more than anything, but Angus had missed Fiona McCurragh far more.

The princess was indeed above trivial things like competition. She was the hope they had for fighting this whole war, and the one thing that had kept him going when he thought all was lost.

Angus stepped away from the firelight. Thirteen months, twelve days since he had last seen her. He wondered whether she even remembered him, or whether in the time that had passed she had moved on, made new friends, perhaps even fallen in love with a lad—someone at Caerdun or another of the clansmen.

He clenched his jaw at the thought. But of course, that was the natural way of things. People did not remain as one left them. They too moved on, grew up, experienced life. No one ever stayed the same.

Then again, she was the princess and heir to her stolen throne. She could not just marry whomever she pleased. She had obligations to fulfil, and she was young yet. When she married, the choice would have to be approved by all the clans. Surely his father would have received some sort of news had such a thing occurred.

But they had been in Cymru for so long. Such news might not have been sent to them because of the distance. Did Scotland think of them as a lost cause?

Angus shook his head like a horse beset by flies, trying to dive away the entangled thoughts. They would find out on the morrow. Then he would see her.

His chest tightened, and he drew in a sharp breath.

Over a year, and he remembered their parting as easily as if it had been that morning. For certain, some things had faded, such as the faces and the sound of their voices. But he remembered well how tightly the princess had embraced him and how it had stung to know it would be a long time before he saw her again. She who knew his deepest fears and yet had never mocked him nor turned him away. She who had seen him at his worst and still offered her friendship.

And he had given her his heart.

He did not know whether she felt the same, whether their friendship was sweetened by an affection much deeper. He had never had the chance to ask her—he had been too afraid, too uncertain of his own feelings. But he knew now, and while he trembled at the thought of seeing her again and seeing her changed from how he remembered her, his heart beat faster at knowing he would soon be with her.

Should she reject him for another, he would always care for her, even if at a distance.

Angus knelt and plucked a sprig of heather that would not bloom for some months yet, holding it gently in his hand as the evening stars pierced the twilight with their wan, glistening light. Behind him, the cooking fires were built and most were eating the evening meal. He would have to join them soon or else risk his friends searching for him once their tasks were done.

He fingered the sprig, so young, so fragile, and kissed it softly before tucking it into his dead brother's clan pin beneath his plaid.

Tomorrow. Only a morn away.

He smiled in spite of himself. Even as just friends, he had missed her dearly. It would be good indeed to see her again.

He turned away from the remnants of the dying daylight and returned to camp.

The next time he saw the sun, they would be home.

~ 2 ~
AT LONG LAST

MISTY swaths of fog lay about the castle walls, hiding the ground beneath its silvery mantle. The eastern horizon paled with dove's gold, a few low-lying clouds resting on the shoulders of the rising dawn. No wind stirred upon the battlements. It seemed as though the whole world held its breath, as if knowing what was to come that day.

Fiona rose early that morning, taking more care than usual to plait her unruly crimson curls out of her face and smooth the wrinkles in her green and ivory woollen dress. She arrayed her McCurragh plaid over her left shoulder, stabbing home her silver clan pin with a delicate boat engraved on it. She hesitated, glancing at her murky reflection in the piece of polished bronze hanging upon the wall. Her brother's pin, its metal smoothed from many years of holding it in her hands during the darker moments in her life, lay on the small table before her. She almost always wore it beneath her plaid, but today... Something in her desired to let go of the past and face the future without clinging to old memories and faded dreams.

Fiona stood back, leaving the pin on the table. She had made up her mind. She walked over to the window and peered out at the misted world touched with amber and waking with the sun. A surge of excitement and nervousness rose up within her, as it had at random moments ever since the messenger had come yesterday. Her thoughts raced and ran into themselves, only one thing standing clear against the emotions racking her consciousness.

They will be here today after so long!

She wondered again what Angus and Malcolm would think of her now, whether they would even recognise her from the young lass she had been. Would they even want to maintain their friendship with her, strained by a year's silence? Or had their new acquaintances, which they surely had acquired, become more desirable? Even if she was the princess, it was rare that lads would be good companions to lasses, even if they had been her bodyguards at one time.

Sighing deeply, she turned and walked out of her room, headed for the Great Hall to break her fast.

Fiona met Annag there, eating with the rest who were up at sunrise. Sitting down among them, she listened absent-mindedly to the conversations taking place around her—mostly servants' gossip—but did not take part. Her mind buzzed with anticipation of what was to come that day and she swallowed her porridge with great difficulty, her throat tight with uncertain eagerness.

Occasionally she smiled at the two wee bairns sitting at the end of the table, who had to have their mother Elspeth's help to ensure their porridge actually reached their mouths and did not end up on the table, on their clothes, or flung at each other. Lilybet, who was little more than an infant, and Ranald, who was only a couple years older, were the youngest inhabitants at Caerdun. Unlike the other women at this table, Elspeth did not speak save to her two children, her voice low and murmuring.

Fiona tried to catch her gaze with a friendly expression, like she always tried to, but Elspeth did not seem to notice. However, considering how occupied she was with her bairns, Fiona did not count it against her. Not everyone had something so potentially joyful to look forward to this day like Fiona did. She pitied Elspeth, so young and so lonely, but Elspeth was not the sort of person to beg for sympathy. Whatever grief she suffered, she suffered in private. Aside from her quiet shyness, Fiona did not know what best to make of her, doubt sometimes whispering in the back of her mind that maybe Elspeth remained distant because Jamie died in her name. She could only try to be a friend, which Annag had told her Elspeth much appreciated, even if she had not found the courage to say so herself. After all, it had only been a year since Fiona had seen through the veil of another's pain, and Elspeth was quite different from that other blue-eyed and dark-haired soul.

Having finished her porridge, Annag rose to her feet and gave orders to several of the women there before exiting the hall, headed to her other duties. No sense in standing idle while they waited for the embassy to arrive.

Fiona left the hall after breakfast as well, the rafters falling silent as the women left it until luncheon. The expectant quiet that remained was peaceful, disturbed only by distant echoes drifting from other parts of the castle through the open door. Fiona wondered a moment how much louder this hall might become this evening if Chieftain McCladden truly returned. If Malcolm were with them, the sound would indeed increase, but she doubted anyone would mind that for the joy of seeing them again. And hearing Angus' voice again...

She blushed in spite of herself as she climbed the stairs to the second floor and continued down the corridor. She was a daft lass to flush so easily, and all for what? Surely it was only that she was overcome with excitement and nothing more. She was a princess, and not a silly maiden who daydreamed the working hours away.

Pushing aside her thoughts, though expectancy hummed ever at the recesses of her mind, she entered another room whose windows faced the main courtyard, the cheerful daylight streaming in. Already there were a couple lasses seated by the fire or the windows, busy with mending or sewing clothes. Fiona smiled when she saw Elspeth among them, her bairns being watched by an older woman who cared for them while their mother laboured.

Fiona was greeted by a shy wave and was satisfied. She crossed the room and sat down at a loom where an unfinished tapestry lay half-woven, the vibrant colours already speaking of stories and songs waiting to be canonised into legend. She slid the shuttle back and forth, a rhythm that was peaceful and almost musical despite having no melody. The sweet sound of harp trickled into her mind at the thought, but oh, she had not practised properly in ages. Preparing for war had taken the place of such things for now.

Strand by strand, the weaving proceeded on from where she had ceased it yesterday, a banner slowly shaping beneath her hands. Whether or not it would be used in battle during the coming months remained to be seen, even though Annag had taught Fiona the art of weaving so that she could fashion this pennant herself: a princess' ensign to be carried into war by her warriors. And while she dreaded the thought of more loss and bloodshed, she felt they needed this, that this endeavour to seek allies had not been for naught. Surely everything had a purpose, did it not?

Her hands came to a halt on the loom for a moment. Try as she might to think of other, ordinary things, like whether she would be able to play with Elspeth's bairns after luncheon, or whether archery might be set aside today for practising horsemanship only, her mind always returned to the homecoming McCladdens. Her pulse raced every time her mind brushed against the subject, and she attempted in vain to keep her trembling hands steady.

After an hour or so had passed in such turmoil and slow progress, she laid the shuttle aside with a sigh of frustration. She could not stand the waiting anymore. However longer it must be, she could not endure it merely sitting here.

Rising to her feet, she left the room to find Annag, whom she had not seen since breakfast. Annag usually came to help with the weaving or knitting when her other duties were done, which were usually accomplished by this hour. But perhaps she was overseeing preparations in light of the coming host; or, perhaps, like Fiona, the anticipation made doing ordinary things a challenge.

Searching for Annag to no avail, first in the Great Hall and then in the Council Chamber, Fiona went outside into the courtyard, halting in surprise at the warmth of the wind, quite different from yesterday. The fresh scent of heather wafted up from the rooms near the ground where the washing of clothes was being done. Fiona inhaled deeply as the delightful spring wind carried the smell of herbs mixed with the woodsmoke from the forge to her senses. The gentle breeze played with the curls hanging about her face, and the young princess hummed a strathspey to herself as she walked across the cobblestone courtyard, greeting various servants as she passed by them.

At last, she found Annag talking with the guards at the gate. Hurrying to her, Fiona stopped when she saw the broad smile on Annag McCladden's face.

"Wha' is it?" Fiona asked, her breath catching in her throat. Had the Scots arrived already? Had she missed them?

"Alan here says that his son, Rhiseart, caught sight of Donald and my sons when he was out riding. He signalled to his father from the first hill jist beyond the castle."

"When will they be here?" Fiona questioned almost before Annag finished her sentence. She could hardly keep the excitement out of her own voice.

"Any moment now, and they will be o'er the hill. Come to the wall wi' me and we shall see them." She grabbed Fiona's hand and pulled her up the stairs to the battlements, where they shaded their eyes against the bright, cheery sunlight, gazing at the road winding south in hopes of catching a glimpse of the returning men.

A few minutes later, a trio of horsemen crested the hill and sped on down towards the beaten trackway leading to the outer defences.

Annag squeezed Fiona's hand as the three forms drew gradually closer.

Fiona's heart jumped into her throat, nearly choking her. Nervousness shot through her veins, a painful tingling that stung her fingers. She slipped her hand out of Annag's and stepped away from the wall, feeling almost sick. The thought of finally seeing her dear friends again suddenly seemed too much to bear. What if she did not recognise them? What if they did not miss her as she had them? What if they no longer cared for her company, and all this expectation was for nothing?

"Wha' is it?" Annag asked softly in a tender voice, turning towards her with concern.

"I...I donnae think I can bear meeting them here." Fiona shut her eyes tightly for a moment, concentrating on the heather breeze and not on the twisting in her stomach. Perhaps she should not have eaten breakfast at all.

"Why is tha', pray?"

"I donnae ken. Mayhaps 'tis because I wish to meet them without others looking on." She did not want other witnesses to her confusion and dismay if Angus and Malcolm did not desire to see her again. She did not want castle inhabitants and who else to see her disappointment and shame. "Besides, I am sure ye want to greet yer family first as well," Fiona added, forcing a smile to her face.

"Are ye sure ye donnae want to meet them wi' me? I thought ye missed them so." There was a kindly twinkle in her hazel eyes.

Fiona nodded. "Aye...I'd rather meet them after the first wave of excitement has passed. I supposed I hae missed them so much the thought of truly seeing them again fills me wi' a sort of terror.... I donnae want the entire courtyard to be watching. I might cry, and then Malcolm will ne'er let me forget it." She tried to laugh, but it was breathy and hardly anything at all.

"Well then, I suppose there is nae holding ye back." Annag smiled in return, resting her hand on Fiona's shoulder for a moment in encouragement. "Where will ye be? I'm sure they will ask."

"In the gardens beyond the inner gate."

"I will tell them so."

Fiona gave a quick, timid dip of her head in farewell and turned away. Swiftly making her way down the stairs and out the innermost gate, she headed for the small gardens. She cast a glance over her shoulder, seeing Annag still upon the battlements, hearing the hoofbeats and faint shouts of greeting from the guardsmen—for the garden muffled much—and watched as Annag disappeared to run down to the courtyard and greet them. Even from this distance, she could note the grin of widespread, pure joy, the raw emotion that rarely graced the resolute woman.

Her heart skipped a beat and she turned away, walking farther from the gates.

Fiona waited for what seemed like an eternity in the gardens, her back to the entrance as she slowly walked farther and farther away from the gate. The muddy beds boasted green shoots thrusting up through the dark soil amid the pearly snowdrops already in flower, promising a beautiful blooming yet to come in the warmer months. Because the gardens were behind the castle, she did not hear anything going on inside the courtyard. Whatever noise there might be was muted by stone walls. The silence, broken only by the whispering wind and the sweet, trilling songs of the birds, became unbearable.

She took long breaths in a vain attempt to calm herself. Her hands trembled with nerves, no matter how she clenched and unclenched them. Surely they should have come through the gates and greeted Annag by now! Were they not to come and see her after all?

Fiona was about to head back when she heard the sounds of gravel crunching beneath someone's feet, growing louder, coming nearer. She knew that stride. Her chest tightened. Yet she did not turn around. She was afraid of what she might see, of how different he might look.

The footsteps stopped. She could almost feel the warmth of his presence behind her and her skin prickled at the thought, everything in her longing to turn around—and everything in her terrified to do so.

"Fiona?" The voice was deeper than she remembered but still had the same gentleness that she loved and had dreamt of ever since he had gone away thirteen months ago. The question was spoken in cautious bewilderment, as if her hesitation made him unsure of whether he had found the right lass.

She could not handle the waiting any longer. She spun around on her heel and then stopped, gaping at the Angus McCladden standing before her.

He stood at least six inches taller than she was, but it was not his height alone that caused her surprise. The scrawny boy from a year ago had changed. His shoulders had broadened and his once stick-thin body now filled out his linen shirt, though he took after the leaner frame of his mother. His piercing blue eyes still startled her, as perhaps they always would, but the rest of his face retained its boyishness, though manhood chiselled itself there in sharp outlines she did not remember seeing before.

She met his gaze at last, and an uncontrollable blush burned her cheeks. She exhaled deeply, tension slipping away from her shoulders, watching him as he stared at her, his mouth partly open in surprise.

"Fiona," he repeated, this time almost whispering it in awe as a smile spread across his face. Scarlet touched his pale face for a moment as if embarrassed at the silence between them, or perhaps it was something else entirely...

She grinned, her throat tightening with exuberant, repressed emotion. "Angus!" she cried, taking a step forward and flinging her arms about his neck. "'Tis been so long!"

"Aye, Fiona, far too long." He brushed his fingers through her fiery locks, pulling her close.

She shut her eyes, holding onto this moment as long as she could. For even a lingering embrace like this could not make up for the months they had been apart. He had been gone so long—they all had—and though the future remained so uncertain, for this moment, she was home.

"We hae been gang a long time," he continued after a moment, drawing back and looking down earnestly into her face, "but I'm home now, and I willnae be needing to gae away anytime soon."

His words struck a fond, much-contemplated memory. She reached up and unclasped a slender silver chain around her neck, pulling up the simple knotwork pendant from underneath her dress and placed it in Angus' palm. "Here. I hae worn it ever since ye gave it to me in An Dùn when ye left." Her voice was quiet, lost in the past, in the spring of many months ago.

He glanced at the necklace that had been his dead brother's and then back at Fiona, his eyes glistening. "Thank ye," he murmured, clasping the chain around his neck and slipping the Celtic knot beneath his tunic. His hands trembled as he opened his mouth to speak again, but the words never came.

A figure appeared at the end of the garden path, peering back and forth until he spotted them. Then he cried out "Fiona!" before running down the path towards her.

Fiona glanced from Malcolm McCladden to Angus before steeling herself for the onslaught. The younger brother still managed to almost knock her over anyway before nearly crushing her to death in a tight embrace.

At last, she pushed him away and held him at arm's length, looking him up and down while laughing breathlessly. "Malcolm!" she squeaked. "Ye're too tall fer me now!"

If Angus had grown, certainly his younger brother had. Malcolm, who had barely reached her shoulder, now stood eye to eye with her. But his humorous, freckled face and the merry twinkle in his grey eyes were the same, as were the flaming curls that lay every which way on his head. And his voice was no longer the high, song-like tone of a young lad, but had deepened to a sweet tenor that had not yet reached its full depth.

"Och, but ye're still the fair lass we left behind." He was still laughing as he gazed from her to his brother. "She has no' changed, has she?"

"Aye, she has changed," Angus replied, looking at her fondly. "Our wee princess is no' so wee anymore."

"Och, I was no' wee back then either!" Fiona protested, her eyebrows raised incredulously, a smirk playing on her lips.

"Aye, she's no' changed tha' drastically," Malcolm agreed, his forehead wrinkled in a frown.

"She's changed fer the better; she looks more a queen than she ever did before," Angus said by way of compromise. He stepped forward and linked arms with Fiona, leading her back towards the castle courtyard.

"Aiee, wait up!" the younger brother exclaimed as he ran up and took the princess' other arm, marching proudly with them up the garden path.

Fiona only chuckled, lightheaded with relief and joy at seeing them both so well and so happy in ways she had never seen them before. The shadow of war and loss seemed indeed a thing of the distant past; perhaps the treaties had gone well? Or perhaps they had not, and the lads had chosen to forget it in light of being reunited with her and their mother again. Either way, she did not wish to ask, did not wish for bad news to darken this moment, did not wish to hear that their time had run out—

She thrust the thoughts aside as they entered the courtyard, which bustled with rushing servants on errands and nickering horses being led away to the stables. The brothers guided her to where Donald McCladden stood talking with Annag.

Donald looked up as they approached, a swift grin spreading across his weathered face. "So, how fares our fine princess?" He had not changed as much as his sons; only the growing number of white hairs in his scarlet beard marked him a year older.

"Well enough. And ye?" Fiona asked shyly, the giddiness at seeing them all again returning.

"I am well, jist weary from much travel. But 'tis very good to be home." He slipped his arm around Annag's waist and kissed her lightly on the forehead despite them being in full view of anyone in the courtyard.

Fiona glanced at the ground, a lump in her throat. The wonder and doubt regarding their quest burned ever in her mind, and she could not remain silent any longer, regardless of how she dreaded the answer. "How was the treaty-making?" She forced the words out, mindful of the way the brothers drew closer to her, as if to encourage her that hope was never fully lost.

"Rest assured, princess," Donald said kindly, his voice warm. "It went better than we had expected. Cymru has agreed to our request and is sending as many men as they can spare without greatly weakening their own borders."

Fiona gasped in shock and relief, nearly feeling sick as the last of her fears melted away like frost beneath the rising sun. The weight on her shoulders was fully and completely gone, and a smile spread across her face, tears springing to her eyes. The death-bound promise to the harper who had been her mentor, and in some senses a father, had been kept.

We did it, Rhiada. Cymru has sent her men.

Her soul nearly sang at the thought. Perhaps now they stood a chance against the Danes.

"The main leaders of the host are but a day behind us," Donald continued, "and many will be staying at other castles and fortress towns, I am thinking. We must provide enough lodging fer those tha' will come here."

"I will see to it," Annag murmured, her voice smooth and sweet like honey.

Fiona glanced at her, seeing the way she looked at her husband with happy contentment. Both the warmth of safety at seeing her second family back together and a twinge of loneliness for not truly being a part of them crept up her spine, despite the two brothers on either side of her.

Donald kissed Annag's hair before letting her go and beaming at his sons and the lass between them. "'Tis good to see ye again, princess," he said. "Ye were greatly missed." He winked, and Fiona felt both Angus and Malcolm stiffen in embarrassment.

She blushed as well, but she could not stop smiling. After waiting for so long, what they had so earnestly yearned for had finally come to pass. However long the road that remained ahead, the path looked much brighter now. At long last, they finally had a chance.

"Come ye both, let's find something to eat." Malcolm interrupted her thoughts, pulling them away. "'Tis nearly noon and I am faint wi' hunger."

"He's been saying tha' ever since we left Cymru," Angus drawled, chuckling.

Fiona laughed, her heart light within her. "I believe yer mother made oaten bannocks fer yer arrival."

"Oaten bannocks!" Malcolm squeaked, his voice cracking. He let go of her arm and raced across the courtyard and into the castle, leaving the two of them behind.

Angus turned to the princess beside him. "Do ye want to gae as well?"

Fiona looked up at him and grinned. "Mayhaps we should, since we hae no' eaten yet either. We must get something before Malcolm devours it all."

That night, the Feast Hall was filled with cheerful voices and sweet harpsong, a welcome celebration after so many dark months in despairing winter. The fire burned high and bright on the large hearth, and the tables were spread full with food that had been set by to last until the harvest. Perhaps it was a frivolous waste, but it was well worth the occasion. Hope, ever a small, burning flame, had rekindled into a beacon that might burn to high heaven. The Scots had returned and brought with them an army to defeat the Danes once and for all, bring justice to the realm, and restore Fiona to her throne.

But she did not think of such things now.

She was content enough to watch Malcolm feast to his heart's content and see Angus listen with delight to the harper's music, speaking to her of the Cymreig music and language and how glad he was to be home. Malcolm interrupted their conversation at times, either to add his own commentary or to tease his brother about something.

Fiona listened to them both, happy to have them home and to be with them again without saying much. Besides, there was not much to say. Little had happened to her, save the ordinary and the mundane, while they had travelled to other lands and stood before foreign kings. In comparison, the life she had lived over the past year was dull. What use would it be to tell them of that?

"Och, and then there was the time," Malcolm was saying through half a mouthful of honeycake, "tha' ye and yer friends decided to go hunting at midnight as the year turned, some crazy idea of finding a white stag seen in the forests nearby." He swallowed, allowing his brother a chance to defend himself.

"Ye would hae gang wi' us had ye kent!" Angus sputtered. "Besides, 'twas beautiful to run on snow beneath moonlit skies, entering in the coming year as if in a song."

Malcolm rolled his eyes heavenward. "Ye still sound like ye hae had too much mead. I would much prefer to celebrate by staying inside by a warm fire and enjoying myself."

"I think," ventured Fiona, "tha' both things can be poetic in their own way. Some prefer fire, some prefer snow, but it doesnae make either less songlike."

Angus gestured dramatically with his hands in agreement, nearly knocking over a young boy serving mead near them.

"But tha' was no' why they were punished." Malcolm cleared his throat and turned from accusing his brother to recounting the full tale to Fiona, who listened intently. "They became lost. In the woods. In the snow." He opened his mouth for the next phrase, but was cut off.

"Aye, but beneath the moonlight, the land looked different!"

Malcolm placed both hands on the table and gazed at his brother square in the face. "Aye, so it did. Yer so-called 'poetic moon' was the very reason ye were lost, and ye want to continue singing her praises?"

Angus wisely said nothing.

"Anyway." Malcolm turned to Fiona with a toss of his head. "They were lost in the woods, even those tha' had grown up by them. They lit a fire and stayed warm until morning when they returned home. The worst part was tha' none of us kent they were gang in all the celebration until late in the night, and most of us assumed they were sleeping elsewhere. But none of us kent where until the next morning when they walked in the castle gates." He heaved a long sigh. "Father didnae let him leave at night fer weeks."

"Only because he didnae want any of us to be attacked by a bear or freeze to death. Otherwise, he didnae mind," Angus returned.

"I think he still would hae minded." Malcolm rose to his feet and stretched, groaning. "I cannae fit in another bite. I'm gang to find Mother now. If I donnae see ye again this evening, good night!" He clambered over the bench he had been sitting on and walked away without waiting for a response.

"Did ye find the stag—the one ye were hoping to see?" Fiona asked in a quiet moment when conversation died to scattered applause for the harper's finished song.

Angus shook his head. "I think we saw it once tha' evening, but I donnae ken fer sure. We had given up on finding our way and built our fire, most of us sleeping close to it and each other fer warmth. I awoke from something, I donnae ken wha', and I think I saw the stag standing amid the trees, watching us." He shrugged, as if to make light of something often spun into legend. "Perhaps it was only a dream after all."

Fiona smiled shyly. "But was it a good dream?"

He grinned. "Aye, it was a good dream. Worth the hours spent shivering in the snowy darkness. The forest sounds different then, more mysterious, more ancient. Beneath the moon and the stars, the world glimmering in white—it was beautiful. I wish ye could hae been there," he added softly.

"Perhaps in dreams, I might."

A sober look crossed his face. "Dreams can be beautiful, but they are nae substitute fer reality. I can escape in dreams, live in a world free of cruelty and war and loss, but then I wake up, and the world is no' wha' I wish it to be, and I am more the sad fer it."

"But can a dream no' be worth fighting fer, to bring it to fruition?" she pressed. She knew he was speaking the truth, *knew* that everything around her would slowly crumble away if all anyone did was wish for what was not. But this deep yearning could not have meant nothing, either. It was too precious to her, the vision of that distant Scotland shining free in the mist, the vision she'd believed in since her days with Rhiada in Caerloch. And those months on that winter's war trail had only strengthened that vision before it wavered in defeat.

"Aye, it can. Yet some dreams can never come true." He looked at something distant in the firelight, something perhaps she could not see, and his eyes darkened. "'Tis our duty to ken which is worth the struggle and to fight fer it. Those dreams, they are worth all the pain and sorrow." He met her gaze.

"Do ye think we stand a chance, now tha' the Cymry are joining us?" Fiona asked a moment later.

Angus shrugged. "I cannae say. I cannae see wha' the future holds. But I do ken this—if ever we had a chance, 'tis now."

Annag came by their table then and murmured something to Fiona, no doubt too quiet for Angus to hear; his face betrayed his confusion.

Fiona rose to her feet, nodding to his mother. She flashed him a quick grin and then was gone, following Annag out of the hall.

Angus watched her go, already missing her vibrant yet steady presence. He had longed for this in all the months he had been away, to speak with her, to share his thoughts with her, for he knew she would not mock him like Malcolm did. In that, she had not changed at all.

For contrary to Malcolm's words earlier, she had changed as much as them. Time slowed for no one. He had expected her to change, of course, but he was surprised nonetheless. She was taller and no longer a bony-limbed lass whose arms and legs were almost too long for her clothes. Slender she remained, but her form was more like that of his mother's now. The lass he had known had grown into a fair young woman. Yet her lightly freckled face was as youthful and beautiful as he remembered. And the fearful look that had so often been in the depths of her soft, green-gold eyes was gone. He prayed he would never see that fear again; but with war surely to come, who knew what the future would hold for them?

Angus drank what mead remained in his cup and took a seat closer to the harper, more interested in listening to the music and being lost in his thoughts than exchanging jests with the servants who had known him as a child, as Malcolm was currently doing.

The song was a mellow one, a song of a lover's loss of his beloved and his going away to war to bury his grief. Angus clenched his jaw, the words striking a chord too close to his heart. He glanced around the hall, searching for Fiona, the slightest dread weighing down on his shoulders.

He caught sight of her and the tension eased, relief flooding his veins. He was foolish, he knew, to place so much in a mere song. But it had indeed hit close to home.

"Is everything all right, Angus?" Fiona asked softly, coming to sit beside him. Her gaze was puzzled and almost concerned.

Were his thoughts that obvious? Or was it only because she could read him so well?

"Aye, I was jist lost in thought. All is well."

As if he had heard, the harper changed his song to something much more light-hearted.

"'Tis good to hear tha' all is well." She grinned, the torchlight catching in her eyes. "We could do wi' tha' more often these days. Jist donnae remain lost in thought," she added in a whisper. "Malcolm will hae something to say about tha'."

He chuckled in spite of himself, warm softness flooding his chest even as they both said no more and instead listened to the harper's music in content, contemplative silence.

Oh, he had missed her!

~ 31 ~

~ 3 ~
A DAY OF FREEDOM

A veiled sun filtered through the windows at Caerloch Castle in the Scottish Highlands, the daylight glimmering silver on the weapons hanging on the walls. Outside the Great Hall's doors, servants could be heard walking back and forth, sometimes greeting each other, but the sound was dim within where Lady Nuith and Lord Erland sat with Nuith's half-brother, Drummond.

"Now that spring has come again, what is your plan?" Lady Nuith asked wearily.

Drummond sipped from his cup of imported wine. "I wish to take a band of thirty men to Caerdun."

Lord Erland lifted a dark eyebrow. "That is a far distance for this soon in the year. That's McCladden territory."

"I ken." Drummond swore softly in Gàidhlig before continuing in Danish. "But where else could they be hiding her? We searched all the other castles and strongholds in the Lowlands during the last year. Unless she truly died like they swore she did, she must be hiding somewhere. And the Highland chiefs had nothing to do wi' the uprising."

"She is very much alive," Nuith commented bitterly. "I would know if that child were dead."

Neither of the other two replied to that.

"But why had you not checked it before? Surely it would be the most secure place to hide her," Erland pressed.

"Simply because of the fact it is too obvious. That is the strongest, most defensible place in McCladden territory, and where—so they said in An Dùn—the McCladdens returned after the treaty was made. We searched all other places in the lower Lowlands, and surely they would not keep her so close to their Saxon enemies in the south. Therefore, she must be hiding in Caerdun." Drummond set his empty cup on the table and gestured for the manservant waiting in the shadows to refill it. "I am also thinking that Donald and his sons are hiding there, and possibly a few other chieftains who hae been missing. If anything, I might find some clue as to where they are, if they be no' there."

"Will they not consider it a threat, to approach such a place with that many men? It has been a thin peace since you searched last summer." Erland did not seem convinced.

"Threat or not, we must have her," Nuith snapped, weariness now fled from her voice. She could hear the words of past failure in her mind. "Drummond did not keep his promise, and neither did the Scots when forced to surrender. We demanded proof of her death in the treaty, but they denied us with some flimsy excuse. As long as she lives, we will never be safe from future uprisings. And our sweet Henrik deserves to live a life without fear, unlike the life we have had to endure for far too long." She turned to her husband with pleading eyes. "Is it not worth it for him?"

Erland wisely said nothing, nodding his head instead.

"I ken I failed where McCladden and the princess were concerned," Drummond said at last. "But I at least killed Rhiada like I should hae done years ago. I will take care no' to incite a rebellion, but I will no' hesitate to use force if necessary." Looking directly at his sister, he added, "It is clear that to go softly allows them time to plan against us. If I hae the chance, I will kill her myself and no' risk another escape attempt." He rose to his feet and drank the last of the wine. "I will leave by next morn."

"Not sooner?" Nuith asked, disappointment in her voice.

"I need time to gather men and horses. It is a long ride, a two—perhaps three—day journey depending on how badly the melting snows hae swollen the rivers. We will need supplies to last us; the land offers little so soon in spring and we will hae nae time to hunt. Are ye satisfied wi' this?"

Nuith nodded sullenly. "Take care," she said, her skirt rustling as she stood. "I have few men I can trust, and I cannot risk sending out my personal guard for a task that should have been done long ago."

Drummond looked her straight in the face, his voice emotionless. "I promise ye, it will be done." Then he turned and left, leaving the servant to take his empty cup and pitcher of wine away.

A cold, wet something landed in Fiona's face, startling her from a deep sleep to abrupt wakefulness.

She sat up with a jerk, fuming like a kettle boiling over, blinking rapidly to get the water out of her eyes.

Once she could see, she stared in bewilderment at Malcolm, who stood at the foot of her bed, laughing so hard he was not making any sound. In his hand was the cup he had used to hurl the chilling water into her face.

"Malcolm, what do ye think ye're doin' in here?" she demanded as she fairly leapt from her bed onto the floor, ignoring the fact she was still in her night shift.

"Ye wouldnae wake up!" He was still laughing, tears running down his face. "Besides, ye looked so ridiculous when—" He broke off in another series of chortles.

"I donnae care! Ye hae absolutely nae right to be in here, Malcolm McCladden, no' without warning! Now get yerself out before I tell yer mother."

"She said to wake ye up in the first place, so I donnae think tha' is gang to do much." Another voice broke in.

Fiona whirled around to see Angus in the doorway, leaning against the door post, calmly watching the entire spectacle. "Wh-wha'?" she stammered in surprise, her cheeks burning.

"Aye, she said tha' we had best spend as much time together as we could since the embassy from Cymru arrives this evening or tomorrow or whenever they come, and then there will be too much gang on fer us to be free to do whatever we want. But come, Malcolm," he called to his brother. "We had better get breakfast so Fiona can change into something a wee bit more suitable fer the horse-runs." He cast a teasing smile at Fiona before leaving, Malcolm following him, still chuckling.

Fiona waited until they had left to heave a groan and run her fingers through her hair. She had definitely not missed their pranks. Besides which, she was no longer the fourteen-year-old they could jest with in this way, even though she was glad they seemed as open and friendly as they had before. She was sixteen now, almost a full-grown woman, and most lasses were married or at least betrothed by her age.

Fiona pulled her hair into a messy plait with a sigh. Annag would certainly hear about this.

She found the brothers in the Feast Hall. Malcolm polished off another oatcake with his porridge while Angus talked to him, discussing potential lodging arrangements for when the Cymreig hosts would come. He finished speaking when Fiona reached them, sitting down beside them to eat her own breakfast.

"Wha' kept ye?" Malcolm asked through a mouthful of food.

"I had to get dressed, dunderheid. I cannae jist slip on a kilt, breeks, and plaid and belt it. I am too old fer wearing those clothes anymore."

"Och, then right glad I am tha' I donnae hae to wear dresses," he responded, licking the oat crumbs off his fingers.

Fiona glanced at Angus, who was busy inspecting the tip of his dirk. He caught her gaze, and the corners of his lips quirked upwards.

"I suppose ye ne'er grew out of tha' old habit, did ye?" she questioned, remembering how he would always check the sharpness of his weapons, something of an obsession for him. But both of them knew the deeper reason why: a fanatic desire to protect and preserve those he loved from harm and death since he had lost the brother he had loved the most.

"Nae, I didnae. But 'tis only been thirteen months."

Before she could reply, Malcolm shot off the bench, headed towards a maidservant bearing a platter of fresh bannocks. He returned after exchanging some words with her, leaving her confused and blushing, and him with the plate in his hands. He plopped triumphantly back down on the bench, a bannock already headed towards his mouth.

"Wha' did ye do to tha' poor lass?" Angus sputtered.

Fiona tried not to choke on her porridge by laughing at Malcolm's expression of feigned innocence.

"I jist told her our princess here was muckle hungry and wanted more bannock?"

Fiona snorted, swallowing hard and laughing through her nose instead. When she could speak, she cried, "Malcolm! I hae ne'er eaten so much at one meal, let alone at breakfast."

He shrugged good-naturedly and grinned. "Well, they were no' meant fer ye anyway."

"Ye shouldnae hae deceived her—tha' was no' kind," Fiona pressed, scraping the last of the porridge out of her bowl.

"Our princess is right, Malcolm. If ye do such a thing again, I'm gang to tell Mother," Angus added. "Anyway, are ye all ready to gae now?" he continued, changing the subject while standing up and stretching.

Malcolm nodded, tucking the last remaining bannock into his sporran. Fiona placed the final spoonful of porridge in her mouth and rose as well, taking her bowl and spoon to the kitchens to be cleaned by someone else.

Then she followed the two brothers out into the lovely spring morning. The sun shone gold upon the world, bringing colour to the dull grey castle stone. The breeze was warm and welcoming, carrying with it the enlivening scent of resurrecting life.

Fiona paused halfway through the courtyard, inhaling deeply and squinting against the bright sun. The courtyard itself was relatively empty at this hour, though she knew it would bustle again once the Cymry arrived. Guardsmen stood over the gate, sharing a jest; she could hear faint echoes of their laughter from where she stood. Some commotion escaped the kitchens, whose entrance was open to welcome the fresh air; perhaps someone was burning oatcakes by accident.

"Fiona!" Malcolm's voice rang out from the depths of the stables.

"Coming!" she cried, striding quickly across the remaining cobblestones. Stepping inside the stables, she could see Angus and Malcolm finish saddling three horses in the dim light before they led them outside. They handed her the reins to one of the mares as all three mounted. She had no horse of her own, not since Sgàil, the horse her brother had given her, had been lost at the end of the last war. Fiona did not know whether Sgàil had been killed or taken by another, but she had bonded with no horse in the same way since. Besides, the danger of being discovered by the Danes or their sympathisers was too great for her to leave Caerdun's walls unaccompanied, and few men could be spared for that. But today—today she could ride, and with her dear friends no less!

Angus looked at them both with a smile lighting up his face. "Ready?" he asked softly, his voice edged in excitement.

Malcolm, always the dramatic one, grabbed an imaginary claymore out of an invisible sheath, raised it above his head, and cried, "Ride out!"

Fiona said nothing, returning grin for grin in answer, the joy of being together with them and doing the things she had missed over the past year leaving her elated.

Without another moment lost, Angus dug his heels into his horse's flanks, old faithful Branwen, spurring his steed onward, the other two following in like suit.

The moors opened wide to them, the braes shining vibrantly green under the golden sun's glow. The wind gusted welcomingly, showering its warm kisses upon them as the brilliance of the speed at which they rode brought blood rushing to their faces, splashing their cheeks rosy red.

They rode until they were out of sight of Caerdun before slowing. They stood together on the crest of the brae, panting from the exhilaration of the ride.

"Sa, tha' was a fine thing." Malcolm spoke first, a wide grin gracing his youthful, freckled face.

"Who says we cannae do it again?" Fiona shot back before urging her mare forward, the others hurrying to catch up with her lead.

A surge of utter joy rose up within her as the emerald moors flew past them, a feeling she had rarely had since she was a child—before the War. She thrust away the dark memories that sprang to mind at the reminder of her past. Today was glorious, and she was not going to let anything—or anyone—ruin it.

She glanced at the dark-haired rider beside her, his face concentrating on the land rolling before him. For a moment, Angus met her eyes and flashed a smile before spurring his horse onwards.

"Aiee! Wait up!" she cried out, laughing, before trying her best to catch up to him, leaving Malcolm lagging behind.

At last, they stopped and dismounted, letting their horses free as the three sat down in the heather, listening to the whisperings of the pleasant breeze blowing about the grasses.

Fiona gazed at the azure sky with the white clouds floating lazily across it, her arms crossed underneath her head as she lay on the heather. Malcolm sat beside her and munched on the oaten bannock he had saved from breakfast. Angus sat on her other side, leaning back on one arm and silently admiring the landscape, beautiful in its leafless desolation. Clumps of cheery, yellow gorse flowers contrasted with the green, an early herald to the full birth of blossoming spring.

"Why can it no' always be like this? So peaceful and without worry of the future?" Fiona murmured to no one in particular after several moments of content silence had passed.

"'Twas like this once—before the Danes came," Angus replied softly, looking at her.

"Aye, or so they say," Malcolm added, putting the last bite of bannock in his mouth. "We all ken I was much too young to ken tha' the world had changed."

"But can it be like it was again?" Fiona's voice sounded almost helpless in its pleading. After all, was that not why the Scots had gone to Cymru in the first place? Or perhaps this taste of freedom without fear of the future reminded her of a childhood long forgotten, when she had been too young to know of the darkness in the world. She wished to have that innocence and confidence to dream again, but perhaps that was not possible. Perhaps the knowledge that something could always go wrong—that there was evil in the world, that wicked men struggled for dominance—would always haunt any attempt to remain fearless of the future.

Angus turned and lay down also, his hands clasped over his chest as he watched the sky with her. "I believe it can. We hae no' lost Scotland yet. We hae something to build a new country on. We jist need to drive out the Danes."

"Aye, but can it be done?" she questioned. Surely he knew as well as she did that it would take far more than simply sweeping the enemy into the sea. But that in and of itself would be its own challenge without trying to heal the nation's wounds and unify the separated clans of the Lowlands and Highlands.

"I donnae ken..." Angus' voice trailed off. "Sometimes I think we can, while other times I am no' so sure. Do we hae the strength to overthrow the Danes and drive them out and keep them out?"

"We did once," she whispered, turning to look at him. No matter how much time had passed, she still felt a ghost of the shame she had long endured knowing it was her father's decisions that had doomed them all.

He gazed at her for a long time before answering, his eyes dark with despair. The soft breeze brushed back the dark locks over his temple, revealing the silver scar from his first battle. "I believe we can heal the broken pieces of this country—surely ye are proof of tha', Fiona. The question is, how can we reach the Highlanders when the Danes lie in between?"

"We hae the Cymry, do we no'?" The hope that had filled her heart the day before melted away, fear taking its place. Were their numbers still too few?

"True, but still I wonder." He turned away and continued, "If we cannae defeat them now, I doubt we will ever be able to. And even if we do drive out the Danes, will it be enough to keep them out? At least fer our lifetime, if no' fer those tha' will come after us?" Angus sighed heavily and said no more.

Neither Fiona nor Malcolm spoke; none of them had answers to that which only time itself could reveal.

"Tell me more about Cymru," Fiona said after several moments of silence had passed.

"Och, much like Scotland, but wi' mountains everywhere," Malcolm commented while chewing on a blade of grass.

"We hae mountains here too, but they're in the Highlands," she supplied, sitting up.

"Well, it was beautiful, but no' as beautiful as here," Angus replied, sitting up as well and gazing around them as if the rolling hillside beneath the spring sun could never cease to enthral him.

"What makes ye say tha'?" Fiona turned to him, brushing aside the crimson curls that the sudden breeze blew into her face.

He shrugged. "Maybe because one's own home is always dearer to him than any other land, beautiful though it may be. Besides, Mother and ye were here."

"In other words," Malcolm piped up, the blade of grass on his lips bouncing with every syllable he spoke, "he was homesick."

"Och, ye were too!" his brother retorted, a wave of scarlet tainting his otherwise pale face.

"Aiee! Can I no' hae a few moments in yer company without ye both arguing?" Fiona sputtered, getting to her feet.

"Nae, we were born to argue. 'Tis our fate," Malcolm said grandly, brushing the strands of broken grass off his kilt.

"Ye sound like Rhiada now," she commented, watching him with amusement.

"Aye, his country has about as many harpers as we hae sheep." He shook his red locks in mock pity. "'Tis nae wonder Rhiada came to Scotland—probably to escape all the competition."

"I highly doubt it," Angus muttered dryly.

"Right, are we gang to get back before midday or wha'? We might miss luncheon, and I ken Malcolm will regret tha'," Fiona added, a grin spreading across her face.

"Last one back will serve at table!" Malcolm shouted before running to his horse, swinging up into the saddle in one movement and riding off, the other two following in quick pursuit.

Fiona and the McCladden brothers arrived back at Caerdun Castle just in time for luncheon, much to Malcolm's delight.

The fluffy white clouds now hid the sun from view at times as they crested the last hill that separated them from the fortress yonder, the brightness of day now vanishing.

As they clattered over the drawbridge and entered the courtyard, they realised they were not the only ones to arrive.

The whole place was filled with men and horses, some of them Scots, but most of them were in tunics and breeks, not the kilt and plaid of Scotland. They jabbered to one another in a deep, guttural language that was quite different from the Scots' Gàidhlig Fiona was accustomed to hearing. And yet their language, which she supposed to be Cymraeg, still sounded beautiful in its own way.

"Is this all the greatest part of the Cymreig host?" she asked Angus as they entered, surprised at the sudden crowd in the normally empty courtyard. There were perhaps some twenty or so standing there; with any luck, this was merely an advance party. If the Scots in all their many hundred clansmen were too few against the Danes, then this would never be enough.

"Nae, of course no'!" he hastily reassured her with a chuckle. "'Tis but the leaders and some of our close friends in the whole war host. Jist like we hae our High Chieftains wi' chieftains under them who hae their own clans in the army, so hae they. Nae," he added, "the others will stay at other places, such as An Dùn, until we send out the Crann Tara. If anything, this is the smallest band; unless I am wrong, 'tis only the king and his choice warriors."

"The king? The king himself is here?" Fiona gasped, her head feeling light. The king himself had come? And here she surely looked a sight, with horsehair and bits of grass still sticking to her dress, and her hair in disarray from the wind. How must she appear to those who had travelled far from their own lands to fight in her name? Certainly nothing like a princess.

"Aye, the king. Who else did ye expect to lead them?"

"I thought maybe it would be one of their High Chieftains, no' necessarily their king." The words tumbled from her mouth as she sought to discreetly tidy her clothing while seated on her horse. "Who will look after his kingdom in his absence?"

"One of his councillors that he trusts. Donnae worry about everything, Fiona, there is enough to be concerned about already." Angus grinned good-naturedly at her, as if he had noticed her discomfort and wished to reassure her. "Come on. Ye will meet him later, I am sure." He swung his leg over the saddle and jumped down, leading his horse into the stables, Fiona and Malcolm following.

Once the horses were safely in their stalls, the three of them returned to the grey afternoon and the many men and youths milling about the courtyard.

Malcolm suddenly yelped like an excited puppy and disappeared among the bustle.

"Where is he off to?" Fiona raised her eyebrows in surprise. "I thought nothing could distract him from luncheon, but I suppose I was wrong."

Angus threw his head back and laughed. "Och well, he is probably looking fer his friends. Speaking of which—" He left her without finishing his thought, likewise vanishing from her sight.

Fiona shook her head and pushed her way through the midst of strangers, trying to follow him. She soon found him speaking hurriedly to a lad she guessed to be Angus' age, who was dark and wiry as were most of the Cymreig brotherhood.

The two youths were chattering as she approached, but the lad Angus was speaking to in their strange tongue stopped abruptly at the sight of her, the words dying on his lips.

Angus turned to see what he was gaping at and smiled at Fiona.

His friend told him something, his soft, hazel eyes never leaving Fiona's face.

Angus' cheeks burned bright red, and he spoke to Fiona in a stiff, guarded voice. "Dafydd here says tha' ye are beautiful."

Her cheeks grew hot, for it was not every day that strangers greeted her in such a manner, but she managed a polite nod nonetheless. "Tell Dafydd"—she struggled over the strange pronunciation—"tha' I thank him."

Angus turned to Dafydd, and another strand of incomprehensible words flowed from his mouth as easily as if he was speaking in Scots' Gàidhlig.

Then Dafydd asked a question to which Angus responded just as quickly, though something in the dry lilt of his voice told Fiona that he was making some sort of jest while trying to be serious.

"Wha' did he ask?" Fiona interrupted, her curiosity overcoming her shyness.

Angus turned to her and blinked as if he had forgotten she was still there. "He asked who ye were."

"And wha' did ye tell him?" She could not keep a smile off her face, bracing herself for the possible jest and wondering what in the world it had to do with her.

"I told him tha' ye are a nasty, mean old ogre in disguise as a beautiful young woman who devours children at night when everyone else is sleeping."

Fiona's mouth dropped open. She expected Malcolm might say something like that, not Angus. "Ye did wha'?" Angus seldom teased her like this... Had he really changed that much? Could she even trust him as she used to?

Dafydd looked from her to his companion, an innocent question written plainly on his face.

Angus' eyes twinkled in mischief, but he did not answer her. He turned to Dafydd instead and spoke to him. It must have been amusing, for the Cymreig lad started laughing, a merry—almost musical—sound.

They said some more words to each other before they exchanged what she guessed to be a brief farewell, as Dafydd took the reins of his horse and began to lead it to the stables, where several other Cymreig men were headed with their mounts.

"Did ye really tell Dafydd tha'?" Fiona asked in a soft voice, the laughter gone, replaced with humiliation.

Angus turned to her and flung his arm across her shoulders, walking with her to one of the main entrances to the castle. "Och, Fiona. Did ye think I would really do such a thing?"

She looked up at him and saw that he was not jesting anymore, for his deep blue eyes were serious. "I donnae ken. But I wanted to ken fer certain." She leaned into him as a chill breath of wind whistled through the courtyard, as if to remind them that winter had not passed entirely from the earth.

"Aye, and there is nothing wrong wi' tha'—" He added something else under his breath, too soft for her to hear.

Fiona glanced up to ask him what it was and stopped. There, amidst the tightest grouping of their Cymreig visitors speaking with Donald McCladden, stood a young man who carried the spitting image of Rhiada. A great white bird, its head hidden in a leather hood, sat on the man's gloved fist, its tethers held in his other hand. Little bells attached to the bird's feet jingled as the man's hand moved slightly while talking.

"Rhiada?" she asked in a bewildered whisper to Angus, who had followed her gaze.

"Nae, 'tis his son, Cynfael. He is their king."

Fiona's eyes widened in astonishment. "Their king?" she squeaked. "Since when..."

"Aye. Did Rhiada never tell ye about his past?"

"He did once, when we first met, but I remember it little."

"He married Cariad, the daughter and only child of the Cymreig king, Brenin. He had a son, Cynfael." Angus paused, letting his words sink in.

"Aye, I remember him speaking of his son once or twice, but I never thought...I never assumed his son would be king."

"Aye, he was the only bloodheir, so naturally he would be king. When we arrived in Cymru, King Brenin had died only a few months prior and Cynfael was now ruler. We were jist as surprised as ye when we saw him in the throne room. I donnae think Rhiada thought his son would succeed the throne so soon when he initially told us to gae to Cymru and seek their alliance."

Fiona turned and looked at the young man more closely. How similar he looked to the harper she had known! The same dark, shoulder-length hair and pronounced cheekbones, the dark eyes that Rhiada must have had once, and a closely trimmed beard, which only lent further to Rhiada's image. "Cynfael ap Rhiada...he looks much like his father."

"Aye, and he has also inherited the bardic talent. He prizes his bogwood harp above even his sword." Angus chuckled softly. "Though, I think ye'll find most of the Cymry treasure their stories and songs as highly as their loved ones."

Perhaps she had only imagined the sudden warmth in his voice as he said this, but she could not have imagined the tightening of his arm across her shoulders. Fiona looked away as a blush heated her cheeks. "Do ye think they will sing some of their songs fer us?" she asked, attempting to speak of something else. "I would like to hear them."

"Och, I'm sure. And ye can meet Cynfael later once Father finishes speaking wi' him. Come, we must eat before Malcolm and all his friendly host devour it all." Angus took his arm off her shoulders and extended his hand to her instead.

Fiona took it gladly.

~ 4 ~
FEAST BY TWILIGHT

IN all the time Fiona had slept beneath Caerdun's sanctuary roof, the Feast Hall was generally half filled—if that. But tonight, with the addition of the Cymreig royal party and a few of the returning Scottish embassy, the place was crowded. No empty seats remained along the tables, and additional benches had been set out in the great courtyard under the light of the stars to accommodate all the celebrating hosts.

Angus, Malcolm, and their Cymreig companions sat inside the hall with Fiona, since it was the McCladdens' castle after all, else they would have been sent out to the courtyard with the other youths to enjoy the feast. The lads talked and jested with their few friends in their native tongue who sat with them, sometimes remembering to translate for Fiona, but most of the time she listened to a language she did not know, smiling when they smiled, yet longing to be a part of the conversation the way she used to be.

Laughter and voices speaking both Gàidhlig and Cymraeg rang up to the rafters of the hall, followed by sweet harp music, often lost beneath the sea of sound. Page boys brought in platters of roast lamb, oat bannocks, honey cakes, ewe cheese, and the last of the winter apples and dried berries, while young maidens helped refill their cups with the fire-hearted mead, sweet with the taste of long-ago summers.

Near the end of the feast, when most were satisfied with food and content to listen to the music or engage in small conversation with one another, King Cynfael rose to his feet and waited as the hall grew respectfully quiet.

He spoke haltingly in the Gàidhlig language, though with a trace of a Cymreig accent, just as Rhiada once had. "I would like to thank Chieftain McCladden fer his kind hospitality to us," he began, his voice deep and rich, enhanced with a distinct, musical tone. "I also would wish to hereby pledge, in the sight of ye all, the allegiance of both myself and my men to a noble cause: to drive out the Danes—or at least subdue them—and restore the rightful heir, Princess Fiona McCurragh, to the throne. Though I know the official oath shall no' be taken until some time hence, I wish to make my intentions clear. I will no' return to my home until the oath is fulfilled or I die in the attempt." He raised his cup to his mouth and drank its contents, setting it down as everyone else in the hall stood and followed his example.

Fiona's throat tightened from a sudden rush of emotion, and she almost choked as she swallowed the mead. Her cheeks flamed, and not only because of the eager gazes fixed upon her. Cynfael was yet a stranger to her, even if she had known his father well. They had never even spoken nor been introduced, and yet he had just pledged himself and his men to defend her even to death. She blinked back the tears and set down her cup very carefully on the table, glad that the eyes that had looked at her before now ignored her.

Once they were all seated again, Chieftain McCladden leaned over and spoke to Cynfael, though they were too far away for Fiona to hear what they said.

She watched with interest as Cynfael walked half the hall's length to the harper and spoke to him. The harper stood up and bowed, placing his harp carefully in its bag and resting it in the corner of the hall. Then he sat down to eat at the feast, no doubt glad of the chance to fill his empty stomach.

Meanwhile, Cynfael summoned one of his bodyguards, who returned presently with an oddly-shaped bag.

Fiona guessed instantly what it was and excitedly nudged Angus with her elbow.

He turned to her from speaking with Dafydd and asked with furrowed brow, "Wha' is it? Is something wrong?"

"Is Cynfael gang to play fer us?"

He glanced towards the front of the hall, studying the Cymreig king for a moment. "Aye, I believe so," he replied with a swift smile before continuing his conversation with Dafydd.

Fiona pursed her lips. A year away from him and Malcolm, and they were far more enthusiastic to speak to their friends from whom they were absent a few days than her. Had they not missed her at all, despite what they had first claimed? She turned away from him, bitterly disappointed. She might not mean much to them anymore, but they still meant the world to her.

Sighing, she pushed the thought away and gave her attention to the king soon to sing for them.

Cynfael indeed drew out his black bogwood harp and began tuning it, brushing against the strings delicately with his fingers. He handled the instrument with such gentle, loving care, as if it were his sweetheart. Once the strings were on pitch, he plucked them in a lilting, dance-like pattern as the hall gradually quieted and turned their full attention to him.

Then the song stopped, and an expectant hush descended upon the assembly.

He started to play again, but this time the tune was a mournful one and did not carry a distinct melody, the chordal harmonies sweetly weeping together. He opened his mouth, serenading them with words in his native tongue, and his voice, though beautiful when he spoke, became almost heavenly as he sang.

Fiona touched Angus gently on the arm, afraid of upsetting him by interrupting him once again, but she did not understand the words and wanted to know why the song was so bittersweet. Yet she did not need to speak.

Meeting her gaze, his lips parted in a knowing smile, and he whispered, "'Tis a love song from his own country. 'Tis of a lover lamenting that he cannae hae his love because she doesnae notice him. He sings, wishing tha' perhaps she will see him one day, but he lacks the patience to wait fer so long." After a pause, he continued, "The singer finishes by stating tha' he will sing and play his harp fer her to woo her wi' his beautiful music."

Her face flushed as he spoke, and she hoped that in the torchlit dimness of the hall he did not see it. "I hae ne'er heard of such a song," she replied at last. "Do we no' hae them in Scotland?"

"Och, aye. But we donnae usually hae the singer require music to win the heart of his lass. The Cymry are far more musical than we are," he added by way of explanation.

Fiona glanced around the room, seeing almost all the assembly caught in the beauty. The Cymry listened with fond admiration for their king, the Scots not knowing the words but equally ensnared by the loveliness of the song.

And then her eyes landed upon Elspeth, who was helping serve at table, the mead jar still in her hands. The woman's mouth was parted, her eyes glistening in the torchlight, and something in Fiona's chest warmed, knowing that in all her pain and loss this beauty had touched her too.

But before she could dwell on it more, Cynfael's fingers flew upwards on the strings in a glissando that fluttered lightly up to the rafters of the hall. Then it vanished away into memory, and the song was over.

Applause and cheering met his performance, and while many asked for more, he declined them with a shake of his dark head and put away his beloved harp, returning to the feast.

The Scottish bard took his place, but no one paid much heed to him. Not because he lacked the skill of the Cymreig king, but because he was playing the sort of music one only listened to as one would listen to the songs of birds while working in the fields, not the sort that required one's whole attention, not the love songs or epic sagas of ancient days.

After a few minutes listening to this, Malcolm, who sat across from Fiona, muttered something under his breath and scrambled off the bench. He made his way to the harper, bending down to whisper in his ear.

Fiona watched the proceedings in confusion, wondering what that lad would be doing now. But when she asked Angus, he only laughed and said to wait and see.

The harper stood and handed his harp to Malcolm, who sat down and positioned it into his shoulder, striking one or two strings as if testing the waters. Then he flashed a grin to his curious audience before striking up a fast-paced jig.

Within moments, many people were clapping their hands in rhythm, some of them laughing—though Fiona soon realised those were mostly his friends. She glanced at Annag, who watched her son with as much surprise as Fiona.

His playing was clumsy and he made almost as many mistakes as right notes, but perhaps that was the point. Sometimes all one needed was a good laugh.

He finished abruptly and stood, bowing with a mock flourish before sitting down again and playing a slow air, his face much more serious and concentrated.

Fiona observed him, the shock wearing off a little bit, replaced with wonder. The lad who had complained about weaponry practice and his ever-present hunger had gained the gift of music! She remembered the time he had danced while she had practised a strathspey, and his enthusiasm to hear her or Rhiada play. Perhaps it had been enough to awaken a hunger in him to learn the beauty of song himself.

The slow air, if not the most skilful playing, was beautiful, and Fiona found herself humming along to it. The sombre melody fit Angus more than his brother, she mused, looking at them both in turn while listening.

As if to prove her wrong, Malcolm finished with a rolled chord and then struck up another song, singing along in his raw-edged tenor some song about seven brothers riding a pig to the market and who were promptly dumped, one after another, into a ditch.

Laughter and thundering applause followed this song, the Cymry just as loud as the Scots. Perhaps the song was originally in their own tongue.

Malcolm bowed dramatically and handed the harp back to the harper with a grin. The man chortled merrily as he took back his instrument. Then Malcolm strode back to his place, clapping hands with many of his companions, who greeted him in Cymraeg.

"Since when did ye learn to play?" Fiona asked as he sat down at the table.

"Och, everyone kens how to play and sing in Cymru. I learned it jist to fit in. Angus, though, he took it a bit further." Malcolm hitched a shoulder and chortled before downing what mead remained in his cup.

Fiona turned to ask his brother about it but discovered a vacant seat where Angus had been. Only Dafydd met her gaze, his eyes shining in the torchlight, and he smiled in greeting. She smiled back, uncertain, and searched for her friend amid the celebrating company.

At last she caught sight of him, seated up near the front of the hall where Malcolm had been only moments before. Angus settled the harp into his shoulder with care, watching the firelight dance on the strings as the hall fell into respectful quiet that almost rivalled when Cynfael had played.

He fingered the strings gently, coaxing a strangely familiar melody that sang in the silence. It was not until he began to sing that she remembered the song she had performed the night she had fled from Lady Nuith and later played in An Dùn. But the words were not the ones she had learned.

His mellow voice rose and fell in cadence with the sweet euphony, memories of that song and of two years ago rushing back to mind.

The firelit hall at Caerloch, singing a song of treason before escaping her prison and looming execution. The moonlit moorland, running with Angus to freedom, falling asleep beside him in the heather. The rain hitting the windows at An Dùn as she played the song again, Malcolm's entranced face, and the pain and longing visible in Angus'; his reaching out to pluck a string and instead pulling at her heart...

Her eyes blurred with tears she struggled to hold back, not only for the melancholy beauty of the music, but also the remembrance that song gave of the many close brushes with death and the irrepressible longing for freedom, and the thought that perhaps she would have to endure it all again—if not worse—before the end. And who was to say that they would be successful now? Hope was always a fragile thing, just a dream.

But perhaps even dreams were worth dying for.

And yet...this was not the song she had sung before. This was something else entirely, something new and hopeful, like the shy breaking of dawn after the darkest night that blossoms into glorious sunshine and chases all the shadows away.

Her breath caught in her throat as she listened, mesmerised, not only by the music and his voice, but also the words.

The sun now rises
High above the mists
The Highlands are calling me home
Driving away night
And bringing hope
The Highlands are calling me home

Our hearts may now sing
My dearest love
The Highlands are calling me home
Day has come again
Hope has rekindled
The Highlands are calling me home

The future is ours
Ours fer the taking
The Highlands are calling me home
Our Scotland is free
Nae more shall night reign
The Highlands are calling me home

Yer hand in mine, love
We'll roam the heather braes
The Highlands are calling me home
Heart of my heart
Home is where ye are
The Highlands are calling us home

Angus finished the song, plucking a high third that reverberated throughout the hall, which had held its breath until now. In the hush that followed, he looked up and met Fiona's gaze across the room, his eyes shining in the dim light and his lips parted in the barest hint of a smile.

She looked away and blushed in confusion, both at the different words and what he had done after the song, but when she glanced up again, he had set the harp aside. A wave of scarlet washed over his face as those in the hall broke into applause, the reverent silence broken.

Fiona clapped with them, if more hesitantly, a jumble of emotions entangling themselves in her mind. She glanced towards the table where Donald and Annag McCladden sat, and saw them both beaming at their son with quiet pride. Perhaps she was the only one who had not known Angus could sing and play.

Fiona gazed at her hands, nervously fiddling with the skirt of her dress as the applause died down around them. Angus had not meant those lyrics for her, had he? Surely he meant them only in a general sense, and the look he had given at the end was only in memory of that song two years ago. Or was it meant to mean more? She did not know, and she hated the uncertainty and confusion. A year since they had seen each other, and it felt like a lifetime in light of how different they had become. He had gained confidence and courage, no longer seeming to walk in the shadow of fearing the future. And she...she still fretted about the littlest of things, such as this.

She might have gone on wondering in endless worry about the intentions—or lack thereof—except Malcolm called to her and playfully suggested she give them a song next.

The blood drained from her face, and she felt light-headed for a moment while she collected her wits. "Nae, I...I hae no' been practising. I hae nothing to sing." She forced a smile to her lips, but her stomach twisted. She had never liked performing, least of all when she had not been expecting it.

"Everyone has a song," Angus put in, coming to sit down beside her again. "None of us here are masters, except fer Cynfael and our own harper. 'Tis more fer the enjoyment of the thing than anything else. Will ye no' play fer us? 'Tis been so long."

Fiona hesitated, nervousness rising up within her and nearly choking her. She had sung and occasionally brought out Rhiada's harp, but she never played as well as King Cynfael and Angus had just done, and never intended to play before the whole assembly. True, none of them might judge her attempts, but she usually only did a thing to do it well—and this time was no different. Besides, her mind was already in turmoil. Could she silence it long enough to think of something to play?

The room grew too hot and she gripped the edge of the table, her anxiety growing to overwhelming panic. "I need some air," she murmured before fleeing the hall with as much grace as she could. She tried not to think of their disappointed, confused faces. She could not play even if she wanted to, not in this state.

The early spring night air hit her like a sudden rain shower, and she drank in its freshness deeply, her head clearing after the smokiness of the hall. She walked quickly across the moonlit courtyard, which had since been cleared of tables and benches, and was now empty save for a guardsman and a maiden speaking together by the well. Tormented by her thoughts, Fiona ascended the stairs to the battlements and leaned against the cold stone.

What was wrong with her? Such a simple request, and she had behaved childishly. What must they think of her now? Angus and Malcolm had both gained confidence and skills while away in Cymru. She? She had learned womanly skills such as weaving and knitting wool, but that was all. She was as timid and insecure as she had ever been. Perhaps she had not grown up at all.

The thought struck her like a shard of ice through her heart. Perhaps some people never grew up.

How was she expected to be queen when she still acted like a child?

A tear slipped down her face. It was no wonder that Angus and Malcolm preferred their Cymreig companions to her. She bowed her head, though she knew a real princess would never lower her chin in defeat. She should be back in the hall, playing for her people like a proper ruler—like King Cynfael had. But how was she supposed to bear it like he did? Was it even possible? Would she ever be who she was supposed to be?

She heard halting footsteps ascending the stair and she turned her face away in shame. Perhaps it was only one of the guardsmen, she told herself, but they never took that way up—and even in the hesitation, she recognised the tread.

"Fiona, is everything all right?"

Fiona squeezed her eyes shut, tears escaping regardless. Of course it would be Angus. For once, she wished it was not him. A year ago, she would not have minded. But a year had grown between them, and neither was the same person who had bidden the other farewell.

"Aye, I am fine," she said at last, the words like ash on her tongue.

He came up beside her, resting his hand on the rough stone of the battlements. "Ye were ne'er good at lying."

She choked a bitter laugh. "Nae, tha' was always ye."

Angus took a step closer. "Fiona, wha' is wrong? Ye hae been strangely quiet and shy all this time; is it because we were gang fer so long? Or hae Malcolm or I offended ye?"

She shook her head, even though both things were true in a sense. "Nae, I..." She paused. He had been her close friend once, even if he had gained other companions since; she could trust him with this as they had once so deeply trusted one another. "It has indeed been a long time. Ye and Malcolm hae grown up—I almost donnae recognise ye. And I donnae ken how to pick up the threads we left behind; they become more unravelled when I try to touch them."

He wrapped his arms around her gently, saying nothing, only listening.

She shut her eyes against the night, his warmth soothing her despite her insecurity and the chilly night air, against which she had not brought her cloak. "Ye both hae spoken mostly wi' yer new friends this eve, and I understand tha', but since I donnae ken their language, I feel almost more lonely than before ye came home."

He tightened his embrace, and she leaned her head against his shoulder.

"I ken I shouldnae care so much. I should be grateful fer the friendship I had; I didnae deserve even tha'. But part of me longs to return to wha' was." She sighed and said no more.

"If things were always the same, I think we wouldnae treasure them as highly," Angus said at last, his voice soft and thoughtful. "Our friendship has been the dearer because of its briefness and because both of us hae come face-to-face with death many times. And no' only tha', but would ye want it to always be the same? Change is frightening and brings wi' it many risks, but perhaps change may even bring about a deepening of our friendship, and would tha' no' be worth it? Change isnae only evil."

She forced a chuckle. "I hae always been afraid of change. Far more often in my life, it brought about bad things. Fer good to happen, I would be much surprised."

"Then I hope ye will be surprised many times over." He let her go and stood, head bowed beneath the moonlight, lost in thought. Then he said, "As fer the other things, Malcolm and I hae no' been the best of friends at including ye. Left so long in a different place, 'tis hard to come back to the old threads, as ye said. It takes more than one to hold it together. But I want to try, and Malcolm does too."

His simple earnestness made her smile, something she remembered from the days before. "Ye both hae grown up, and I still feel like a child."

He laughed incredulously, but there was still warmth in his tone; he was not mocking her. "A child? I didnae think it was ye at first in the garden yesterday. Ye hae grown too, in yer own way."

She shook her head. "Nae, I meant tha' I am still as timid and fearful as I hae always been. If—if we somehow win against the Danes, I donnae think I'll make a very good queen."

The moon, pale and bright in its waxing beauty, passed behind clouds, leaving them shrouded in gloom.

"I may hide it well, but I still hae the same fear I always had," Angus replied. "Some things donnae change. I am thinking tha' fear is something we must always fight all our lives; it isnae something we grow out of, though we can to some extent. But fear is no' a mark of inability, only when we let tha' fear rule us. And when the fear is rooted deep in our past, it creates a wound tha' only love can heal." He exhaled softly, silent for a moment; perhaps he was lost in the past, remembering his fallen brothers, remembering Sioned and Duncan. "Jist promise me ye willnae bear the fear alone."

She looked at him, shadowy and uncertain in the dim light. "Aye," she said at last. "I promise, if ye will do the same."

The moon shone on her face once more, and he placed his hand over his heart. "Aye, I promise."

"Now Angus," she said with a mischievous smile, "since when do ye play the harp and sing?"

He grinned. "I wished to learn it ever since I heard ye play and sing so beautifully. So I asked Cynfael to teach me, since Dafydd claims he cannae teach it himself."

She blushed at his compliment, but held her smile nonetheless. "Well, ye play better than I ever did. And ye sang well, though I didnae recognise the words. Did Rhiada no' teach me the rest of the song?"

Angus shrugged and glanced down at the courtyard below them, where a small band of men left the main entrance to the keep and talked with one another on their way to the tower, most likely to sleep. "I believe he taught ye all of the song tha' exists." His words were hesitant.

She furrowed her brows in confusion. "Then where did the new words come from? Are they Cymraeg? Do they hae such a song and ye merely translated it?"

He was silent for a moment, and when he did speak, insecurity was woven into the undertone of his words. "I wrote them. The song was so bittersweet and I wished fer it to hae more hope, to be written in light of victory, no' in dread of defeat."

Fiona looked at him in astonishment, wondering how the lad who so oft despaired of beauty and light for fear of losing it forever had become a poet, a songmaster in his own right.

Another question formed in her mind, one she could not gather the courage to ask. For whom was the song meant? Scotland? Herself? Or had Angus found a lass in Cymru who had won his gentle heart? She was terrified of what the answer might be, so she remained silent.

"I think 'tis best now tha' we both get some rest, princess," he said, breaking the awkward quiet between them. "Who kens wha' tomorrow may bring." He led the way down the stair and bade her goodnight, departing for his room.

Fiona entered her chambers. She crossed the room and gazed out her window, lost in her thoughts. Outside the walls, the moon shone on empty stone, once warmed by human touch and now left to the sighs of evening. The milky light glowed on heather moors, bending beneath a whispering breeze. Among the swaying brush, the sweet sound of harp echoed in her mind. She steadied the questions swirling in her heart and asked them silently into the night.

The moon did not answer.

~ 5 ~

DUNGEON SANCTUARY

RAP. *Rap. Rap.*

The insistent knocking woke Fiona out of a deep sleep. She opened her eyes, seeing light grey on the horizon outside her window. The sun had not even risen yet. Who was knocking? Had Malcolm woken early again?

"Who is it?" she croaked, sitting up and rubbing the sleep out of her eyes.

"Angus. Are ye awake?"

His urgent tone sent a shiver down her spine and she pushed aside the bedclothes, reluctantly leaving her warm bed and tiptoeing across a chilly floor to the door. She opened it a crack, enough to see him in the dim hallway. "Wha' is it?" she asked, expecting the worst.

"A messenger jist arrived all the way from Caerloch this morn, rode without stopping except to exchange horses. Drummond is leading a band of men here to look fer ye, and they are no' far behind him."

Her heart stopped beating, ice trailing through her veins, and not merely because of the draughty air. A year of hiding, of dreading every group of horsemen that rode up to the castle gates, and now it was happening. "How does he ken this?"

"He's a spy, playing the part of a servant. Mother didnae want to tell ye last night because the messenger arrived so late, and she kent ye would worry and no' be able to sleep, and ye worry enough as it is."

She barely heard his explanation through the fear pounding in her mind. "Wha' must we do?" Her voice was dull and despondent in her own ears.

"Ye need to dress quickly. I will help wi' the rest once ye're wearing more than yer shift." He took a step backward into the hall and clasped his hands behind him.

Fiona closed the door, her hands shaking. Her thoughts could not form themselves into intelligible words. Panic darkened her senses to the point that had Angus not given her instructions, she might have sunk to the floor and remained there, trembling, until Drummond and his men came.

Must no' focus on the fear, no' on things I cannae control. Jist dress. Ye hae survived this before.

But there were only so many times one could escape death.

She dressed as quickly as she could, slipping into her dress and woollen stockings, for the morning was a cold one. Then she opened the door, allowing Angus to enter.

With a sympathetic glance at her, he walked to the chest at the foot of her bed and opened it, hurriedly taking out the garments within it and putting them in a wicker basket, placing her bow and other things on top.

"Wha' are ye doing?" she asked in confusion. Were things truly this serious?

"Putting these in Mother's room, beneath her own clothes. We need to make it look like ye are no' here." He finished a moment later, articles now a disordered pile. "Turn yer bed over so there is nae warmth on top. I will come back."

His words sparked movement in her and she did so, pulling off the sheets and woollen blankets, turning over the featherbed mattress—how Annag had spoiled her—and replacing them.

By the time she finished, Angus had returned and spread ashes over the remaining embers in the fireplace, deathly grey replacing the once-living red. He rose to his feet and looked at her, his eyes dark. "Ye ready?"

She gulped down the lump rising in her throat and tried to ignore the hunger pains in her stomach. Her life was more important than food. "Where will I hide?"

"In the dungeons. I will be wi' ye." He offered her his hand and she took it, her hand cold and clammy.

"Wait!" She slipped her hand out of his and ran to the side table, snatching up her brother's clan pin that she had forgotten to wear the last few days.

Angus inhaled sharply, meeting her eyes, the relief on his face clear. Oh, if she had forgotten and the Danes found that...

"Do ye hae anything else laying about tha' I donnae ken?"

She shook her head, not trusting herself to speak, and took his hand again.

He led her out and closed the door, shutting out the growing daylight. Then he set off down the hallway, Fiona following in dread.

"Wha' will ye do about the Cymry?" she managed to ask, trying to think about something other than herself and her own impending demise.

"Cynfael and those tha' cannae speak Gàidhlig will also be in the dungeons. Father believes the Danes willnae check there since we hae no' used those rooms fer as long as he has been chieftain."

"But Cynfael speaks our tongue easily enough?" It was a question more than a statement as they stepped out into the courtyard, the air chilly and damp. She shivered, stepping closer to him for warmth. Fiona cast furtive glances towards the shadows beneath the battlements and the black mouth of the closed gate, expecting at any moment to see the Danes' armour with their mocking ravens.

"Aye, Cynfael does," he replied, his breath puffing in the air, "but he looks too much like his father. Drummond will recognise him easily." Angus entered the kitchens, grabbing a small bundle—she supposed it to be food—and continued on, leading to the tower where a small table and chairs had been pushed aside, revealing a trapdoor.

Fiona had never been in the dungeons, since they were used for nothing more than occasional storage these days. She wondered if they were anything like those at Caerloch, or worse. Better to hide there, however musty and damp, than be captured and executed, but she could not shake the feeling of dread as Angus yanked open the trapdoor, revealing stone steps leading to yawning blackness beneath. She was still afraid of the dark, even if she was sixteen.

They descended the steps, entering a narrow corridor at the bottom, the gloom thrust back by a couple smoking torches set in brackets on the walls. Casks of a sort stood at the foot of the stair with dust on them. The air felt close and confined, a damp stench of death and slow decay. Fiona was glad she had not eaten breakfast, for the reek was enough to make her gag.

Angus hesitated, looking with longing at the torches flickering on wet walls before moving on without them, leading her into the dark. They passed a cell, in which she could see a number of individuals sitting in the dimness, their eyes glinting in the faint light, though naught else was visible. It was the Cymry, no doubt wondering why they had come to Scotland only to hide in ancient cells.

Angus reached the cell at the very back, where the torchlight almost could not reach, and fumbled along the wall with his free hand for the key before unlocking the door and leading her inside. He put the bundle of food and the key into her hand and said, "Wait here," before leaving her.

She stepped back towards the door, watching him walk towards the stair and run up, exchanging words with whomever was up there. Their voices ceased, the trapdoor shutting with a resounding bang, and someone shoved the table back on top of it, or so she guessed from the rough, grinding noise that followed. Then Angus returned to the depths, his footsteps light and even on the stair, his mellow voice breaking the silence as he spoke to the Cymry. They said something in reply, and he took the torches and doused them in a bucket of water beneath the bracket.

Fiona gasped in spite of herself as the light vanished. The darkness was so thick she imagined being able to grab it with her fingers. Terrors unnamed flooded her mind, somehow seeming more real without light to thrust the shadows away. Every drip of water, every exhale from the Cymry in the cells with her, seemed far too loud in the quiet.

She heard footsteps and someone closing the cell door with a creaky bang.

"Fiona, may I hae the key?"

She reached forward, finding his hand, and placed the cold metallic object in it. "Must we be locked in, truly?" Her voice was feeble against her will. She prayed none of the others could hear it.

"Aye. Best they think nothing amiss down here. If they glance in the cells, perhaps they will think us mere shadows of prisoners and no's the ones they are looking fer." Angus finished locking the door with a final, ominous click. She heard him grunt in exertion as he twisted his arm to reach the hook outside the door, upon which he hung the keys.

And then all became silent.

The darkness was stifling. She longed for light and fresh air, even though she knew she would be seeing and feeling neither for some time—unless the Danes came to the belly of the castle. And oh, how she hoped they would not! Better this crepuscular gloom than that!

The stale air caught in her throat, her breaths shorter and shallower as the seconds passed since the torches were snuffed out. Everything felt so close and yet so distant, the only real thing the blood roaring in her ears; all else was a cold void around her.

"Where are ye?" Angus said softly, his voice sounding far away. But perhaps that was only because she had been lost in her own mind.

"I'm here," she answered, still clutching the bundle in her hands as if her life depended on it.

A moment later, his hand found hers and she clung to it, stepping so close to him that their shoulders touched. She needed to know he was real, that this was not all a horrible nightmare she could not wake from.

He led her gently to the back of the cell, taking the bundle out of her hand. "We can sit down. These cells were cleaned out long ago."

She sat down beside him, still close to him, and shut her eyes, panic rising in her throat. "Wha' will they do about the full stables?" she whispered.

"I am sure Father has a good excuse. Tha' is no' fer ye to worry about."

"Wha' about Malcolm?" she persisted.

"He's in the castle somewhere. I donnae ken where; there was enough gang on wi' trying to hide those we could. He wished to be wi' his Cymreig friend Merwyn, but Father said 'twould be better if he was visible where Drummond could see him and therefore no' seem a threat as he might if he were hiding—as though he were guilty."

She felt him shift his position against the cold wall behind them. "Why are ye hiding here, then? Should ye no' be wi' yer family? If Drummond—"

"I donnae think Drummond will harm them; he cannae risk it without some sort of revenge on behalf of the other Lowland chieftains, especially Bryce MacClydno. Drummond fought wi' us before; surely he remembers tha' our loyalties between the clans hae been repaired, and even as small as we hae become wi' the losses of our finest men, we are still no' a force to be laughed at. We may no' hae open war, but there are other ways of fighting against them, even if they are no' as effective."

Fiona considered this. "Aye, tha' may be so, but ye and I ken how treacherous Drummond can be. He might still try to harm them fer his own personal revenge against the last war."

"Father can hold his own if Drummond threatens either him or Mother. Should such a thing happen, and I doubt Drummond would stoop so low as to allow his emotions to control him, Malcolm has a means of escaping to let the other chieftains ken."

"Ye should still be wi' them," she replied, her voice firm, despite that they both whispered—though the Danes surely could not hear them.

"Mother kent tha' ye might be afraid, hiding down here wi' strangers in the dark. Someone has to protect our princess, even if 'tis jist from herself." His voice was soft and tender, no mockery in his tone. "I would much rather be hiding away wi' ye than worry about ye the whole while."

Tears sprang to her eyes, warmth flooding her veins instead of cold fear. "Thank ye, Angus. I am glad ye are here wi' me."

"Always, princess."

She shivered in the silence that followed and leaned closer to him instead of the damp wall at her back. "I hate this darkness."

"As do I," he whispered back. "But we will see the light again. We can brave the dark. Jist...meanwhile...try to sleep if ye can. It will make the waiting seem less."

She laid her head against his shoulder as he placed his arm around her. "Will ye wake me if—" She wanted to say, if the Danes came, or if Annag came to say it was safe, but she was afraid to say either of those things for fear that the worst might happen.

"Aye, I will. Donnae worry about it. Sleep well, princess."

She did not know whether she ever closed her eyes or simply stared into the darkness long enough to become unconscious. All she knew was that the cold seemed to grow less and less. And then she was lost in a world where the sun always shone and the heather bloomed purple, and she and Angus and Malcolm rode upon the hills all day and the Danes never existed.

A pity it was only a dream.

Elspeth stood trembling at the window of her room. Grey light came through the glass, illuminating the forms of her children, Ranald and Lilybet, on the floor, who stared up at her. Ranald had been playing with his wooden horses, and Lilybet had been holding her wee doll made out of scraps of yarn, but now both toys lay forgotten on the floor. The Danes had come through here just minutes before, only to realise she was not the princess they were seeking.

She still felt the bruising on her arms where their leader had yanked her roughly to her feet. Her pulse still raced as she struggled to keep back the sobs threatening to escape her. But she must remain calm; she must remain fearless for her children's sake. They did not understand those strange men, did not know that those men were responsible for the death of their father and her beloved husband.

She could see them now in the courtyard below her window, some of them holding the horses upon which they had ridden here. Most of them, though, were still searching throughout the castle, swearing at the servants and treating most of them—especially the women—brusquely. She hoped, as all of them did, that they did not discover the entrance to the dungeons, that they did not search there. Else all would be lost. And she shuddered to think of how they might enact revenge against finding the Scottish princess and the Cymreig hosts here.

Would it all come to this, to be defeated on such a grey morning? Would their rising rebellion be stamped to ashes before it had a chance to flame into freedom?

Her heart broke for Fiona, who must be just as frightened as she was, hiding down there in the dark. And...it also twisted in fear over the safety of the man whose faery-like voice had sung so sweetly the night before, the king of a foreign land who reminded her in some ways of Jamie, reminded her that she had been young and free once. A stranger he was to her, aye, and certainly he had a lass of his own back home. But she remembered the days when she had loved a man like that, a man who had been slain before his twenty-third birthday. And somehow, in the remembering, the old wound hurt the worse because she knew she would never have that chance again.

Certainly never, if the Danes discovered their princess and allies.

She could not save Jamie. She could scarcely save herself or her children. And she was helpless to save this young man and her princess as well.

Elspeth could bear it no longer. She turned away from the window, pulling the shutters closed against the daylight. The fire burning on the hearth shone brighter in the dimness, reflecting on the wood-covered stone floor.

She sank to the floor, gathered her frightened children into her arms, and grieved for all that had been lost and for all she had yet to lose.

Fiona awoke to a void.

Startled into wakefulness, she straightened and stared wide-eyed into nothing, confusion and terror melding together into a scream that rose into her throat.

"Shh, Fiona. 'Tis all right," Angus whispered into her ear. "I'm here."

She closed her eyes, used to the stench of the place by now, but not the chill. "How long since this cell was last used?" she whispered, weary of the oppressive silence.

"No' since my grandfather's time," he replied just as softly. "He was a bit of a tyrant, worse than King Daibhidh. He thought everyone was attempting to murder him or somehow steal his chieftaincy."

"Wha' did he do to them? Did anyone even try?" she prompted, glad to think of something other than the darkness and growing hunger in her stomach.

"I donnae think so since he died of old age. Father doesnae really speak of him; I learned most of this from Mother's father, Mac-Clydno. Anyway," Angus sighed before continuing, "my guess is tha' Bram McCladden did those things out of guilt, since he had taken over the clan by murder and treachery, and so he suspected many of plotting against him fer the same reason. He tortured them and abandoned them in the dungeons without a proper trial. My father, the lesser son, took to the defence of the Saxon border and so escaped wha' may hae been his death—ironic, tha'. His older brother disappeared, and it was no' until his father died tha' my father found his brother's corpse down here, along wi' others. He buried them wi' decency and has no' used the cells since." Angus chuckled, a breathy sound. "I donnae think we are sitting atop any decayed bones, at any rate."

She elbowed him in the ribs. "I donnae find it funny."

"Och, me neither. They deserved better." He hesitated. "So do ye...and the Cymry. All of us, I suppose. Lady Nuith is becoming as paranoid as ol' McCladden had been."

Fiona could not think of a reply, and so they fell into silence.

That was the worst part, the waiting and the darkness and the quiet. No light, no way of keeping time. Endless, eternal black. How had prisoners lasted in such conditions? It was enough to make anyone go mad.

She fidgeted, if only to remind herself this was not all some bad dream.

"Are ye hungry?" Angus asked softly, shifting beside her.

"Aye, I didnae get breakfast." Her mouth, as well, was as dry as earth without a summer's length of rain.

He slipped his arm off her shoulder and a few moments later placed an oatcake in her hand.

She bit a piece off, the dryness not helping.

"I hae a flask of water too," he said, settling the skin into her hand.

Fiona drank from it sparingly so there would be enough for them both. "Thank ye," she gasped, glad to have something to slake her thirst.

"Always, princess." The sudden lilt at the end indicated he was grinning.

She nudged him playfully, smiling in the darkness.

"Aiee," he squeaked as softly as he could. "Keep tha' up and I'll hae a nice bruise beneath my ribs."

Fiona snorted and finished eating the rest of the oatcake.

She heard Angus chewing beside her, but that sound soon ceased and the awful quiet resumed its pace, broken only by their breathing. Then it became loud in her ears, and she strained to hear the muffled sounds she had heard before.

From time to time, she could hear shuffling from the other cell, but it was distant. All of them kept silent, hoping they would be unnoticed, unfound.

"They're searching above us, I think," Angus whispered, stiffening beside her.

She swallowed hard, glancing towards what she believed was the ceiling, and curled up next to him. Nothing could be heard through the thick stone, but sometimes muffled sounds came from the trapdoor at the end of the corridor.

Those sounds ceased.

There was nothing except silence. Endless silence.

Perhaps they will pass on by the dungeons... Perhaps we can escape...

And then a grinding. The bang of the trapdoor being thrown open.

Fiona's breathing skittered to a shaky stop, and the world spun around her. She groped for Angus' hand, clenching it hard when she found it.

They were coming.

After all this time, it would come to nothing.

She would die.

For a moment, the thought was a calm one. Perhaps she might see the daylight again, one last time...

But then, surely Angus and Malcolm and Annag and Donald and all else she loved would likewise die.

She squeezed her eyes shut, stars dancing beyond her vision.

"Stay wi' me," Angus hissed in her ear, gripping her hard to prevent her from becoming unconscious.

Footsteps echoed down the corridor, voices speaking Gàidhlig and not Danish. A lit torch reflected on the grimy walls, distant and faint.

"They hae gang—ye can come up now." It was Donald McCladden's voice.

Fiona nearly swooned from relief, her head throbbing from the tension. A sob escaped her lips.

They were safe. She would not die today. They had a chance to keep fighting. The nightmare had ended...for a time.

A chorus of voices cheered from the other cell where the Cymry had waited and keys clattered, clicking open the lock.

Angus lifted her to her feet and half-supported, half-carried her to the door, which he unlocked. He led her outside, closing the cell and hanging up the keys amid the voices talking, voices that swirled around her head.

The torch felt too bright and her eyes hurt to look at it as they passed Donald, heading up the stairs. Guardsmen greeted them, relief clearly etched on their faces. Malcolm was there too, grinning at her encouragingly, but it still felt so far away.

Angus brought her outside to the courtyard, where fresh air kissed their faces. She gulped it in as if she had been drowning underwater all this time, and reality came a bit closer, though it still hovered far beyond reach.

Then she caught sight of Annag running towards them, embracing them both fast. Fiona inhaled the sweet scent of her heather soap, and the wind and grey skies and warmth of their embrace finally became real.

And Fiona wept.

~ 6 ~

HIS FATHER

A fire burned brightly on the hearth in the Great Hall. It was late afternoon, and the happenings of that morning remained a distant nightmare that most had done their best to forget.

Fiona sat on one of the benches at the table, resting her chin on her hand, watching Donald McCladden speak about that morn. The McCladden brothers were beside her, their friends close by. The smiles and laughter of the night before were gone, replaced by solemnity. All of them knew—if they had not before—how serious this really was.

"None of us kent the Danes would strike this soon. My wife, Annag, kent tha' the Danes had been searching the Lowlands fer the princess, my sons, and myself last summer. I didnae think they would resume their hunt this early in spring, but it has happened. Thankfully, none of ye were found and they did nae damage besides disgracing us and leaving a wreck behind. Fer tha', we should be grateful. It could hae been much worse." Donald paused, allowing Cynfael to translate to those of his men who were not fluent in Gàidhlig. Donald knew the Cymraeg tongue, but it was easier this way, better that Cynfael still be their leader.

Then he continued. "But wha' is of greater concern is the fact we are running out of time. Lady Nuith never believed we would keep the peace treaty. Our spies report tha' she is preparing her forces, even calling fer reinforcements from other Danish settlements to help her. If they should come o'er the water, they will be too many fer us to defeat, even wi' the help of our allies." He gestured now to the Cymreig king and his men. "I had thought we would hae more time to assemble our hosts, but 'tis no' the case. Within three days, I want all able men tha' can be spared from here to set out fer An Dùn. I will send out the Crann Tara to the other High Chieftains this evening, telling them of the news and asking them to prepare as well. I ken tha' ye came from yer own mountains and valleys fer this very cause, but now ye ken wha' is truly at risk. If ye wish to return home, this is yer chance to do so without disgrace. Else we will gladly welcome yer aid." He finished speaking and sat down, awaiting what King Cynfael would say.

Silence fell heavily upon them all as they considered what Donald had said. Fiona felt nothing, only a dull sense of importance, exhausted from what had happened earlier. She knew the threat was real, but she felt only dread at the thought of the future.

She had survived the first two wars, but was she strong enough to withstand this coming one? She was of little use when it came to a real crisis; this morning's events were proof enough of that. How could she lead her men into war if she could not even keep enough presence of mind to protect herself when in danger?

Cynfael rose to his feet, his fingertips resting on the table as if to support himself. He looked at each member assembled there in turn, as if to read their thoughts before he spoke, much like Donald did. But the way he expressed himself was wholly like his father. "About a year ago, Chieftain McCladden and various representatives of the Lowland chieftains, along wi' their best warriors, arrived at the capital of my country. They asked fer one thing: support and forces against our common enemy, the Danes. After long deliberation, I agreed to help support the Scots in their desire fer independence. My men and I, taking leave of all that was dear to us, set out fer a country that was no' our own to fight fer a cause we firmly believe in. I still hold fast to that decision and will do so until death. My father, Rhiada, fought wi' ye as well as he could, encouraging and protecting the young heir, Princess Fiona McCurragh, in the midst of danger and certain death. I—and those wi' me—can do nae less." He sat down, and silence took the place of his words.

A chill crept up Fiona's spine at his words, feeling the same security about him that she had with his father long ago. She only prayed he would not meet the same fate.

Donald McCladden stood. "Tonight, I will tell the rest who live at this castle the news and find out how many will fight wi' us. Once we arrive at An Dùn, King Cynfael, ye and yer men as well as our hosts will take the oath of loyalty together. 'Tis then tha' we shall make plans fer launching the continuation of the war. Fiona McCurragh." He turned to her now. "'Tis entirely yer choice whether to come wi' the war host or no'. I will leave tha' up to ye to decide."

Silence followed, and Fiona realised they were waiting for an answer. She rose to her feet, her mouth dry. She licked her lips, shyly meeting the gaze of everyone who looked upon her, finding courage in the kind glances of Donald and his sons. "If 'tis all right, I would like some time. I donnae hae an answer ready yet."

"Of course, princess," Donald replied. "I will give ye as much time as I can."

"Thank ye," she murmured, sitting down again.

Angus reached over and brushed her hand with his own, meeting her glance with a quick smile of encouragement.

"Unless ye all hae any more questions, I shall dismiss ye and see ye again this evening."

Silence followed the chieftain's words.

"Until this evening, then." He bowed his head to her and then to the Cymreig king before leaving the hall, the others following him.

"I shall see ye later, perhaps?" Angus whispered to the princess, his eyes searching hers as if to reassure himself that she was truly all right after the events of a few hours ago.

"Perhaps," she replied, touching his shoulder gently before he exited the hall.

She heard footsteps from behind her and turned to see Cynfael lingering, his gaze on Fiona. She straightened, wondering what Rhiada might say, were he here to witness her finally meeting his son.

"I am sorry we hae no' had a sooner moment to speak, princess," Cynfael said, standing before her and giving a short bow.

"Between preparations fer the feast yesterday and the Danes' sudden arrival this morn, there has been little chance fer such conversation," she offered. "Donnae take it to heart—yer majesty." She added the title hastily, the words seeming odd on her tongue. Though she was royalty in a way, she had no idea how to address him. It was always her brother who had been in her father's presence when entertaining rulers of other lands, not she. She had been kept hidden away, out of sight of her father whose strange moods were only worsened by seeing her.

But Cynfael only smiled, a warm smile that lightened his thoughtful face. "How strange this world is. We both heirs to the thrones of our kingdoms, and yet we were no' originally destined to be so. I, the son of a mere harper. Ye, the younger child and daughter of King Daibhidh. The mystifying ways fate works astounds me betimes.... But please, simply calling me Cynfael will be enough. Ye never called my father by anything but his name, though he was both harper by trade and heir to his father's stolen lands."

Fiona raised her brows in surprise. Rhiada had never told her that; he must not have thought it important. But all she said was, "As ye wish—Cynfael." She slipped one foot behind the other and dipped her head in an awkward curtsy.

"Thank ye, princess."

"Do ye remember much of yer father?" she asked him, noting the way his smile faded, a look of interest and almost desperation taking its place. She wondered if she had offended him, whether she should have kept silent on that matter instead.

"A wee bit, jist snippets, mere glimpses of him throughout the years." He paused, turning to look out the window, where the bright sun pierced through a few lazy clouds in the heavens. "I remember very little of him before he was blinded, jist memories of him tossing me in the air and trying to teach me to use a sword and speak yer Gàidhlig tongue. And then he was gang fer a long, long time. When he finally came home, he could nae longer see." Cynfael's voice was tight. "Mother's heart was broken to see him so despairing, sitting by the fire like an old man. Were it no' fer King Brenin, who took pity on his daughter's husband and one of the best among his teulu, I donnae think my father would hae found hope again."

Fiona was silent, unable to picture a Rhiada in such darkness, even though she had sometimes caught glimpses of such, but only when he spoke of the reality of their situation. "Wha' did King Brenin do?" she asked softly.

Cynfael turned to her, the edges of his mouth quirking upwards, looking much like his father in that instant. "Sent his harper to him.

My father learned a new skill, one that would carry him further than his spying skills of former days, and one that brought healing. Donald told me that he was instrumental in rescuing ye from the Danes. Were it no' fer his music, ye might hae remained a prisoner."

"Is tha' why ye took up the harp?" she asked, remembering how gently he had handled his instrument the night before. "To bring beauty into the brokenness tha' life sometimes brings?"

He shrugged one shoulder. "Mayhaps. I also love the music; it brings comfort that I sometimes cannae find elsewhere." He looked at her closely, and there was a sadness in his eyes that she could not mistake.

Perhaps he was thinking of his father. She ached for him; it had been months before playing the harp had ceased to make her think so much of Rhiada and thereby cause her pain.

"I still hae yer father's harp," she said gently, not wishing to intrude upon his thoughts.

His gaze flicked up to hers with a surprising intensity. He took a step nearer. "My father's harp?"

"Aye, Angus McCladden took it wi' us when we fled the Danes after the Battle of the Pass, and I hae kept it ever since. Would ye like to hae it?"

"Does it no' belong to ye? I wouldnae wish to take yer last remembrance of him; Donald said ye loved him dearly." A trace of a Scottish lilt crept into his Cymreig accent in an endearing way.

A blush spread across Fiona's face, captivated by this young king already. "Aye, I do, but I thought perhaps ye might wish to hae it, since ye possess the skill and love fer the music tha' Rhiada had."

"I thank ye, though truth be told, I sought the music because I wished, in some way, to hae kinship to the man I hardly kent." Cynfael was silent for a moment, lost in the past. Then he finally said, "My father entrusted it to yer care. I would that ye keep it; I already hae a harp of my own."

She nodded, grinning now. "Then I shall."

"Good. Now, princess, I donnae wish to keep ye from yer other tasks. But I hope we may speak again before the war overtakes us. I should like to hear ye play sometime." He flashed her a grin. "I must return to my men and make sure all is well fer the war trail." He bowed his head and left her, his footsteps light and purposeful as he left the hall.

Fiona watched him go, musing over his words. The thought, while it terrified her still to think of playing for him, did not seem as averse as before. His father had taught her; Cynfael would understand her struggles in a way that a hall of feasting men would not.

She shook her head, driving the thoughts away. There were more important things to worry about now.

"Wha' do ye think is gang to happen?" Fiona asked that evening in Elspeth's quarters, helping watch her young children. Supper was still being prepared, but Fiona preferred to stay as long as she could in these warmer, more homely rooms than in the draughty, vaulted halls filled with so many individuals. She was exhausted by the scare of that morning and needed to gather what strength she could. She did not want to disappoint those awaiting her presence later by hiding away from the noise and conversation sure to come. Weariness did not lend wisdom, and she did not wish to make a decision about the war trail while worn out.

Elspeth McBride looked up from spooning porridge into wee Lilybet's mouth. Her son was on the floor, playing with some wooden toys and telling himself stories in a quiet voice. "I donnae ken, Fiona," she replied. "Who kens wha' the future will bring."

The princess sighed deeply and stared into the flickering light of the fire. She wished she could speak to Annag, who was seeing to the meal that night, even though Elspeth, when she did speak, usually had good advice of her own. "The future seems very dark to me."

"As I am sure it does to all, even Donald McCladden and the Cymreig," was Elspeth's steady reply. "I am surprised they are staying, even though they desired to come. It shows good strength of character to remain, wi' the threat of danger happening so soon."

"Aye, well, as the son of Rhiada, I would be surprised if King Cynfael left after this," Fiona reflected, looking into the fire now. "He promised he would stay. And if he is anything like his father, he will follow his cause to the end, even if it means his death."

Elspeth opened her mouth to reply even as she directed another spoonful of porridge into Lilybet's mouth. But before she could speak, Lilybet attempted to snatch the spoon, impatient that her food did not come soon enough. "Shh, take it a wee bit easier, darling," Elspeth murmured.

Fiona watched her, noting a blush fading from her face, though perhaps that was from the embarrassment of her child acting so when Lilybet was usually so well-behaved. It was still a shock to her, that a lass not much older than herself should be a mother of two children. "Do ye remember Rhiada?" she asked after a long pause had lapsed between them.

Elspeth hesitated, staring at the floorboards a moment before returning to her daughter. "Nae, I never met him. I had never been anywhere but our village of Claddandach before I came here, and he was already gang beyond the sunset then."

"Och, I am sorry, I had forgotten. It seems like ye hae been wi' us always."

A small smile graced Elspeth's lips. "'Tis nae matter, princess. Ye hae enough things to think about and remember."

Fiona swallowed, leaning back against the chair she sat on. Her face burned. "Maybe so, but I should remember those things too if I am to be queen someday like they say."

"One cannae remember everything. I doubt King Cynfael remembers all the details of those who live in his castle, let alone his kingdom."

Fiona shrugged. "Perhaps no'. But I am sure he remembers the important things; I'm sure he would remember someone coming to his castle fer refuge."

Elspeth sighed, wiping Lilybet's mouth clean and setting down the empty bowl of porridge. "Perhaps he would. But I didnae come to his castle, did I?"

"Are ye angry wi' me?" Fiona asked suddenly, grateful for this chance to speak to her so freely, but also wanting to be certain there was nothing in between them.

Elspeth looked up at her, her brows furrowed. "Why would I be angry wi' ye, princess?"

Fiona hesitated before answering, thinking each word through before speaking them. "Because if it were no' fer me, yer husband wouldnae hae been summoned to fight against the Danes, and he would still be alive, and ye and yer children and yer husband would still be in Claddandach." She could hear Angus arguing with her in her head about how wrong she was to think like this, but she ignored it. She needed to know the truth from Elspeth.

Elspeth thought a moment, rocking Lilybet to sleep in her arms. "Nae, Fiona, I am no' angry wi' ye nor anyone else. Jamie chose to gae of his own free will. We both kent the cost. And he might hae died fighting the Danes or Saxons anyway, regardless of yer involvement. There is nae anger, only grief, and of tha', ye are no' responsible. And I will only say this more: be careful, Fiona. I pray tha' ye willnae hae to suffer the loss I hae, but I am warning ye. Ye love the McCladdens much, as ye should. Yet yer love alone willnae keep them safe. War claims all, and when it claims those ye love, nae one can ever replace them."

Firelight danced in flickering shadows up to the rafters of the Feast Hall that evening. It was late, the feasting—such as it was with the threat of war hanging over their heads—long since over, and most were retiring for the night. Some of the men left to change out the guards and keep watch for any further threat of the Danes. But some still lingered, small groups of them engaging in quiet conversation, peaceful murmurs that rose and fell like waves gently lapping at the shore.

Fiona helped the last few of the servants not busy in the kitchens with clearing the tables and preparing the hall for the next day. Sleep was far from her, despite the happenings of early morning, and while she longed for rest, fear dogged her steps like an unwanted companion. So she worked instead, hoping sheer weariness might help silence her thoughts.

There were perhaps five other servants still in the hall, working with her and bringing the dirtied cloths and dishes down to the kitchens, sweeping from beneath the benches what the castle dogs had not eaten. None of them spoke to one another, all working with a singular purpose, content to finish the work before bed. The grand feast of yesterday remained but a memory. Amid the peatsmoke, an echo rang of the warmth of humanity that had filled this hall before. But tonight, there had been little harpsong. Celebration had been replaced with foreboding—the cold reality of the Danish threat seeping in through the walls of what should have been a safe fortress.

"Do ye need help?"

Fiona jumped at the voice behind her and turned to see Angus, one hand resting on the table beside them.

"I thought ye were asleep long ago," she replied, her voice soft, not wanting to disturb the others still in the hall.

"Nae. Father wanted me to oversee the changing of the guard, tha's all. Besides, I couldnae sleep if I kent ye were awake."

Fiona hesitated a moment, rubbing her forehead, which had begun to ache over the last hour. "Aye, if ye wish to help. We are almost finished anyway." Then she added, by way of explanation, "I cannae sleep, even if I wished to."

"Is it because of wha' happened this morning? Or are ye thinking of an answer fer Father?" he asked gently, picking up the bench so she might more easily sweep out from under it.

"Both, I suppose," she said, not speaking again until they had replaced the bench. "I donnae ken which is the best decision, especially in light of wha' happened this morn, and I hae no' had the chance to speak wi' Annag about it yet."

"I understand." He lifted and then set back down the last bench at the end of the long row of tables. "Ye need no' feel obligated to come wi' us, princess. 'Twould probably be safer fer ye if ye were no' wi' us." He met her gaze, his eyes pleading with an unspoken request.

Her head whipped towards him at such a sudden suggestion. The expression that met her—what thoughts burned in his mind to cause him to look at her so earnestly? "Aye, 'twould be safer, but I think Rhiada would wish me to gae. I ken he isnae here, but would it no' give courage to our warriors to see before them the very reason they fight? If no' the reason, the hope of such?" She sighed, leaning on her broom. "And yet, if something were to happen to me on tha' field, I ken it would destroy tha' hope, and tha' is the last thing I wish to do. We hae had so little so far."

He laid a hand on her shoulder, the warmth bringing her out of her thoughts. She realised how cold she was in this draughty place with so few people left in it.

"Fiona, princess, we hae hope now, the like of which we hae no' had since the Danes first came. If we ever had a fighting chance, this is it. Of course," he continued, his touch unchanged as he looked away towards the floor, his face hidden, "Malcolm and I would wish to hae ye wi' us too, but we understand if ye donnae come. If anything, we might rest easier kenning tha' ye were out of harm's way."

"Nae one is truly out of danger, Angus. Ye and I both ken tha.'"

A servant passed by them, carrying out a bundle of soiled rushes that had been laid out on the flagstones prior to the feast that evening.

The maid stopped, taking Fiona's broom and gathering the last of the swept rubbish, adding it to her own.

Fiona thanked her, to which the maid responded with a blushing nod and curtsy before leaving them alone.

"Aye," Angus answered, once the servant was out of hearing. "But this place is defensible. Ye would hae a better chance here than out on the battlefield."

None of them spoke for a time, Fiona gazing absent-mindedly at the last group of men speaking together at a far table. Around them, the servants slowly extinguished the torches and candles, banking up the fire for the night. The light faded into the dimness of a peaceful night, and she suddenly felt very worn out. If not for Angus' hand resting on her shoulder, she might have wavered on her feet.

"And yet," she finally replied, her voice hoarse, "I ken tha' if I stayed back, I would be constantly worrying about whether ye were all right. Wondering how the war is gang, wondering who has perished and who yet lives, wondering whether we are gaining ground, whether we are finally succeeding in wha' my father failed to do years ago. And I donnae ken whether such worry is worth me staying here in safety. I may be protected by these walls of stone, but my heart will be lost, susceptible to every arrow, every sword-stroke tha' may take the lives of those most dear to me. And if my heart is thus broken...who is to say I will be a better ruler than my father was?" Fiona looked up at him, tears smarting in her eyes. "Wha' if, all along, I become nae better than he? Will a ghaist ascend the throne and this country fall to pieces, no' from the axe of the Danes, but from the mistrust and betrayal of one another? If we cannae heal our country's deepest wounds, wha' chance do we truly hae fer freedom once the Danes are gang?"

Angus did not reply at first, reaching up with his other hand to wipe away the tears that had slipped down her face. Then he embraced her. His voice was soft as he murmured into her hair. "Fiona, ye are no' yer father. He was ever unstable of mind. Yer mother grounded him, and once she was gang, he and his country fell to pieces. But the rot had begun before his time, and while the Lowlands hae begun to heal, the Highlands... Who can say where their hearts lie? Perhaps we must first drive out the enemy without before we dare to deal wi' the one within. But tha' is no' yer fault. And should the worst happen—"

His voice broke, and it was some time before he could speak again.

"Should the worst come to pass, ye will find the strength to continue in spite of it. Ye hae borne more on yer young shoulders than yer father did at yer age, and ye are far stronger than he was. Donnae despair, princess," he said, pulling back and tilting her chin up to look at him. "We may find our courage yet. Hope cannae be lost forever."

She nodded, wiping the traces of tears off her face. "Thank ye, Angus. I ken ye speak the truth—I ken it is the truth—but oftentimes I forget it, and must needs be reminded of it."

"Always, princess. If tha' is how I can best serve my queen, I will do it gladly."

At the sudden lilt in his voice, she glanced up, seeing a warm grin on his face in the dimness of the hall. She smiled, her fears fading away.

"But now, I think we had best get some rest. Today has been harrowing, and ye need yer strength fer whatever comes next." He placed a hand on her shoulder in farewell. "Rest well."

"And ye, Angus." She watched him leave, the cold suddenly more acute now that he was gone. She did not waste much time in following his advice and retiring for the night. Her fears remained, but they no longer seemed as overwhelming as they had.

~ 7 ~

THREADS OF WAR

COME on, Ranald, jist a few more steps," Elspeth said, short of breath as they ascended the stair. Lilybet squirmed in her arms, sucking on her fingers and sometimes putting her slobber on her mother's dress. Elspeth's other hand held onto her son's as he hiked up one step and then another, going up the tower. It was after breakfast and time for Fiadh, their nursemaid, who had no bairns of her own, to watch over them while Elspeth helped with the weaving or whatever else was required of her.

A door closed above them, rapid footsteps racing down the steps.

Elspeth flattened herself against the wall as best she could, pulling her two children close so as to be out of the way of whoever was coming down. But the stair was narrow, and when the figure came round the turn, he had scarcely enough time to pull himself back before colliding with them entirely.

"*Mae'n ddrwg iawn gen i!*" The words fell out of his mouth before he gained control and repeated in the Gàidhlig, "I am so sorry! Forgive me—I should hae taken more care..."

Elspeth met his hazel-eyed gaze and the blood rushed to her face in dismay, ashamed they were not more presentable to face a king. She was acutely aware of the children on either side of her, clothes messy from playing in the gardens, and of her own hair falling loose from its plaited crown. "Nae harm taken, yer majesty." Were it not for the steps preventing such an action, she would have curtsied, but as it was, she could only bow her head.

"Nae, but 'tis I who is at fault…Elspeth?" King Cynfael replied, his dulcet voice resonating in the stair.

She made as if to take a step backward at the hesitant sound of her name, but the cool stone wall met her back. "How do ye ken my name?" she gasped. How would a king know about her, she the wife of the smallest clan's High Chieftain, now a poor widow?

"I asked Donald McCladden, fer I had mistaken ye as the Scottish princess when I first came. He told me about ye, back in Cymru when news from Annag arrived; I am sorry fer yer loss." There was no mistaking the pity and compassion in his eyes.

She looked away, struggling to keep Lilybet from suddenly diving out of her arms. When she got her daughter situated, she replied, "I thank ye, yer highness. But such is the cost fer fighting fer freedom. I ken my Jamie wouldnae think his sacrifice in vain." Her words were bitter in spite of herself. She tried to be grateful that he had died honourably, but oh, why had he been the one to die and not one of the other chieftains who did not have a young wife and children to depend on him?

"Nae need to remember my title; I am but a guest in this country. My kingship has nae power here. But…" He paused, searching her face with concern. "Do ye no' hae family wi' whom to seek refuge? Or hae the Danes taken that too?"

Elspeth shook her head, holding Lilybet closer to prevent her from wiggling so much. "My parents died of fever when I was little more than a bairn. Jamie's father died fighting the Saxons ere his son took his chieftaincy. His mother yet lives, but she is weak and crippled and is wi' her people. I didnae wish to burden her in her poverty, I a young mother wi' two children. She has enough to worry her without tha'. But I hae nae complaints." Her voice was sharper than she had meant it to be, being roughly defensive of what little pride she had left. "Annag McCladden has been very kind to give me a home and work by which to support myself and my bairns. I would no' wish to dishonour her goodness."

"Och"—it was his turn to blush now—"I didnae mean to dishonour anyone. I was merely curious, if ye had family, why ye wouldnae be wi' them." He swallowed, looking away for a moment. He ran a hand through his dark hair, thrusting it out of his face. "Forgive me, I didnae mean offence. Annag is a wise woman; she reminds me much of my late mother. I am glad she has been so kind to one who has lost so much fer freedom. But surely, there will be another to comfort yer sorrow before many years pass."

She did not answer at once, instead squeezing Ranald's hand gently; her son was growing impatient with the seemingly endless talk and no movement. "Nae, I donnae think tha' will be. The men the Danes hae no' slain are mostly too old or too young, or hae loves of their own. Besides, who would wish to love children no' his own when he could find a free lass?"

"I think...I think there are men indeed like that. They jist may be hard to find amid so many others." His words, with the grave way he said them, made him seem far older than his twenty-something years. "Donnae despair, Elspeth McBride. Yer story is no' over yet." He paused, looking away again. "I must no' keep ye. But I would that we speak again." His gaze flickered up to meet hers, almost shyly, before he glanced at Ranald and smiled, his grin giving wings of joy to his face.

Something inside her fluttered in spite of herself, and not just because her boy, so timid and wary for his two years, gave a bashful smile in return.

Then Cynfael bowed his head and continued on his way, leaving her in greater turmoil than before their paths had crossed.

"Come, Ranald," Elspeth said softly. "We are almost at the top." She tugged at him gently, and they finished ascending the stair to the second floor. She surrendered her bairns to Fiadh and entered the weaving room where the other women already sat at work, Annag and Fiona included, and picked up the mending she had left unfinished yesterday.

Though she worked as steadily as ever, her thoughts were in confusion. A king from another country, scarcely older than herself, had surrendered all to fight for another's cause, and yet he did not care so much for himself as for others, enough that he would remember her name and her past and speak so kindly to her! Yet it could never be more than that, despite what her longing heart, starved for affection, might yearn for. Fair he was, the sort of king poets would sing of, with a compassionate spirit that would make any mother proud. But her heart was broken, and with two bairns dependent on her, there was nothing that would make any man, let alone a king, desire to love her. And if a man could not love her children as well as herself, then he was not worthy of her affection.

Her story may not be over yet, she mused, but she was fairly certain of its ending. She had resigned herself to her fate, and better that this king be gone from Caerdun's walls before she lost her heart beyond all recall.

Fiona glanced up as Elspeth entered the room and sat down, picking up the never-ending pile of mending. Elspeth did not meet her eyes, her expression a troubled one, and Fiona had no wish to embarrass her in front of all the other women in the room by asking about it. So she returned to her weaving with a quiet sigh, the shuttle resuming its tuneless rhythm.

The end of this banner was not so far off anymore. Perhaps another day of steady work, and it would be finished in time for the Scots to take it with them as they set off on the war trail as originally intended. She was glad that the Danes had not found it nor destroyed it when they had so roughly searched these rooms yesterday. Maybe Annag had hidden it well among other things—how else would they have done nothing about it? Unless they had found it and considered it proof of an uprising, leaving it alone to seem as if they had not found it in order to move more quickly against the Scots....

Fiona slid the shuttle across with a louder clack than usual, which sent a few surprised faces her way. She flushed, not wanting to draw extra attention to herself. After all, it was not their fault her mind was not at rest, ever weighing the choices in her mind which she knew might impact her future far more than any of them realised.

In the coming war, should she stay in safety and yet risk her heart? Or should she go to put her mind at rest and risk all in return? Was it worth it?

Fiona glanced up at Annag, still wishing to speak with her before time ran out, but not in the hearing of others, not even Elspeth.

A small gust blew in through the open window, bringing with it the warmth and freshness of budding trees. Fiona took a breath, the sweet air playing with her senses, even as Annag looked up and met her gaze, a question in her eyes.

Laying aside her embroidery, she rose to her feet and stood behind the princess, inspecting her work. "'Tis well done," she murmured, stroking the lass's hair in encouragement. "Ye donnae need to work more on it if yer mind needs to rest. I will see to it tha' it is completed in time, sweet one," she said softly.

Fiona tilted her head back to look at her, leaning against her slightly as Annag laid a hand across her shoulders. "Thank ye. But leaving this willnae resolve my thoughts, I fear."

Annag stepped away and opened the door to the room, Fiona following as they left it to the spring breeze and the other ladies still at work.

"Everything all right, princess?" she asked once they were out in the corridor, the dimness startling after the daylight that had poured through the open window.

"I cannae decide on an answer fer Donald, and I am afraid of choosing the wrong thing and regretting it forever." Fiona blinked, her eyes still adjusting to the gloom in the draughty hallway. "I spoke wi' Angus about it last night, but he couldnae advise me further than tha' he would understand whatever I chose." She sighed. "I ken he meant to be helpful, but it has done little good."

"And keeping yerself in turmoil over it willnae make it seem any easier," Annag replied. "Make yer decision and trust tha' it is the best and only choice." She laid a hand on Fiona's shoulder. "We make miniscule decisions every day tha' change the course of our lives and donnae realise the impact we make. If we were to panic over such small things, let alone the bigger questions, we would be in much agitation. This instance, while the effect may seem more monumental, is no' so different."

Fiona said nothing, only listening with head bowed. She knew Annag's words to be the truth, and yet it did not make it any easier. "Wha' would ye do in my place?" She looked up to meet the woman's hazel gaze in the faint light of the corridor.

"I would gae on the war trail. Better to risk it all than live kenning I could hae had another chance to speak wi' those I loved best, to hear their voices and laughter.... I went wi' Donald in our early days—though I didnae fight alongside him—until I had my first son, Sioned, and then I stayed back and ruled in his stead until he came home. But my decision shouldnae influence yers; 'tis nae the same."

Fiona was silent, thinking about what she had said. Indeed, she had already begun to lean so, but she was still afraid. She was no longer a wee lass for whom the decision had already been made. She was a woman in her own right, a queen yet uncrowned, and the way of life she had become accustomed to over the last year would be abruptly changed if she went. And yet, would it not be worth it in the end?

Annag seemed to understand her hesitation, for she said no more on it besides, "Perhaps spending time wi' my sons, getting a taste again of the war trail, will make this choice seem less of a burden." She smiled warmly before taking her hand away from the lass's shoulder. "I will see ye later, princess."

Fiona watched her go, a shaft of light appearing and then vanishing as the door opened and closed, leaving her in grim silence. She squared her shoulders. Perhaps Annag was right. It had been a long while since she had spent time with Angus and Malcolm in such a way. And war trail or no war trail, she had missed it deeply.

Dust mites danced in the hazy, weak sunlight that made its way through the open door of the stables. Angus glanced up at them, tempted to stop and dream of more restful days without the imminent shadow of war, but he knew better than to pause the work. Especially when they were so near the end.

Laughter rang out from the other end of the stables; Merwyn must have said something utterly ridiculous, for Malcolm's head was thrown back and Angus could hear him gasping for breath from here. But whatever conversation followed was spoken too quickly and too interspersed with chuckles for Angus to make much sense of it.

"Wha' did he say?" Dafydd asked from beside him, his voice low and murmuring as he tried to speak in the Gàidhlig and not his native tongue.

"I donnae ken." Angus let out a whistling chuckle. "Clearly something amusing." He caught Dafydd's swift grin in the dimness and returned it.

Angus straightened and wiped away beads of sweat from his forehead with the back of his hand. Someone—perhaps it was his father, perhaps someone else—had thought it a good idea to put the now-immense job of cleaning the stables in the hands of the young warriors. He did not mind the work, but for this many horses, it was definitely quite the chore. Yet they were nearly finished, and soon would be out in the open air once more.

He turned back to shovelling out the rest of the soiled straw from this stall while Dafydd spread fresh bedding in its place. It would not do for Malcolm and Merwyn, who by the sound of it had spent far more time exchanging jests than actually working, to beat them at the end.

"Wha' do ye think they'll hae us do after this?" Dafydd asked a moment later as they closed the stall door and set to work on the next one.

"Weaponry practice, most likely," Angus grunted, setting to work at shovelling out the worst of the mess. Two more stalls to go. He did not take the time to glance down to the other end to see how far Malcolm had gotten.

"Do they think we hae become..." Dafydd hesitated, searching for the right word, "...less able to fight since we journeyed over the mountains?"

"I donnae ken. I jist think they donnae wish to risk us losing our sharpness in between now and when we actually gae to fight. Tha's how 'tis always been. We hae enough men now, perhaps, but we cannae risk it in any case. Rather to always be practising than lose too many men fer lack of it."

"Do I hear ye being against practising as often as ye breathe?" A familiar voice, a female voice, broke into his concentration. Angus looked up, sweat running into his eyes, his face burning from embarrassment and also exertion, to see Fiona McCurragh coming up towards them, her unbound curls bouncing with every step.

"I didnae say tha," he retorted, wiping his forehead with his sleeve. He tried to laugh, but it felt shallow and airy. "Did Mother send ye?" he asked a moment later, trying to think of something to say when his mind offered nothing else, seeming to focus only on Fiona before him. The light from outside formed a natural glow around her, while he and Dafydd were dirty from cleaning the stables.

"Aye, she said I needed to take a rest from weaving. She suggested I gae practise wi' ye instead of wi' the servants like I used to." She did not continue, and he was left to guess if maybe there was another reason. Considering it was his mother, there surely was.

"We will be finished soon," Dafydd answered, his voice soft and awkward as it always was when he tried to speak the Gàidhlig.

Fiona flashed a dazzling smile. "Well, I shall wait fer ye then outside on the grounds!" She spun on her heel and left, disappearing around the corner of the doorway.

Dafydd let out a low laugh. "*Mae hi'n merch hyfryd iawn,*" he murmured, returning to raking out the stable muck, his face flushed.

Angus looked at him warily, torn between accepting Dafydd's declaration of Fiona's beauty as his friend and being defensive of his own interest. But all he said was, "Aye, she is."

Two stalls later, both of the lads none the less perspiring for it, they dumped the load of soiled straw and manure at the back of the stables for someone else to carry out to the nearby fields. Then they hung up their tools even as Malcolm and Merwyn did the same.

"So, where are we bound now?" Malcolm said, heaving a great sigh. "I'm starving."

"We're gang to weaponry practice, o daft one," Angus replied. "Ye'll hae to wait to eat until 'tis time to actually do so. Besides, Fiona's coming wi' us."

"Och, she is? Well, tha' makes it a wee bit more bearable." Malcolm let out a whoop and skipped out of the stables, his tall, lanky form nearly hitting some of the support beams overhead as he did so. Merwyn followed him at a slower, more uncertain pace.

"Well then," Angus said, turning to Dafydd with what he hoped was a teasing smile on his face, "are ye ready to fight the princess?"

~ 8 ~

A QUEEN'S COURAGE

THE sun was warm upon Fiona's hair, despite the cool gusts sweeping across the practice fields and rippling the banners above the gates of Caerdun. The clash of weapons and shouting of corrections filled her ears as she watched those sparring on the plain. The grass was soft beneath her as she leaned back on her hands, her ankles crossed, the folds of her dress tucked underneath her to prevent the breeze blowing them away.

She heard footsteps coming near and glanced up to see Angus approach, his sword now belted about his waist. "Ye finished, then?" she asked.

"Wi' the stables, aye." He sat down beside her, inhaling deeply. "Malcolm may try to satisfy his hunger before this," he added after a moment.

"As he would," she commented with a laugh, breathing in the sweet scent of growing things and moist earth from last night's rain. "We often practised much longer than this, while ye all were away." She paused, looking at him intently. "But no' as much as when we would spar by the stream in An Dùn."

"Aye, I remember," he replied, his voice soft in remembrance. "And yet it served us well, when it came time to fight."

She nodded, turning away again, the choice still weighing heavily on her, woven with memory and longing for days long ago. "Ye will be returning there first, before making other plans?" It was half question, half statement.

~ 91 ~

"I believe so." He said nothing else, but she could feel his gaze still on her, warmer than the sun.

She wondered if he expected her to have an answer, whether he wanted to know more of her struggle.

Do ye wish me to gae wi' ye? Would ye rather hae me by yer side as I do ye? Or must we be parted yet again?

A loud whoop sounded from behind him before she could speak, the moment lost in the playful wind.

Malcolm slid to a stop, nearly falling over on the grass, laughing breathlessly. "I won!" he squeaked before doubling over to catch his breath.

Fiona glanced from Angus to his brother, and then to the two Cymreig companions now arriving behind Malcolm. "Ye won?" she asked.

"Aye," he gasped. "I said whoever got here first didnae hae to spar first." He jerked his thumb in the general direction behind him. "So I get to rest fer awhile." He plopped down onto the ground, his legs crossing over each other, his pleated kilt resting slightly above his freckled, bony knees. He lay down and covered his eyes with his palms, his chest rising and falling as his breathing slowed to normal.

"'Twould be rather hard to beat ye wi' yer long legs," she commented, a smile playing on her lips despite the wistful surge in her heart. It was still a struggle to reconcile this Malcolm with the wee lad she had known a year ago.

"And his appetite," she heard Angus mutter beside her, his brows drawn together as he squinted against the daylight.

"Och, I heard tha'!" Malcolm cried but made no further movement.

The pair sparring before them stopped and stepped apart, bowing to each other before sheathing their weapons.

"I believe ye, Fiona, are next?" Angus said.

Something in his tone, light and teasing but also dangerous, made her look at him sharply, searching his face for what he meant.

There could be no mistaking the dancing yet guarded light in his blue eyes.

"Are ye sparring wi' me?" she asked, her confusion evident in her own ears.

"Nae, Dafydd is." Angus glanced at his companion, a roguish grin spreading across his face.

What did that grin mean? Fiona looked at Dafydd's uncertain expression. It did not seem a kind thing to force his friend so—and why now?

Dafydd stared at the grass at his feet, his face pale. He glanced up, meeting her gaze and blushing violently before looking away again.

Fiona clenched her jaw, frustrated by whatever sort of game Angus was playing. But there was only one way to end it, and she was not going to wait for them to resolve it among themselves. Rising to her feet, she gripped her familiar sword hilt. She stood before Dafydd, waiting until he met her gaze before saying, "Ye ready?"

He answered by stepping towards the flattened grassy area, his eyes never leaving hers, and pulled out his blade, holding it level to his face.

Fiona unsheathed her sword, the blade flashing the sunlight in her eyes a moment, blinding her. In a true fight, she would have been caught and possibly disarmed—or worse—but Dafydd was polite enough to wait until she could see before advancing.

She knew how to distance the fact she was fighting someone often much older than her, how to blank out a familiar face—replace it with one of an enemy. But this was different. Dafydd could not understand her tongue well, but he was no Dane; he was unfamiliar, and his methods of approach were not what she was used to from the Scots or the enemy.

Nonetheless, it took only a minute of defending his blows to realise that he had a rhythm too. Unlike Angus, ferocious and passionate like an angered cat, and unlike Malcolm, nearly playful and teasing, this had an almost melodic-rhythm. The way he thrust and pulled back, his footwork stepping forward and then back and sideways, the way he parried blows and turned them in his favour all spoke of a dance.

Fiona could not help the smile on her face, though sweat began to bead and roll down her brow as she quickly figured out his weaknesses: he paused too much when he led with his left foot—perhaps he had had an injury and was ever after cautious. A moment later, she tripped him and placed her booted foot onto his blade before he could grasp it, her sword pointed at his neck.

"No' bad, lad of Cymru," she said, stepping back and allowing him to rise.

"Thank ye, Princess of Scotland," he said stiffly, jerking his head down in a bow. "I hope yer trust in our skill is no' lessened by this fight."

She furrowed her brows, glancing to Angus and the others around them who had been watching, wondering what he meant. "Nae, nae," she said at last. "Jist be lighter on tha' left foot. I wouldnae wish fer a Dane to thus trip and slay ye."

He nodded, still seeming half terrified, and returned his blade to its sheath, going to sit beside Merwyn and Malcolm.

Fiona sheathed her sword and walked off the sparring ground as another pair took their place, still lost in thought. She sat down beside Angus, looking at him intently until he gave her his full attention. "Wha' was tha' all about, anyway?" she whispered, not wishing for anyone else to hear. "I thought he was yer dear friend?"

Angus grinned. "Aye, he was and is. Only he said something about ye being so lovely tha' I thought it only fair tha' he fight ye first. He must respect ye as a princess and future queen, and no' jist as a bonnie lass."

Fiona glared at him, unamused. "'Twas no' very kind, Angus. I think ye would ken better how to tell him so without embarrassing him in this way."

The grin vanished, and his next words were hastily spoken, as if he were now ashamed of what he had done. "Fiona, I meant nae harm. Besides, whether 'tis ye or an enemy, skill is skill. He can fight well; I hae fought wi' him enough times to testify of tha'. But I kent he was nervous about the prospect, and I ken tha' the only way fer him to become greater than his fear is to face it. I wouldnae wish fer the same sort of thing to happen out on the battlefield. I highly doubt it would, but I donnae wish to take chances—nae wi' those I love."

She searched his face, seeing only earnestness and something else she could not understand, let alone describe.

"Can ye forgive me fer offending ye?" he said next, still speaking in a low voice as Malcolm and Merwyn rose to fight.

Blood rushed to her face at the intensity in his gaze and she looked away, ashamed she had thought wrong of his actions. "There is nothing to forgive, Angus. I should no' hae assumed the worst. But I would wish fer ye to apologise to Dafydd so there is nae bad blood formed between ye, no' wi' war soon to come."

The breeze blew between them, cool as it kissed her face. She felt a sudden warmth as Angus laid his hand on hers and she looked up to see him gazing at her, sincerity softening his face. "Aye, I will. Donnae worry about it, princess."

Perhaps it was because she had thought of days long ago. Perhaps it was because of the wind playing in his hair and the sun shining in his deep blue eyes. Perhaps it was also because she had yet to make the choice that would cost her dearly, not just because of the war, but because of him who her soul realised she treasured far above anyone else. For her next words tumbled out of her mouth before she had thought them through: "May I fight against ye next, then?"

He laughed. "As ye wish." He jumped to his feet and held out a hand to her.

She took it, looking into his eyes as he did not immediately let go. Her brow wrinkled in confusion. "Are we gang to wait fer Malcolm to finish?"

"Why should we? There is room enough. And I remember several pairs sparring last time I lived in this place." He flashed a grin and stepped back, his hand going to the hilt of his sword.

Fiona did not reply with words. They had often had multiple persons practising at once before, but she did not wish Malcolm to think them impatient. Though, knowing Malcolm, it was unlikely he thought that.

They drew blades together, Angus' smile slowly fading into a look of quiet concentration, though she still saw a light dancing in his eyes.

He thrust first, stepping forward and drawing back as she parried. It had been more than a year since the last time they had duelled, but she remembered his rhythm well, the balance between frenetic blows and carefully placed strikes. They were still evenly matched, neither of them gaining long before it shifted in the other's favour. When she glanced at his face, she did not see the fear or anger that he had often fuelled his movements with as before, but a careful, thoughtful expression. This dance of blades had poetry humming within it.

With a pang in her chest, she realised how much she had missed this: missed the days when they were equals, all children—even though Angus had been sixteen and considered nearly a man—children facing a war too big for them, and who faced it with courage and hope anyway. But a year *had* passed, and none of them had remained children; they had each grown, and coming back, some things made them feel more like strangers.

Fiona nearly lost her balance as Angus advanced with a series of cuts and thrusts, bringing her back to the present. Gritting her teeth, her face flaming in embarrassment—she had trained better than this—she defended his attack and slowly but surely pushed him back.

He parried a couple of her blows and then held his sword upright to his face, the winged corners of a smile peeking at either edge of the blade. "Well done, princess."

She hesitated, her sword pointed towards the trodden grass. "Is tha' it?" Her chest heaved and she was glad of the reprieve, but she had not seen him pause like this before. Unless it was part of some jest.

"Aye. 'Tis good enough fer now. I donnae desire to weary my princess overlong wi' the blade." He sheathed his sword and rubbed his sweaty forehead with the back of his hand. "Come, I suppose ye're hungry?"

She slammed her sword into its scabbard, a tired grin spreading across her face. She was definitely winded, and yet some part of her longed for that feeling, not just for this day, but for every day, like they had used to experience what seemed so long ago. If she went with them on the war trail, she would have that again, and she would yearn for them if she stayed behind, perhaps far more than she would for comfort and routine.

She bit her lip, lost in thought. Annag was wise to have sent her to the practice fields; if anything, this made her choice clearer and easier than if she had remained inside, stuck weaving that tapestry.

Angus turned and began heading back to Caerdun. Malcolm and Merwyn strolled ahead of them, chattering about something in a chaotic mixture of Cymraeg and Gàidhlig and somehow understanding what the other was trying to say. Dafydd shadowed his friend in silence, his footsteps almost inaudible on the grass like a deer. Fiona followed them all, lengthening her stride in spite of her dress to match Angus' pace.

He greeted her and then leaned closer to whisper, "I wish to speak to Dafydd...to apologise," he continued, looking into her eyes. "I'll meet ye in the Feast Hall."

She nodded and picked up the edges of her skirt to run and catch up with Malcolm. She'd see him later at any rate, but first, she must speak with Chieftain McCladden before she could doubt herself and change her mind once more.

"Dafydd," Angus murmured, dropping behind to speak to his companion.

Dafydd glanced up, the sun shining in his hazel eyes, and dipped his head in acknowledgement. "Aye, Angus, did I do something wrong?"

"Wha'?" he sputtered, his face crinkling in confusion. "Wha' made ye think tha'?"

Dafydd shrugged a shoulder. "I only thought, since ye made me fight wi' the princess—"

"Nae, nae," Angus interrupted, laying a hand on Dafydd's shoulder. "I meant it in jest, to tease ye since I saw how interested ye were when she came into the stables." They stopped walking now, the noise of the groups still practising on the field sounding behind them. "But it was wrong of me to push ye forward like tha', and I am truly sorry. I didnae mean to embarrass ye in front of her. Will ye forgive me?"

Dafydd smiled broadly, his lips parting, and he placed his hand on Angus', releasing it from his shoulder. "Of course, *fy ffrind*. There is nae hurt taken. It was wrong of me to take such interest; she is yer princess, perhaps soon yer queen, and I ken ye care fer her as more than jist a friend."

"There is nae wrong in taking interest," Angus replied. "I hae nae claim on her.... I donnae ken her heart," he continued after a moment, looking away towards the figures fading from sight into the castle. "'Tis only a fool's dream she would care fer the son of a Lowlander chieftain."

"Nae." Dafydd shook his head emphatically, his smile gone, seriousness replacing it. "Fools donnae dream, they merely sleep. She cares fer ye deeply; there is a bond beyond that of mere acquaintance. Ye lived through the last war; that creates a sort of trust nothing else does. Besides"—he flashed a grin—"I'm sure yer lassies are jist as strange as ours; she might be hiding her true feelings."

Angus playfully punched him in the shoulder, biting back a laugh. He knew Dafydd meant well, but with war once more on the horizon and Fiona most likely staying behind, he was almost afraid to wish that she might return his longings in the same way. And who was he to make promises about the future when both of them knew he might not even come back?

But what if she did go? His heart leapt at the thought, eager to not be parted from her after so soon returning. His elation faded a moment later, knowing that greater vigilance would have to be spared for her protection. He would not want her to fight on the field; he cared too much now, and the excuse of having too few men as before was gone.... Aye, she would be safer staying behind. It would be best for them both. And if she had any sense, she would choose to stay.

"Come," Dafydd said after a moment, pulling him back into the present. "Methinks yer brother may eat all the food before we can."

Angus rolled his eyes heavenward. "He'll certainly try."

Fiona breathed deeply, trying to calm her nerves as she walked the short distance from the Feast Hall to the Great Hall after luncheon. She had been unable to speak to Donald McCladden during that time as he had been deep in conversation with King Cynfael and the other Cymreig leaders, and she did not desire to disturb their council—not in front of everyone else also at the meal.

She knew what she wanted to say, and she knew that Donald would not try to persuade her otherwise in her decision once made. But it was not those things that caused her heart to flutter like the whinnies of a nervous horse. No, she knew that this choice would be irrevocable once made, and that was what terrified her: the fear of somehow making the wrong decision and it costing her dearly. And yet she knew, just as strongly as she had been reminded during the laughter and jesting and casual conversation during luncheon with the McCladden brothers, that she would not choose otherwise.

She only hoped that it truly was the right thing.

Squaring her shoulders, she pushed open the door to the hall, entering the reflective quiet disturbed only by the low murmuring of Donald and Cynfael. They were bent over what looked like a map of Scotland, worn and stained by use throughout the long years. As she approached, her footsteps seeming to echo in the barren tension of preparations for war, her eyes wandered across the flourished burns, dotted trees, and rigid mountains. Based on the layout and style of writing, it was perhaps from before her own father's time; but the land, like the wind and sea, remained the same regardless of who lived and loved and died on it.

Their conversation ceased as they became aware of her presence, both of them greeting her wordlessly, Cynfael's dark eyes glinting with something of acknowledgement. The silence left in her wake seemed somehow heavier for it.

"Princess Fiona," Donald began, dipping his head in a quick bow, "how may we be of service to ye?" His blue eyes were merry, though his reddish brows were still drawn in what appeared to be concentration, though it might be something else. War and the inevitable deaths of men were never an easy task to scheme for.

"I wished to speak to ye about gang wi' ye on the war trail," Fiona began, her voice weak but growing steadier the more she spoke. "I apologise fer being unable to speak to ye sooner on this."

"Nae matter, ye still had time left. So...ye are coming then?"

She could not read his tone. Curiosity, almost; concern, most likely. "Aye, I wish to gae, if tha' can be arranged."

In the silence that followed, she swallowed, gazing at the floor now as she gave her reasons, which perhaps were not needed, but she wished to say them all the same. She clenched her hands at her sides, trying to calm her racing heart, drawing what strength she could find to speak clearly and firmly.

"I understand my presence may be a risk, since I will be far closer to the Danes than I would be here at Caerdun. But even as ye and Rhiada said two years ago, perhaps my presence will inspire courage in the hearts of our men. Even wi' our combined numbers"—she glanced at Cynfael—"valour is always a welcome weapon against the enemy. And besides, should the worst happen, I willnae be much safer here, should the Danes' might overcome the country when Scotland's best men are slain and gang."

She pulled herself up to full height and looked Donald straight in the eyes, seeing him as an equal, or perhaps her commander beneath her rule. She continued, her voice firm and steady now. "I would much rather put my life at risk, the same as those fighting fer me and fer Scotland, than sit back here and worry as the days gae by whether we still hold the field. I would no' play the coward by staying behind."

She inhaled sharply, the last words more murmured than declared but without the usual tremor of shame: "I may be a lass, but I will no' be my father."

Donald looked at her fondly, admiration shining in his eyes. "Aye, princess, one could never accuse ye of being as yer father in his last days. When he was younger, aye, he shared tha' same passion, but ye hae yer mother's sweetness and caring. Ye will make us a fine queen someday. I would welcome ye among us as we set out, and I am sure all the rest of our army will do so as well."

"Thank ye, Donald," she replied with an exhale much louder than she intended it to be, an invisible burden sliding off her shoulders, her cheeks warming.

"I will speak wi' Annag about finding ye suitable war gear; we hae been discussing this should ye make tha' decision. Would ye like to choose yer own bodyguards, then?" he added, a smirk playing at the corners of his mouth.

Fiona smiled in spite of herself. "I would like to take back yer sons, if they are willing."

Donald laughed. "I donnae see why no'. Would ye prefer to ask them or leave it to me?"

"I would...I would ask them," Fiona replied, "if I may. Though perhaps 'tis better if ye speak to them first."

"Of course, princess. I will speak to them. There will be time in between now and after we arrive in An Dùn, donnae worry." Donald bowed his head, a twinkle still dancing in his eyes. He turned to Cynfael. "We can discuss this later wi' Fiona and the other chieftains then," he said, gesturing to the map before them.

"That is well," Cynfael murmured, his low, melodic voice once again taking Fiona by surprise. "I will also be glad to hae ye, princess."

"Is there anything ye might need to ask of me?" she asked, grateful for his willingness.

"Nae," Donald replied, shaking his head. "Ye may gae. I am sure ye need to pack yer things fer setting out wi' us."

"Thank ye, I will see ye then at supper tonight, I trust." And with that, Fiona turned and left the room, something winged still fluttering in her chest. Once outside the hall, she attempted to breathe more deeply to calm it, even as she set out for the battlements in search of someone she knew would care very much to know whether she was going with them or not.

Out in the open air, the wind once again toyed with her hair but with gentle playfulness, as if welcoming her back, and so she did not mind. Few noticed her swift passing as she ran across the courtyard and quickly ascended the steps to the battlements, pausing only to catch her breath.

She caught sight of Angus standing on the far end, doing his own share of guard duty, his form grim and steady as he gazed out on the moors facing north. She approached him softly, but he still heard her, turning to her with an inquisitive expression on his face, a wordless question hanging in the air.

"I am gang wi' ye," she said quietly, reaching down and taking his hand in hers, cold in the spring air.

His shoulders relaxed, his dark brows no longer furrowed, though something flickered in the depths of his eyes, something that seemed almost fearful despite his next words. "I am glad, princess."

She stepped closer, releasing his hand, and he placed his arm across her shoulders as both of them looked to the north, the distance hidden by the afternoon haze.

She had asked Donald to speak with his sons before she would, but part of her wished she could ask Angus now, to know not only would she be marching with him, but that he would be honour-bound to remain by her side.

But perhaps it was for the best to wait. It had been one thing when they had been children, but to ask him now whether he would sacrifice his duty as a soldier to become her personal guard.... There was more than one allegiance to consider, and he might very well be forced to choose between his country's safety and hers at times should he accept. It was no light matter, and certainly not when her heart hung in the balance. Malcolm, it was an easy question; Angus, it meant something far more. Aye, she would ask him, but not yet. She did not wish to ruin this moment by an ever nearer recognition of war.

So she said nothing and merely leaned her head on his shoulder. She still had this, at least. And she did not want the moment to end.

"I am glad ye are gang," he murmured, breaking into her thoughts. His voice was soft, as if it were some great secret shared only between them two. "Whatever this coming storm brings us"—he nodded towards the darkening clouds in the distance—"I am glad to fight by yer side." And his arm across her shoulders tightened.

~ 9 ~

RETURN TO AN DÙN

THE Scots and Cymry rose earlier than their wont at Caerdun that last grey dawn, all preparing for the warband's departure, even if many of the castle's inhabitants would stay behind. The servants bustled around, preparing breakfast and ensuring everything was ready.

Elspeth was among them, her children still fast asleep in their beds. She was glad of this chance to work hard in silence without the guilt of knowing she should be caring for her bairns, though Fiadh was more than willing to watch over them. Besides, this busyness kept her thoughts from overtaking her. The princess was leaving them, and some small part of Elspeth wished she could do the same, if only so she could prove her worth in return for the kindness shown by Annag and the other women at Caerdun. But she had two children and no knowledge of weaponry, and she knew war had no place for her.

Ye are a fool, she told herself in rhythm to her footsteps as she ran up and down the spiralling stairs on the last few errands, making sure everyone's clothing and gear was taken out of the rooms they had slept in.

She closed the doors softly behind her to now-empty chambers, their occupants not to return—if ever—for a long time. Pausing to regain her breath, she returned the way she had come, walking down the dim corridor. In the distance, she could hear raised voices coming from the lower halls and courtyard where all were gathering for the leave-taking.

Not long now, and silence would reign in their place. And the quiet left behind would be all the heavier for the emptiness.

"Elspeth!"

She froze, glancing over her shoulder to see Cynfael approaching her, his long stride bringing him to her in a matter of moments.

"Am I keeping ye?" he asked, his chest heaving from quick breathing. Clearly Elspeth was not the only one rushing around this morn.

"Nae, there is but little left to do before ye leave," she answered, bewildered by his question. Her pulse raced faster in spite of herself. What could he possibly want with her, he a king and she now little more than a peasant?

"I wished to say goodbye," he said, looking her earnestly in the face.

The blood roared in her ears. "Goodbye—to me?" she sputtered, her cheeks burning. "We hae spoken but once, and tha' in passing."

"Aye, Elspeth McBride, to ye." Cynfael's face was solemn, his eyes dark and hidden. "Perhaps in more peaceful times, we might hae had a better chance to become acquainted, no' rushed by things beyond our control. I ken I cannae promise I will return, but, should we win against the Danes, I would wish to speak to ye again." His words were hesitant, and not only because Gàidhlig was not his native tongue.

Elspeth stared at him, clenching her jaw to keep it from falling open in shock. "Me?" she said again, knowing she must sound like a silly bairn. "But I am nae one, jist a mother widowed by the war." Surely he had spoken such words to other women. A handsome young man—now a king—he certainly would have no end of admirers, perhaps those better suited to him than herself. If anything, he should spend his efforts to woo the Scottish princess and form a stronger alliance between the kingdoms, though perhaps the McCladdens had told him otherwise.

"Aye, Elspeth, ye." His voice was soft, like the whispering wind had been when she had stepped into the courtyard that morning. "I would wish to speak to ye again, should we win our way back. I am sorry I cannae promise more, and that we ken each other so little, but, all the same, will ye wait fer me?"

She did not quite know how to find the words to respond. *He wishes to speak to me again.... Had Donald or Annag McCladden spo-*

ken to him about me? Why else...perhaps.... "Aye," she managed to say at last. "I will wait fer ye."

"Farewell, Elspeth," he replied, bowing his head as if she were some great lady. But his voice, ever melodic, had a melancholy tone that touched the depths of her soul far more than his words did. "May we meet again under clearer skies."

Then he was gone, passing her by to join his men below, taking her bruised heart and half-buried dreams with him.

Horsemen assembled in the main courtyard, most already mounted while stable boys ran hither and thither among them, fulfilling last-minute errands. While a good portion of the army would be on foot, those would come later at An Dùn. This part of the warband would all be riding—at least, for the present.

Fiona stood beside Annag within the doorway to the keep, more than happy to wait to swing into the saddle. It would be a couple days of riding before they reached An Dùn, and it had been a long time since she had ridden regularly. The last two days had flown by so fast it seemed that each day consisted of rising early and preparing for the departure, only to fall into bed each night exhausted. The tapestry had to be finished and weapons sharpened and gathered for those who might assemble in An Dùn without a blade. Food had to be packed, each warrior carrying a week's ration of oat bannocks and dried fruit, with some dried meat and ewe cheese for the first few days. And what cloth could be spared had been gathered for tents against foul weather or torn into bandages.

Fiona had wanted to spend the last few days of freedom with Angus and Malcolm, but it seemed that was not to be. She scarcely saw her friends at all those two days, and when they did happen to meet, there was no time for an exchange of words aside from a brief greeting. She would have to wait until An Dùn to speak to them, it seemed.

Beneath her cloak, she wore her usual dress, with a leather jerkin made to fit her form. Annag had seen to it she had proper garments— for war or otherwise—before setting out. Fiona had clothes more suitable to wear for battle, should necessity call for her to risk her life alongside her warriors instead of merely being a symbol to them, but fine mail and outer tunics were not as comfortable for long riding since she was not used to wearing them.

Upon her plaid, draped over her left shoulder, she had placed her brother's clan pin instead of her own. She was setting out for war at the age he had been when she had last seen him, and she wanted to have a piece of him with her, almost as a sort of shield against whatever the future would bring. The past was behind her, but she could still hold onto the memories as a light in the dark.

Donald, Cynfael, and two other Cymreig leaders who had also not yet mounted stood at one end of the courtyard, briefly going over the plans as to what villages they would be riding through to save their rations for the days beyond.

Cynfael once again had his hooded bird sitting on his leather gauntlet, whose covered head turned at times as if to better hear the secrets whispered in the wind. The king looked far more intimidating with the gyrfalcon sitting on his wrist than without it, and a chill shivered down Fiona's spine at the thought of such a graceful beast and a kind king turning deadly and feral in the heat of battle. She had only heard stories of fighting with birds of prey, and knew of no one else who used them. If she had a chance, she would have to ask him more about it.

Malcolm threw his head back with a hoot from where he sat atop his horse near her, his friend Merwyn chuckling with him, and her thoughts were forgotten.

Angus and Dafydd stepped into the courtyard, leading the last of the horses out of the stables. They looked at Malcolm, who was still laughing, and Angus said something to his companion, who grinned in response. Angus returned the expression and caught sight of Fiona, greeting her with a cheerful nod. Then the pair mounted, waiting with the rest as the day grew ever brighter, still tinged grey and hinting of coming rain.

Breezes brushed over the battlements, warm and sweet with the smell of heather, tossing the horses' manes and rippling the banner that Annag, Elspeth, and Fiona had woven over the past year. The emerald dragon on its blue field fluttered in the air, seeming to take flight some moments and falling straight in others. The colour was bright enough in the greyness, brilliant blue like cloudless sky. And the sound of curlews calling carried over the castle walls, the sure sign of spring.

As if the birdsong was a signal, Donald McCladden called out, "Mount yer horses! We ride out soon!"

The Cymreig leaders obeyed at once, but Donald came and kissed his wife farewell before bestriding his horse, looking at Annag with pained longing at being parted again so soon.

Fiona turned to Annag, attempting a smile. She threw her arms around Annag's neck and held on tight, wondering how long before she would see her again, wondering whether they would once again bring her tragic news when they returned—if they did at all. "Thank ye fer everything," Fiona said, though her voice threatened to break. Her chest was tight with all the words she wanted to say and yet did not know how to speak, but she knew that she would never be happy if she stayed behind.

Annag pulled away after a moment, brushing aside a loose strand of Fiona's hair and tucking it behind the lass's ear. "Donnae think about the road ahead. Take one day at a time, dearest. I am always wi' ye in thought. Remember, courage is pressing onward in spite of fear." She kissed Fiona lightly on the forehead. "Gae now, lass, and win back yer own. May the road rise to meet ye, and may the wind be always at yer back."

Fiona nodded, not trusting her voice to speak. She remembered saying those words to her brother years ago, and he had not come home, taking instead another path, the Warrior's Road. That traditional farewell held nothing but bittersweet memories for her now. It felt more of a bad omen than a good one to hear it spoken as they set off on the war trail. But perhaps it was time to let go of the past. The words themselves had no harm.

With a quiet grunt, she mounted her horse, riding beside Malcolm and Angus out of the gate. As they passed beneath the raised portcullis, she glanced behind her at the lady standing in the courtyard.

Annag raised a hand in farewell, and Fiona waved back before turning to the road that unwound itself before them.

An Dùn and a war trail lay ahead, and who knew how much sorrow and suffering would be endured before the end. Was freedom worth the price they must pay? It had been high enough the first time. She only prayed it would not be so now.

She looked at Angus and Malcolm where they rode now a bit ahead of her, faces set towards the misty, opening skies. She was glad to be with them as they set out once more for war. Whatever lay ahead in the days to come, they would no longer be separated.

"Come, princess!" Malcolm cried, slowing his mount to let her ride up.

She grinned and spurred her horse onward, the familiar feel of the saddle reminding her of the McCladdens' breathless ride from nearly a week before. More flowers bloomed on the braes now, new life sweeping over the land. Aye, perhaps spring had come for Scotland too.

Elspeth raced up the stairs to the battlements, ignoring the presence of the guards as she peered over the stone walls, gazing at the war host slowly disappearing into the rising grey dawn. She remembered the last time she had seen such a departure, when Jamie had embraced her, a smile on his face that did not reach his eyes, and his words—spoken far too lightly—that he would be back before she realised he was gone. Only the painful memories remained now, and other dark figures against the blooming landscape riding to war as the land breathed new life.

She felt the warmth of another person's presence and she turned to see Annag come stand beside her.

The woman placed a hand on Elspeth's shoulder, her gentle touch easing the tension in Elspeth's shoulders.

Perhaps she knew—or at least guessed at—Elspeth's thoughts.

"We must hope tha' they will come home, dear one. Jamie wouldnae want ye to despair."

A tear slipped down Elspeth's face despite her struggle to remain calm. "The spring is dark without him," she murmured, her throat tight.

"But tha' doesnae mean the light will never shine again. Ye hae yer children, and ye hae us. Ye are loved still, and we would hae ye stay here as long as ye need. Ye donnae walk the path of grief alone." Tendrils of dark hair played about Annag's face, strands that had come loose from the braided crown on her head and now framed her face. Her brow was creased in empathy, her voice soft. "I ken this must hurt, thinking of other days. Take as long as ye need, Elspeth. We will be waiting fer ye, when ye are ready to return." She took her hand away and left her, returning to her many tasks that remained despite the warband's going.

Elspeth watched her leave, and then looked one last time at the horizon as the warriors vanished from sight. Annag was right. Thinking about the past would change nothing. And besides, there was plenty to occupy them both until they came back. She could only pray they did, that Annag might not endure further loss, not like Elspeth already had.

Snatches of song and laughter could be heard among the ranks as they rode east to An Dùn. Malcolm's bubbling laugh rang out often, almost as if he were singing with the calls of the curlews and occasional raven, though what he was laughing at exactly, Fiona could not say.

She was one of a few who did not participate in the joyfulness of the others. The excitement of finally setting out on this new—if dangerous—adventure had worn off, worry taking its place. So instead of jesting and making small conversation with the other riders, she gazed at the greening lands they passed through, her mind on what Annag had said, repeating the words over and over until they seemed to form a chant with every step of the road her horse took. Squaring her shoulders, she breathed in rhythm with the words humming in her mind.

Courage is pressing onward in spite of fear. Spring air filled her lungs, and the writhing in her gut slowed.

Courage is pressing onward, she repeated as she took another breath, *in spite of fear*. The painful tingling in her wrists faded. The phrase rang truer than it ever had before as she recited it yet a third time—and only as it echoed did she start to believe it.

"Ye look very serious." A deep voice broke into her thoughts.

Startled, Fiona glanced up to see Cynfael riding alongside her, his hair nearly black in the gloomy daylight. "I was merely thinking 'bout something Annag McCladden said to me before we left," she replied wistfully.

"And wha' was that?"

"'Courage is pressing onward in spite of fear.'"

The king was silent for a moment, watching the road before them.

"There is much truth in that. We would all be the wiser, mayhaps, if we paid heed to it."

Fiona nodded solemnly. "Aye. Annag possesses much wisdom. I doubt I will ever ken as much as she does."

Cynfael chuckled. "Ye are young yet. Wisdom comes wi' age, and often through hardship do we learn the lessons we wouldnae learn otherwise."

"Yer father said the same once," she said, her voice wistful.

A sad look crossed his face, and he looked at the bird still resting on his wrist before turning his eyes to the road again. "Aye, that is where I heard it from, long ago, he and my mother."

"Is yer mother still living?" she inquired after a pause.

"She died a few months before we left fer yer country, Fiona. She was no' in good health, and I didnae wish to leave her behind and hae her join my father in death without my being there—which is why I hesitated to answer Scotland's plea fer help against the Danes." He was about to say something more when Donald McCladden called to him from the front and, with a nod to Fiona, Cynfael spurred his horse forward to answer the summons, leaving her once more to her thoughts.

She glanced around, finally spotting Angus and Dafydd riding together some distance behind her, discussing something she could not hear. She looked away, not only because it was unsafe to ride and not look at the path ahead, but because the loneliness was painful enough. She did not wish for jealousy to come between them, even if it meant the suffering of her own closeness with Angus. His and Dafydd's friendship must be allowed to flourish, especially now, when trust between swordbrothers could mean the difference between life and death. Perhaps it was unwise to ask the McCladdens to be her personal guard when it might pull them away from other companions. She must not strain the new friendships, no less those between allies.

But she still missed the days when the three of them were close. No war trail was the same, it was said, but she had not thought of the difference being this. Mayhaps, once she had spoken to them, it would change. They already shadowed her and were never out of her sight—which was perhaps Donald's doing already—but until she had a chance to speak to them once they arrived in An Dùn, to ask them herself, perhaps it would remain as it was. Yet maybe she was merely overthinking it, as she often did.

Her shoulders relaxed, and she exhaled at the thought. Yes, perhaps it was merely that.

By twilight on the second evening, the war host from Caerdun Castle crested the final hill and rode hard on the last stretch of road to An Dùn, entering by the south gate as the evening fires were being lit. They were greeted by enthusiastic cheers. Stable hands ran to take care of their horses while others told them where they could eat and sleep, and the captain of the guard hurried to speak with Donald and Cynfael. It was too dark for Fiona to see who it was, and she did not recognise his voice. Perhaps it was not the same guard as two years before.

Malcolm and Merwyn began unloading things from the horse-packs, telling her that she was the princess and should not have to work as hard as them while Angus and Dafydd busied themselves with stabling the horses, promising to see her at suppertime—if not before.

She watched the two young lads for a bit. Malcolm constantly switched between the Gàidhlig and Cymraeg with the rapidity of a squirrel, leaving Merwyn to stumble in his replies. Fiona smiled to herself at the chaos, having given up trying to help since every attempt resulted in a shrill declaration from Malcolm that she should rest.

Not knowing what else to do, she walked down the chariotway to the centre of the fort, wrapped in her cloak for warmth. It was chilly this evening, the spring air almost biting, and for a moment she was whisked back to an An Dùn of the past. She could almost hear the clangs of training in the distance, almost savour that first taste of porridge—and kindness—from the first place she had learned the meaning of "home".

She made her way to the McCladden croft and opened the door to dusty darkness. It had not been lived in since she and Annag had departed for Caerdun last spring, when the embassy had left for Cymru.

Fiona entered, a different flood of memories coming back as she took in the dwelling she had lived in, which now seemed so long ago. Fear, hope, pain—all mingling together in a sort of bitter homesickness. She remembered the other faces that had been here, Duncan McCladden's and Rhiada's, faces she would see no more.

She paused before the fireless hearth, strangely empty without Annag nearby it, and her fingers brushed the cold, rough stones. Rhiada's voice spoke in her mind, unbidden.

"Life is full of battles. Ye cannae escape them. Ye can only prepare to stand yer ground and fight them...."

She leaned her head against the chill hearth stones and closed her eyes, her chest tightening at the memory. "I did fight," she whispered, her voice thick with emotion, "and I am still fighting. And it has cost me much."

She stepped back before turning and ascending the stairs leading to the second floor.

It was pitch dark, the windows shuttered against the dying light of day. She walked gingerly through the room, her hands outstretched to feel anything before she would run into it. Her fingers touched stone and she knelt down beside the cold fireplace, her hands locked around her knees, and she looked around her in the empty blackness, long without life.

Leaning her head against the wall behind her and closing her eyes, it all came rushing back.

Returning to An Dùn after fleeing the Danes, Duncan's cold body buried on unknown ground to the north, and Rhiada's left to the wolves. The numbness wearing away into grief that kept her from sleeping. Angus comforting her, offering hope when she had none.

She opened her eyes, seeing nothing but dim light coming from the cracks in the shuttered windows. It felt ages ago now. So much had changed, yet they were still fighting for the same cause. And her fear remained. Did some things never change at all? Or was it only the bad things that lingered, and all that was good changed beyond memory?

The floor was cold beneath her, seeping through her clothes, and she had nothing with which to light a fire. She rose to her feet. Malcolm and Merwyn's voices reached her from down below; they were most likely unpacking their things. This place would be far more cheery when they returned to sleep. Meanwhile, there was supper to be had—below, she could hear one of the lads calling her name, no doubt summoning her to eat. And whenever she got the chance to speak to either of the McCladden lads without a crowd about them, she must ask them about becoming her guards.

As painful as the past had been, the future still held promise. For as chilly and dark as this evening was, spring was indeed coming. Not even the Danes could stop it.

~ 10 ~
OF DAYS BEFORE

FIONA stepped outside the McCladden croft, her eyes adjusting to the brightness of gloomy twilight, a sharp contrast to the blackness of the empty home. Then she saw Angus standing by the door, looking directly at her, a question in his blue eyes. Malcolm and Merwyn were nowhere to be seen.

"Angus? Was it ye tha' was calling me?" she asked, confused.

"Aye, I had something to ask ye and I thought ye might be here. Malcolm said he saw ye walking this way, at any rate." His voice was soft, as if he understood the pain and hurt, the memories from two years ago that this place brought back to them both.

"Wha' did ye wish to ask me?" she asked, wondering if it was about being her guard, or perhaps something else entirely...

"Father says we are still waiting on most of the chieftains to arrive, so tomorrow is a day of rest fer us. I was wondering if ye would wish to gae riding wi' me on the moors in the morning. If ye would rather rest, I understand. But if no', I would wish to spend our last free moments together before we head off to war." *Before the matter of killing takes the place of living life as it was meant to be lived.* The words hung unspoken between them.

She stared at him, surprised but also delighted. Perhaps he also knew that she would not want everyone else about when she asked—surely Donald had spoken to them by now—and even if not, this would solve the issue of finding when to speak to him. "Aye, I would love to gae," she answered at last with a smile. "I hae missed spending time wi' ye the past few days. When would ye wish to leave?"

"After we break our fast. And will ye bring yer sword?"

Fiona blinked. What did her sword have to do with it? "Aye, I can," she replied, mystified.

He returned her smile, his shoulders easing. "Good." He glanced down the chariotway that was vanishing into the dusk. "Would ye like to help Malcolm and I finish putting our things in our croft? Supper is nearly ready, but Father said he'd like tha' to be finished first. He said ye can sleep up in the second loft; the rest of us will be in the main one."

She nodded and followed him to where Malcolm and Merwyn stood by what remained of their saddlebags. The rest of the Cymry still milled about the entrance to An Dùn, most of them greeting their companions already there and being led to housing places. The fortress town was once more becoming the living hive it had been two years ago.

"Aiee, young lad," Malcolm squeaked as Angus bent to pick up the saddlebags, "ye are forbidden to touch these things. They belong to Chieftain McCladden himself."

"Och, donnae be daft now," Angus muttered, taking them anyway despite his brother's attempts to snatch them back.

Fiona chuckled and gathered her own. "If ye are so familiar wi' Chieftain Donald, then I donnae suppose ye would ken tha' this is his eldest son?" she asked, smirking.

Malcolm's grey eyes sparkled and he winked at Merwyn, who grinned. "Ah, forgive me, I didnae recognise ye at first." He bowed towards his brother and then picked up his belongings, strutting down the main road like a king of the roost. Merwyn followed behind, chuckling, even though Fiona guessed he had understood but little of what Malcolm had said.

"Sometimes I think he enjoys making himself look like a fool," Angus drawled as they followed him.

Fiona laughed. "Perhaps tha' is his calling, to be a jester and nae so much a chieftain's son. There are worse ways to earn a living. Being a jester isnae so ignoble simply because ye hae nae desire fer it."

He shrugged, but she could see him smiling in the dim light. "Neither is being a princess."

"Point taken," she replied, her shoulders drooping. The laughter was gone from her voice now.

Angus sighed. "Fiona, why do ye shy away from it so?"

"I...I ken so little of how to be one. 'Twas my brother who was meant to be ruler one day, no' me. I remained in the shadows save when Douglas led me out of them. And should we somehow win this war, I am supposed to be a queen. I ken even less of how to be tha'. One can choose to be a jester. I didnae choose to be a princess, nor a queen."

They had reached the McCladden croft by now, where Malcolm was already inside, instructing Merwyn on making a peat fire on the hearth to give light and warmth against the cool evening. Angus paused before the doorway, his hand fiddling with the leather strap of his saddle bag.

"Perhaps," he said at last, "perhaps none of us can really choose who we are. Malcolm doesnae choose to be a jester; he is one in his heart. I donnae choose to be a warrior or a harper; I am the first out of necessity, the second out of desire, but the skills were already there. And now I must become a chieftain after my father, to which I was born—perhaps—to be, even if I didnae expect it to come about in the way it did."

In the way my elder brothers were all slain, were his silent words. But Fiona did not draw attention to it.

"Ye were born the daughter of King Daibhidh and Queen Fionnuala, the sister of Prince Douglas," Angus continued. "Ye are meant to be a princess, and ye will find tha' ye hae the skills to be the greatest queen Scotland has had yet when ye need it most. Perhaps it is tha' who we are meant to be is already laid before us, even if we donnae hae the eyes to see it. And is tha' no' a comforting thought?"

"Maybe," she replied, despair in her voice, as always when she thought of it. "But sometimes I think tha' the path before us is no' the true one, only wha' we think or desire in our hearts. And if tha' be so, then who is to say we are truly becoming wha' we are supposed to be? I...I am afraid of disappointing the very ones who risk their lives fer my sake. I donnae wish fer them to regret such a sacrifice, all because I am chasing a dream tha' Scotland has lost."

"Och, Fiona," he pleaded, turning to look at her, "there is nae regret. Even should ye fail in some way, or disappoint yer people in one aspect, it doesnae mean tha' ye are no' meant fer this. All of us fail at some point. Failure doesnae mean unredeemable defeat." He laid his hand on her shoulder, warmth flowing from his touch like a light flaring in the darkness. "Ye will find yer way. I ken ye will."

She met his gaze, watching as the slight breeze ruffled his dark curls, seeing the reflection of the fire within the croft burning in his eyes. "And if the path seems to forever remain in darkness?" Her voice was barely a whisper.

Angus did not reply at once, only entering the croft and slinging down his saddlebags to the floor before giving her his full attention. He spoke softly, not wanting Malcolm to hear. "I thought so too, once. But I was wrong. I hope ye find yer way, sweet lass. 'Tis nae joy to wander in the dark."

"Angus, do ye ken if supper is ready yet?" Malcolm asked, sitting back from creating a successful blaze, whose heat Fiona could feel from the doorway. "I'm hungry."

"Naturally," his brother said, rubbing a hand across his eyes. "Come on, let's gae find out." He gestured for Fiona to follow him, and Malcolm and Merwyn scampered behind them, listening to the birdsong that echoed in the evening stillness.

Fiona sighed with contentment, pushing thoughts of gloom and fear away as she walked with Angus. His shoulder brushed hers at times as they made their way to the Great Hall in the centre of An Dùn, and she was glad to have him beside her. Though now was not the time, she realised how, more than ever, she wanted him as one of her guards. For not only did he protect her from enemies without and thoughts within, he guided her through the unknown.

She did not want that to ever change.

The next morning dawned a rosette gold, the rising sun painting the low-lying clouds in soft blushes, as if the world itself rejoiced to see the light again. The Scots and Cymry rose with the sun, eating an early breakfast, and some explored the fortress town. Malcolm, after eating his fill, lay down on his straw mattress and promptly fell asleep again. Soft snores filled the McCladden croft. Outside, Dafydd and Merwyn remained with the Cymreig company, likewise dozing or having casual conversation in the sunshine.

Returning to the croft after breakfast, Fiona buckled her sword at her waist, wondering once more why Angus thought it necessary. Was he taking her somewhere unsafe and wanted her to have the means to defend herself in case something happened?

Thrusting away her thoughts, she glanced at Malcolm fast asleep. A soft spring breeze blew cool through the open windows, breathing life into the long-shuttered place and playing with his mess of fiery curls. He muttered something in his dreams and then rolled over, burying his face in his arms.

Fiona smiled and shook her head, traipsing downstairs and out into the village, meeting Angus at the north gates. He held the reins to his mare, Branwen, and to her own horse that had replaced Sgàil.

He greeted her without a word spoken, and they mounted and rode out of the gates.

They went north, past the gorse bushes where Fiona had once hid from the Danes, past the forest path that led to the archery range where they had practised so often years ago, and then through moorland she had travelled but once—and that by moonlight, when Angus had fled with her from *The Raven's Wing*. She wondered whether that tavern was still there, or whether Lady Nuith had burned it to the ground for unknowingly sheltering the Scottish heir and letting her escape. But their path wound northwest and across barren hills. Best to keep away from any potential Danish spies.

Angus finally stopped at a small stream, which was brown and swollen with the spring rains. He alighted off his horse, letting her free to drink from the stream before tying her reins to one of the scraggly trees on the streambank. It would not be good for the mares to eat the spring grass.

Fiona followed suit, gazing around her with interest, the landscape somehow familiar, though she could not place it. She did not remember the stream being this broad and this deep before. Surely it was not the same place her brother had trained her....

Angus stepped closer to her, as if sensing her thoughts. "Do ye remember when we first met?" His voice was soft, but there was a warmth to it, a warmth that blazed in the half-smile playing on his face.

The light of remembrance washed over her then, almost as bright as the sunshine.

"Ye and I fought wi' swords," he continued, standing so near she could almost feel his breath against her cheek, "and ye were shocked to discover ye were in the Lowlands."

She chuckled, glancing around them fondly now. "Aye, I remember. I thought fer certain ye were a thief, or one of Lady Nuith's men sent to punish me." Her smile faded. "When I returned to Caerloch, I remember wondering if I would one day be restored to my father's throne, and Lady Nuith and her husband gang out of my life, ne'er to return. If I had kent wha' it would cost us all..." She gazed at the ground beneath her, her voice betraying her guilt, and she did not finish.

Angus reached up and brushed aside a stray lock of her hair. "Some things are worth fighting fer, and ye donnae fight alone. Yer people choose freely to stand wi' ye, nae matter the cost." Then he stepped back, an enthusiastic grin spreading across his face, driving away the shadows that gathered in her soul. "Come, let us duel, like we did here so long ago."

She drew her sword in reply, touched that he too seemed to miss the old days and wanted her to relive them again with him.

Together they returned blow for blow, the glen ringing with the sounds of steel against steel. The ground beneath their feet was soggy with recent rains, sucking at their boots and almost hampering their movements. Yet they were evenly matched; every time it seemed one of them would win against the other, their opponent would deflect the blow in some way and the duel would go on.

But something in the casual way Angus fought made Fiona feel as though he were holding back, as if he did not wish for her to feel incompetent by easily defeating her. It seemed too easy for him, while she had to constantly be on her guard to retaliate his strokes. Unlike the last time they had duelled, he no longer seemed surprised by her skill.

After a few minutes thus spent, they pulled back, both of them panting.

"Ye did well, even wi' the mud against us," Angus gasped, sheathing his sword.

"I thank ye, but ye also did well." She placed her sword in its scabbard, scrutinising him closely.

"Wha'?" he asked with a breathy chuckle. "Do I hae a tree sprouting between my ears?"

Fiona laughed in spite of herself. "Nae, nae. 'Tis only...it seemed like ye were no' as serious about it as before."

Angus leaned against one of the trees on the banks, crossing his arms. "I am always serious," he replied, though his grin said otherwise. "Nae, Fiona, I didnae wish to overtire ye. And besides...I am afraid I would win against ye too easily now. We are no' children anymore, and in some things a lad will always be stronger than a lass. I didnae wish to shame ye, no' wi' a war soon upon us." His grin was gone now, and the soberness in his tone and his blue eyes reminded her too much of pity.

She blushed in spite of herself and looked away, fiddling with the hilt of her sword. "Do ye no' wish fer me to fight in battle, then? I trained alongside everyone else at Caerdun"—her throat tightened in disappointment—"and I donnae wish to think it was all fer nothing. I won against Dafydd, and I fought in the last war. Wha' use can I be if I cannae hold my own in a fight?" She shut her eyes a moment, struggling to keep her voice steady. "I cannae give speeches like yer father, nor direct men in battle like the High Chieftains. I cannae even find courage to play the harp before my people. I'm supposed to be the princess, but I donnae ken wha' I am meant to do! I donnae even hae Rhiada to guide me this time."

"Fiona, tha' is no' wha' I meant." Angus took a step forward so he was standing before her, and she had no choice but to meet his gaze. "Aye, I wanted ye to come wi' us on the war trail, but no' so ye could fight. I ken ye did before, but we had so few men—and none to spare to guard ye—tha' ye fought alongside us in battle. 'Twas a wonder tha' ye were no' seriously harmed then, and we willnae risk it now when we hae men a-plenty. 'Twould no' be fair fer us to travel all the way to Cymru and seek an alliance of men only to put our princess on the front lines.

"Yer purpose is no' to defend yer country wi' a sword; tha' is mine. Mine, and tha' of every other man and lad who swears loyalty to ye. As fer speeches...I—I donnae ken how to give them either. There are other ways to lead and inspire yer people than warfare and speaking fine words, or even playing harp. Ye are our princess, a symbol of hope and courage to us, whatever comes our way. And the chieftains, certainly Cynfael as well, will help guide ye."

Fiona swallowed, looking past him at clouds drifting across the sky, encroaching on the brightness of the sun. "I understand," she said at last. *Am I merely jist a symbol, and nothing more?* For once, Angus' words offered little encouragement. *Perhaps I should no' even hae come...* "It was wrong of me to think tha' things would be the same as before."

"Fer the sake of all we suffered, I certainly hope tha' it willnae be the same as before." He sighed and ran his hand through his hair. "Fiona, please, donnae misunderstand. There is nae shame in keeping ye back. Jist because yer purpose is different doesnae mean tha' it is no' as important and valuable as anyone else's, if no' more so. Ye may no' fight on the battlefields, but I also cannae sit in yer throne and wear yer crown."

Fiona chuckled in spite of herself. "Ye would look sillier than Malcolm, methinks."

He hummed in amusement. "Am I forgiven? I truly didnae mean to hurt ye or shame ye, princess."

She nodded after a moment, wrestling with disappointment and longing for purpose. She hated feeling useless, no less because Angus had said her role as a warrior was better left abandoned. What right did she have to request he protect her when she could not even protect herself? But the question burned within her, and she knew someone must take up the task, especially now. "Aye, Angus, there is nothing to forgive. I...I only..." She hesitated, struggling to find the right words. "I only wish, since I willnae be fighting, no' like ye—and if ye are willing, of course—whether ye would become one of my bodyguards, as ye and Malcolm were before?" Her gaze flickered shyly to meet his, a blush heating her face against her will.

He stared at her a moment, though whether it was from surprise—surely he had already known!—or something else, she could not say. "Of course I am willing," he sputtered when he found his voice. "'Twould be an honour to serve ye in such a way."

"Wha' is wrong?" she pressed when he said nothing more, a sudden stab of fear snaking its chilling way across her shoulders. This was not like Angus, not like the Angus she remembered. Why was he so surprised? Had he not expected it?

He looked away, his jaw clenching. "Nothing is wrong...'tis only, provided Malcolm is also wi' ye, would I be allowed to fight fer ye, when it comes to tha'? No' jist if ye are in danger, but actively defending ye upon the field?"

She reached out and laid her hand on his shoulder. "I wouldnae keep ye from tha', Angus, no' if tha' is wha' ye wish." The words tasted bitter on her tongue. Perhaps she should not have asked him—given him this clearly unwanted burden. "Are ye sure tha' is all?"

He turned back to her, his lips pressed in a firm line. And in his eyes, she saw a wordless struggle, as if there was much he wanted to say and yet could not find the courage to speak. His eyes looked beyond her, as if he could find the words upon the distant braes.

Then the blood drained from his face.

Fiona whirled around. A distant shadow stood on the hill directly north of them. Her heart froze. "Angus? Wha' is tha'?" She could not keep the panic out of her voice.

"We need to ride back—now." He turned and hastily loosened the reins of both their mounts.

Wind arose, whistling through the budding branches of the trees, and Branwen whinnied nervously. The skies were growing darker, as if it was soon to rain.

"Angus, wha's wrong?"

"I saw someone—something—on those hills, up there to the north, I am sure of it. I think it may be one of Lady Nuith's spies."

She shivered, though only partly from the growing coolness in the air that comes before rain. "Why would they be in the Lowlands—out here, where there is nothing?"

"I donnae ken, but we cannae risk being seen, no' wi' the war about to start. If they ken we're coming..." He did not finish his sentence, but he did not need to.

He hoisted her up into her saddle before mounting Branwen, his brows drawn together with worry.

Without another word spoken, they rode off towards An Dùn, Fiona leading, Angus behind in case of any danger. And as raindrops began to fall from the sky, a tear slipped down her face, soon followed by another and then another.

Must every moment of freedom be tainted by the enemy? What had Angus wanted to tell her before he had caught sight of a threatening figure? Would they ever have another chance to simply be equals and dear friends without the roles of princess and bodyguard, under the shadow of war estranging them?

Fiona reached up with one hand and quickly dashed the tears

away, though it did not stop them from falling. How selfish she was to think of her own heart when the heart of the country was at stake!

And yet...should she not wish for better times? Was that not why they fought?

She risked a glance and saw Angus riding a good pace behind, looking over his shoulder in case they were being followed.

Even here, even in the blossoming of spring, they were not yet free.

"Where is Angus?"

Malcolm glanced up from reworking a worn leather strap and replied in the Cymraeg tongue, "I do not know. Why?"

Dafydd looked around him, his lips tightening. Fine mist fell behind him where he stood within the doorway of the stables. "I saw both he and the princess leave this morning, and the princess rode through the gates just now without him. But I cannot find Angus anywhere."

Malcolm shrugged. "He is probably around here somewhere; I doubt she would leave him that far behind. Perhaps they raced back and that is why she was alone. Why do you not ask Fiona herself?"

Dafydd raised his dark brows in surprise.

"What is it?" Malcolm asked when he heard no answer, an insecure grin on his face. Was Dafydd alluding to something he did not know about?

"The princess was crying when she returned."

"She was wha'?" Malcolm jumped to his feet, the leather strap falling to the ground, forgotten. In like manner, he seemed to not have noticed he had switched to the Gàidhlig.

"Aye, she was weeping as she came in," Dafydd explained, still speaking his native language. "Everyone saw the tears on her face. I do not know why, perhaps I am merely thinking too much of it, but I thought at least you should know."

Malcolm rubbed the bridge of his nose. What *had* his brother done? "All right, I will try to see wha' I can do." He picked up the leather strap and placed it in Dafydd's hands. "Ye need to practise yer Scots more. Gae take this to the stablehands inside; tell them I finished it."

Dafydd groaned and walked deeper into the stables.

Malcolm watched him leave and then shook his head. "Aiee, Angus, Fiona. Wha' hae ye done this time?" He set off down the centre of the village. *Where could Fiona be?* Knowing her, she would want to be alone, but had she gone to their croft or to one of the towers? No, the guardsmen were in each one now, watching the moors for any approaching army from either side. At least he could check the croft.

Fiona sat in the shadows of the loft, listening to the rain softly drumming against the thatched roof. Tears had dried on her face, and she leaned against the wall, lost in her thoughts and confusion about what had happened out on the moors.

She had not mistaken the look in Angus' eyes before he had seen that distant shadow. If that figure had not been there on the braes, would he have found the courage to speak freely to her about what warred within him? Or would he have warned her not to ask anything more of him because he cared for someone else? Though, surely, if that were so, Malcolm would not have been able to remain silent about it. Or...would he have told her he cared for her in the same way she did him?

She rubbed her hand across her face, closing her eyes a moment. She thought she had made the right choice by going with them, but did anyone think of her safety as a burden? Even though Angus had said he was glad she was going with them, was he bitter about being asked to be her bodyguard? Or was it something else?

She knew she cared much for him. But whether it was for mere friendship's sake, or something more, she could not say. Did she love him like Annag loved Donald, like her mother had surely loved her father so long ago? Did she wish to be wedded to Angus, should they both survive the war?

And then she realised that the thought was not so frightening.

She trusted him like she trusted no other. He had seen her at her worst and offered her only comfort. She could not bear the thought of living without him, apart from him. But was it enough to mean love? And did he return her feelings? Or did he only see her as a princess in need of protection? Was she hindering him from fulfilling his purpose even as she struggled to find hers?

"Fiona?"

She straightened where she sat, startled, and rubbed her face hastily. Hopefully no one would see she had been crying, though perhaps it was already too late for that.

A moment later, Malcolm came up the stairs, his brows creased with worry. They eased when he caught sight of her, but only for a moment. He knelt beside her, wiping away what tears remained. "Fiona, wha' is it?"

His sweet earnestness might have made her smile at any other time, but it only pained her further. "Many things, Malcolm, many things." Her breath quivered.

"Does Angus hae anything to do wi' them?"

Her heart skipped a beat and then groaned within her. "Wha' makes ye think—"

"Dafydd is the one who mentioned it, actually," he interrupted before she could finish. "He said he saw ye both ride out and then ye came back alone, crying.... Wha' exactly happened between ye two?"

"I donnae ken how to put it simply." She shrugged. "'Tis no' even his fault, I..."

"Can ye give me more details than tha'?" He gestured wildly with his hands.

"I asked him if he would consent to be one of my guards as we set out to war, but he seemed almost upset by it." The words stuck in her throat, her hiccuping breaths gradually fading away. "He seemed as if he would ask me or tell me something tha' he clearly cared much about, but he caught sight of a figure—maybe a Danish spy—and so we rode back as quick as we could. I donnae ken why Dafydd didnae see him ride through the gates; I thought he was close behind. I jist...I jist wish I kent why he seemed so *strange* about it. I thought such a request would bring him joy.... And I ken 'tis so selfish to think of myself, to worry about something insignificant when there is a war coming, but..." Her voice faltered, and she did not continue.

"Hmm." Malcolm cupped his chin in his hands, resting his elbows on his kilt-covered knees. "I think I ken perhaps wha' it might be, wha' Angus might hae said, but I cannae tell ye. Angus keeps his secret thoughts close, and 'tis only fair I donnae say my suspicions. I donnae ken why he would act tha' way, though I am sure there is some daft reason he thinks is important fer it. Wha' I do ken is how much ye trust each other. If it is important, he had better tell ye soon.

There should be nae secrets between sword brothers—er...lads and lassies?" His freckled face scrunched up as he searched for the right word. Giving up, he only said, "Since we are heading to war, 'tis best to ken whom ye can trust no' to stab ye in the back. No' tha' Angus would do tha'," he added hastily with a forced laugh.

But Fiona was in no jesting mood. "Ye think I donnae ken tha'?"

"Nae, I ken ye do. But I donnae ken wha' else to say. I am no' a poet like ye and Angus and Dafydd." He sighed softly. Then, "Are ye choosing anyone else as yer guards?"

She glanced up, seeing a twinkle in his grey eyes despite the dimness of the room. "I was gang to ask ye, as well. I jist...never managed to do it before we left Caerdun."

"Well, dear princess, I would be honoured. Even if my daft brother thinks differently fer whatever daft reason." He rose to his feet, giving her his hand. "Come. Ye cannae hide in the shadows all day. Someone might come looking fer ye. Even wi' the rain, 'tis nae so bad outside. Perhaps we'll find Angus too."

Together, they left the house and rejoined the Cymreig company, taking shelter in one of the larger halls from the storm. Fiona listened to conversations in a tongue she could not understand, though Malcolm tried his best to make her one of them.

But her mind was elsewhere, confused and distracted.

For Angus was not among them.

The Great Hall in An Dùn was filled that night, even fuller than Angus remembered the previous evening, though he had not heard of any of the other chieftains arriving yet. Perhaps it was all of his father's clansmen finally arriving.

Though taller than many of the assembled warriors, he still stood on tiptoes, glancing around the hall for a familiar redhead whom he had not seen since earlier that day. At last, he espied Fiona sitting beside his brother and Merwyn, who seemed to follow Malcolm and his antics like a faithful hound.

Making his way through men and lads finding places to sit down for the evening meal, Angus finally slid onto the bench beside Fiona. She looked up, seeming surprised to see him, and something in his chest twinged with disappointment.

Was she angry with him for something?

"I wondered whether ye'd come," she said, but he could hear that her heart was not in it.

"Fiona, wha' is wrong?" he asked in a low voice, leaning his elbow on the table and giving her his full attention.

Her crimson brows furrowed. "Where hae ye been all this time? Dafydd said he didnae see ye ride in earlier, and none of them hae seen ye until now."

Something in her accusatory manner cut him deeply and he leaned away from her, realising the source of her distress. "I am sorry, Fiona, but there was nae time to tell ye. Once we were in sight of An Dùn, I pulled back, and when I saw ye safely within the gates, I returned the way we had come and ensured we were no' followed."

"Ye could hae told me. I was worried something had happened, or tha' ye were hiding from me."

"Wha'?" he exclaimed, almost too loudly, for a few heads turned in their direction. His next words were spoken more softly. "Why would I hide from ye?"

"Ye seemed upset by something when I asked ye to be my guard. And then ye were jist...gang. Wha' else was I supposed to think?"

Och, Fiona, I was no' upset by tha'—only my own inadequacy to perfectly defend ye and my country; only my inability to control my feelings; only my cowardice in failing to ask ye, to tell ye how much I care fer ye, how much I long to be more than jist yer guard...

He realised a moment too late that she was still waiting for an answer. She had turned away from him, her lips tightened.

He laid his hand on her shoulder, forcing her to look at him. "I am sorry, Fiona, but yer safety was my first concern, and I didnae wish to risk any potential ambush, even tha' close to An Dùn's gates. No' when ye are supposed to be hiding. It was a great enough risk riding out north, and tha' is my own fault."

"Then why did ye no' tell me once ye were back? Surely it didnae take ye the whole afternoon."

Oh, how he hated the disappointment in her eyes. The war had not even begun, and he was already failing her. Even Malcolm, who glanced their way with interest, gave him a sympathetic shrug.

"I didnae ken where exactly ye were, and I thought it best tha' Father and Cynfael—and whoever else—kent wha' had happened. If it was truly a spy, they needed to ken."

She looked down at the bowl of stew someone placed before her, rubbing her forehead with one hand as if deep in thought. "Do ye think it was a spy?"

He sighed, taking his hand away from her shoulder. "I donnae ken fer sure. Might jist be a shepherd looking fer a lost lamb. But we couldnae risk it, even if it was. They might see us and report to Lady Nuith—"

"I ken the risk, Angus." She met his gaze now, and he could see sorrow and guilt in her eyes. But before he could say anything, she continued, "Forgive me. I was wrong to doubt ye. Ye donnae hae to tell me yer every movement. Ye donnae owe me tha.'"

"Nae, but I am yer friend as well as yer guard. And wi' war coming, I donnae wish fer ye to think ye cannae trust me."

She gave a half-hearted smile in response before beginning to eat her stew, and said no more.

But he could not help but think there was something deeper that now lay between them, something that could not be healed by casual words, though he could not say what it was. Once, he could have trusted her with his heart, but it seemed she could not even trust his words now. If she wanted him to be honest, truly so, did he risk it in the event she did not return his feelings? He had faced death and survived, and yet he could not bring himself to reveal his deepest longings to the one who held his soul captive. Perhaps Fiona was right. A year *had* grown between them, and he wondered, with cold dread threading his veins, whether they had not just grown separately but apart.

~ 11 ~

The Hunt

LORD Erland sat in his lesser throne at Caerloch Castle, fingers splayed across his face as he rested his head in his hands. Pale daylight shone through the windows, another dawn coming to life; nothing spectacular about it. No vibrant colours shot through the sky, no low-lying clouds hovered at the horizon to lend character and hue to something that happened every morning.

Then the door at the end of the Great Hall burst open as a figure entered, wearing chainmail overlaid with a tunic boasting Lady Nuith's crest of crimson ravens. His firm step echoed in the still hall, his stride steady and familiar, as was his short black beard.

Lord Erland straightened in his chair, suddenly interested in the report Drummond brought. If he had returned this soon and so early this morning, he could only be bearing important news.

"Sir," Drummond greeted, his black eyes roving the room, no doubt in search of his half-sister, for whom the dispatch was really for.

But before he could ask regarding her whereabouts, a side door opened and Lady Nuith swept in, clothed in a deep violet gown, whose split sleeves revealed an ivory underdress. She stepped up the dais and sat down in her throne, her skirts rustling with the movement. Her eyes snapped to Drummond, scrutinising him and no doubt forming her own opinion of the news he must carry.

"Well?" she asked curtly when he did not speak.

"Our search was more or less successful. Nae sign of the princess, but I did find Chieftain McCladden and his youngest son there—

though where his other son is, I couldnae find out. It would appear they are holding to their terms of the treaty, save I saw a great many men at An Dùn as we returned here, the number of which isnae usual fer that place." A glimmer of triumph beamed in his eyes despite his words, and Lord Erland looked quickly to his wife to gauge her reaction.

Her dark eyes lit up with cruel interest. "What else did you find?"

"Nothing that I care to share at present." The warning edge in Drummond's voice was unmistakable. But his half-sister was either deaf or foolish.

"You do know that I can have you arrested and thrown in the dungeons for rebellion," Nuith put in coolly.

Drummond flashed a defiant grin, his teeth gleaming, and Erland shuddered where he sat. "I do, jist as much as ye ken that as soon as ye do so, my men will besiege this castle and overtake it, and ye will be without this castle and the throne within. I might even hae mercy and spare yer miserable life."

Lady Nuith shot to her feet, bristling, gripping the armrests of the throne so hard that her knuckles shone white through her skin. Her nostrils flared as she spoke. "My men are just as loyal to me, and I can very easily call in reinforcements."

"Asbjørn is loyal to whomever he considers his authority, which in this instance, would be me. Ye made the mistake, dear sister, of choosing men fer yer guards whose allegiances are as treacherous as yer own."

Erland winced. Drummond's accent, bleeding through the Danish tongue even as he spoke of Nuith's own betrayal of King Daibhidh, would not calm matters.

"We will see where his allegiance truly lies, when the time comes," Nuith replied at last, her voice low and threatening. "I have no further need of you here. You are dismissed."

"I will leave of my own accord when I choose," Drummond snarled. "If it were no' fer me, ye wouldnae hae news from the Lowlands, and ye wouldnae be able to make plans against those Scots. Donnae forget it." He wheeled and left the room, his firm stride echoing in the stillness following his words.

"I know we have been waiting for a sign of rebellion," Erland began softly when he was gone, "though I am not sure whether this is such, but what had you been planning?"

Lady Nuith returned to her throne with a sigh. "Last autumn, before the winter storms set in, I sent word to those we still have ties to in Danesland for reinforcements against a Scottish uprising in the spring. And as soon as the winter snows began melting in the mountains here, I sent messages to the lords in the Highlands. Whether all the messages arrive safely or not, we will have an army worth destroying the rebellious Lowlanders for good. I will not make the same mistakes we made in the past. It is time we put a final end to this."

"Is there a reason for the sudden urgency? We do not know for certain if she is even alive." He was treading dangerous ground, but he hoped she would not take offence. She knew he was loyal, unlike her half-brother.

Nuith turned and looked at her husband, her forehead creased with worry. "She is alive, I know it. I have not set eyes on her since the day she played for us—but always she haunts my dreams. Elusive...mocking. I see her as the child she was when her father first introduced the two of us and told her I was to be her new mother. She squinted at me, and after looking me over, stated quite clearly: 'She's nae my mother.' She never accepted me, as her people likewise did not, and therefore, I never accepted her. Her father cared for her little, but more so than he did me—it seemed at times. Not that it mattered. He was cold-hearted and had no love left in his heart. His attempt at peacemaking had broken him."

She broke off, her eyes dark with bitter memory.

"Her brother was dead long before I came, else I might have had to face opposition from him as well as his horrid sister. The Scottish servants, before I sent them away, resented me for being a Dane, even if my father had remarried a Scot—the fools. As if they did not realise they were already defeated." Nuith clenched her hands into fists. "They are all gone or dead now, save *her*. I suppose she hates me as much as I wish to see her dead. I know you never thought much of her, Erland, but you were the one who held me back from killing her at the start. You told me to wait until the feast and then we could blame it on one of our guests' servants—save our necks from Scottish reprisal. And look what good it did us! *She* is still alive and probably even now is leading the Scots into yet another attempt to overthrow our rightful rule. *She* is a threat to our son." Lady Nuith looked at her husband. "If anything happens to him because of her—I will hold you responsible."

Erland did not answer for a moment, looking at the doors to the hall while musing on her words. "If there is any way I can best serve you, my lady, in this as in all things, may it be known."

A smile spread across her thin lips and the crease on her forehead relaxed. "Since Drummond is no longer of use to me, that is good hearing." Without another word, she rose to her feet and left the room.

Lord Erland watched her, his chest tightening, only releasing slightly as she disappeared from view. He knew what her unspoken words meant, and he would do well to obey them. Rising to his feet, he called to the men-at-arms at the end of Caerloch's throne room. "Bring to me Asbjørn, at once."

Drummond gazed out the small window that overlooked the courtyard, his jaw set in irritation. How he hated having to bow to his sister's every whim. Since when was she the ruler of the Highlands and not him? He actually possessed Scottish blood. If it were not for her constant meddling, he would have accomplished his goal long ago. Of course, others had hindered rather than helped him, like Lachlan. But it was Nuith who had stood in his way far more than they.

"How fares the world, MacDougall?"

Drummond glanced up to see Asbjørn, the captain of the guard at Caerloch, walking towards him, his dark eyes glinting in the daylight. "What do ye think?" he answered back in the Danish tongue.

"I take it that your search proved fruitless? Lord Erland just spoke with me, but he said little pertaining to whatever you might have found," Asbjørn said softly from beside him, his gloved hand resting on the stone windowsill.

Drummond spat onto the rushes-strewn floor. "Nae sign of the princess yet. Perhaps she truly is dead, or else very well hidden. But I did find Donald McCladden and his youngest son, though his elder son was missing. And he had far more horses in his stables than guardsmen to ride them."

"Did you discover why?"

Drummond shrugged. "They were more of the sort of breed that Chieftain Eachann has, and we also discovered a gyrfalcon. We donnae hae birds of that sort here, let alone one that belongs to a king—or a princess. Wi' the news that the spies brought today, I am certain that they are planning another rebellion." He swore under his breath.

"Did you tell Nuith this?" Asbjørn asked, a black eyebrow raised.

Drummond laughed mockingly. "She meddles in my plans enough." His mirth faded. "I told her I found the McCladdens, but I didnae mention anything beyond that. Let her think she is on the throne and that I am in disgrace. I am making my own plans now, and we ken who the men will follow." He glanced at the captain, as if to ensure his secrecy.

Asbjørn's lips lifted in a sneer. "I hold little love for her and her silly fears about that girl. We all saw her many times, such a little slip of a thing—I would be more afraid of the chieftains than the princess herself. So make your plans. And if there is any way I can help, let me know. My men are tired of Nuith, to the point that perhaps even wee Fiona might be a better ruler." He said this last part under his breath, peering around the hall to make sure no one hid in the shadows.

"Fiona irked me because of her timidity, but she would be easy to mould, I think, given the chance. My anger was more towards Rhiada, but I slew him; even he couldnae survive that. But Princess McCurragh, I think, is alive—whatever the Lowlanders might say. I donnae think they would rise up again this soon if she were truly dead, even if they had allies."

"Unless they seek revenge."

Drummond scoffed. "They donnae hae enough of their own men fer that, and who would care enough to help them fer only revenge? Nae, I believe she yet lives, and so does Nuith."

Asbjørn grunted in agreement. "It will be hard, I am thinking, to get her away from the Scots without swift retaliation—unless they can trust we intend to put her back on her throne."

"We must win them over, but they trust me little after what happened at the end of the last war. I will need more than jist myself, especially should we try to kidnap her." He gave the man a knowing look.

Asbjørn nodded. "When you need me, you know where to find me. I must return to my men, but you have my word. I stand for liberty, and not the sort Lady Nuith believes in." He clasped his hand over his heart. "For peace and freedom."

Drummond placed his fist over his chest. "Fer peace and freedom, whatever the cost."

Fiona rose early that morning, greeting the pinkish-grey misty dawn before anyone else in the McCladden croft was awake. She dressed quickly and gathered a spare bundle of clothes among other things, glancing at those sleeping on the floor below to ensure their slumber was not disturbed.

Sneaking down the stairs, she paused as one step creaked beneath her weight. She looked hastily around the room, but only one person stirred for a moment before turning over, his face flushed from sleep. Fiona passed him as she made for the door, realising it was Angus, his eyebrows drawn together even in his dreams. She paused, gazing at him, filled with both longing and confusion at the events that transpired yesterday. But she did not want to wake him to speak of it now; he needed his sleep.

She stepped gingerly across the muddy pathways of An Dùn, heading to the hall where the warriors gathered for mealtimes. The air was crisp but not too cold, and the sun promised to shine fully that day instead of hiding behind a silver veil of cloud. The ground glistened with dew, and fairly soon, her leather shoes were damp.

Fiona entered the hall adjacent to the feasting place, which served as the kitchens. She greeted the women already preparing porridge for breakfast, her heart fluttering with slight embarrassment at the request she voiced a moment later.

"Would it be too much trouble if ye were to heat some water fer a bath?" Her voice was steady, much to her relief. She did not want to overburden her people, though Annag had said two years ago that it was no trouble—and much safer than washing in the forest outside the gates. But Annag was not here now.

One of the women, who seemed to be the head cook, nodded and gave a toothy grin. "Aye, nae trouble at all, yer highness. We was wonderin' if ye'd be wanting such afore ye take to the road ag'in." She reached up a hand to tuck away the greying hair escaping her plaited bun. "If ye donnae mind waitin' a few minutes, we can prepare a place where ye can wash in privacy." She then barked a few curt commands, and two of the younger women bustled about fulfilling her orders.

"Thank ye," Fiona murmured, feeling very much out of place as more women entered the kitchens to help with breakfast. *I should be helping them, no' getting in their way.* She looked at the flagstones beneath her feet. Her face burned in spite of herself. "I donnae mean to impose." The words were softer than she intended.

"Och, yer highness," the head cook replied, patting her hands on her apron before coming over to Fiona. "'Tis an honour to help in such a humble way. Methinks ye will be a kind ruler. Remember us, the lowly folk, when ye become queen. Tha' is all we ask."

Tears smarted in Fiona's eyes. "But how can I help ye in return, beyond remembering?" Perhaps this woman, old enough no doubt to be her grandmother, held the answers she sought.

"Be fair in yer judgments, but donnae fear mercy. Show kindness to the outcasts. Unify the broken clans. Love yer people as if they were yer own flesh and blood."

Fiona sighed. "Tha' is much... I hope I will ken how to do so, when the time comes."

The woman smiled and touched the princess' cheek. "Aye, ye will. The knowledge doesnae come to anyone all at once. Life teaches ye how. Ye jist must be willing to learn."

The two young women reappeared around a corner, faces ruddy with heat. "Yer bath is ready, yer highness," the taller of them said, her brown hair sticking to her cheeks. "We partitioned it off wi' sheets, and one of us will stand guard, jist in case."

Fiona smiled. "Thank ye."

"If ye will come wi' me?" she returned, gesturing with her hand.

Fiona bowed her head gratefully towards the head cook and then followed.

Fiona washed as quickly as possible, not wanting to keep the woman from helping longer than necessary. Besides, Angus and Malcolm might worry if she did not return soon. Dressing in clean clothes, she left the others, which she had washed, to dry amidst the other linens. She combed her hair before gathering the bag which had carried her clothes, trusting her hair to dry the rest of the way on its own as she returned to the croft. She thanked the women once more before stepping out of the kitchens into the morning.

The sun rose ever higher as she walked, warming her back, the golden light spilling across the ground as if offering her comfort. And the wind was still and silent, a reverent hush.

Placing her things in the upper floor of the McCladden croft—which was empty, the straw mattresses piled to one side of the wall—she made her way to where the men stood in lines for breakfast.

The people of An Dùn had been kind enough to share their own scarce supplies remaining from the last harvest to feed their war host, but it would all run out within days if things did not change sooner. Even hunting would not help much this early in the year, only delay the inevitable. If the other bands came within the next day, they could leave. Else they were hurting rather than helping those they would soon pledge to save.

"Fiona, where hae ye been?" Malcolm squeaked when he saw her, his creased forehead easing, no doubt in relief.

"I was in the kitchens, washing."

His shoulders eased slightly, but that was all.

"Ye must no' hae seen me returning," she continued, "wi' the hall standing in the way." She laughed, but it ceased when Malcolm did not return it. Did they think she had—

"Ye promise ye didnae gae elsewhere?" he blurted before she could finish her thought. "We thought perhaps ye had gang to the stream, like before, or some other daft idea. Angus and Cynfael were about to ride out in search of ye if ye didnae—"

"Fiona!"

She whirled to see Angus running towards her, his face flushed, and he came to a stop, panting. The look in his eyes was not one she'd care to see again.

"Fiona, where hae ye been? We hae been looking all over fer ye, and nae one had seen ye, no' even the guards—"

"Wheesht!" Malcolm cried, gesturing wildly with his hands and casting sheepish glances at those looking in their direction. "She's here and safe, and tha' is all tha' matters, aye?"

Angus scowled, his nostrils flaring as he tried to regain his breath. He continued in a softer tone, "Could ye no' at least hae told one of us where ye were gang? I thought ye might hae left An Dùn, like last time, and especially wi' wha' happened yesterday..." His voice trailed off as she turned her face away, tears smarting in her eyes.

She stepped out of the line, Angus following, as she walked up the main path and stopped at the door to the McCladden croft, where they could speak without a crowd gathered around them. "Aye, I ken," she replied. She tried to calm the guilt that threatened to drown her beneath its sticky clutches, but her voice was already unsteady. "I didnae wish to wake ye; ye needed yer sleep. And I didnae think it would matter, since I didnae leave the gates. I was never in any danger, I promise." She quickly dashed away a tear that slipped down her face, afraid to meet his gaze.

"Fiona...I am no' angry wi' ye."

She felt his fingers gently brush her damp hair away from her face, but still she did not look up, her face burning in humiliation.

"'Tis only I was worried where ye were when we all awoke and discovered ye were missing, and tha' nae one had seen ye. None of us thought to check the kitchens."

"I didnae think I would be gang long enough fer anyone to notice," she replied, the words sticking in her throat as another tear slid down her face.

But he brushed it away this time, his hand lingering on her cheek. "Fiona, look at me."

She dared to glance up, seeing only sympathy and compassion in his eyes, turned into a sapphire sea by the rising sun.

"Next time, tell one of us, even if ye're simply walking down the street. These are dangerous times, and we cannae be fools. Better to be laughed at fer caution than to lose everything because of one's pride."

She nodded, swallowing hard. "I ken. I...jist didnae think, and I am sorry."

Angus cleared his throat, looking away from her for a moment towards the centre of An Dùn. "If...if ye also need time to be alone—I ken tha' will be hard enough in the coming days—jist let Malcolm or I ken. Malcolm can keep his mouth shut when he needs to, and ye ken I can. Jist donnae wander off again without us kenning, please?"

"I promise I will no', Angus," she replied, some of the tension in her shoulders easing away.

"Good. Now—" He inhaled to speak again, but she cut him off.

"But only if ye promise me no' to do the same." She winced at the coldness of her tone, but it was too late to take it back. "I want to be able to trust ye, Angus, but trust must gae both ways."

He gazed at her, understanding flickering in his eyes. "I promise," he replied after a moment, his voice warm. "But I am also at fault. I was wrong to vanish without a reason yesterday, and I see now how cruel it was to leave ye like tha'. I am sorry, and I hope ye will forgive me. I will try no' to do so again."

"I do, Angus, I forgive ye." She reached out her hand, but he did not pull her into an embrace, so she merely rested it on his arm instead.

"I am glad, princess. Now, both of us need breakfast, methinks." He gestured for her to walk ahead of him, but she waited until he was by her side, wanting his companionship, before returning to the hall where men and lads were still entering in for the morning meal.

She did not know why he remained distant, but as much as it pained her, she did not want to force an answer from him. Not now, not in front of the eyes of everyone else.

Fiona sat with Angus alongside Malcolm and their friends as the morning sun poured in through the unshuttered windows. They said little, focusing their attention on spooning down the hot porridge. It was a welcome warmth, though the morning was not cold.

Angus nudged her elbow as they finished eating, catching her gaze before leaning over to murmur, "Would ye mind gang wi' Malcolm today?"

Her brows furrowed. "Wha' do ye plan on doing, then?"

"Father wishes fer some of us to test the lads here on their skill wi' a blade before we set out. If I hae yer permission, would I be able to help them wi' tha'? I wouldnae wish fer ye to hae to sit and watch tha' all day, and it might intimidate them," he added with a quick but nervous grin.

Fiona shook her head in disbelief. "Angus, ye are my bodyguard, no' my slave. Of course I wouldnae mind. Ye donnae need to ask my permission, and ye certainly donnae hae to be fastened by my side all the time. Ye didnae do so before, in the last war."

"Aye, I ken, but things are different now." Something in the tone of his voice and the quick glancing away of his eyes told her he meant more than them simply being older. "I promised I wouldnae disappear without telling ye where I was, and I donnae want ye to feel alone."

"May I take yer dishes?" Malcolm interrupted, looking at them both and leaning dangerously over the table.

"Och, forgive me," Fiona replied, feeling somewhat flustered, handing him the empty wooden bowls and spoons.

The lad winked before hurrying away, leaving the pair of them alone as the rest in the hall finished eating and left.

"Thank ye fer asking, Angus," she said after a moment, struggling to know how best to express the confusion she felt at his reservedness. "But please...I ken ye are my guard, but ye are also my friend. I willnae think less of ye because ye hae more responsibilities now."

He smiled, but it was forced and did not lighten his eyes as it usually did. "Friends?" he replied softly, so softly she was not sure she heard him.

"Aye, Angus, always." She rose to her feet, trying to ignore the sudden tightening in her chest at his response. What on earth did he mean by that?

"I'll see ye later then?" she called as he stood and began to walk away.

He turned and looked over his shoulder, nodding. "Aye, princess." He bowed his head and left, his familiar figure turning into a silhouette in the sunlit doorway before vanishing altogether.

Fiona bit her lip in frustration. She had done nothing wrong, had she? Of course they were friends, this should not change it—she had wanted it to bring them closer together. And yet...it was seeming to do the opposite.

But perhaps it was not that. Perhaps it was the dual responsibility he now had, first to his father as his heir, and to his country and herself, that was bearing down on him. That, and the coming war. She remembered how he had been so nervous the last time. Perhaps it was only that.

She rolled her shoulders, exhaled the breath she had not known she was holding, and stepped outside the hall.

The sun had risen higher in the morning sky and, after the dimness of the hall, the light was momentarily blinding. Fiona blinked hard, the warm sun kissing her freckled face with delight.

"Where are ye off to?" she asked Malcolm, who appeared close behind her and began excitedly discussing something with his companions who had been waiting for him.

He turned to her, a dancing light in his grey eyes. "We are gang to hunt. Would ye like to join us, yer highness?" His voice rose as high as a girl's in a teasing lilt, cracking at the edges.

"Och, stop wi' tha', Malcolm!" she said, rapping his arm playfully. "Aye," she added, "I would like to join ye. I hae nothing else to do."

"Wha' is this?" Dafydd's gentle voice broke in.

Fiona turned in surprise, having expected him to be with Angus. His use of Gàidhlig, though haltingly spoken, was not far from being fluent, though she had never tried to hold a proper conversation with him before.

"We are gang hunting," Malcolm answered eagerly. "Would ye like to join us, or keep my dull and unexciting brother company?"

Whether Dafydd actually understood the barrage of insults Malcolm slung out or not, he said nothing regarding them. "Angus has duties of his own to attend to. He told me to join ye."

"Well, come on then! Let us no' wait any longer." The fiery redhead all but leapt down the path, seeming in all his eagerness like one of the animals soon to be killed.

Fiona hurried back to the croft to grab her weapons: a short hunting bow and quiver of arrows; her dirk was already belted around her waist. Then she ran up the chariotway towards the gate, where Malcolm and his friends were already waiting.

"Sa, this makes us a happy fivesome, does it no'?" the lad greeted her, grinning all the while.

"Malcolm, since when has 'fivesome' been a word?" Fiona retorted, laughing.

"Since I forged it from the fires of my imagination," was the swift reply.

The other three Cymreig lads laughed with them, but Fiona wondered how many of them actually knew what they were saying.

As they walked out the north gate of An Dùn, Malcolm turned and asked something in the Cymraeg tongue to his companions. They nodded, a couple of them smiling in response. He offered no translation to Fiona, and so she followed them in silence. She inhaled deeply as they stepped out into the sunny countryside, the warm sun shining down from a brilliant, blue sky.

Like the colour of Angus' eyes. The thought slipped into her mind before she could stop it. The painful ache in her chest came back, and she looked down at the ground as the group headed for the forest. *Why does it seem like he is afraid of my presence? Did I hurt him somehow or disappoint him in some way? Or is it something else?*

She pushed the thoughts from her mind. She could think on it later; now was not the time.

The forest was filled with light as the leaves, which normally hid the sun during the summer months, had not fully bloomed yet. But the foliage was a bright green, and the budding undergrowth hid the darker branches of occasional brambles that tried to snag at their clothing as they passed.

As they went deeper into the woods, past the stream and archery range, they took greater care to be silent, lest they alert any possible game. It would have been much easier to track down an animal had they hounds with them; but only the greater warriors had them, and they perhaps were in use elsewhere. Fiona was sure Malcolm must have already asked that. He was never one to do something the more difficult way.

An hour or two passed in which the sun climbed ever higher, and sweat began to bead on Fiona's forehead as they sneaked through the forest, following tracks of deer that sometimes were lost and then found again. Her stomach was beginning to growl, and she figured she was not the only one. Malcolm must think they were close, or else he would have had them turn back for luncheon. Unless, of course, they had brought some food with them, but even then, he had not called them to a halt.

As if he had heard her thoughts, Malcolm stopped in his tracks, his scarlet brows drawn together and his finger lifted to silence the others.

Fiona strained her ears to hear anything besides their own breathing and the gentle spring breeze amidst the tree branches high overhead.

Something crunched faintly on last autumn's leaves, not far away.

Malcolm squatted down and slipped his strung bow off his shoulder, the others imitating his movements as softly as they could. Then he motioned for them to follow him. He stepped lightly in a different course than they had been going so as to be downwind of the animal—whatever it was.

Within moments, Fiona caught sight of it and the air left her lungs. She had seen few living deer in her life, never having had much occasion to venture into a forest, but none this beautifully graceful. It seemed almost a shame to kill it, yet they needed the meat for the war trail ahead.

Reaching behind her, she nocked an arrow to her bow as the others became aware of the hart ahead. She glanced at Malcolm before drawing it back, signalling that she wanted to claim first kill.

He grinned, nocking an arrow to his own bow and letting the others know with a gesture of his hand to wait until she had shot.

Aiming carefully down the shaft, she moved her arrow a bit higher than the place she was hoping the arrow would land, and let loose the shaft.

With the softest *wisht* sound, the barb pierced the deer, a red stain soon appearing on the light hide. The injured animal took flight but did not succeed in getting far.

The other lads let fly and the stag stumbled, though still pressing onward as if to escape death.

Leaping to her feet, Fiona took after the creature, hearing the footfalls of the others close behind her. They followed the blood trail a short distance before they found the stag in its final death throes, fallen on the forest floor.

Malcolm rushed forward and slit the animal's throat with his dirk, laying a hand on the animal's neck until the shuddering ceased. He wiped his blade clean and thrust it back into its sheath. "Right," he said, getting to his feet. "Who will help me carry this back to An Dùn?"

Fiona laughed. "Ye should hae brought a horse, daft one."

"Och well, I didnae," the lad replied in irritation, scratching his pate. As was often the case, Malcolm had not thought his plan through as well as he ought to have.

"We could find some sort of...pole; tie the legs—to carry it back," Dafydd said, gesturing with his hands when the right words were harder to find.

"Ye hae got an idea there. Come on, then." Malcolm motioned for the other lads to follow him, leaving Fiona to stand by and guard the creature.

They returned within a few minutes, carrying with them a good-sized limb. Malcolm began peeling the bark off with his dirk while the others searched for something to tie the legs with. One of them finally took off the string from his bow, and after much struggling, managed to get the deer and the pole tied together.

Malcolm and Dafydd tried to lift the pole up, but set it down before the deer ever fully left the ground, groaning at the unexpected weight of it.

"Here," Fiona spoke up. "Hand me yer weapons and I'll carry them back. Ye can bear it back together."

Malcolm translated to the other two lads and they nodded in agreement.

Handing over their bows and quivers to the lass, they gripped the tree limb.

"*Un, dau, tri!*"

With a heave, they hoisted it onto their shoulders, a couple of them stumbling to regain their balance with the added weight.

"Ready?" she asked when they appeared to be settled.

"Aye," Malcolm grunted in a strained voice. "Lead us back."

She did her best to guide them out of the forest, glad that she had paid close attention the first time, else they would have been hopelessly lost. She meandered at times through the trees, trying to lead them along paths where they would not have to clamber over obstacles like fallen trees or briar patches.

The sun was just past noon as they came out of the woods and set off determinedly for An Dùn. It shone hot on their backs, and Fiona was certain the four lads were sweating just as hard as she was, if not more so for carrying the heavy deer.

The guards hailed them in with shouts of delighted surprise and opened the gates without the five having to demand entrance. One deer was not much, but any little bit would do. Besides, Fiona was sure they were not the only hunting party going out this day.

Once inside, several grown men hurried forward to take the heavy load from the young shoulders of the four lads, but they politely refused with youthful pride, continuing on their way to the Great Hall. They did not slow their pace until they arrived, though Fiona could tell by the frequent swaying among them that their muscles were beginning to weaken.

At last, they stopped outside the opened double-doors of the place and stood still, Fiona watching in amusement as they seemed to be expecting something to simply come out and take their burden off their shoulders.

Whether they were or not, a moment later, a couple men and lads stepped out and began to relieve the four of the deer.

Malcolm and the other three rubbed their shoulders and necks hard, but they were grinning all the while and chattering to their companions about the whole adventure. Fiona was certain they would be bragging about it at supper, if not for days to come. She thanked those who had taken the hart when she suddenly stopped short at the sight of one of them.

"Cadwal?" she sputtered in surprise.

The lad glanced up at her, his brown eyes showing recognition. "Yer highness," he answered with a slight bow, unfazed.

She wondered if he remembered the time he had not given her the respect the McCladdens demanded and had gotten duly thumped for it. But she only said, "Ye hae grown so!" Like the McCladden brothers, he now stood at least a few inches taller than she.

"We all hae, yer highness," was the only response she got before the lad disappeared inside with the rest.

"Who was tha'?" Malcolm asked.

"Cadwal."

"Wait, wha'?" Malcolm squeaked, causing several heads to turn their way. "*Tha'* was Cadwal?"

She nodded, still shocked.

"I almost didnae recognise him without the black eye he got last time ye were here."

"Malcolm, donnae be ridiculous. I am sure we saw him when we returned from the war during tha' winter."

"I ken, but he's grown so. He was still a short bairn tha' autumn."

"Aye, indeed, though ye were as well, if ye remember," Fiona retorted. "I only realised it was him because of his forehead shape; it sits heavy o'er his eyes. And his nose," she added, trying not to laugh. It was not a kind thought.

"Wha's wrong wi' his nose?"

"Angus broke it, remember? 'Tis crooked now, poor lad."

Malcolm snickered. "I daresay he deserved it. I would hae done worse had I been strong enough to match him then."

"Wha' are ye doing, loitering about and wasting precious time?" A stern voice broke in, and Fiona glanced up to see Angus approaching them, a scowl on his face that swiftly turned into a grin at the lads' shocked expressions.

She ached to meet him, but she hung back, feeling timid and awkward in his presence. After his strange behaviour at the end of breakfast, she was not sure what to make of him. His gaze met hers a moment and he dipped his head in acknowledgement, but that was all.

"We hae jist brought back some fresh meat; we can take some time before gang inside," Malcolm shot back. "I daresay ye hae no' done as much useful good as we hae today." He stuck his tongue out for good measure before entering the building, though whether his irritation was towards his brother's assumption of laziness or because he was hungry was more than she could say. "We'll most likely gae out again later," he said over his shoulder, grinning at Fiona before disappearing inside, followed by Merwyn.

"How did it gae?" she asked softly as Angus made to walk past her.

He stopped, turning to face her, squinting against the daylight back the way he had come. "Well enough, methinks. We are no' finished yet." He met her gaze again, hitching one shoulder in a shrug. "Ye donnae hae to be ashamed of yer growing army at any rate, princess."

She smiled, her cheeks suddenly warm, and she knew it was not only because of the bright sunshine. "Tha' makes good hearing."

"Angus!"

Both of them turned to see Donald McCladden striding up towards them, his brows drawn together against the sun.

"I would speak wi' Angus fer a moment, if ye donnae mind, princess." His eyes twinkled as he approached.

Wha' is this about? "Aye, I donnae mind," she answered aloud. She glanced at Angus, who stood looking at the earthen path at their feet. "Will I see ye after luncheon?" she asked softly, hoping he would say yes. While she understood what kept him, she missed not having him beside her.

Angus nodded but said nothing.

Donald bowed his head towards her before gesturing for Angus to follow him.

Turning away from them both, she stepped inside the hall, feeling empty, as if she had left something important behind her that she could not easily regain.

Fiona wandered outside after the midday meal. Malcolm was preparing to go with his companions and some others on yet another hunt while the weather stayed fine. Some other warriors this morning had returned with the rewards of full traps, and Donald McCladden hoped that with enough provision, they could stay in An Dùn until the other chieftains arrived. Those not busy hunting or at weaponry practice helped the Lowlanders prepare the fields for the planting soon to come, as if in payment for all that the inhabitants of the fortress town were sacrificing for them.

"Was it good hunting?" a soft voice said behind her, and she whirled, her heart swelling to see Angus standing behind her, an uncertain look in his eyes.

"Aye," she blurted before regaining control of her emotions and continuing in a more subdued tone, "Aye, it was a good hunting."

"Will ye gae out wi' them again?" he asked, glancing away from her to the buildings around them.

"I..." She watched him, her chest throbbing with repressed feelings. What she would give to ride out with him back to that stream, to relive those happy moments once again, for him to speak what was on his heart— "Will ye be gang out, once ye finish judging the swordsmanship?"

"Father wants those tha' can be spared to ride in search of the coming warbands. I thought tha' perhaps, wi' yer permission, I could gae wi' them and help."

"Do ye think ye cannae help by remaining here? Wi' the rest of us?" It was hard to keep the bitterness out of her voice.

He finally met her gaze, his eyes dark and guarded. "Fiona, tha' is no' wha' I mean, and surely ye ken it." There was almost a challenge in his question, and she was afraid to meet it. "I want to best serve ye and my country, and by doing this, I may be better able to serve than simply remaining by yer side while we wait here in An Dùn."

"Aye, Angus, do wha' ye must, if ye think tha' is the right thing to do," she finally said, her mouth dry. "I suppose I should ne'er hae asked ye to be one of my guards," she added in an undertone, beginning to turn away.

"Fiona—" Angus began, and she heard him take a step nearer when another voice cried out, heading towards her.

"Princess!"

It was Cynfael, a broad grin on his face and his gyrfalcon on his wrist, hooded as always when she saw the bird.

Fiona turned, her throat tight, but Angus was no longer there. Her eyes smarted, but it was too late to take back her words now.

"Princess, is...is everything all right?"

She blinked back the tears and forced a smile to her face. "Aye, is there something I can help ye wi'?"

"I am going hunting wi' Gwyn"—he gestured to the white bird of prey on his wrist—"and I thought I'd ask ye if ye wished to accompany me. I ken there has been little action fer any of us, and thought ye may like a companion."

Fiona hesitated, her heart still hurting, but what good would it do to stay in An Dùn and mull over things she had no control over? "Aye, I will come, if only so tha' ye donnae call me princess. 'Tis no' fair if ye insist I call ye Cynfael."

His eyes gleamed. "Aye, I concede. I only did it out of habit and because I didnae wish fer anyone else to think I was being disrespectful."

"I understand," she replied as they made their way to the north gate.

~ 12 ~

MANY MEETINGS

"NOW," Cynfael said as they walked the path between the forest and the fields, out of earshot of any guards, "tell me truly, is everything all right?"

Fiona stiffened. He sounded much like Rhiada in that moment. "Nae," she said after a moment. The grasses which rustled as they passed seemed very loud in her ears.

"Is it Angus?"

She looked at the young king suddenly. "Is it tha' obvious?"

Cynfael shrugged, pausing a moment. Glancing around them, he took off Gwyn's hood and whispered in his own tongue to his bird, who looked at Fiona with bright, piercing eyes. Then, cautioning Fiona to stand back, he threw his arm up, and the bird shot into the sky.

"Another form of hunting," Cynfael said by way of explanation. "She is a mighty hunter, but even deadlier in battle."

"And yet," Fiona said, wondering if he would answer her original question, "she is beautiful."

"Aye, she is." He looked at her now. "Nae, 'tis only obvious to those wi' eyes to see. Donald spoke to me about ye both, that there might be an understanding of a sort between ye. I ken Angus has no' been wi' ye much the last few days, unlike before, and ye seemed upset when I approached."

Fiona was silent, inhaling the sweet smell of things blossoming to life under a warm sun as she watched Gwyn nearly disappear into the sky. "Aye, something has come between us, but I donnae understand wha' it is, and I hae no' found the courage to ask him wha' it might be. I thought...I thought tha' asking him to be one of my guards would be a good thing, as he was before, but..." She flicked her gaze away from the sky and towards Cynfael. "All was fine when I had asked him, but he seemed as though he would say something more, yet he never got the chance. And now, it is almost as if he is purposefully avoiding me if he can."

"Companionship is a difficult thing," Cynfael said, beginning to walk into the moorlands where Gwyn had flown. "And the more deeply ye care about someone, the harder it feels when something comes in between. 'Tis challenging, in the days of war, to be able to speak to someone without other ears hearing, but I hope that whatever has come between ye is mended ere we march." He looked at her sadly. "War is nae place fer broken hearts, especially if it is truly so small a thing as ye say."

Fiona bit her lip. "Perhaps if he was the same lad I kent a spring ago, but sometimes he feels a stranger to me. He is nae longer a lad, and I..."

"Time changes outward appearances, Fiona, but no' always wha' lies within." Cynfael paused in his steps, the wind suddenly tossing his thick, dark hair behind him. "War changes lads into men far sooner than they otherwise might hae been, but souls, even if wounded, remain the same."

The wind ceased, and the silence carried the faint jingle of bells. Cynfael set off at a slight jog, Fiona picking up her skirts to follow. Within a few minutes, they came upon Gwyn strangling a ptarmigan when Cynfael called her off.

Following Cynfael's brief instructions, Fiona took the twine he gave her and tied the poor ptarmigan's legs together as Cynfael let Gwyn fly off again.

"Donald spoke to ye about Angus and I?" Fiona asked, her curiosity gaining the better of her.

Cynfael smiled, a twinkle in his eye. "He said he didnae ken fer sure if there was an understanding, but that ye were very close."

"Was there a reason?" she pressed, wondering now how much Donald and Annag knew—or guessed. Did they know her heart better than she did herself?

Cynfael furrowed his brows a moment before answering. "Aye, I suppose ye could say that," he said at last. "I had asked him, when he proposed an alliance, whether it could be strengthened by a marriage and no' only by oaths and a blood swearing."

Fiona's face grew hot, her heartbeat roaring in her ears. She had not thought of that—that such a thing might be required of her because she was the rightful heir to Scotland's throne.

As if he noticed her discomfort, he continued, "That was when he mentioned Angus. Donnae worry, lass, I hae nae desire to come between ye."

Her shoulders eased, the relief leaving her lightheaded for a moment. "There is wisdom in it, though, even if I could never see ye as such." She glanced up, hoping she had not offended him, but he gestured with his hand for her to speak on. "But I donnae ken if there is anyone else...who might, in my place..." She shrugged. "Perhaps in the Highlands, but I wouldnae ken. It will be hard enough to unite those clans without requiring tha' as well."

"There is someone," he murmured, his eyes watching Gwyn on the horizon. "Elspeth McBride."

"Elspeth?" Fiona sputtered, too shocked to say anything more.

"Aye. Donald spoke about her. As the wife of a former High Chieftain, and though of the smallest high clan, they are most vulnerable to the Saxons—as are my people—and such an alliance is no' so strange after all. But I will no' wed anyone against their will, no' even to protect my country, unless I had nae other choice."

She was quiet as they continued roaming the moors beneath the spring sun, musing on Cynfael's words. "Hae ye spoken to her?" she said at last.

"Very little. But I did ask if I might speak to her when we returned, though I didnae say wha' about. I didnae think 'twould be fair to ask such a thing on the eve of war, nae less since she lost her beloved in the last one."

"Do ye fancy her?" Fiona tried to smile, but it was too serious a thing to treat it lightly.

"I donnae ken her much beyond wha' I hae heard. Aye, she is fair, and there is room enough in my heart to love her bairns as my own—should it come to that. I can grow to love her, and fer my country's sake I would, even were she plain and cold-hearted. But that must be something she chooses, when the time comes. Fer now, I hae nae claim on her, nor will I presume such."

"Do ye think I should seek such an alliance fer Scotland?" Fiona asked softly, standing still a moment. She both dreaded his answer and craved it all the same. She wanted direction, to know she was doing the right thing. Destiny was a hard path to carve for one's self alone.

The corners of his mouth quirked upward. "Methinks ye donnae need to worry about such a thing until Scotland stands free of the enemy. And besides, a coalition between a Highland princess and a Lowlander chieftaincy would be a good thing." He winked, and she looked away hurriedly, ashamed to so easily blush.

They spoke little for the next half hour, following Gwyn as she soared in the bright blue skies, striking the birds flushed from the shrubbery as Fiona and Cynfael walked on the moors.

Once Cynfael had a couple more birds as game, he hooded Gwyn as she sat on his wrist, holding her tethers in his other hand. Fiona willingly carried the birds for him as they began to make their way back to An Dùn.

"Ye are much like yer father," she said, finally breaking the silence. "Ye hae much wisdom despite yer youth." She looked at him now, squinting against the sun beginning to lean into the west. "I think ye will make a good king."

He met her gaze for a moment, fondness in his eyes. "I thank ye, Fiona. I think ye will be a fine queen fer yer people, should we win this war. Ye hae courage and strength, even if ye donnae believe ye do."

"I wish I had yer wisdom and insight, though. I feel ashamed I cannae lead my own army and must leave it up to the chieftains alone. I donnae wish to become my father."

"I never kent yer father, though Donald and my own father told me enough of him. But I donnae think ye would. 'Tis no' wisdom alone that makes a good king, but also humility and self-sacrifice. And that is rarely something that one is born wi', but something one must learn, and one can only learn it through hardship."

"Well," Fiona added dryly, "there is nae lack of tha' these days."

She heard Cynfael chuckle beside her. "Aye, perhaps hardship is a constant companion in the days of war, but it is still true. When faced wi' hardship, how we act is a true telling of who we are. Ye chose to come wi' yer men, even though staying behind would hae been the easier choice. That is courage. And ye care about yer friendship wi' Angus and donnae wish fer whatever has passed between ye to remain so. Those are the makings of a queen, no' a coward."

They drew near the gates now as Malcolm and his companions walked through, the evidence of another fruitful hunting visible even from where Fiona and Cynfael stood.

"I thank ye," Fiona murmured. "I will try to do wha' is right. 'Tis only, he is riding off, and I donnae ken if I will get another chance to speak wi' him."

Cynfael turned to her as they approached, his gaze firm, yet kind. "Then ye must make one, Fiona. War doesnae give anyone second chances."

Angus was gone by the time Fiona and Cynfael returned. Cynfael had given her a sympathetic look, but Fiona did her utmost to swallow the bitter taste in her mouth and continue on. She was Scotland's princess, and as such, she could not wallow in self-pity just because an awkwardness lay between her and her dear friend. So she threw herself into helping the women of An Dùn with the final preparations for the war trail.

Three days passed, three days spent gathering weapons, double-checking rations, and taking farewells. Fiona spent most of that time on her feet, rushing back and forth between the dwelling places, stables, and the forge, only to fall in bed at night utterly exhausted. But the busyness kept her thoughts at bay, both of Angus and of the war.

Fiona did not wish for the army to stay longer in An Dùn, having seen the low food stores, for she did not want to burden her people while they waited for the remaining chieftains to arrive. Chieftain McCladden and King Cynfael had seemed relieved at her suggestion, and so McCladden sent messengers after the scouts searching for the coming warbands, and the rest of them had set out north.

That was two days ago now, two days of fair weather and high spirits. Fiona rode at the head of the first company alongside Cynfael and Malcolm. Angus had not yet returned, though surely he would before the Scots encountered any Danes.

Bryce MacClydno and Hamish McLairdun had joined up with them since they had left An Dùn, and their numbers slowly swelled greater and greater the farther they marched towards Drumdae. They numbered some thirteen hundred with the Cymry, and Fiona's confidence grew even as they marched to war. Already their numbers were nearly what they had been in the last war, and two of the High Chieftains had yet to arrive—not to mention if the Highlanders finally joined them. Surely they had received the messages by now.

Donald had said, when Fiona asked why the Scots seemed more numerous, that even with their losses from the last war, the chieftains had had more time over the past year to train and gather their men, even from the most secluded of glens, than before. But all the same, when Fiona glanced behind her as they rode, many of these Scotsmen were lads scarce of age to bear a sword or ancient men who should be resting at home. And so her hope was tainted by guilt and a sickening knowledge that if the Scots did not win this war now, they never would.

The following evening, as the sun tinged pale gold, the clouds hanging low, the Scots and Cymry arrived at the south fringes of Drumdae forest. Fiona gazed long at the familiar budding trees as they drew ever closer, her heart torn though the breeze blew warm and soft in welcome. This place haunted her dreams. Memories of her first battle came to mind, and she fancied she could hear the echo of clashing swords upon the distant hills. She remembered the grief of the McCladdens losing yet another son and brother, of losing Elspeth's husband High Chieftain Jamie and far too many other men, grief that yet plagued her with guilt, even if it was not her fault. And amid that wave of anguish came the warmth of when Angus had helped tend to her wounds after his own broken heart had been revealed to her, their friendship strengthened by shared sorrow. And then of the days that followed, Rhiada singing a lament, a lament that would never now be finished unless she or Cynfael—or perhaps Angus—took up the song again.

"Strange," Malcolm said from atop his horse, breaking into her thoughts, as Donald called the company to a halt.

"Wha' is strange?" she asked, glancing at him beside her, though she was fairly certain she could guess.

"I was merely thinking how strange it felt to be back, after all this time.... We were so young then. At least I was. Angus and ye, I think, had already tasted what war could do. I had only wished to no' be alone." His seriousness caught her off guard. Perhaps he too remembered the days where he grieved Duncan, having stolen his way into the warband only to be robbed of those he loved most. She wished he would not have to endure such again, that neither of them would have to.

"Aye," she replied at last, just as solemnly. "We hae grown much since then; in some ways, we are still growing up." She smiled, sadness tainting it. "But I donnae think ye are alone, no' anymore."

He nodded. "Nae, princess, I am no'. But come," he added, changing the subject with a swift grin, "we hae yet to reach the trees. We can think and talk after we hae rested and eaten."

Fiona laughed. "Ye are always thinking of yer stomach, Malcolm."

He threw his head back and laughed merrily with her. "Someone has to!"

"Donnae worry. I am sure we will all hae a chance to eat tonight," she said in reply, shaking her head.

Then Donald McCladden called out for them to continue the march. Malcolm only muttered under his breath and remained silent until they finally arrived at the eaves of Drumdae forest.

Donald ordered them to dismount and begin setting up camp for the evening, his words repeated by Cynfael in the Cymraeg tongue. Fiona watched with interest as the older men began preparing cooking fires and instructing the younger lads to set up tents and picket the horses. Malcolm led her horse away with his to be picketed for the evening, leaving her standing alone with their belongings. Meanwhile, Donald and Bryce selected a handful of youths to send into the forest to set snares for small animals; it was too late in the evening to begin a hunt.

"Princess!" Donald called to her, and Fiona stepped forward, glad to have something to do rather than simply keep still and watch everyone else bustle with activity.

"Aye, my chieftain?" she asked, cheerful despite the weariness of travel.

He grinned, his blue eyes catching the light of the sinking sun that struck his copper hair like sparks of fire. "Bryce has suggested we send out a few bands of scouts to look fer any sign of the other chieftains yet to arrive. I thought perhaps ye would like to be wi' them, in case Angus returns. I think ye might hae missed him the last few days."

Aye, though perhaps no' in the way ye think... Fiona's face grew hot and she glanced away at the camp slowly settling into routine. "Aye," she said, turning to him again, a lightness in her heart at the thought that Angus might be beside her by twilight. "I would like tha'."

"Dafydd!" Donald hailed, gesturing for the lad to join them. In a hesitant mixture of Cymraeg and Gàidhlig, he spoke to him, repeating the same question.

Dafydd nodded, looking shyly at the princess. "I would be honoured, sir, if the princess doesnae mind."

Fiona shook her head. "Nae, unless Malcolm is able to come?"

Donald furrowed his brow, looking at the picket lines. "I think he is best put to work here, fer now. Ye should be safe riding southwest wi' jist Dafydd. But at any sign of danger, any feeling tha' something isnae right, ye both ride back here as quick as ye can." He began translating it to Dafydd, but the lad gestured with his hand.

"I followed wha' ye said." For good measure, the lad placed his hand on his sword hilt as if to reassure McCladden, and Fiona bit back a smile.

"Right then, I'll see ye at supper." Donald bowed in Fiona's direction before turning away to oversee something else.

Dafydd hitched a shoulder and headed towards the picket lines. Fiona followed in amusement. She supposed Donald had chosen Dafydd because she was familiar with him, and surely Donald trusted him. But perhaps he had also chosen him because it was good for her to become better acquainted with those who would soon be fighting in her name, no less because she had struggled to do so of her own will. These men and lads—they were more than mere names, ranks, and faces; they were flesh and blood, with as many dreams as she had and with just as much to lose. Besides, if the Cymry were to be in alliance with them, it was best she learn about their people—and from who better than one of their own?

Dafydd managed to secure two reserve horses kept for such a task, handing her the reins and helping her into the saddle with as much care as he did everything. Without a word spoken between them, they rode out of camp into the glowing dusk.

Fiona squinted into the sunlight as they rode towards the west, gathering the courage to speak to her companion. It was only mid spring and darkened early, but the light would continue to hold for another hour. "Hae ye ever done scouting before?" she asked once they had ridden a good ways from the camp.

"Nae, no' really," Dafydd answered, struggling over the words a bit. "I was never old enough to gae on these expeditions." He laughed. "I suppose nae one thought me trustworthy and...sensible enough. Jist hunting, nae scouting."

She laughed with him. "Aye, I suppose the same fer myself, though I also think the real reason was tha' nae one wants to endanger me. Most of the scouting is done up north where the Danes are." Her smile faded.

"There is much sense in that, princess. Yer life is worth too much to risk it needlessly."

She did not say anything for several minutes. Only the soft soughing among the grasses met their ears.

"So," she began after a moment, "do the Cymry hunt any different from the Scots?"

Dafydd shook his head as their horses slowly moved across the moors. "Nae. Except maybe we understand the forest and hills more. We see them as a living thing, no' jist land and trees. And the creatures that live there—no' so different from the legends at times."

Despite his struggle with the language, Fiona stared at him in wonder. Here she caught glimpses of a world much older than her own, one far more mystical and poetic, a world nearly forgotten. Perhaps it remained still among the Highlands, but she had long been estranged from those mountains.

She turned away, spurring her horse onward a few paces and cresting another low hill. She squinted against the sunlight.

Dafydd joined her a few moments later, his horse nickering to hers in some unknown conversation.

"Do ye see anything?" he asked.

She shrugged. "I see something dark, but it might only be rocks."

They looked at it a moment longer, the wind slowly rising, tickling their faces and tousling Fiona's loose curls. She reached up to brush her hair out of her face and glanced at Dafydd, who was gazing at her. He turned away, a faint blush rosying his cheeks.

"Is something wrong?" she asked, a prickling of discomfort worming its way up her spine. It should be Angus riding beside her, looking at her like that—not Dafydd. But perhaps Angus already knew that; perhaps that was why he had Dafydd spar her first at Caerdun, weeks ago. Perhaps it was because of some stupid idea of his that he did not deserve her, that her hand would be best given to that of their allies, as to why he remained distant. Or perhaps he did not care for her in that way at all but only as a friend, and as a friend, believed Dafydd was best suited for her.

Fiona bit her tongue. She should not let her thoughts grow so wild and beyond reason. Surely Angus would not do so without first asking her, would he?

"Nothing is wrong." Dafydd broke the silence. "I was only thinking of something."

Fiona turned to him; she had almost forgotten she had asked. "And wha' was tha'?"

"I donnae ken how to put it in yer language properly," he protested, staring now at the horizon, the setting sun shining gold in his hazel eyes.

"Then say it in yer own. Angus has always told me it is a beautiful language. If it isnae so important, it shouldnae matter much anyway."

Dafydd stared into the distance for several minutes before finally speaking. "*Mae'r tywysoges yr Alban yn brydferth.*" His voice became very gentle, almost like when Angus used to speak with words meant only for her ears, when a strange light shone in his eyes that was not from the sun.

"'Tis poetic, I will admit," Fiona replied after a few moments had passed, the awkwardness making her skin prickle. Then, "Those rocks look much like men, and by their garb, methinks they are Scots." Without waiting for a reply, she rode onward as if to flee the memory, Dafydd soon following.

The land sloped away before them, the sun disappearing into the glen's rising as Fiona drew near a company of marching men. Their tartan weave was that of the MacDonald clan and those beneath him, but Angus was not with them; he must have ridden out to find Alastair. She could not quench the deep disappointment at not seeing his face among the company.

"Hail and well met, yer highness!" Eachann MacDonald cried

as she approached, raising his hand in greeting. "'Tis good to see ye well!"

"Hail and well met, Chieftain MacDonald!" she responded, pulling up her horse before his and placing her fist over her heart. She forced a smile to her face, pushing away her hurt. Even if Angus had gone in search of Alastair, she would see him soon.

The entire company behind Eachann slowed to a halt, horses nickering to one another.

"Is Donald's company already at Drumdae, then?" the chieftain inquired. "We were told we had jist missed them when we arrived in An Dùn two evens ago."

"Aye, as is Bryce, Hamish, and the Cymreig contingency. Alastair is yet on his way; we expect him soon."

"Ah, tha' is well." He glanced at the youth horsed beside her, nodding in greeting. "And who is yer companion? His face seems familiar."

"Dafydd, one of the Cymry," the lad answered in his soft, accented voice. "We stayed in yer holdings on our way to Caerdun Castle."

"Aye, I remember now. Ye speak the Gàidhlig well, better than I expected," Eachann replied kindly.

"Thank ye."

Eachann spoke a few sentences in Cymraeg to Dafydd, who flushed with pleasure and answered back in the same tongue.

"Shall we gae on?" Fiona asked when they seemed to have finished, listening with as much interest as she imagined much of Eachann's men would—unless they also knew the language. Though the words sounded lovely, the sun was setting, and they were still a few miles out from Drumdae.

"Aye, might as well," Eachann replied. Then he called out to his men, and they went onwards. They arrived at the plain with Fiona and Dafydd riding as escorts while the sun bid its final, golden farewell before leaving the land in shadows.

Fiona left them once men arrived to greet the new band and take their horses. After picketing her horse, she joined Malcolm and his friends, who were waiting for her around one of the fires as twilight came on. Angus had not yet returned, and her heart sank a little at not seeing him among them.

"Hae ye eaten yet?" she asked teasingly as she came to Malcolm, forcing away her thoughts.

"No' yet. I was waiting fer yer return." He grinned. "Nothing worse than being stared at while eating."

Fiona chuckled, and the tension and discouragement slowly slipped away from her shoulders. "Aye, especially by someone who is probably still hungry after eating camp porridge." She elbowed him playfully in the ribs.

Malcolm yelped. "Aiee! Donnae remind me. I certainly hope they are feeding us more than tha'."

Fiona laughed and followed him to one of the cooking fires as he poured out in full his commentary on that food source, realising even as she did so how grateful she was for his companionship. As much as she yearned for Angus to be beside her, she was not completely alone.

Chieftain Alastair McThraedan and his men arrived later that evening by the light of the moon, famished and weary. The Scots already assembled were more than glad to share what remained of supper with them, the last of the Lowlander host, as Chieftain McCladden gathered the rest of the chieftains and Cymreig leaders to hold a council.

After greeting Alastair, whose blond hair had silvered further over the past year, Fiona went in search of Angus, who surely must have returned also. Faces that had grown familiar over the last few days passed her on their way to the council, guard duty, or to rest early that evening. In the darkness, the land seemed strange, especially with the ghaistly forms of tents that had been set up, though the weather was fair. But at last, she heard the sound of a familiar tread and Malcolm and Dafydd's voices raised in greeting.

She paused, almost in view of them, her hands suddenly tingling with nerves. She felt faint. Would Angus be glad to see her? Or would he remain distant and shy? Fiona swallowed, inhaling deeply. She remembered Annag's words, of pressing onward in spite of fear. And so she put one foot in front of the other, moving forward. There was only one way to know.

She stepped out of the shadows as the lads walked right by her, and noticed that Angus met her gaze instantly, almost as if he had been expecting her.

"Och well, we'll see ye after ye hae something to eat. Father wants us fer the council, so donnae stray too far," Malcolm said, meeting her eyes with a grin before he and Dafydd set off in the flamelit darkness.

"Ye had a good hunting?" she said to Angus after a moment.

He did not reply at once, only gazed at her, his eyes never leaving her face, almost as if he wanted to memorise every detail. His expression was hard to read in the dim light, but he seemed more tired than anything else.

"Aye, princess, I did," he said at last. He took a step forward and enveloped her in an embrace, resting his head against hers.

She tightened her arms about him, relief flooding her veins at having him back and his treating her as dearly as he had a year ago. She felt his shoulders loosen, and she closed her eyes, savouring it as long as she could. Perhaps...perhaps it would be all right after all.

Around them, the sounds of the encampment slowly faded into the quietness of a spring night, the eaves of the forest rustling gently, the horses whinnying softly, and the low melodious voices of men speaking to one another in friendly conversation.

A burning log snapped violently near them, and as if startled back into reality, Angus pulled back, running a hand through his dark hair. "And ye...ye hae been well?" he asked.

"Aye, jist tired. We hae been marching long, and who kens wha' the next few days will bring." She watched him, curious and yet yearning for him to say something more, too afraid to ask what had come between them, with him so worn out from endless riding.

"Fiona, I..." His voice trailed off and he looked away at a distant fire, as if he expected to find the words there. "I am sorry fer no' being a friend to ye in the way I should hae been before I left. Will ye forgive me?"

"Aye, Angus, of course," she replied, her words nearly tripping over themselves. "I wished tha' ye hadnae gang away, of course, but I understand, and I donnae wish to keep ye captive here against yer will."

"I am no' a captive to ye, Fiona—I hope, anyways." His lips twitched at the corners into something like a smile, and she smiled back, her face warming at his familiarity and nearness to her. "I suppose I jist needed time to think, as much as help ye by searching fer Alastair. Coming back after a year...I—I was afraid tha' perhaps something was lost between us, tha' I had lost something, and so I went searching fer it."

"And did ye find it?" she asked softly when he did not continue.

He met her gaze unflinchingly, and the walls he had hidden behind melted away in the light of his smile. "I found tha' it was right beside me all the time." And he slipped his hand into hers.

Fiona squeezed his hand gently, her chest tightening with deep emotion that she could not put words to. Tears smarted in the corners of her eyes.

"Now I donnae suppose Malcolm has eaten all the food, has he?" Angus asked a moment later.

Fiona laughed, a tear slipping down her face that she quickly brushed away. "Nae, though I am sure he tried. Come, there is plenty fer ye."

She led him gently through the camp, weaving her way around the few tents and sleeping men towards the centre where the High Chieftains sat, Malcolm among them, a couple of them still eating. Angus sat down beside her and took the bowl of porridge offered him, devouring it as if he had not eaten in days.

As the last few men gave their empty bowls to Angus, who took them to be washed, Donald McCladden cleared his throat. Straightening his back and adjusting his plaid, where he sat on the upturned log, he began to speak. "Greetings to the newest clans among us, MacDonald and McThraedan." He bowed his head towards Eachann and Alastair, who acknowledged it with the same.

"Greetings to McCladden and our princess," they both replied, and Fiona placed her hand over her heart in return.

"I trust the treaties went well," Alastair added with a grunt as he adjusted his position. "I see new faces amongst us."

"Aye, they did," Donald said. He gestured to Cynfael, who stepped in among them and sat beside Fiona, giving her a reassuring look.

Fiona dipped her head in return, though she was a bit sorry that Angus would not be beside her anymore. But that was a small sacrifice; she was glad enough that their friendship seemed restored between them.

Cynfael spoke for himself, his voice clear though he did not seem to raise it. His melodic tone rose and fell like a cadenza in rhythm with the flickering flames. "I am Cynfael, son of Rhiada ap Derlyn, who was wi' ye in the last war, and king of the northernmost mountains of Cymru. I and what men could be spared hae joined ye, that together we might finish wha' those before us could no', and destroy the threat of the Danes."

The fire crackled in the silence, and Fiona sighed quietly in contentment. Though they were gathered for a dark and gruesome thing, his words, spoken so calmly and with such confidence, filled her with courage. Courage that blazoned like a homing beacon of light against the shadow that had lain over Scotland so long.

"We are glad to hae ye wi' us, fer better or fer worse," Donald said after a moment.

"And we hope 'tis the former," Bryce added, a bitter edge to his voice.

Angus stepped into the circle of light, meeting Fiona's gaze before sitting down in the only empty seat left, beside his father. She gave him a half-hearted smile, not wanting to distract anyone from the matter at hand, and his blue eyes twinkled kindly like a starlit night in response.

"Wha' are the plans then, fer the present—if any plans exist at all?" Alastair asked, his voice rough at the edges, as though he had been sick and was still recovering.

Fiona felt a chill at the thought. He was old, older than any of them, and should be safe at home, not about to march to war.

"Tomorrow night, when all hae had a chance to rest after the hard travel of the past few days, we shall hold the oath-taking," Donald McCladden answered. "Formerly we hae tested our strength wi' the sword dance, but the Cymry donnae ken tha', and as allies, we wish to bond ourselves together in something tha' we both will recognise and honour. Therefore, we shall follow the Cymreig custom and swear an unbreakable oath as many of our ancestors did in days of old."

Eachann nodded, murmuring his agreement as he closed his eyes a moment against the firelight. "Aye, 'tis a good plan. Bind us in unity and honour as well as common loyalty."

Hamish and Alastair voiced their consent before Donald raised his hand for quiet.

Beside Fiona, Malcolm sneezed and then looked around with a sheepish grin, muttering an apology. Fiona elbowed him playfully before turning her attention back to the sombre discussion.

"We hae prepared long and hard fer this day," Donald continued, gazing at each of them in turn as he spoke. "We all ken wha' is coming. This is our final thrust, our last attempt. If we lose this war, there willnae be another—ye all ken tha'. We hae lost much in the last eight years. Freedom comes at a costly price, sometimes more than we expect to pay. But it is in my heart tha' we hae nae other choice. We owe it to those who hae gang before us, who hae given their lives fer this struggle, fer our country, and fer our princess." He looked at Fiona now and she returned his gaze.

She sat straighter on the log, wishing she had words of wisdom to add to that. But she did not. Cynfael could sing words that resounded in men's hearts. She felt the passion, but she struggled to bring those intense sentiments into words others might understand.

"We cannae let the Danes win, no' after all we hae lost." Bryce MacClydno spat into the fire in the centre, as if to emphasise his words. The spittle hissed in the flames. His passionate hatred against Scotland's enemies had not dulled over the past two years, though the darkness of his hair had faded more and more into white. "We hae already spent enough fer this cause to justify it many times o'er. I would rather die than hae the Danes win against us once more."

"As would I. But we cannae think of jist ourselves, but also our people and our princess," Donald chided his father-in-law gently. "This is no' jist fer our own clans but fer all, and it is fer this tha' we are united.... We will discuss plans fer the actual fighting tomorrow after the oath-taking, especially if our scouts bring news between now and then, but there are some I feel we should speak of tonight, now tha' we are finally all gathered together."

"I am in agreement." Cynfael spoke, his voice ever strong and deep. He leaned his elbows on his knees, tossing his thick hair behind his shoulders, sitting forward as if to better hear them all.

"As am I," Fiona added, her voice soft in comparison with the men. Angus met her glance with a half smile, and there was a warmth in her heart that was not from the heat of the flames before them.

And so they began, discussing the numbers gathered, the ranking of the lesser chieftains, how Cynfael would divide his men—especially those with little knowledge of the Gàidhlig—and so on.

The dim light of the fire and the endless droning of deep voices after a long day spent in the saddle eventually began to lull Fiona into a drowsy state, and she found it hard to fight back sleep. She looked from one face to another, attempting to find something to focus on during the council meeting. The discussion did not demand her presence, since it was of things that were not of crucial importance to her. She might have been permitted to slip away and sleep, but she knew she should stay and listen. It was her duty as princess and future queen; in this, as in many other things, she needed to think of her people before herself. Besides, between Cynfael's many questions and suggestions, Bryce's short but fire-hearted comments, and Malcolm's fidgeting, she could not doze off for long.

A log snapped on the fire, a spark of light leaping up towards the sky. The brightness shone upon a young face sitting near it and she glanced towards him, realising a moment later that it was Angus.

Her throat tightened and her chest ached with something akin to homesickness as she gazed upon him, wishing for a moment he was sitting beside her instead of Cynfael. He, who could understand her almost better than she could herself, might be able to explain things to her, make her feel more a part of this than she was. The flamelight shadowed his high cheekbones and strong jawline, his deep eyes darkening so that they resembled the twilight shining with the luminance of the stars.

How fair, how pure, how noble he looks, bespoke her heart. At once, the fear of the coming war was replaced by something else, a surfeit of longing to know whether he cared for her in the same way she loved him. To know, should they win the war, whether there was a future for them together. But she did not dare ask, not with danger so near, not with him promised to be her guardian. She did not want there to be an awkwardness or distance between them, not when they had repaired whatever it was that had been between them already.

Fiona looked away, crossing her arms over her chest, and not because of the sudden chill whispering across the plain, causing the fire to dance higher for a few moments.

Annag oft spoke of courage, but it was not only marching to war or self-sacrifice that required it. Sometimes one needed courage when facing change or the uncertain future. And that sort of courage was the greatest of all. Because it did not deal with a danger that one would never face in the same way again, but rather with the familiar. For whether one desired it or not, life would be changed forever.

~ 13 ~

AN UNBREAKABLE OATH

WIND whispered about the castle walls, silvery dawn spreading across the land. Songbirds twittered about the tower's eaves, wherein lay their nests. Somewhere a curlew was calling, waking the world into life. Mist swirled thinly about the land beyond the castle's gates, hiding the ground from plain view, but Alan MacCaelan could hear above the birdsong and gentle breeze the unmistakable sound of hooves. And they were headed directly towards the castle.

Alan closed the window, the latch clicking into place, and turned to dress for the day. He had scarcely finished when a knock resounded upon his door.

He opened it himself, seeing the startled face of a servant who surely did not expect him to be awake this early.

"Wha' is it?" he murmured, not wishing to wake his young wife.

"A messenger jist come, sir. He bears a letter from Chieftain Mc-Cladden—in the Lowlands," the servant replied just as softly. "He's ridden hard; his horse is nearly foundered. Wha'e'er it is, 'tis important, sir."

Alan's dark brows drew together. "McCladden? Wha' does tha' madman want o' us now?"

The servant blinked. "Nae, this is his son. Bram died some years ago."

Alan rubbed his forehead, sleep still hazing his senses. "Och, right." Bram McCladden had stopped coming to the gatherings of

King Daibhidh long before the Danes came. And so Alan never met the man, nor his sons, save so long ago he hardly remembered. The elder son had been new to manhood and Alan in contrast a very young lad; he did not recall ever speaking to them. "I donnae suppose ye ken which son?"

The servant shook his head. "I cannae read. I only told ye wha' Arran said it was."

Alan nodded, stepping out into the hallway and closing the door. "Verra weel." The words, spoken in his thick north Highlander accent, felt almost like a verbal sigh. "Lead the way."

He followed the young lad down the corridor and the spiralling steps to another hall that opened into the courtyard. The early spring morning air bit his bare hands and face. It seemed remnants of winter still hung on this far north, even though the last few days had been quite warm.

A man stood by the gates, holding the reins of his horse, who indeed looked well spent. Beside them stood Arran, captain of the guard at MacCaelan's castle, the morning light shining fiercely in his face so that his harsh features resembled a bird of prey more than usual. As for the messenger, he looked like he had slept little in the last few days—which was probably the truth, if he bore news from the Lowlander chieftain.

"I am Chieftain MacCaelan," Alan addressed the man directly, searching the messenger's blue-grey eyes and realising he was much younger than he had thought, more a lad than a full-grown man.

The lad merely handed him a piece of rolled parchment with a nod. "This is fer ye," he said, his voice weak. "McCladden said to make sure it arrived safely." As he withdrew his hand after placing the parchment in Alan's, the chieftain could see a dirty bandage hidden up the lad's sleeve.

Alan gazed at him a moment longer before gesturing towards the kitchens. "Arran, see tha' this young man gets warm food an' a place to rest. An' see tha' his wounds are properly taken care of. Och, an' make sure the stablehands care fer his horse as well as they can."

Arran grunted and led the messenger off, who was still stammering his thanks.

Alan turned away from the gates and looked at the seal, recognising the McCladden crest of crossed swords behind a shield. He broke the wax, unfurling the parchment, the words a coal black against the creamy paper, seeming as if to burn into his memory.

To the Highland chieftains,

May the sun shine upon your fields, and may the rain fall softly upon the earth. May good health and fortune follow you until our paths meet under clearer skies.

It is unknown whether you still hold faith to the true throne of Scotland. Since King Daibhidh's death and Lady Nuith's seizing of the throne, we have long remained in doubt as to the old allegiances. We tried two years before, despite your silence, to take back the crown, and failed, losing many men.

But this is not to open old wounds. We wish to seek your aid in trying, one final time, to destroy the hold of Danish tyranny and take back our land for our own and restore it to the true heir. We once held faith together. We seek to renew that ancient oath.

If you do not join us, we consider you to hold loyalty to your new queen, and for that we account you faithless and accursed, for you have forsaken your own in their direst hour of need.

If you should join us, follow the cries of the raven and the eagle, for they hunt the sound of battle.

In memory of the ancient oaths,

> *High Chieftain Donald McCladden*
> *High Chieftain Bryce MacClydno*
> *High Chieftain Alastair McThraedan*
> *High Chieftain Hamish McLairdun*
> *High Chieftain Eachann MacDonald*
> *And the clans beneath them*

Alan MacCaelan looked up from the parchment, the blood pounding in his ears. Around him, the castle was waking up to life, but he scarcely heard it. Instead of the familiar stone walls of the keep and inner walls of the courtyard, he saw the words, the cry for unity and the threat of just vengeance if they failed. He could not blame them; he would certainly have written the same in their place. And only three of the chieftains' names were ones he recognised...and recognised only from his father, whom he had succeeded within the past few years.

Had the Danes taken that much from the Lowlanders as well? And what did Chieftain McCladden—he could not recall ever meeting Donald—mean by the true heir to the throne? Did one of the McCurraghs yet live, despite the declarations made by the Danish rulers at Caerloch? Or had they found another heir? News was always slow to reach them, so far north, and they had heard nothing of this—if it were true. If there had been other messages two years ago, they had never reached the Highlanders.

Alan took a step forward and then another, slowly making his way towards the kitchens, even while lost in thought.

No, they had not forgotten the Danes. Not up here in the north, not here in his chiefdom, farthest away from Caerloch and yet where the threat was closest. Aye, they knew the threat of the Danes all too well. Every passing summer brought more and more settlements that slowly encroached inward, a noose ever tightening about the Scots' necks. They were far outnumbered, else they would likewise have tried an uprising, if they had had any hope of victory.

But now the Lowlands were calling for him to join them, and the news had arrived mere weeks after a command from the Danish stronghold at Caerloch to do the same, against a possible rebellion in the Lowlands.

If they joined the Lowlanders and they lost, the Highlanders would suffer the greatest. Yet if they won...

His pace quickened.

He stooped to enter the kitchens, which were a few steps lower than the courtyard, and saw the Lowlander messenger eating porridge as though his life depended on it.

"Arran," Alan said, and his captain jumped to his feet, no longer focused on the Lowlander.

"Aye, sir?"

"Saddle my horse and spare two of yer men to ride wi' me. I hae need to speak wi' the other chieftains on this matter, regardless of whether they hae received this summons or no."

"Aye, sir, 'twill be done. How soon would ye wish to leave?"

"As soon as may be. There is nae time to waste. I will return to the courtyard shortly."

Arran bowed his head and left, leaving the messenger behind.

"Rest here as long as ye need," Alan said to him amid the bustle of cooks preparing breakfast around them.

The messenger swallowed, his throat bobbing. "I thank ye, sir, but I wish to return to my swordbrothers. We need as many men as we can hae."

Alan merely looked at him, but the devotion in the young man's face was unmistakable. "Sae be it. Ye may take any horse frae our stables as ye wish. Yer own willnae bear ye back, I am afraid." Then he turned and left the kitchens.

He needed to speak to his wife before he left, lest she worry too much. With their first child on the way, he did not need her to suffer undue anxiety on his behalf. There was enough of that already.

But all the same, she did not need to know that they might very soon be at war.

That second evening, the combined war hosts of the Lowland Scots and Cymreig allies, an army some two thousand strong, feasted together as the sun sank in the west. A golden glow lay across the land, the shining light casting an almost ethereal warmth upon those sharing food together, as if they belonged to a much older, almost forgotten world.

While some might have considered it foolish to squander the meagre provisions they had, it was more important to unite the varied warriors into a loyal brotherhood. And so they regaled that night, complete with harpsong that was sometimes broken by fiercely bright piping. Cameron MacClaerthun, their piper in the last war, had joined them once again, having come with Chieftain Alastair's men. That afternoon had been filled with his music as he taught the Cymry the different songs used by the Scots to signal moves in battle.

King Cynfael himself played for the company once much of the eating was done. Drawing out his bogwood harp, he tuned it and sang song after song for them all, not just in the Cymraeg but also in Gàidhlig, his voice ringing in the cool night air.

Fiona listened to the music with bittersweet melancholy, remembering the first time she had heard Cynfael sing. When they had sat beneath the roof of Caerdun's hall, which had echoed with the joyous voices of men, their fears forgotten. Now they sat with solemnity at the edge of war, a band soon to be united by sworn oath to be faithful unto death, friendships already formed to be forged into something unbreakable.

Yet even while surrounded by the comforting warmth of near friends, Fiona felt only chill foreboding inside. For though sunfire dissipated into cloud-wreathed, smoky twilight, storms were darkening the horizon. These days of peace on the cusp of conflict would not last long. And perhaps that was why the music and laughter seemed all the brighter, even if harshly so, because one did not sing in the face of turmoil and live unscathed.

At last, Chieftain Donald McCladden called for their attention, and the harpsong and scattered talk died away, the peaceful silence of the night replacing them.

"Ye all ken why we are gathered here on the eaves of the Forest of Drumdae. Eight years ago, we fought against the Danes in an attempt to drive them out. Few of those who battled that day returned alive. Six years later, we attempted it again. We won a few victories, but in the end we lost—and at great cost. Some of ye might be wondering wha' the point is, why the pain and suffering when in the end it yields nothing. Why are we still fighting? I often ask myself the same question. I fought wi' many of ye six years ago. I hae lost two of my sons in this war, this war tha' is still happening....

"I sometimes wonder if, had I kent wha' it would cost me, whether I would hae made the decisions I did. But the thing remains—we cannae change the past. We can only regret it, learn from our mistakes, and move on.

"Eight years since this war's birthing, we are still fighting fer the same cause. We want our freedom. We want to ken tha' we can live in peace, tha' we can gae out to the forest to hunt fer a day or longer, return home, and ken that our wives and bairns are still safe. We want to journey openly to other glens, visit other clansmen, without being accused of plotting fer rebellion. The Danes destroyed tha' security. We want it back. We want our country back. We want our throne back, our true heir restored to it, and no' to be replaced by our enemies. 'Tis fer these things tha' we fight—and will continue to fight.

"We hae wi' us our Cymreig allies and the united hosts of all the Lowland Scots. We hae yet to receive word from the Highlander chieftains, to whom we sent a plea to reunite beneath the true crown; it remains to be seen whether they are loyal to the old ties. We are a strong army, aye, but the Danes are still—surely—more. Thus we hae gathered to join forces and fight together fer the last time, fer if we donnae win this time, we shall be too weak to ever do so again. In our combined strengths, we hae more of a chance to win than by ourselves.

"Yet this is an alliance tha' should only be made wi' willing hearts. I ken the fear tha' battle brings. Many of ye will be facing it fer the first time. Cowards hae nae place on the battlefield. If ye donnae wish to fight among us, leave now, and ye leave without disgrace. Fer once ye hae taken the oath of bonding—the oath tha' cannae be broken—ye cannae leave and retain yer honour unless released from it. Loyalty, strength, and honour—these things unite us. Break it, and all sense of justice is bereft. So choose now which way ye shall gae. I willnae hold it against ye."

Silence replaced his words. The wind whispered across the plain and in the forest near them, wrapped in the last dying glories of the sunset, but that was all. Even the fires dared not snap against the waiting hush.

Fiona glanced about, and though she was not certain, she did not see anyone leave. All had their eyes focused on Donald, as though he were a master storyteller and not their war captain, as though he were telling them a song of heroes and not soon leading them to possible death.

After a long pause, Donald McCladden spoke once more. "So let us begin." He called forth all the leaders and chieftains and they gathered about him, the flame-light throwing strange shadows across their faces.

Alastair McThraedan brought out a great sword, bound carefully in oiled wrappings. He untied the cords gently and withdrew the weapon buried beneath.

Fiona gasped as the light from the fire glanced off the blade so that it seemed to shine with an inhuman glow, as if it had been made by faeries and belonged to heroes in days long ago. What it was made of, she could not tell, only it seemed to be of some transparent material like glass, a spiralling design carved into it and set off by emeralds.

Without a word being spoken, the High Chieftains each brought out their own dirk and drew it across their shield hands before setting them upon the sword blade. Donald McCladden held out his other hand to Fiona, gesturing for her to come near.

Rising to her feet, Fiona walked through the firelight and stood before the High Chieftain. Butterflies found their wings in her stomach, and the gravity of the situation suddenly weighed her feet like stones to the earth. But when she met Donald's eyes, she saw only kindness and encouragement in his gaze, and she knew—whatever the future held—she, and those who swore this oath, whose breakage was punishable by death and eternal disgrace, would not regret this moment beneath the stars.

She drew her dirk, hearing the soft *shh* from the leather sheath, and winced at the icy feel of the knife slicing across her palm, fiery pain trailing in its wake. Laying her throbbing hand on the ethereal sword, a sudden, humming warmth from the blade kissed the wound, the blood of those who had gone before meeting her own. Awe washed over her for a moment, a chill that sent her trembling to her bones, but then it was gone.

"Would ye stand here as yer men swear to ye?" Donald murmured to her softly as she sheathed her dirk and clenched her hand, longing only to bandage it. "Angus will see to it, I am sure," he continued with a quick smile, as if he had guessed her thoughts.

Fiona gave him a slight nod. Then she stepped back beside the five High Chieftains, feeling as though she had suddenly become part of something much larger than just herself, something much more ancient and much more sacred.

The Cymreig leaders stepped forward to lay their hands upon the sword still held by Alastair, the oldest among them.

Cynfael's thin fillet of gold resting on his hair glinted in the firelight, catching her gaze. His eyes flickered up to meet hers a moment as he placed his hand on the sword. An earnestness blazed in his glance, one that bespoke of his passion and loyalty to this cause, and she looked away hurriedly, ashamed. Here was a king worth following, but what was she? A timid lass to inherit a crown passed down to her by blood, not because she had earned it. But oh, how she longed to—to be like Cynfael. Perhaps in the days to come, she could prove her worth, even if she at this moment felt worthless.

Then the McCladden sons came up. Malcolm's face shone with

excitement but also a soberness he did not have two years ago. Something stirred inside Fiona, for this war had already changed even the youngest among them, even the brightest of souls.

Angus did not meet her gaze at first, and his face was set in determination, raised up high and not hanging down as if timid or ashamed. At the last moment, he looked up, and the fear she expected to find in his eyes was gone, replaced by a humble confidence that was unlike anything she was used to.

His dagger flashed in the light as he cut his right hand instead of the left, which everyone else had done.

Fiona wondered at it, why he—so particular about weapon practice and being best able to defend oneself, would risk himself like that. But this was not the time to ask why.

After placing his hand upon the sword, he stepped up to her, holding out two strips of cloth with which to staunch her bleeding as well as his.

"Let me tie yers first," she whispered, taking one of the cloths from him and tying it securely around his hand.

Angus opened and closed his fingers into a fist, testing it. "Aye, 'twill do. Thank ye," he whispered as men continued to walk forward and swear upon the blade.

She nodded, taking the other bandage. She tried to tie it around her own hand, failing miserably. Warm, sticky blood continued to trickle across her palm, making it worse.

"Och, Fiona!" His breathy chuckle was warm against her cheek. "When will ye ever learn to let people help ye?"

She glanced up, her cheeks burning, but there was nothing but kindness in his gaze.

"Here, let me." He took her hands in his own, and she trembled at his touch, his fingers warm against the spring's chill evening air. He tied the cloth around her hand, knotting it gently, and then looked at her for a moment. But his eyes were veiled, hiding his heart within. "There, tha' should hold well enough."

"Thank ye," she murmured, remembering the other time he had bandaged her hands, the way the fear and weariness of that battle had melted away into trust. How different that time had been compared to this, a battle yet to be fought and a future yet to be seen, not just for Scotland and those gathered to fight for her here but also for themselves. She searched his face. Their young hearts had not even time to blossom into something more, if it was even meant to be.

He hesitated, holding her gaze still, his blue eyes full of unspoken emotion. He opened his mouth again, only to close it and look away. "Always, princess," he murmured at last, the words resting on his tongue as though he longed to say more, his voice thick as if holding back tears—and shame. Before she could stop him, he turned and left her alone as others continued to move forward for the oath-taking.

She ached at his leaving, yearning to know what he wished to say, yearning to know his heart, whether her affection was returned.

She wiped away the tear that had slipped down her face, realising too late which hand it was. She sucked in her breath sharply at the pain before attempting to ignore it. Something within her throbbed far worse than the shallow cut on her palm. The blood would stop, the wound heal.

Could longing be satisfied as easily, especially if not returned?

Och, ye daft one, ye selfish lass, she chided herself. *How can ye think of only yerself now when all this great host is pledging themselves to ye! This is about more than ye, more than Angus.*

But in her eyes, he was the very image of a Scotland free of war, and above the warriors she respected, above her beloved heather braes and rolling glens—despite herself—he mattered most.

Donald McCladden gestured for Fiona to return to her former place as the rest of them were seated once more. Alastair McThraedan raised his bandaged hand for silence, still holding the sword in the other.

Only the horses nickered to one another in the quiet that followed, the earth itself seeming to hold its breath.

Alastair raised the sword into the air, glass stained red in the moonlight, and brought it down upon the central fire around which they were gathered, holding the bloodied side of the blade to the flames. After this he spoke, his voice resounding with an unearthly echo: "Thus we pledge our lives, our freedoms, and all tha' we hae to free our country, win back our land, and restore our princess to her throne. As we bound ourselves by blood to this blade, so may our blood be drawn should we fail to keep our oath. Only death or fulfilment by mutual release shall free us from it. May this oath hold us, bind us, unite us, until the dawn returns and freedom is won."

Then he began chanting in rhythm the ancient oath that was

from ages past, of a time far beyond Fiona's reckoning, a vow she had nearly forgotten.

As they spoke it together in unison, their voices sounded like that of no mere mortal army but of an unstoppable force that no blade could touch, no earthly power could ever harm.

If we break faith with you, may the green earth gape and swallow us, may the grey seas roll in and overwhelm us, and may the stars fall from the sky and crush us out of life forever.

Fiona glanced at Angus across the fire, his eyes fixed upon the flames. A sudden gust tousled his dark curls, but he did not flinch. His jaw was set, his brow creasing. There was no turning back from this for him either, no matter his old fears.

Stubbornness straightened her spine. If he could find his courage in this, then certainly she could as well.

"So it is done," Donald said into the deep silence that followed. "Ye hae sworn an oath tha' cannae be taken lightly. From henceforth, we are all one until we hae succeeded, or death has found us first."

"So be it," they replied solemnly, their voices ringing across the plain.

The fires flared brighter as dark, billowing clouds stole over the moon and stars, casting the land in deepest shadow. And around them, the wind began to rise, carrying with it a dampness that could only mean one thing.

A storm was coming.

~ 14 ~

STORM CLOUDS

DAYLIGHT spilled over the castle of Caerdun. The sounds of servants bustling to and fro as they prepared for the day awakened Elspeth. She stirred, opening her eyes and seeing her two children beside her, still fast asleep. Their faces were flushed with warmth. Lilybet's thumb was partly out of her mouth, and her brother's arm lay across her protectively.

Elspeth sat up, ignoring the weariness of a night with ill sleep, and looked at them, sadness seeming to darken the room. It should be Jamie there, with Ranald and Lilybet in their own bed beside her. But Jamie was not.

He had loved spring best; she remembered that well. Of how the wind became sweet, bearing promises even when it brought rain. Of the vivid colours of wildflowers he would bring her. Of taking her hand and running out with her to the moors, laughing and dancing amid the blooming grasses.

Yet a second spring had come when he was not at the door to whisk her away, not there to kiss their children, not there to tease her and make up for it with an embrace.

Elspeth bent over her sleeping bairns and gently touched their foreheads with her lips, lingering with pity. Then she arose and dressed, thrusting the memories away. Dwelling on loss would not bring Jamie back.

A thought crossed her mind then, of how the young Cymreig king fared, and she shut her eyes tight a moment, ashamed. It was not her right to think of him so, especially after reminiscing of Jamie. She had no claim upon the king, even if he had shown undeserving thoughtfulness to her, and it was wrong to think he could even care in such a way. Surely he had a lass at home. She was little more than a stranger, and though once the wife of a High Chieftain, was now far beneath a king's gaze.

And yet he had asked her to wait for him. For what other purpose could he have, unless he meant to help her in some other way?

Not that it mattered, she chided herself as she made her way to the kitchens for breakfast. With her fate so far, Cynfael might not even return. She had loved before and had lost. She did not want to lose such again.

"The water is so cold!"

Fiona's voice hung in the glen, the wild wind whipping about her hair and dress, drenched with mist from the waterfall. She turned and looked back at him. The warm sunlight shone on her fiery hair, and an eager smile lit up her face. "Come, Angus, wha' are ye afraid of?"

"Nothing," he replied, laughing as he walked forwards to meet her on the mossy rocks.

Then the light from the sun vanished and all became darkness. Angus looked around, panic seizing his chest. The water glowed with an unearthly hue, the droplets on Fiona's wet clothes and hair shining with the same eerie sheen.

Since when does water shine and the sun turn into darkness? he wondered, a cold heaviness weighing him down. Had they been swept into a faery realm? "Fiona!" he called. "We should turn back. Something isnae right."

She turned to face him, her brows drawn together. "Wha' do ye mean? There is nothing wrong—"

Her words were cut off by the sound of many horsemen dashing through the forest.

"Fiona!" Angus cried out in warning, rushing towards her.

But it was too late.

One of the masked horsemen pulled up beside her, snatching her up in an instant and spurring onward, his chainmail shimmering in the odd light.

"Angus!" Fiona screamed in desperation, the sound lingering in the glen and even louder in his mind.

"Fiona!" he cried, trying his utmost to get to her. But it seemed that an unseen force slowed him down, for he could move no faster than if his legs were in thick porridge. "Fiona!" he shouted again, but she could no longer hear him.

The last thing he saw was her pale, frightened face, her fingers outstretched towards him as she struggled to get free. Her voice cried his name, echoing over and over again in his mind.

Angus sat up with a jerk and glanced around him, seeing dim dawnslight through the tent's opening. His chest heaved with hurried breaths, and his clothes were damp with cold sweat. He buried his head in his hands and groaned.

"Angus, wha' is wrong wi' ye?" a voice asked sleepily. The person it belonged to sat up, his tartan blanket falling from his shoulders.

"Nothing—'twas jist a dream. Gae back to sleep, Malcolm. 'Tis no' sunrise yet." He lay down himself, staring at the grey tent material above him.

It was not the first time he had had that dream. Nor, he feared, the last.

The details varied, but it was always Fiona and him in some sort of misty forest. Always he felt like something was wrong, but it was always too late. Always the horsemen came and took Fiona away, and he was absolutely powerless to stop them. It was too vivid—and had happened too many times—for him to simply dismiss it as a machination of the mind.

But what did it all mean?

He turned his head and glanced at Dafydd, who was still fast asleep. If anything, that lad, raised among Cymreig mystics who believed everything had meaning, might know what to make of this. Of course, he might say what Angus already knew—that he should speak with the princess and tell her all his heart before they marched out for war. Anyone with any sense knew that.

And yet he was afraid at times to even be near her.

Seeing her—her swift smile, her thoughtful expressions, hearing her laugh—it broke him. Knowing that perhaps she only wanted him as a friend was almost worse than when he had been apart from her in Cymru all those months. And that worsened the pain, for he could live with uncertain hope, but not with the knowledge that his deepest desires would never be realised. Now he was ever torn between remaining her friend and companion, and knowing the truth.

Throbbing pain coursed through his veins, pain such as he had not felt since Sioned had died all those years ago. Except this was worse, for with this anguish he feared he would break from that which had once healed his old wounds.

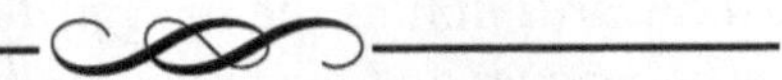

Angus awoke again some hours later, hearing the camp stirring to life around him, conversation coming through the tent's walls.

How could I hae slept fer so long wi' nae one waking me? he wondered, casting aside his tartan blanket and getting unsteadily to his feet. He remembered his thoughts from only a few hours before, and resolve hardened itself within him. Even if he did not speak to her of everything, he at least wanted to warn her in some way. With war upon them, perhaps it was a sign of some cruel fate to befall her, and he would do all he could to prevent it.

"Angus, 'tis a wee bit late fer ye to be sleeping still." An energetic voice broke into his thoughts.

He glanced up, seeing his brother peeking into the tent. "Aye, Malcolm, but I'm awake now."

"Och, ye're all scowlly today, more so than usual."

Angus drew his dark brows together in confusion. "'Scowlly' isnae a word."

"I jist fashioned it into one."

Angus shook his head. "Ye're impossible." He tightened his belt around his waist, slipping his dirk into its sheath before stepping outside the tent.

Malcolm followed closely behind, whistling a strathspey. He stopped for a moment to say, "Father wants me to gae wi' the lads into Drumdae. I wanted to let ye ken before I left. Fiona's wi' Cynfael at present if ye want to find her."

"Why are ye gang into the forest?" Angus stopped, staring at his brother. Did his father want them to hunt—at this hour—instead of weapon practice? Or were they to spy out the hills—though why would his father send young lads for such a thing instead of trained scouts?

"He wants us to gather things like pine twigs, as well as wood fer the fires. He's sending other lads out on the moors fer heather and thistle buds. He wants us to make symbols, like wha' some of us wore in the last war to tell friend from foe, since the Cymry donnae wear the tartan."

"I see," Angus replied, "though the thistles and heather willnae be blooming yet fer some time."

Malcolm shrugged. "I ken, but tha's wha' Father says."

"Where are ye off to?" Dafydd asked, coming up to them, his hair damp from washing in the stream nearby.

"Off to the forest," Malcolm shot back cheerily.

"Something tha' needs doing," Angus replied a moment later, shaking his head. Sleep still hovered close against his will. His stomach twisted within him at the memory of his dark dreams.

"Ye are worried about it," Dafydd said softly, an understanding light in his eyes.

"Aye, perhaps I am." Angus rubbed his forehead.

Malcolm sauntered off, still whistling, leaving the pair alone.

"Is it about the princess?"

Angus nodded, looking at the dewy ground at his feet. "Aye, though more than tha'. I hae been dreaming...and 'tis no' any pleasant dream." His gaze flicked up to meet his companion's. "About the war."

"Is there any way I can help?"

Angus was quiet for a moment. Perhaps Dafydd might understand it better, but he could not bring himself to speak of yet, to put the terror into words and therefore make it more real. It would be hard enough to tell Fiona. "Nae, Dafydd. I...I wish to warn her, if I can. I donnae ken if I hae the courage to do anything more."

"I wish ye the best wi' it." Dafydd laid a hand on his friend's shoulder. "I think perhaps," he continued, switching to his native tongue, "that Fiona may yet feel the same about it as you, in matters of the heart. She seemed very lost without your presence by her side the last few days—before you returned."

"*Diolch, fy ffrind.*" Angus smiled weakly before turning to leave, and as he walked through the enormous encampment, he gazed around. Where was the red-haired lass that caused him so much confusion?

Sunlight peered through the faint, hazy clouds that had arisen with the dawn, playing in golden shadows on the ground. The air was cool but promised to warm as the day progressed, and Fiona sat at the fire more for comfort's sake than to flee the chill of spring.

She had already eaten breakfast. Now she spoke with Cynfael as he plucked the strings of his harp and gently tuned them in between answering her.

"Did yer father teach ye much of the instrument?" she asked. "Or did ye learn from another?"

Cynfael's gaze remained on his harp. "Aye, he taught me a little, but I learned my country's songs from listening to the other harpers. My father kent some of them, but mostly the tunes of other peoples ,as it aided him when he travelled through their lands. I ken very little of yer strathspeys, fer instance, though I would like to learn them." He glanced at her, a sparkle in his dark eyes.

Fiona laughed. "I am afraid I would make a poor teacher. I never quite mastered them, nae matter how hard Rhiada tried."

"Och, but I thought he only taught ye fer a few months," Cynfael replied, sitting back and running his hand over the strings. Their sweet sound filled the air and men nearby paused to listen, only to turn away when they realised he was not going to sing.

"Aye, tha' is true enough. I wish I had been more diligent practising wha' he did teach me, though," she said with a sigh.

Cynfael laid a hand on her shoulder, his hand that had been bandaged after the swearing the night before. "Methinks it may hae been too painful, the memories still too near, in the months that followed after my father died," he murmured. His hand fell back beside him, his eyes focused far away. "Perhaps, should we win this war, ye may hae the chance to learn them again."

Fiona watched him, her chest tightening at the thought. It almost seemed too daring to even whisper those words aloud. Of course, they most certainly wanted to win—why else ally themselves with the Cymry? But it still seemed too distant a thing, even though the oath-taking from the night before was still fresh in her mind. Could they dare to even think of victory before the first blades of war were to be crossed?

But aloud, she only said, "Should tha' chance come, would ye teach me some of yer country's songs?"

"I would be honoured, Fiona," Cynfael answered with a grin. "The melodies and stories are in some ways quite different, but I think ye may like them still."

Fiona returned his expression, almost seeing in Cynfael's place his sightless father, who had shared the same enthusiasm for music and song that could heal wounds when words failed.

Strange, that, to think of healing when death and hurt lay on the horizon. But perhaps Cynfael, like Annag, could see in the misty future the days that must surely come, in which healing would be needed more than anything else.

She heard footsteps and glanced up to see Angus approaching her, his brows drawn together and a worried look in his eyes.

"If ye would excuse me," she murmured to Cynfael before rising to her feet and stepping towards Angus.

"Fiona, may I speak wi' ye?" he asked softly, glancing at the king behind her.

"Aye, of course. Is there something wrong? Has something happened?" Her voice rose higher, anxiety overcoming her good sense. If anything had happened, surely she would have heard noise in the camp, would she not?

"Come wi' me. I donnae wish fer jist anyone to hear us." He led her to the outskirts of the camp by the fringe of the forest and sat down on a fallen log, beckoning to her to do the same.

"Well?" she asked after a moment of silence, her pulse racing. She did not look at him, but instead gazed at the camp rising with the sun, golden light spilling on the verdant plain. It looked warm and inviting, unlike the cool air beneath the forest's shade. She did not like this sudden worry, not when she had wanted to avoid that until they had news of the Danes...unless that was why Angus was speaking with her.

"Ye will probably think me mad," he finally said, "but there is something that has been bothering me of late and I wish to tell it to ye." She could hear his hands fiddling with the handle of his dirk.

"Why? Wha' is it?" She looked at him now, even more confused and worried than before.

"Because it concerns ye, in a way."

Fiona gazed into his blue eyes, searching for an answer but seeing none. The breeze blew softly between them, ruffling his dark hair, and he glanced away, swallowing.

His voice was hesitant when he finally spoke, but he managed to say it all without stopping for too long, his hands moving slightly in suppressed gestures. "Thrice o'er the last few weeks, I hae had this dream. 'Tis always ye and I. We're always in this dark, misty place. And ye are calling to me to come join ye, and I start walking towards ye—and then I feel like something's wrong and I try to tell ye, but it does nae good. Always, dark, mail-clad horsemen carry ye off and I can do nothing about it. Ye are always calling out to me to save ye, b-but I cannae."

She said nothing, the blood suddenly cold in her veins. She could almost see it in her mind, with a clarity that horrified her. She had never dreamt it, and yet...

"'Tis too much of a coincidence fer me to merely dismiss it," he said, breaking into her thoughts and giving an awkward shrug.

"Wha' do ye think it means?" she asked at last with a soft sigh, afraid to think too deeply on it herself.

He shrugged. "I donnae ken...Fiona." He sighed heavily. "I wish I kent, if only to ken how to better protect ye and prevent such from happening."

"Do ye e'er dream anything else?" she asked after a moment, watching the camp. She could hear the sounds of the lads in the woods, their calls carried on the wind as they laughed with one another.

"Aye," he murmured, his voice gentle.

She glanced at him, seeing that his eyes were on the camp as well. A wistful look lay in them.

"I hae dreamt of us, after the war." His cheeks flushed. "The sun is setting, all aglow, and yer hair is aflame wi' the light." He flashed a smile at her and she smiled back, the chill from earlier driven away by the warmth of companionship.

"So we win in the end?" Her voice was soft.

"In my dreams, aye, we hae won. And we are both very happy. Exhausted by the war, by loss, and by the grief caused by it, but we are happy."

"It sounds like a good dream." She drew her knees up to her chest, tucking in her skirt around her feet. "I hope it comes true."

"Aye," he replied, turning to look at her and leaning back on one elbow. "I hope so, too."

Birds twittered in the trees above them, sweetly singing among the pleasant breeze in the contented silence that followed as they sat together in mutual silence.

Then he rose to his feet, giving her a hand up, and she embraced him tightly. He stiffened, as if surprised, before wrapping his arms around her protectively.

She leaned her head on his shoulder, her forehead against his neck. She could feel his heartbeat, fast like her own had been when he first asked to speak to her, but then it slowed, almost matching the rhythm of hers.

She felt him gently play with the loose strands of her hair, his fingers entangling themselves in her curls, and she sighed softly. She was unwilling to let the moment between them pass. It was rare enough to speak with him, to spend time with him undisturbed, like in days before. She knew it might not happen again for a long time.

He inhaled, but whether he intended to say anything more was ruined by the cry that sounded close by.

"Fiona!"

"That'd be Malcolm, no doubt," Angus said, releasing her. He looked away, his jaw clenched, and she felt a pang of bitterness that the moment was gone.

"I'd best be off then," she replied, trying to sound more cheerful than she felt. "I may see ye later, after practise?"

He glanced up and smiled. "Aye, perhaps so."

"See ye then." Fiona grinned by way of goodbye and turned, heading back towards the camp.

Her heart sang, feeling as light and free as the birds flying against the blue sky. She was glad of those few moments, of that embrace, even if she did not know whether he cared for her as much as she did—in the way she did. Still, she wondered whether Angus had indeed meant to say something to her before she had been summoned back to the camp.

She stopped and looked back over her shoulder, but Angus was no longer standing beneath the forest eaves. The question that burned in her mind must wait. But, with any luck, not too much longer.

With the storm clouds of war forming on the horizon, who knew how much time any of them had.

~ 15 ~

TREMORS

"OUR scouts have news of the Scots' movements. They are en-camped at the Forest of Drumdae, just south of the border." Asbjørn pointed to a shaded area on the parchment map. "It is clear that they are preparing for a war trail. They number a couple thousand, including a small cavalry—though where they have gained so many more men is beyond me. I thought they had been decimated in the last war, but it appears it did not take long to gather their strength again."

Lord Erland nodded, the black ink landmarks blurring as he tried to envision a Lowlander uprising of that size. Surely, after the last two wars... "So, captain, what do you suggest?" He needed Asbjørn to think he was giving him the choice out of thoughtfulness, not because he did not feel he had enough wisdom to make a decision here. The last thing he wanted was Asbjørn, as well as Lady Nuith, to think him incompetent in matters of war. He had fought in wars before, but had never led them, and there was a stark difference between following orders and giving them yourself.

"Gather your armies and strike before the Highland chiefs join them—if they should do so. We intercepted a messenger riding north, who carried a letter pleading for the reunion of all the chieftains. He is now in the dungeons awaiting his fate," he added before Erland could ask. "Perhaps that is how they have such a large army already, though we have not seen bands of such a size moving this far north.

Nonetheless, we must attack them and end this rebellion before they can overwhelm us. I do not know if the Danes will answer Lady Nuith's summons." Asbjørn straightened and looked Erland in the eye. His face bore as much emotion as if he were merely commenting on the cloudiness of the day.

"Do you doubt their loyalty?" Erland asked, his voice threateningly soft. He did not manipulate nor let his emotions get the better of him as his wife did, but he knew when to become dangerous. If Asbjørn had any sense, he knew it too.

Asbjørn hesitated, as if choosing his next words carefully, and Erland felt satisfaction at his caution. Perhaps this captain of the guard would learn to respect him. "Nay, only their willingness to always rise for Lady Nuith's call. They are also wearied by war. Besides, it takes time to summon men. They may not arrive quickly enough, even with the best of intentions.

"As for the Highlanders, aye, they swore an oath, but so did the Lowlanders many times, and yet they are once more on the war trail. I do not doubt that there may be some, still, who are loyal to the Scottish cause. It would be dangerous to assume otherwise; there is always the risk of a knife in the back among these savages."

"Hmm." Erland thought for a moment, weighing the risks in his mind. If Nuith's captain of the guard thought this was the best decision also, surely he could not be blamed if it went awry. "Prepare our armies and strike them hard at Drumdae. Perhaps we can end this rebellion before it grows any more."

"It shall be done," Asbjørn replied solemnly. "But who shall lead them?"

Silence hung between them. Drummond was no longer in Nuith's favour as a war captain, but Asbjørn could not so easily abandon his post here either...

"I will place the army in your hands," Erland said at last. "I trust your judgement; you will not let us down. Choose another man whom you trust to be captain of the guard in your place. As for Drummond, he is not under my jurisdiction, and I cannot answer for him. If you want the added strength of his men, best you be asking him."

"I will do so, sir." His face remaining blank, Asbjørn bowed his head and walked out of the room, his stride firm and steady.

Erland studied the map once more. The Forest of Drumdae seemed so small in comparison with the rest of Scotland—and so close to Caerloch, only a few days' ride away. He knew the forest was much larger in real life, but it was hard to imagine the place as more than those tiny black marks, never having been there himself.

The door opened, but he did not look up to see who was there. The familiar footsteps told him enough.

"So I heard you have mustered our forces?" Lady Nuith said, wrapping her arm around her husband's.

He only gazed at the map. "Aye, I have."

"Why are you looking at it so intently? 'Tis just a map, after all."

"This map is more than a mere map. 'Tis an outline of the future. These plains here and here"—he gestured with his finger—"will be the bloody burial grounds after battle. Who knows who will emerge victorious?"

She stiffened beside him. "Do you doubt our forces?" Her voice was icily cold.

"Nay, I think Asbjørn has enough cunning to outwit them, should their numbers be more than our own."

"Then why do you question such a thing?"

"It was more of a rhetorical question than anything else." He looked up and met her gaze. "I do not wish to gamble on something that will always be uncertain. I do not doubt we have a chance to crush this uprising before it bears fruit, but I do not wish to tempt Fate. They nearly succeeded the last time."

Nuith scowled, her eyes dark. "Aye, but they do not have their harper and claim they no longer have their princess. Whatever reason they have for rising up again, they are fools, and it will end like all the others: in bloody defeat. They cannot recover the lives of men they have already lost."

"Aye, that is true. Forgive me; I was wrong to doubt. They have no hope, only a fool's hope." He bowed his head a moment.

"And fools never win," she replied, a smile on her lips.

But even he could see that she seemed unconvinced, and the shadow of fear ever flickered in her eyes.

"Sa ha, I heard ye are to lead the forces now," Drummond said with a sinister chuckle as he passed Asbjørn down the corridor.

Asbjørn knew better than to cower. But he had not expected this reaction and was afraid. Anger he knew, fear he knew, but laughter?

Drummond never laughed save when he won, and to everyone else, this appeared a defeat. "I am sorry; I never asked for it. I expected you to be named."

Drummond shook his head. "Nay, Nuith doesnae trust me. Besides," he added in a softer voice, "'tis best ye are out there. Ye hae a shrewd mind. I can best plan in the shadows and strike where they least expect it. I am gathering my men and will meet ye north of Drumdae. Engage in battle if I donnae arrive in time and fight the Scots like ye promised Nuith. Jist keep the princess alive. Ye may kill whomever else pleases ye, but she must remain alive. I plan on capturing her myself."

Asbjørn smiled, the smile of a conspirator, though he kept from wringing his hands nervously. He understood now why Drummond had laughed. "Aye, that I will do."

"Good." Drummond straightened and added in a louder tone, "Now I am off to my own holdings." And then he was gone down the hall.

Asbjørn watched him leave before slipping away himself, and the place where they had spoken was left to the dust. His blood trembled within him, equally flooded with anticipation. He only wished that he could see Lady Nuith's face when she found out what her half-brother had done. Nuith would be pleased and might even forgive Drummond, but only for a short while. For then she and Erland and their child might be in the dungeons themselves or perhaps even dead. He did not know how far Drummond planned to go; he could only speculate. Drummond always held his pawns close to him instead of pushing them all out on the board.

A dangerous game, to be playing so many pieces at once. But oh, how he enjoyed it. How they both did!

Bright sunlight penetrated the thick cover of clouds and shone upon Fiona. She sat against the rough bark of a tree at the edge of Drumdae, her eyes closed, feeling the pleasant warmth from the sun. The gentle breeze toyed with her hair, whispering no doubt that spring had come at last, bringing with it new life—and also death upon the ends of glittering blades.

From a distance, she could hear the noise from the camp, the horses whinnying at times, men's voices, the clash of weapon practice, and the field forge at work shoeing a horse. But here, all was quiet save for the wrens singing sweetly in the trees.

Perhaps moments of peace like this can still be found amidst the turmoils of war, she mused.

That morning, after speaking with Angus, she had spent her time helping Malcolm and Merwyn give out the pine twigs, heather sprigs, and thistle buds for the warriors to place in their clan pins, which the Cymry wore as well.

The faces of those men, both young and old, came easily to mind even now, and she blushed to think of their humility as they had approached her, bowing their heads and murmuring her name, or something to the effect of "princess" or "yer highness." The younger ones often flushed and stuttered the words, no doubt out of shyness—except for Cadwal, who had said it quite emphatically, though he did not meet her eyes.

But perhaps the most memorable part of it all was hearing Malcolm and Merwyn chattering to each other. Malcolm never stopped for a pause in between talking to Merwyn about all sorts of things, from childhood memories to Scottish traditions, and instructing the less-experienced warriors on how to wear the symbols.

Fiona laughed at the recollection, her eyes still shut against the sun.

"Aye, and then when Cadwal didnae open the gate—och nae, Dafydd, if ye only hae it lying in there like that it'll fly out the minute ye start running, and then where would we be?"

Dafydd's ears had burned bright red, and he looked away.

"Here, let me," Fiona had said, giving Malcolm what she hoped was a stern look, and then had helped the other poor lad get his done properly.

"A fairer sight was rarely seen, than the faery lass who was a queen." A familiar voice broke into her thoughts, bringing her back to the present.

Fiona looked up to see Angus walking towards her from the camp, no doubt returning from weapons practice or some other such duty, and her face grew hot. "Angus! Stop flattering me! Ye ken I hate it." She smiled in spite of herself. Despite his teasing, she was glad to have him back, the Angus she knew so dearly, even if he was behaving more like Malcolm—like a jester—than the sober lad he usually was.

"'Twas no' flattery but the truth," he replied, sitting down next to her. "I can heap praises upon my queen and mean it in all honesty."

She raised an eyebrow. "Even resorting to poetry? Was tha' something ye learned in Cymru as well as the harp?"

He only grinned in response.

Fiona shook her head helplessly. "Besides," she continued, "I am no' the queen yet. I scarcely hae a kingdom to call my own, let alone a crown."

He stared at her, the smirk fleeing from his face. "Fiona, since when does a thing make someone something? Am I no' a swordsman or archer if I donnae hae a blade or bow in my hand? Is Cynfael no' a harper if he doesnae hae a harp?" He paused, searching her face. "'Tis the actions of a person tha' makes them wha' they are, no' any physical object."

She looked down at her hands. She picked at the ends of threads on her skirt, musing on what he said, and acutely aware of his eyes on her.

He reached up to gently brush away the loose curls that had fallen over her face. His fingers were cool against her skin, warmed by the sun. And when he spoke again, his tone had softened to a bare whisper. "Ye are a queen, Fiona. Yer crown has been stolen and our country desolated, but tha' doesnae change the fact tha' ye ought to rule—tha' ye were born to rule."

She glanced up and saw the hint of a smile playing on his lips.

"Ye are a queen to me, Fiona, *my* queen, and 'tis an honour to be yer servant."

Her face flushed again and she looked away, uncertain what to make of the flood of emotions that surged through her veins at his words. She was foolish to care for him so, with the threat of losing him looming closer every day. But all she said was, "Thank ye, Angus. I only wish to one day feel worthy of such loyalty."

He remained silent for a time, and she finally glanced up to see him still gazing at her intently, as if he meant to memorise every detail of her face.

A grin spread across her face at his solemn yet earnest expression, and a quiet laugh escaped her lips. "Wha'? Do I hae oat crumbs in my hair still from breakfast?"

"Why would ye—" he sputtered, his face wrinkled in confusion.

"Malcolm decided to use my hair as a napkin as some sort of jest, and it took forever to get all the bits of bannock out."

"Best ye donnae let him do the same once ye're on the throne," he drawled, glancing towards the plain and rolling his eyes heavenward.

Fiona chuckled. "I didnae let him do anything. He was too quick fer me to stop him!"

Angus shook his head, grinning. "Nae, nae," he said a moment later, "I was only thinking...of how poets might describe ye in song."

She raised her eyebrows in disbelief. "Is tha' so? How might they describe me? A timid mouse too small fer the crown she's meant to hae?"

He snorted. "Nae, no' at all." He looked at her again, as if pondering his words before answering. "Nae, I was thinking tha' they might speak of yer appearance. Ye are no' timid, nae more so than anyone in yer place, and certainly too tall to be a mouse."

She smiled but said nothing as he continued.

"Ye can look very much like a queen when ye want to be. Especially...when the sun shines on yer hair like gilded fire, or in yer eyes like emeralds tha' nae gem can capture, or—" He broke off suddenly and turned his face from her, and said no more.

"Angus, wha' were ye gang to say?" she asked softly, glad to have yet another moment to themselves and equally reluctant to have it end so soon.

He sighed and shook his head. "Nae, it doesnae matter."

"Well, I thought they were very pretty words, though I donnae think I deserve them."

"Ye deserve far more than tha'," he replied in a very quiet voice.

But before she could reply, they heard footsteps approaching quickly, and she glanced up to see Malcolm running towards them, and he did not have his usual smirk on his face. If anything, his face was red, beads of sweat forming on his brow as he drew near. "Fiona! Angus!" he gasped, panting from sprinting all the way from the camp. "Father wants ye both. Scouts hae come from the north at last. They're making plans now—and they need ye to be there. Best hurry."

Doom crashed into Fiona's heart, and her next breath came painfully. "Thank ye; we will gae at once," she replied, her voice strangely calm. She struggled to get to her feet, seeming to be pulled down into the very earth below her.

Angus guided her, his arm at her elbow, as they walked through the maze of tents and cooking fires to the makeshift council ring. Her hands were cold and clammy, and all from the few, brief words Malcolm had said. Why else would they be summoned except to be told that war was now upon them? Of course, this was why they had set out, but she dreaded to hear the worst. It was one thing if the Scots were attacking, but if Danes had already been seen marching out...the bloodied battlefield northeast of them might see yet another brutal conflict.

The leaders and chieftains were assembled in the centre of the camp, much as they had been the last couple of days, making plans and strategies for any possible confrontation with the Danes. Except that none of them were sitting this time. All of them were on their feet, weapons girded as if they expected the crimson ravens to descend upon them right there and then.

"Fiona, Angus, ye hae come in good time," Donald McCladden said as they came up, his face grim.

"Wha' is the news?" Fiona asked, dreading the answer.

"The Danes are mustering their forces to fight against us. We had desired to march on them at Caerloch at least without them kenning, but 'tis hard to conceal a force this large, even in the Lowlands, even here on the moors."

The air left her lungs as if it had been knocked out of her, and her vision darkened. Already, it seemed, the tide was being turned against them.

Angus placed his hand on her shoulder, and she felt a small ounce of lost confidence return. She took a breath, the world coming to light once more. But still, fear hovered close around them.

"Wha' are yer plans, then?" she questioned after a moment when no one spoke. Perhaps they were waiting for her to assume command, or at least attempt to. "Do ye ken their numbers yet or where they are heading, exactly?"

King Cynfael shrugged, answering for them all. "Until we ken their exact locations and guess their intentions, we can do nothing. We only ken they are heading towards Drumdae, roughly, which means they hae spies of their own. We hae been here scarcely a few days."

"Which is why we must send out more scouts," Bryce added. "Without them, we are blind to the plans of our enemy. And we cannae jist sit here. 'Tis bad fighting ground. I suggest we move northeast, put as much of the Lowlands behind us as we can."

"We hae been victorious on tha' ground before now," Eachann put in, stroking his beard.

"At bitter cost," Fiona replied, the words sticking in her throat. "I donnae wish to lose the best of our fighting force at the first battle."

Donald met her gaze, his blue eyes sad yet kind. "Neither do we. But Bryce is right; the ground here is no' suitable fer a battle. And though I loathe to fight on former skirmish grounds, Eachann is right: we did win tha' conflict. If we can get there first, we may hae enough men to easily overwhelm them should we claim the hills. Besides, Drummond isnae here to play the traitor in our midst."

Bryce spat at their feet at the mention of that name and swore under his breath—though all present heard clearly what he said.

"I agree wi' Donald," Alastair put in after a pause. "'Tis our best course of action at present. This way we might also prevent the Danes from attacking our own people as they come. I only wish we had enough time to escape into the Highlands and wreak havoc on the Danes there while we await news from the other chieftains."

"If the news ever comes," Hamish muttered, and the silence that followed spoke much regarding the feelings of the others.

Fiona glanced away bitterly. Even if his words were true, even if they echoed what they all feared, it would have been better if he had not said them. To speak such doubt aloud almost made it seem more real, more certain, and they needed what hope they could muster.

Cynfael cleared his throat, flicking his hair back out of his eyes where it had fallen when he bent his head in thought. "We didnae send out the summons in vain. At least, whatever the coming days bring us, we ken that we tried our utmost to win the Highlanders to us. And should we perish in the end, we will no' perish in regret. Their faithlessness shall be a curse to them. I say we march on, choose better ground, and then await further news from the scouts."

"Any objection?" Donald asked, looking at each of them in turn. When none came, he said, "Tell yer men to prepare to march. We may yet reach the hills by sundown."

The chieftains bowed their heads and left, some of them murmuring "yer highness" to Fiona as they turned away. Their words were like summer sun on winter's snow, but they could not melt the icy fear within. Though she did not cower or tremble as she might have done two years ago, neither did she feel brave and strong like Cynfael was, speaking words of fire against the dark.

Fiona did not linger in the empty space, but neither did she go to gather her things immediately. She walked across the field, Angus following her silently like a faithful shadow. Instead of returning to the forest's edge, she strode to the cusp of the plain facing eastward. She stood there, a spring chill blowing into her face. Tears trickled down her cheeks, and she closed her eyes.

She felt Angus' arms wrap around her, but he said not a word.

"I wish Annag was here," she forced out after a few minutes had passed, her voice unsteady.

"Why is tha'?" he whispered into her ear.

"She would ken wha' to do. She would tell me to be strong, tha' I hae to be strong fer my people...strength I donnae feel at all now." Her voice rose higher, trembling at the edges. "How can I lead my people if I shudder at the mere thought of the coming war?"

Angus waited for her to calm down before answering. "Aye, I wish Mother was here, too. And I am certain Malcolm and Father wish the same. But she isnae. We probably willnae see her until we return from this war. Yet, Fiona," he continued, leaning his head against hers, "ye will be strong, ye will remain courageous in the face of danger, and ye will emerge victorious from this war. Donnae listen to the fears. Ye will be strong until the end. And when the end comes, as it surely will, ye will find tha' ye had the strength to face it all along." His lips brushed the tears on her cheek, and he released her. "I must get back; I need to tell Malcolm and Dafydd to gather their things. But if ye need me, ye ken where to find me. Otherwise, I'll see ye when we march." He smiled encouragingly before turning and walking back towards the camp.

Fiona watched him go, a sudden warmth rushing through her. Surely he did not say those things—or kiss her so—out of mere friendship? Even were it mere friendship, it was close and precious and not the sort to be shared with just anyone. But besides, his words were true—they had to be true. He was not the sort to lie to her. Perhaps her courage would come when she needed it most.

Her confidence returned, a small measure of peace washing over the torn earth. Her fingertips found her cheek with feather-light touch. Her tears were all but gone.

But then she looked north, where the horizon darkened with a coming spring shower. And, somehow, it seemed that she could feel in the ground beneath her feet the tremors of the coming Danish host.

~ 16 ~
# WITH BATED BREATH

THE noonday sun shone hot and bright on Dafydd's head, per-spiration breaking across his skin as he and his companions sheathed their swords and returned to their sleeping places. Except they were not to rest but to prepare to march, eating a sort of lun-cheon on the way.

King Cynfael's words echoed in his ears: "*We are marching north-east. We will encamp at nightfall, but best prepare for the worst. Our scouts have no news yet of the Danes being this close, though they are headed this way, but this is war. Anything is possible.*"

Dafydd had fought skirmishes with Danish pirates on the Cym-reig coast at times, but they were small things. Most of his experience came from the practice ring or sham fights—and hunting. He had not seen war for himself, not felt the blood mist sweep over. But strangely enough, he felt no fear. Only a coldness settling in the pit of his stomach, almost refreshing beneath the warm spring sun. The breeze felt strangely sweet then, reminding him of how beautiful life was, when it might end for him within the next few days.

Gathering his bedroll, weapons, and other belongings, he glanced up to see Angus walking towards him. His brow was knit in thought.

"*Sut mae'r tywysoges?*" Dafydd asked, his voice low so those around him wouldn't hear.

"The princess is fine," Angus replied in the Gàidhlig, still whis-pering. "I left her facing the plain. She needs time.... We all kent the reason fer our marching out, but I suppose none of us realised we might be fighting this soon, especially her. Perhaps none of us hae truly recovered from the losses of the past wars."

This last part was spoken so softly Dafydd had to strain his ears to hear. He said nothing in reply, only laid his hand on Angus' shoulder. He did not know the story—had never asked about it. For this was something Angus must tell freely of his own accord. He had heard enough from Malcolm to piece together what had happened, the deaths of those very dear to them in recent wars, but that was all.

"Will ye be riding wi' Cynfael?" Angus asked with a slight sigh, as if shaking off painful memories.

Dafydd shrugged, a grin spreading across his face. "Nae, I think Dewi is riding wi' him to care fer Gwyn, his huntress. He has more experience than I, at any rate. Methinks my king doesnae wish to hae me overburdened on this march."

"He is a good king tha' way," Angus agreed, looking across the plain as men tore down what few tents had been set up, saddled up their mounts, and prepared to head out. The clouds hid the sun at times, shadowing the open space as if sorry to see them go so soon.

"I am sure Fiona will make a good queen likewise." Dafydd slung his pack over his shoulder, about to turn away. But he heard a strange sort of sound, almost like the breath had strangled itself in Angus' throat, and he looked at his friend and sword brother, confused at the dark expression on his face. But then it was gone, the familiar smile in its place.

"See ye when we ride out," Angus said, a tightness remaining in his voice.

"A good hunting," Dafydd replied, grinning once more. He wished to reassure his friend that all would be well, but then he left, heading towards the picket lines.

"I am starving, positively dying of hunger, and yet Father decides tha' this is the best time to ride out—as if we somehow are faster wi' nothing in our stomachs," Malcolm wailed to the brilliant spring sky, attempting to look his most forlorn. The mare beside him whinnied as if in agreement.

Fiona laughed in spite of herself. She ignored the heads turning their way as they stood amid the picket lines. "Och, Malcolm! Stop yer aching. Yer father said to eat along the way. And who kens? Perhaps we may find some game ere we reach the fields north of Drumdae, and then we will hae more than porridge and bannocks and wha' stuff is given to us from the villages nearby."

Malcolm let out a sound that indicated he was not comforted as he finished tightening the saddle girth. "Aye, but when I eat while doing something, it doesnae fill the hole inside." He jammed his fingers into his stomach as best he could, despite the layers of linen shirt and woollen plaid covering it. "See? This is all empty. I am surprised I donnae find my fingers sticking out the other side!"

"I suppose we should jist hae ye frightening the Danes away wi' yer cryin' instead of bothering to send our warriors against them," Angus drawled, coming up to them as they prepared their horses for riding.

Fiona looked at him, her face warming at seeing him again.

Malcolm snorted, tossing his mess of fiery curls like he were a colt. "Aye, ye jist might after this. A man is meant to eat at his leisure, no' stuffing bread into his mouth while he runs on his feet."

"Ye stuff bread in yer mouth regardless," his brother retorted.

Fiona laughed with him, managing to finally say, "Angus speaks truth. We hae all seen how ye eat."

Malcolm's mouth dropped open in mock astonishment before he closed it, a twinkle in his grey eyes. "Well, wha' can I say, I'm a growing lad. Ye two elders can chew at yer desire. Life's too short to slowly eat tha' bannock stuff."

"'Tis no' all that bad to eat bannock," Dafydd remarked as he strolled up to them, Merwyn shadowing his footsteps.

"No' all tha' bad!" Malcolm spluttered. Settling his things upon his mount's saddle, he made to step around the horse when he tripped over a large stone, and a piece of most unwholesome language escaped his mouth.

Fiona gasped in shock, too horrified to say anything more. It was one thing to hear one of the warriors not known to her speak in such a way, but Malcolm? Who was hardly of age to go to war in the first place?

Angus grabbed his brother by the shoulders and stood him upright, exclaiming, "Wha' did ye jist say?"

Malcolm furrowed his brows, biting his tongue. "I said—"

Even Dafydd, who paid attention now, raised his brows.

"Donnae ye ever say tha' again!" Angus snapped. "Wha' would Mother say if she heard ye?"

"But Grandfather says it all the time and Father never stops him!" Malcolm replied, confused.

"Bryce MacClydno doesnae shout it to the world; he usually says it under his breath," Fiona shot back. "At least when there are younger ears about," she added. "And most of the other men do the same, like the good men they are."

"Our *seanair* can say wha' he likes," Angus retorted, still gripping his brother's shoulders. "He has been at war fer many long years and has seen terrible things. Jist because he has an excuse to swear when he's angry doesnae mean ye are allowed to say it. And like Fiona said, most of the men are decent enough to hold their tongue around a lass, which is more than ye can say!"

"Bryce is yer grandfather?" Merwyn squeaked. "However did that happen?"

The gelding beside them snorted his agreement.

"Our mother is his daughter, but she doesnae share his fire," Malcolm explained, no doubt glad for once to take the focus off of himself.

"Malcolm, promise me ye will never repeat those words again, tha' or anything else *Seanair* says," Angus pressed, not wishing for his brother to escape the subject.

"I promise," Malcolm mumbled, his cheeks burning red.

Satisfied, Angus released his brother and stepped back. "Good. Sometimes men say things to better control their feelings, such as anger, but ye donnae hae the same excuse."

"Nae one does," Dafydd interjected softly, looking at them both. Fiona noted that his voice seemed like music, even though he spoke a tongue not readily his own, through his carefulness in choosing the right words. "'Tis the mark of a great man that he shouldnae give vent to his feelings in such a manner. There are far nobler ways to express anger or grief than to use foul language or brutal force to make its meaning kent. That is wha' makes the best of men."

Angus nodded his agreement, and Fiona likewise kept silent. There was nothing to be said to that, not after Dafydd had put it so eloquently.

"I need to finish taking down the camp," Malcolm muttered, his face still quite red. "I'll see ye as we march." He waved his hand towards them in a farewell, disappearing among the horses. Merwyn followed him, casting an apologetic look over his shoulder.

Angus turned towards Fiona, shaking his head. "I sometimes donnae understand how he will be fifteen autumns this year."

Fiona grinned up at him, jabbing him playfully with her elbow, glad the tense moment had passed. "No' everyone can be as serious and sober as ye, can they? Let him laugh. Marching while satisfying his hunger is the least of our worries. He could be concerned about the coming conflict, or worse."

The mirth vanished from Angus' face, the wonted dread of two years ago taking its place. "Aye, tha' is so. Let us pray he stays this merry when we encamp again." His voice was low, almost as if he were merely putting his thoughts into words for her rather than holding conversation.

"Are ye worried fer him?" she asked as Angus placed his arm across her shoulders and they headed towards their own horses, Dafydd having vanished somewhere else. The smell of horse and leather surrounded her, and the familiarity was suddenly a comfort amid all the unknown.

"I am worried fer all of us." He took his arm away, and her shoulders were suddenly cold. He forced a smile to his face, but his eyes remained dark, and not because they were shadowed against the sun. "Do ye need help mounting up?"

"Nae, I can manage," she replied, smiling back. Securing her things to the saddle, she swung herself onto the horse's back as he did the same with his mare, Branwen.

She glanced around her, seeing the last of the lads gathering up the remaining tents and stowing them away. Those marching on foot found their companies and greeted each other, some exchanging rations to eat as they walked. The rest of them mounted their horses, a sudden tingle of nerves shooting through her hands at the thought of what was coming.

The cry of bagpipes—Cameron's doing—filled the air, a quick strathspey calling all to silence. It ended in a shriek a moment later, and only the wind dared whisper then.

"Ready to ride out?" Donald McCladden called, his command mimicked by the other chieftains and also by Cynfael in the Cymraeg.

And then the company surged forward, horses in front, behind, and to the side, flanking those on foot. Their faces were turned northeast, towards the war to come. Only the wind, the forest, and the trampled grass remained behind.

Rain spat down from the heavens by late afternoon, a warm rain that nonetheless quenched any optimism the war host had about the coming days, leaving them soaked to the bone. It let up by twilight, but the clouds lingered, obscuring the sunset through the trees of Drumdae as they arrived.

The hills remained theirs and the Danes were nowhere in sight, which cheered Fiona considerably, but she still shivered in her damp clothes as they prepared fires to warm themselves and dry out their garments as best they could before sleeping. Little was said beyond the necessary instructions to set up camp, see to the horses, and choose guards to stand watch through the night.

She watched as groups of warriors passed her, some on the way to guard duty, others to find their companies and settle for the night. Many of them met her gaze, some in quick, shy glances, others giving warm expressions and bowing their heads as they went. Most wore the tartan and some did not, but upon the left shoulder of all of them she could see the heather, pine, and thistle in their brooches. A few of the warriors who had ridden that day still had their shield hand wrapped in a bandage from the oath-swearing, and some of the older men raised it in a salute as they passed her. It served as a reminder that their loyalty held true, despite the weather, and she smiled back, glad of their wordless encouragement.

She might not know their names and only recognise some of their faces, but they all knew hers and had sworn to defend her with their lives.

Angus and Malcolm stayed close to her as they ate porridge—better to have warm food in their bellies this night, Donald had said—and occasionally glanced out in the gloom to the hills before them. Though no words were said, she was sure they were thinking of the last time they had been in this place, when they had danced with blades, fought with blades, and lost their brother to them.

Memories of that autumn and winter, two years before, came to mind as she lay down to sleep, the McCladden brothers on either side of her for warmth as before, since the fires had been doused to prevent being spotted by any unfriendly eyes. She remembered Rhiada, the sword dancing, Lachlan and his evil intentions, and her first taste of battle...

She only hoped, as she drifted off to sleep, that she would not lose so much again in the coming days.

"Shall I take a party out hunting?" Alastair McThraedan asked of Donald the next day as still no word of the Danes' approach had been given. "Our food supplies are running low and there isnae much game to be had in Drumdae forest. 'Tis still too early in spring."

Grey sunlight beat down on them as the few chieftains had gathered in the centre of the camp. The air remained damp from yesterday's rain, but it was very warm. Almost too warm, and that and the irritating impatience of waiting were wearing men's tempers thin. No fights had broken out, but some choice words had been exchanged between some, complaints voiced by others, and a tense restlessness lay upon them all.

"I ken tha'," Donald answered, his voice edged with frustration. Frustration because as the head of this army, it fell upon his shoulders to provide for those beneath his care, and because there was so little he could do. "We kent, setting out from An Dùn, tha' this might happen if we didnae take supply wagons wi' us. 'Tis only...I fear separating the companies wi' battle so close. I donnae wish to tire the men out more than necessary, especially after the long march yesterday."

Alastair nodded, his greying hair nearly white in the strange daylight. "I donnae wish to do so either, but I ken many of them are weary of endless weaponry practice. Perhaps this is a good chance fer them to spend their strength in better ways, and also fill their stomachs."

"I agree," Bryce said, his voice mellow with exhaustion. He had volunteered for guard duty last night, and there were sleepless shadows beneath his eyes. "Besides, I doubt the Danes would march upon us this quickly. Take a few companies out, small bands, and we willnae lack too deeply should the worst happen."

"I can lead one," Alastair pressed, though he spoke kindly.

"And I the other," Eachann murmured. "Bryce and Hamish can rest—"

"I am no' a babe; I can withstand until tonight," Bryce snarled, though there was a teasing twinkle in his dark eyes.

"Bryce can train the men here if he so desires," Eachann continued dryly, "and Alastair and I can take a few hunting parties, unless Cynfael also wishes to come wi' us."

Cynfael grinned, a lock of dark hair falling into his eyes as he bowed his head in acquiescence. "I shall, if Donald permits. Gwyn is eager to stretch her wings after yesterday's march."

Donald sighed heavily, though he could not help but smile. "I see I am outnumbered. Take yer men then and gae, and I wish ye a plentiful hunting. We need it sorely. Hamish will be glad of a respite, in any case, though I believe he is already resting after last night."

The three chieftains departed, but Cynfael remained, watching McCladden, a concerned look on his face.

"Aye, is there something wrong?" Donald asked, his voice soft as men moved about them.

"Is there any hope that the Highland Chieftains will join our cause?" Cynfael asked, his arms crossed over his chest. His boyish mirth of just moments ago was gone, the soberness of manhood and kingship taking its place. He stood stiffly straight, squinting against the daylight.

Donald closed his eyes for a moment. Always so much that could so easily go wrong. War could never be simple, could it? "Even if they do, I doubt they will come before the Danes reach us. Some of the men hae suggested marching right into the Highlands and seeking an answer there, but the risk of ambush is too great. If they are against us, we would be surrounded by enemies... Nae, I would prefer to fight on familiar ground—especially where we hae the advantage—than move positions and leave the Lowlands unguarded."

"Do *ye* think they will join?" Cynfael said, his voice reminding Donald much of the king's father.

Oh, how he wished Rhiada, with his wisdom and encouragement, were here now. "There is always hope, Cynfael," he replied at last, "but hope cannae clothe the men, nor feed us. It cannae heal the wounds or bring back the dead. Hope fer the Highlanders' coming, tell yer men to hope fer it, but donnae trust it. They never came to our aid in the past.... Hope fer their coming, aye, but fight as if they never will. We cannae risk otherwise."

"Maybe so," Cynfael said. A sudden warmth tinged his voice, but Donald was afraid to look up, afraid to see that he only imagined it. "Aye, it cannae provide fer our needs, heal our hurts, or restore to us the dead, but it gives us a *reason* to keep on fighting. My father gave his life, hoping that the day would come when the throne would be restored and the clans reunited, and by my oath I took up that same cause. So aye, I will hope. Because my father did, and were he still alive now, I donnae think he would say he gave his life in vain."

Donald looked up now, his vision stained with tears.

Cynfael stepped closer, a light burning in his eyes, and Donald was reminded acutely that he was the age of his sons, of Sioned and Duncan...had they lived....

"We hae returned to this field wi' a stronger host and wi' our princess still living," he continued, speaking of Donald's people as if they were his own. Perhaps he did it on purpose, but something in the natural way he said it seemed to speak otherwise, that he had truly taken this all as his own. "If ever we hae a chance, 'tis now. And I will hold faith to that, whether or no' the Highlanders come. And I will fight fer that even when all is lost. No' only because I swore an oath, but because I cannae do any less." He placed a hand on Donald's shoulder, his face set, and Donald knew these words were not spoken from a momentary passion but from the depths of Cynfael's soul.

He only prayed he would not regret them before the end.

"Forgive me, o king," he said, bowing his head to the younger man. "We had lived without hope so long tha' to hae it again seems but a mercy before death. I keep a strong face before my men, before my sons, before my princess. Naught but Annag kens the truth, tha' fer us who lived through the first war, we are afraid to believe tha' our dream might hae fulfilment after so much loss."

"There is nothing to forgive, my chieftain," Cynfael replied. "'Tis easy fer me to speak those words. I hae no' suffered as ye all hae. Ye tell us to take courage, and I hae. I only wish to remind ye to keep some of that courage fer yerself." He took his hand away. "I must gae."

"I wish ye a good hunting," Donald said, and though he wore no smile, he knew Cynfael saw it anyway.

The king flashed a grin in return. "Perhaps we shall hae bigger game to hunt soon. Gwyn is growing impatient." Then he turned and left, calling to his men in his melodious tongue, answered by cheers.

Donald sighed as he left, his shoulders easing. He felt like a fool, falling to despair so easily. Perhaps Annag was right; he needed to rest. Perhaps, if they won—how he dared to even think the thought—after all this...a time for rest would come. All of them were weary in their souls of this long conflict, and the first battle of this new war had not even yet begun. Who knew of the griefs they would yet endure! And yet, if they won, the losses—dear Sioned, dear Duncan—would not be in vain...

"Father." A youthful voice interrupted his thoughts.

Donald glanced up to see his son watching him, an unreadable expression on his face. "Aye, Angus?" He straightened, searching his son's eyes.

"Scouts Kenneth and Murdock hae jist returned. They say the Danes will be here within two days."

Donald stared, what conviction had returned fleeing away. "Two days?"

"Aye, though possibly before then. They might even be here by tomorrow."

"Where are the scouts? Do they ken the Danes' numbers? Is there cavalry?"

Angus said something over his shoulder, and the two scouts came around the side of the nearest tent, both of them young, bearded men with wild, wind-blown hair and cheeks reddened from the hard ride. They bowed their heads and awaited questioning.

"Wha' is yer report? How many men march against us?" Donald McCladden asked.

Kenneth answered first. "Around five, six hundred, most of them foot soldiers, the rest on horse. I would say only fifty more are on horseback."

"We believe they are only an advance group, sent to keep us distracted while they gather more men," Murdock explained.

Donald nodded, his chest tightening. It seemed the most rational choice, were he their leader. "Hae ye word from any of the Highland chieftains?"

"Nae, no' us. Perhaps the other scouts might, but we donnae." Murdock shrugged his shoulders. "I wish we did. I am sorry."

"A few hae ridden back into camp wi' us on our return," Kenneth added. "They delivered the summons; some were met wi' kindness, others wi' coldness, but none wi' hostility. Yet they were no' given an answer and were no' told to wait fer one."

"Thank ye; ye may gae," Donald replied, gesturing with his hand to dismiss them.

The pair bowed their heads once more and left. Only Angus remained behind, watching his father in silence for several minutes. The sun, fitful all that day, vanished behind thick clouds, and Donald nearly shivered in the absence of cheery light.

"So wha' happens now?" Angus questioned at last, his voice soft.

"We prepare fer battle," came the matter-of-fact reply. "And hope we survive to win." There was a comfort in cold, plain words. If he let his emotions rule him, he might not be able to remain steadfast before his men. And oh, how they needed their courage for what lay ahead!

"Do ye think we can win against them?"

"Fer this battle, I believe so since we yet hold the hills against them and are nearly twice their size, unless their numbers grow in between now and then. It also depends on who's leading them; their numbers are less, but wi' a crafty leader"—he did not say Drummond's name, but Angus surely guessed who he meant—"they might win the field against us. As fer wha' may happen in the future..." He did not finish his sentence but instead looked up at his son, the words hanging in the air between them.

Angus gazed at the ground, his jaw clenched, his hands in fists at his sides. His eyes were dark and clouded as he avoided his father's glance, as if he was afraid of letting anyone see his heart. It was a sight Donald knew all too well from years before, and it filled him with far more dread than news of the coming army.

"Angus, is everything all right?"

He swallowed, nodding his head, and then left, still not meeting his father's eyes.

Donald felt a heaviness in his chest that no thought or reassurance could ease. It was for this that they fought, that their children and those to come after would no longer live in fear and captivity in their own land. He only prayed they would succeed before it was too late and the burden was given to the next generation instead. He had failed enough; he had sworn he would not fail his sons—and his country—again.

Away from the crowding tents in the centre, the bright grey sunlight seemed to mock the bloodbath inevitably arriving in a matter of hours. Sucking in a breath, Angus walked through the camp, twisting and turning to stay out of the way of the other soldiers, heading for the outskirts and the woods where he might be alone.

"Angus!"

He checked and craned his head to see Fiona McCurragh coming towards him, her forehead creased in concern.

"Is it true wha' they say," she said when she stood beside him, "tha' the Danes will be here tomorrow?"

He nodded and looked away, the old fear rising in his throat, nearly choking him.

"Angus?" She touched his hand with her own, her fingers cold despite the warm spring air. "Wha' is it?" she asked softly, that none passing them might hear.

He shook his head, not wanting to thrust her away, but not wanting to think of it. It was better not to think of it, because then the fear did not seem so overwhelming. "'Tis nothing of importance."

"Ye're afraid, are ye no'?"

He flinched away from her words, wishing that this once she would not press him so. And yet, deep down inside, he wished she would, that he could break to her and she not turn him away.

Glancing around them, she took him by the arm and all but dragged him to the edge of the camp. She sat down with him in the grass, under the eaves of Drumdae, her hand on his shoulder. "Speak to me, Angus. Get it out. Ye'll need to hae clear brains if any of us are to survive tomorrow."

"Aiee, Fiona. Jist—wheesht...I'll speak when I'm ready.... The words are no' there yet." He sighed heavily as she took her hand away, but he could not ask her to put it back without seeming untoward. Even friendship did not stretch that far. So instead he picked up the long blades of green grass at his feet and twisted them in his hands, only to cast them aside and tear up more from the ground.

Fiona watched him wordlessly, no doubt knowing that forcing him would not help matters in the slightest. He knew she was only there to listen.

Angus cleared his throat at last and she looked at him as he began, the words halting at times as if he were thinking them through aloud.

"Aye, perhaps I am afraid, but no' in the sense most people would think. I hae been in the heat of battle before—tha' doesnae scare me. Neither am I frightened at the sight of blood." He paused. "'Tis only the old fear, fear of dying or of watching the ones I love die. Tha' is wha' I hate most about war—the losses and the threat of such." He glanced up at her and did not look away.

"I ken," she whispered, her voice strained as if she too remembered. "I ken the pain. And yet, ye said freedom was worth the cost once. Is it still?"

"Aye, it is. Forgive me fer doubting." He forced a smile to his face, but tears still formed in his eyes. "I cannae count the sacrifice of so many fer naught. Sioned and Duncan believed in the cause. I am a coward to fear tha' other lives are no' worth it."

"'Tis nae shame, Angus. I lost my brother too, but I still am afraid of losing others I love. The things we value the most hae high costs. Douglas believed it was an honour to die fer his country, and therefore so must I. Freedom never loses its worth, though men may corrupt the idea of it."

"Aye." He rubbed at his eyes, forcing the tears away. "Forgive me tha' I ever doubted."

Fiona returned his smile, but it did not reach her eyes. "I forgive ye. All of us face this fear at some point. 'Tis nothing to be ashamed of."

"Maybe, but I thought I had conquered the old fears—only to realise they had merely lain dormant all this while."

She laid her hand on his a moment, and he was comforted by such a simple action. "Perhaps," she said, "perhaps fear is something we must fight against our whole lives, even as ye said before."

Angus sighed heavily and gazed off into the distance, his chest tightening.

"But perhaps we can become stronger by it," she added hastily. "Tha' in learning to constantly fight it, we become who we were meant to be. An individual's strength is measured by the hardship they hae endured, I am thinking...." She groaned. "I am no' as good at words as ye are."

He only chuckled, turning back to her. "The words donnae come any easier to me than ye. Difficult things require much thought, and wha' we say in our minds doesnae always make sense spoken aloud. But perhaps ye are right after all."

Fiona blushed. "Thank ye."

He laid his hand on her shoulder, glad of her warmth that reminded him how real and bright life remained, even in the cold shadow of fear. "We should be heading back," he said softly. "Last thing we need is my father worried about us missing." He rose to his feet and held out his hand to her.

She took it, her free hand smoothing out the wrinkles in her skirt, and they walked together back towards the camp.

That night, Fiona found it hard to sleep. Tossing and turning for hours, she at last lay still, staring up at the tent covering above her, dark save for where the fitful moonlight shone through. Try as she might to breathe normally, her heartbeat fluttered and her fingers tingled with nervousness for the next day, when the Danes might come.

No fires thrust back the darkness outside the tent. With the Danes so close, it would not do to be surprised during the night by blades beneath the moon. At times she could hear the guards walking the perimeter of the camp, calling quietly to one another, encouraging one another as the night dragged on and sleep hovered close.

But sleep was far from her, dread taking its place. And this time, there was no Rhiada to speak to, no Annag to give her advice. And the rest—Angus, Malcolm, Cynfael, Donald—they needed their sleep just as much as she. So she waited in anxious trepidation alone, with no one to help calm her fears.

That was the hard part, the waiting. She could handle the adrenaline of battle and the weariness afterward, but the waiting was far worse. Sitting, ears straining to hear the sounds of the coming host, the ground trembling beneath one's feet, waiting with bated breath for the order to charge. And the questions that plagued her thoughts, perhaps, were truly the hardest part.

The most important question of all rang over and over in her mind until her head seemed to throb.

Will we survive the storm?

∾ 17 ∾

RISING TEMPEST

EYOND Caerdun's gates, the distance remained shrouded in mist, as dark and inscrutable as the future.

Elspeth gazed at it, her vision blurred. Her mending lay momentarily forgotten in her lap. Lost in thoughts of the past, she tried desperately not to think of the band of men and the lass they fought for many leagues to the north. And especially not to think of the king among them, whose face was so full of light, who might so easily be crushed in the face of war.

"Elspeth?"

She turned, startled, to see Annag approach her where she sat in the window seat, high above Caerdun's walls. "Aye, Annag, is something amiss?"

Annag shook her head, coming to sit beside her. A warmth graced her face, a look of understanding and pity in her eyes. "Nae, nae. 'Tis only...I hae been thinking about travelling to An Dùn and awaiting further news there instead of remaining here."

Elspeth's brows furrowed, and she adjusted herself to face Annag instead of the gloomy distance beyond the walls. "But I thought Caerdun was far more defensible?"

"Aye, it is."

"Then why do ye wish to gae?" But in her heart, Elspeth was already beginning to understand.

Annag sighed heavily, glancing out the window a moment. "There has been a dark foreboding in my heart, a dream I cannae forget tha' haunts the night hours. It may mean nothing; it may mean everything. But I cannae rest here anymore, so far from Donald and my sons and my princess. An Dùn is no' the same as wi' them, but it is much closer. And should the worst happen, tha' the Danes would win, well.... 'Twould only be a matter of time before they overcame us all. I would rather die near my husband than suffer without him alone." She looked into Elspeth's eyes now, her eyes brimmed with tears. "Ye must ken...wha'..."

Elspeth nodded, her chin quivering in spite of herself. She leaned forward and laid her hand on Annag's. "Aye, if I could hae done the same wi' Jamie, I would hae... 'Tis a hard and bitter thing to be alone." The words stuck in her throat, but she forced them out anyway. "Gae, and hold to hope tha' the worse doesnae happen."

Annag placed her other hand on top of Elspeth's. "Would ye wish to come wi' me?" Her voice was low and strained, almost husky.

Elspeth's gaze shot up. "To An Dùn? But why me?"

"I thought perhaps ye would prefer tha' to being left here alone. I ken ye donnae hae many other friends in this place. And besides"—a hint of a smile played on Annag's lips—"I think mayhaps ye would care to hear any news ye could of a certain Cymreig king."

Elspeth gasped in horror, her face burning. "Is it— I didnae think— I donnae—"

Annag chuckled and her tears fled away. "Och, Elspeth. I was young once, too. I saw the way ye gazed at him at the feast, and I ken he has spoken to ye before. Donald mentioned it as well, tha' Cynfael had spoken to him concerning ye. There is nae shame, fair lass; Jamie would want ye to be happy, I am sure, and Cynfael is a noble and honourable man."

Elspeth looked at the mending in her hands and stabbed the needle through another stitch, desperately trying to think of anything else, anything but her aching heart. "And if I lose him—"

"Love is never lost," Annag replied, her voice firm but gentle. "It may be broken, shattered beyond redemption, but it will heal, and it is never in vain."

Elspeth said nothing for a time. Outside a wind was beginning to rise, whispering of thunder soon to break upon them—if the darkness on the horizon was any indication.

"I will gae," she said at last. "When do ye wish to depart?"

"Within two days, if we can. A small band of guards shall gae wi' us and return once we hae arrived. I am more than willing to assist ye in anything ye might need. And yer children are more than welcome."

Elspeth nodded. "Thank ye, Annag. I am loath to be parted from them," she added with a slight smile.

Annag rose to her feet, planting a kiss on the young woman's hair. Then she was gone, leaving Elspeth to the darkness gathering outside the castle walls.

A storm was coming...but maybe being closer to him, to the small, selfish hope she had left, perhaps she could withstand the breaking. At least better than not at all.

Angus awoke in a cold sweat and sat up, his hands racing across the tartan blanket to reassure himself he had only been dreaming. The feel of wool beneath his fingertips slowly brought back reality, and his breathing slowed to a normal pace. He rubbed his face on his sleeve and opened the tent flap.

He gasped at the cool gust that burst upon his face. The sky paled towards early morning, but the golden—if fitful—warmth from the day before had vanished behind black, impenetrable clouds.

Ironic, he thought, that the storm should come the same day as the Danish one would break across the land. Was his dream, likewise in eerie daylight darkness, a warning?

He rose and dressed, fumbling in the dim light for his clothes and trying his best not to wake his sleeping companions. They had not been requested the night before to attend a dawn council as he had, and if they were to battle that day, they would need their rest.

Once properly clothed with his sword and dirk in his belt, he went outside, his woollen cloak pinned securely around him.

The wind moaned through the cluster of tents and the few smoking cooking fires, ruffling the newly budded trees of the forest, their limbs creaking eerily. The horses neighed with uncertainty, but no other sound of human habitation was audible. It was almost as if he were the only one there, a mere shadow in the faint haze of the rising tempest.

The gusting breeze and rumbles of distant thunder brought to mind the vivid dream that had awoken him in the first place. He had dreamt again of that misted forest, when Fiona was carried off and he could do nothing to stop it. This time, however, every miniscule detail had stood out so much more sharply than before that he found it hard to think it a mere machination of his weary mind.

But he had a council to attend and a battle to face, and dreams, however terrible, had no place in that. He shook his head as if to drive the memory from him.

Stepping carefully across the dewy ground, he looked around him for any evidence of anyone else awake besides the sentries patrolling the camp's borders. The gales grew only fiercer and colder, and he wondered if it would hinder them in the battle to come. Arrows, no matter how skilled the archer, would be useless in the gusts.

Ahead, Angus saw a tent illuminated by a light from within and he hurried towards it, perceiving it to be his father's by the banner over the entrance. Slipping inside, he saw Donald, Alastair, Bryce, Cynfael, and Fiona already standing around the rough table that had been set up, a lamp of sorts set in the middle. None of the other chieftains or leaders were there yet.

They glanced up when Angus entered but said nothing, continuing to speak as if the interruption had never happened. Meanwhile, he stepped around to Fiona's side and stood beside her, relieved that his dream was still just a dream.

"Did ye fight wi' the wind on yer way here?" she whispered to him beneath the murmur of the leaders' talk.

"Wha'—?" he sputtered, his brow knit in confusion.

"Yer hair. It looks like Malcolm tried to make something out of it and, having failed, left it in tatters." She laughed softly, a breathy sound.

He attempted to smooth it down but imagined he had little success. "Fiona," he prompted a moment later.

"Aye, Angus, wha' is it?"

"I had tha' dream again."

She looked up at him and the blood drained from her face, visible in the uncertain lamplight.

He winced. He did not mean to terrify her, but she was not a bairn. She was a young woman who had faced worse, and she should know. With conflict surely coming that day, it was best she be prepared, no less because he would not be beside her but fighting to defend her.

"Do ye think the Danes might...?" She did not finish. With the

Scots' numbers against them, there was little doubt they would resort to treachery.

He nodded. "'Tis wha' I fear."

She shivered, though it might have been from the stormy chill seeping through the tent walls.

He reached out and set his hand on her shoulder, and she inched closer to him as they listened to the leaders' plans.

"We'll hae to wait to hear from the scouts before deciding whether to set up on the distant hills, or perhaps closer to here," Donald was saying. "I personally believe it best if we put as much distance between us and the forest as possible so we hae more ground to fall back on—if need be."

"Do ye think they may try to ambush us in the forest from the other side?" Alastair questioned. "Danish territory lies on the northwest as well as the east."

"Possibly," Donald said, his eyes dark. "There is always a risk. But there has been nae sign from tha' direction, and it makes more sense to send the men from Caerloch. Else they hae to travel through the mountains, and 'tis no' kind territory. If ye are worried, we can leave a small band of men behind jist in case, but I donnae wish to split our forces unless absolutely necessary. Cynfael, hae ye anything to say?"

The Cymreig king glanced up, his arms crossed over his chest. "War is always a risky undertaking, and this time is nae exception. My only concern is how we will fight wi' archers in the storm, if the Danes will truly come today. The rain might ruin the fletching, and the wind will prove a hindrance."

Bryce and Alastair nodded their agreement.

"If need be, we will hae to do without our archers, but I pray it willnae come to tha'," Donald replied gravely, stroking his greying beard. "We will place them on the hills nevertheless, so they may still hae a chance. I say we place the foot soldiers in the centre behind so they are protected until the main attack, and hae the rest on horse to flank them and prevent them from being cut off."

Eachann entered the tent then, dark circles beneath his eyes. Perhaps he had slept as poorly as he had, Angus mused.

Donald briefed him on what had been discussed so far.

"If the arrows will prove hard to shoot in the wind and rain, we may use those meant fer flame," Eachann said when he finished.

"Those are more of an intimidation than of deadly use, but they can still be painful. 'Tis better than nothing at all."

Cynfael agreed. "We use them often against the Saxons and usually wi' success."

Bryce grunted in approval. "Anything tha' may help us is welcome."

"Then, Eachann, I will put yer company in charge of tha'," Donald concluded. "If ye need any more archers, ye ken where to find them among us. If tha' is all, ye may leave. Tell yer men to break fast and prepare fer battle should it come."

Without another word spoken, the chieftains dispersed.

Fiona and Angus glanced at each other before stepping out into the windy darkness, whose damp earthiness smelled of rain. The horizon was grey and sunless, only the growing light hinting at dawn.

"Fiona." He stopped her before she left for her own tent, no doubt to dress for war.

"Aye, Angus?"

"Will ye promise me something?"

"I hae to hear wha' it is before I make any promises." The lightness in her voice and the round shape of her words told him she was smiling, even though he could barely see her face.

"Promise me ye'll stay behind wi' the reserve company when the battle commences. I donnae want anything to happen to ye."

"Staying behind doesnae necessarily guarantee tha'. Battle is an uncertain thing, and it can change so quickly." The smile was still there, though her voice sounded sad now.

"I ken, Fiona." He sighed softly, an echo of the breeze around them. "But if ye are in the forefront of the field—and something happens—I will ne'er forgive myself. And neither will the rest of us, I am certain. Please, Fiona," he pleaded when she did not respond.

"I will, Angus," she responded, stepping up to him and locking her arms around his neck tightly.

Almost out of instinct, he wrapped his arms around her, feeling the quivering warmth from her body against the cold wind around them.

"Yer father said the same anyway before ye came," she murmured into his ear. "He wishes fer Malcolm to stay wi' me, so I willnae be quite so alone."

"I am glad of tha'. 'Twill put my heart at ease if I can ken ye are safe," he replied.

Then she pulled back and said, "I must prepare to leave," before turning and walking away, her shadowy form vanishing quickly.

Angus inhaled deeply, still feeling the tingling memory of her embrace as he looked towards the eastern sky.

It was growing brighter, indeed, but still it would never reach its full daylight. The clouds only darkened and the air seemed to lie still, only to roar again with a ferocity that was almost intimidating, as if it were mocking the warriors.

Try to fight against me; try, and watch yerselves fail.

"Princess!"

Fiona glanced up from where she was tightening the laces on her leather jerkin to see Cynfael headed towards her. His mail shimmered in the fitful light, granting him the appearance of some otherworldly hero, and for a moment, the breath stuck in her throat at the horrible thought that he might die all the same, just like his father.

"Princess, wha' is wrong? Ye look as if ye caught sight of the Danes yerself!" He spoke teasingly, but his face betrayed his concern.

She shook her head, forcing the dark thoughts away. "Nothing; 'tis only nerves. I was no' expecting anyone to call my name since I am no' to be fighting wi' them." She gestured with her hand towards the groups of soldiers slowly donning their armour, such as it was, and weapons. At any moment, they expected scouts to arrive with news of the Danes' movements, though Donald wished to ride out ahead anyway.

"There is a purpose in that, Fiona," Cynfael chided gently, helping her tighten the laces on her bracers, his nimble fingers tying them much faster than she could one-handed. "We wish to protect ye, and wha' is the use of fighting this war if ye are out in the front fer all the Danes to focus their attack upon?"

"I ken, but it still seems cowardly, like something my father would hae done." Her words tasted bitter on her tongue.

Cynfael hesitated, his hands tying the last of the cords together and then dropping to his sides. "Fiona, there is nae shame in this, only wisdom. It would only be cowardly if ye hung back out of fear."

She did not reply at first, only looked away, grabbing her sword belt and securing it around her waist. She wore a kilt and linen shirt beneath her leather jerkin like any of the other warriors, though the plaid was the McCladdens' dark blue and emerald weave—her own tartan of green and brown would make her an easy target. Once her hair was plaited back, she might pass for any one of the Scots at a distance. "It still doesnae make it easier," she finally murmured, casting an eye on the shirt of mail made for her and deciding it was not worth donning if she was not to fight.

"Perhaps no." Cynfael let out a light chuckle. "But 'tis the right thing to do, especially to obey the command of the chieftains. That is a good enough example to yer men—submission and obedience to higher authority. Take care of yerself, Fiona. Who kens the way this battle will flow when it comes. Ye may see fighting yet."

She glanced up now to see his face and felt a twinge in her stomach at the apprehension on his face. *Wha' a fool ye are, to always be thinking of yerself,* she chided. "I will try, my king. If ye promise to do the same," she added.

A swift grin crossed his face, and he laid a hand on her shoulder. "Aye, my princess, I promise." Then he left her.

Pipes skirled through the air, startling and fierce, her pulse quickening its pace along with it. Cameron MacClaerthun was calling them to march out now.

She closed her eyes for a moment, trying to steady her breathing before she went in search of Malcolm and Angus, if only to assure herself they were ready and armed.

The storm was nearly upon them now.

The time of waiting was ended.

~ 18 ~
the breaking

THE rolling sweep of the emerald landscape blurred before Asbjørn's vision, the greying skies and fitful wind whispering into his thoughts as he strategised all possible outcomes of the battle this day. His horse nickered as a breeze whistled among the marching men, shrieking in dismay.

If this weather did not let up, both the Scots and Danes would be hard-pressed to forgo any archers. A shame, that; they offered much protection from a distance. Then again, the weather in Scotland was as fickle as a woman. It might change before they ever joined against the Scots before Drumdae, if the spies' reports were true about the Scots' encampment there.

The booming *hiran-hiran* of a horn broke into Asbjørn's thoughts, the outside world growing clear once more. He looked up to see a contingent making its way towards him, bearing the Danish colours: the scarlet raven upon a banner blacker than the clouds around them, flying violently in the wind. He peered intently, but in the gloom, he could scarcely see the leader of this mail-clad group of a hundred-something soldiers.

"Hail and well met, Asbjørn!"

"Drummond MacDougall, I almost thought you would not come," he retorted in irritation.

"Well, if ye hae nae need of my men, I will turn and head back but fer one thing."

"Which is...?" Asbjørn waited patiently, though inwardly he groaned. When would all the secrecy end? Curse Drummond and his wily ways!

"It will take two leaders if we are to successfully pull this thievery off. Without a present commander, it is hard to control an army in the heat of battle. And the Scots will suspect something amiss."

"I see," Asbjørn stated, looking closely at the man on horseback before him. "Well, we could always use more men in any case. Do you have specific instructions for me, then?"

The marching men slowed to a halt, the silence void of their marching, torn by the winds and crackle of thunder in the distance. This battle would be hard enough without a storm at their backs. Had the Scots summoned it by some strange magic? Were the legends of the ancient druids true?

"Aye, I do," Drummond said, bringing Asbjørn back to the present. "I will place all but a few I hae already chosen in yer charge; they are to obey ye as they would me. If the Scots hae their princess wi' them in their camp as I suspect they do, I will enact the plans we made already. Those wi' me will separate from yer company once the battle is thickest, ride to the southwest and double back through the forest if need be. If she is fighting wi' them, it will be a simple matter to find her. Few men hae hair as wild as hers. I daresay we may hae her before the sun sets this day, should she be among them. If she is no' wi' them, well, we are fulfilling Lady Nuith's orders nonetheless."

"Sounds easy, does it not?" Asbjørn could not keep the hint of mockery out of his voice. Drummond's cool calculations and wild scheming unnerved him, and this time was no different. As his superior officer, he felt he could still treat Drummond with a hint of contempt without fear of reprisal from Lady Nuith should she hear of it.

Indeed, it sounded easy—seemingly too easy. What if the princess was not even in the army? Who knew how many men's lives they might waste trying to find her? Either way, he knew that, regardless if the princess truly lived or not, regardless of whether she was safely hidden away in the Lowlands or travelling with the warband as she had before, they were commanded to put down this uprising. This scheme regarding the princess was something else altogether.

"It willnae be easy; nothing ever is," Drummond replied determinedly, his eyes glinting fiercely black in the light. His horse side-stepped, restless in the growing thunder, and tossed his mane. "But I hae waited fer this many years now. And having come so close, I will no' shirk my duty, even if others may consider it a cowardly act," he added pointedly.

Asbjørn wisely decided to ignore that comment. "Says the one who was fighting on her side two years ago," he drawled instead, looking to the distance where the Scottish army was surely waiting for them.

Drummond made no verbal response, and when Asbjørn glanced at him, he saw that the man's face was darkened with suppressed wrath.

A chill ran down his spine. The battle had not even begun, and he already had angered the one who could easily kill him. It would be such a simple accident, and no one would be the wiser...

"We might as well not keep the Scots waiting longer than necessary," Asbjørn said at last, his chest tight with sudden fear. "And my men and I do not wish to fight in the thunder and rain. Carry on."

Fiona watched the sky grow darker as the war host prepared to head out to agreed positions on the far hills. In the distance, she fancied she saw the arrival of the Danes, their armour glittering cold and fierce in the strange half-light of day.

The archers were already setting out with Chieftain MacDonald and a couple of the Cymreig leaders, some of them carrying torches that they struggled to keep aflame in the rising wind. Rain was coming, which would douse them altogether, but it was worth a try. Anything to give them the advantage.

Behind them marched the standard bearer, carrying aloft the banner Fiona and Annag had spent so many months weaving. The cloth billowed tight against the wild wind, the end of the banner held fast to the pole by the man carrying it, the dragon threatening to take flight before it had ever seen battle.

Then came the foot soldiers armed with spears, their swords belted about their waists. She had overhead Bryce and Hamish commanding them to overlock their shields to form a wall to protect the foot soldiers and archers, who would fire while being safely sheltered from the enemy. Three wings of cavalry flanked either side, a small company waiting behind them all in reserve.

Fiona watched them depart, trying to calm the flutter of nerves tingling in her body. A hand gently squeezed her shoulder, and she turned to see Angus standing beside her, girded for war, the fine mail beneath his jerkin glimmering like stars in the dim light.

"The clouds are dark." She spoke softly over the din of warriors preparing for the imminent conflict.

"Aye, but behind them still remains the clear blue of spring. This storm willnae last forever, princess. And when the sun shines again, we willnae remember the shadows tha' befell us before."

She smiled faintly at his words, embracing him tightly, his chain-mail cold and hard, protecting his heart—and she prayed likewise his life. She shut her eyes tight as his arms encircled her. "I only hope," she murmured, "tha' we will live to see the end of it."

"Donnae be afraid, Fiona," he breathed into her ear. "Good always triumphs o'er evil in the end. The sun will shine upon us again." He was silent, but she felt his breath catch, his pulse suddenly racing, and she wondered whether it was the thought of the coming conflict or something else. Then he whispered something in Cymraeg, so fast she could scarcely catch it, and let her go.

She felt the absence of him keenly but she said nothing. The sooner the waiting was over, the better.

"Take care of her," Angus said to Malcolm, who approached and stood beside her, his hand resting idly on his sword hilt.

Malcolm flung his arms about his brother. His freckled face was suddenly pale, no doubt as the realisation that the battle had finally come sank in. "I will. Take care of yerself, oh reckless one."

Angus laughed, but it stuck in his throat. "Same to ye. If ye hae complaints about being hungry, blame them." He jerked his head in the general direction of the approaching Danes, and then his joy faded. He looked at Fiona, emotion welling in his eyes, and then he turned away, joining Dafydd and the rest as they jogged towards the hills.

She watched him go, squaring her shoulders even though her heart fluttered in fear. If anything happened to him—to anyone—on that field...

No, she must not begin thinking those thoughts. She must be courageous, even as Annag had said.

It was proving much harder than she thought.

"Ye ready?" Angus asked of Dafydd as they joined the archers and strung their bows.

Across the plain, a dark contingent of soldiers and horsemen was slowly making their way towards them, spreading out in battle formation. The Danes were coming. But strangely enough, Angus felt only an eerie calm.

"Nae, but I hae nae choice," his companion replied as rain began to spit upon the ground, a herald of a deadlier deluge soon to come. "I hae practised oft enough. I ken how to kill a man"—Dafydd said these words sourly, as if he had bitten on a bad berry—"but I hae ne'er killed so many, no' like this."

"The first time is the worst," Angus whispered, thrusting back his hair out of his eyes, though the wind threw it back a moment later. Aye, he remembered the last battle far too well. "My first time was on these hills, two years ago."

Dafydd turned to look at him, reaching for an arrow and nocking it to the string while the enemy came ever closer. An unasked question hung between them.

"I came away unscathed save fer a cut here"—he held back the dark curls that fell over his temple, showing a silver scar—"and wi' one less brother."

"*Mae'n ddrwg gennyf,*" Dafydd murmured.

Angus hitched one shoulder as Eachann barked an order for them to reform their line into something more defensible. "Fiona was more injured than I, physically so. But we came away from tha' wi' our friendship bonded stronger than before." He turned to Dafydd as they stepped back and waited, muscles tense for the order to draw and fire. "If anything happens—if the worst should come—and I am unable to return, make sure Fiona escapes safely."

Dafydd nodded solemnly. "I will, *fy ffrind a brawd.*" He placed a hand on Angus' shoulder before drawing back. They turned now towards the Danes, who they could glimpse over the Scots' shield wall, their faces visible now in the distance, stark against the black of their armour.

"Hold the line!" Eachann called, repeating it in the Cymraeg tongue. "Wait fer the order!"

Angus set his face against the rain.

This is fer ye, Fiona.

Let the storm break. He was ready.

Cynfael stroked Gwyn's white, feathery head gently, murmuring to her under his breath. His horse beneath him tossed his mane, snorting in the pelting rain that was slowly beginning to soften into a fine drizzle.

"Sa sa, fair lass," he whispered in his native tongue. "The time for true hunting has come, my fair one. May you ride on swift wings and bring vengeance upon those who destroyed my father. Steal their sight even as they stole his. May justice be done, carried in your talons. Just wait a few moments more, my queen of flight."

He glanced up ahead, where Donald waited atop his mount. They were all waiting, waiting for the clashing sounds and cries of men to tell them the battle had joined. But all remained silent save the lightning raging above, whose splinters of thunder and rain fell on them below.

Soon that would change. And his father's blindness and death would be avenged.

Cynfael smiled.

Angus watched the Danes approach and form themselves into a fighting formation. He glanced at Dafydd beside him, but his companion showed no fear—only cool determination, and it gave him courage. He looked to Chieftain Eachann slightly ahead of him, who was leading the archers at the forefront of the battle.

After several heart-racing moments of vigilance, Eachann raised his hand, and the archers behind him lit their arrows on the torches shielded from the rain.

Angus could feel the heat against his hands and prayed they would not have to wait long to fire.

"Draw!" the chieftain cried, the command followed in Cymraeg, a deafening echo.

Angus willed it to terrify the enemy before them, steeling his courage.

Death before disloyalty. The oath, spoken years before at the first war council, resounded in his ears.

"Aim!"

He heard around him the clink and chime of mail for those fortunate enough to wear it, the creak of leather for those without. He felt the tension in the air, the breathless anticipation for the command to fire, the straining of muscles for this moment when war would truly begin.

Death before dishonour.

"Fire!" Eachann's voice thundered.

The wind stopped, as if expecting this, and thus blessing the whistling of hundreds of shafts that shrieked through the air. Angus heard a sickening crunch as they pierced through armour and the screams of men who did not anticipate facing death this quickly. It did not disgust him this time, only hardened his resolve. They fought in hopes to never fight again.

"Draw!" The High Chieftain brought him back to reality.

Angus pulled his next shaft from his quiver. It would be regular arrows this time. No need for a show now. The shield was taken away, and the torches hissed into extinction.

"Aim!"

Lightning flashed, exposing the field of men waiting to kill and be killed more brightly than if the sun had shone that day.

"Fire!"

Thunder crashed, the ground seeming to shake beneath their feet.

Again, the sound of arrows meeting their mark and the fearful exclamations at the appearance of death.

But this time, the Danes began surging forward, and Angus could almost feel the Scots bracing for the onslaught behind their shield wall between the hills.

Asbjørn ducked a stroke from the youth before him, a youth strangely not wearing the Scottish dress but neither wearing the armour of his own men. He swore under his breath as the lad nicked a weak spot in his armour, but he ducked under the lad's next stroke. His blade stabbed home through the leather armour, already battered and worn by other swords.

The lad fell at his feet, the life fleeing his eyes.

But Asbjørn had moved on. He caught sight of Drummond, who was still on his horse, calling to his men.

Curse this rain that blinded his vision!

Drummond turned and met his gaze a moment, giving a quick nod before appearing to flee the field.

Asbjørn's men turned to him, and he shook his head. *He always has a plan of his own, curse him.* The last thing they needed was to lose the field. None of them had caught sight of the princess, but perhaps she was not with them at all. If any of these barbarians had any sense, she would not be fighting, a mere lass. Even though Drummond had told him of her exploits before....

"Sir, why is—" one of his men asked, dodging a blow from an enemy Scot.

Arrows still fell, though few and far between now. Too much risk of killing their own men save for those who had sharp sight.

"Drummond has his own orders. Hold the field," Asbjørn snarled, still trying to press forward against the unbreakable shield wall the Scots had established before the Danes had ever arrived.

He turned to see whether the man had obeyed his orders, only to see him fall to a well-aimed arrow.

Asbjørn stepped away and met the next threat. Now was not the time to dwell on anything except survival and holding what ground they had gained. If Drummond did not prove successful, he would hate to hear Lady Nuith's words when she discovered they had failed to conquer this "small rebellion". The Scots' cavalry had already ridden out, and he suspected this was not even their full force yet.

Where had they gained so many men?

Where was their princess?

Or had Drummond planned a trick of another kind?

Fiona hugged her arms across her chest. Her feet ached from standing still for so long, yet she was afraid to sit down. The nerves were too intense if she did so. The distant din of battle sounded from the field, and while she was relieved it never seemed to come closer to them, she longed for it to be over. She was nearly sick with anxiety regarding the well-being of them all. For if the Scots lost... But she had known that risk and had come anyway. She had to fight against her fear, else it would defeat her completely. If she was to be queen, she needed to be brave—and this would prove in yet another way whether she had courage or not. Staying in Caerdun would not teach her this, and besides, she would have worried still.

Beside her, Malcolm hopped from one foot to the other, no doubt as restless as she was. At least the rain had finally thinned to a mist, the ground soaked with the drizzle earlier, and the thunder had ceased at long last, the air barely stirring. But still the battle waged on, even though the small band of reserves had not yet been called for.

She let the hood of her cloak slide back, weary of the muffled sounds that came through it. The mist kissed her exposed face, but she did not mind. It was far gentler than the downpour earlier.

"Do ye think they will be done ere nightfall?" she asked, finally breaking the tense silence between her and Malcolm.

He shrugged. "I hope so. Else they will hae to fight in the dark and without supper to refresh their spirits. Though I daresay the Danes can gae without it."

Fiona smiled, though her lips trembled. "I am sure ye cannae think of a worse fate fer them."

He shook his head, his curls flinging damp water everywhere, but there was a momentary grin on his face. "Nae. Nothing can be worse than fighting on an empty stomach."

Her own stomach growled as if to answer, but she had no appetite, even had they had rations on hand. Those were back at the camp, a brisk walk away. The thick clouds above them hid the light, and she had no idea how late in the day it was. It could be noon, afternoon, or early evening for all she knew. And though water fell gently from the heavens, she was parched.

She glanced around them, seeing only the youngest and oldest warriors, some of them sitting on the wet earth or leaning against spears, endlessly waiting. She could slip back to the camp and see if they had any skins of water—or into the forest to the stream close within its tree-guarded borders—quench her thirst, and rejoin Malcolm in a matter of minutes.

"I am gang back to camp; I am thirsty," she said, letting her arms fall to her sides.

He turned to her, a concerned look in his grey eyes. "Do ye want me to come wi' ye?"

She shook her head. "The danger is ahead of us, no' behind. It willnae take me long, and if ye come, ye will want to get something to eat, and then it will take long."

"True," he admitted, looking away to the hills from where the sounds of battle still came. "But if ye are no' back soon, I will come fer ye. Else I will worry."

"I understand," she said, putting a hand on his shoulder for a moment.

He flashed a quick grin. "Donnae want Angus coming after me and saying I neglected my charge."

She smiled, a true smile this time. "Aye, we donnae want tha.'" Then she turned on her heel and walked quickly back the short distance to camp, following the trodden earth from that morning.

Aside from a couple tents, it was a mere ghaist of the camp it had been before with all the inhabitants gone. And though she searched hard, she could find very little besides rations left behind so as not to burden the warriors.

She sighed, straightening. *Looking fer the stream it is, then.* Best she hurry before Malcolm came looking for her.

With one last glance over her shoulder, she headed into the gloom of Drumdae. Beneath the trees, it was nearly dark as night, and the light that did come through was uncertain. The blooming leaves trembled at the slight breeze, but all else was still. Even the battle faded away into nothing as she approached the faint gurgle of the stream, and in the quiet, the hairs on her neck prickled.

She knelt in the muddy earth, cold against her bare knee where her kilt ended, and quenched her thirst. She took one last gulp of water, already regretting drinking so much at once after so long with nothing, and rose to her feet.

All went eerily silent.

Blood pounded in her ears and she took a step backward, the wind whispering no more. Even the rain ceased from dripping down into the wood. She turned on her heel to run back to camp and to Malcolm, when the ringing in her ears faded away. She froze.

Hoofbeats rang out in the quiet, hoofbeats that were growing louder with every moment. And the riders were not her men.

Fiona watched them come in petrified horror, her feet stuck to the forest floor as if hammered there, unable to move. A soundless scream rose in her throat, and in the next instant, earth became sky and sky became earth.

Her head ached as she bounced upside down on the back of a horse, but it was nothing compared to the dark despair in her mind. She should have had Malcolm come with her! How could she have been so daft?

She tried to wriggle her way off—no matter the risk of being trampled by the rider behind them—but her captor only tightened his grip on her. She could scarcely breathe, scarcely see, scarcely think!

A sob tore from her lips as they broke the cover of the trees and mist once more fell on her face—not in welcome but in mournful warning.

She was going to die.

~ 19 ~
A CRUEL TWIST OF FATE

PIPES skirled through the air, a shrill cry of victory, hollowed by the wind driving the mist into the Scots' relieved faces.

Angus watched the Danes flee the battlefield, his sword hanging limp in his grip as he continued to pant from the last duel, but he did not feel relief. His hand ached from the healing cut that had been worn again and again by the use of his blade. But that had been his own choice; he had never trained with a shield on his right hand—though the sword had always felt better in his left—and he had fought with a shield today.

"Angus!"

He turned to see Dafydd walking towards him, the lad's face covered in sweat and streaks of dirt, and there was blood staining his shirt sleeves. But it did not appear to be his.

"Aye?" Angus asked, having caught back his breath.

"We won?" The way the lad phrased it only echoed the doubt in his own mind.

It had been too easy, far too easy. Even with the loss of men—though their numbers had yet to be counted—the Scots had won this battle with little struggle. Even with superior forces, the Danes would never have fled the field this soon. Unless...

He slammed his sword into its sheath and turned, walking quickly among the hills where only a short while ago, the struggle between life and death had raged.

"Wha' is wrong?" Dafydd murmured, following him.

Angus squinted against the fine rain veiling his vision. "I donnae ken. But their retreat—tha' is no' like them to give up so easily. Else we would hae won years ago."

"Where are ye gang?" Dafydd continued as they picked their way around bodies, both dead and living. Some of them cried out in pain as they passed, but Angus did not slow to tend to them. There were enough men doing so already.

"Back to camp."

"Ye fear fer the princess?"

Angus quickened his pace in reply, breaking into a run. He could hear Dafydd's light footsteps behind him as they made their way back.

The light was dimmer here where the forest met the plain. Already there were soldiers milling about, setting up tents and preparing to tend to the wounded being brought back. The princess was nowhere to be seen.

Dread slowed him down, but his nerves writhed ever more swiftly within him. He murmured apologies to men as he wove past them, hardly knowing what he was saying.

Then he caught sight of a lad with fiery hair, and fear gave his feet wings.

"Malcolm!" He pulled his brother up from where he crouched on the ground, and froze when he saw the tears falling freely down his freckled face. And then Angus saw the few bodies lying beside them, thrust through with spears.

It was—suddenly—very hard to breathe.

"Malcolm, where is she? Where is the princess?" He could not keep the panic out of his voice.

"They took her!" Malcolm sobbed, his hands shaking. "She was thirsty—told me she'd be faster on her own. But she didnae come back! And then—and then they rode through—"

The edges of his vision darkened, the old fear threatening to drown him. "Who?" he demanded. His voice grew distant amid the blood roaring in his ears. He seized Malcolm by the arm, ignoring a muted yelp. "Who was it?"

"Peace, Angus!" Dafydd's hand gripped his shoulder, tethering him to reality.

"The Danes!" Malcolm hiccuped, his eyes swollen and his face red. "Drummond—she was on his horse! I donnae ken how, but they took her."

Angus stepped backwards without realising it, his head light.

"They were so fast. One moment we heard hoofbeats, the next—" His brother could not continue, his shoulders heaving, one trembling finger pointing to the slaughtered reserves at their feet.

"Why did ye no' protect her?" Angus found his voice at last, though it was as unsteady as the wind. "Why did ye no' stay wi' her? I entrusted her to yer care, and—"

"Angus!" Dafydd yanked him back, speaking more sternly than he had ever heard him before. "Can ye no' see it is no' his fault! They would hae come even if she had stayed here, and then ye might hae a dead brother as well as a lost princess."

Malcolm whimpered, but Angus did not look at him. He could not. As much as he knew Dafydd spoke the truth, his heart was splintered, and he did not know how he could keep it from shattering altogether. Sioned's face came to mind unbidden, yet another person he could not save from the Danes—his and Duncan's. *No' Fiona, no' my princess too...* Angus shut his eyes, trying to remember how to breathe.

"He bears enough guilt—look at him!" Dafydd cried. "Leave him be. Find yer father, tell him wha' happened, and then we can try to get her back."

Angus turned, his knees threatening to give way. His ears began ringing, the sounds of the battle's aftermath dying away. He felt so light, so empty, and yet so heavy he feared he would sink to the earth and never rise again.

He heard Dafydd's voice but not the words he said. And then Dafydd slung one arm across his shoulders, his other hand gripping Angus' arm, and half pulled, half supported him as they made their way back to the battlefield, where the High Chieftains were gathered between the hills.

Dafydd called Donald's name, Cynfael's, and they turned, suddenly running towards them, their faces etched in concern. Dafydd explained in rapid Cymraeg what had happened, Angus feeling too lost and numb to speak, only grateful that his friend kept him from slipping away from reality entirely.

Donald and Cynfael held a quick discussion, and then Cynfael was running, shouting orders in both languages, a cry that was picked up and carried by all who heard it. A remnant would remain to tend to the wounded and bury the dead, and the rest would set off after the Danes, heading for the glens south of Caerloch, where Drummond was undoubtedly heading.

Angus tried to feel relief, tried to feel hope, but all was darkness. He had tried so hard to protect her, tried to ensure that no one would sneak back and hurt her—and he had been powerless all along.

The air felt cold as Dafydd slipped away, perhaps on some errand. Angus wavered on his feet, struggling to breathe, overwhelmed by helplessness.

"Angus, *mo mhac*."

He looked up to see his father's arms outstretched, an understanding look in his eyes.

Angus took one step forward, buried his face in his father's shoulder, and began to weep.

The doors to Caerloch's Great Hall swung open with a resounding bang. Asbjørn and Drummond entered, dragging the Scottish princess with them. She stumbled across the stones, her hands and feet bound, only a small strip of cloth between her ankles allowing her to take very small steps. Her hair and clothing were dirtied from the rough couple days of riding from Drumdae, and her weapons were gone. Drummond had seen to that the first time they had stopped to water the horses.

All the same, despite her dishevelled appearance, Asbjørn could not help but admire the lass who had refrained from crying or screaming since they had first carried her off. She had remained silent, though she was not gagged, and only her eyes belied the burning emerald fire of fear and anger within.

Lady Nuith rose up from the throne, surprise evident on her face.

Asbjørn noticed that at the sight of her, Fiona pulled herself up to her fullest height, setting her shoulders back and her chin up. Her gaze was steady, meeting Nuith's without flinching, and her chest rose and fell in even breaths. Despite facing down her enemy, helpless to defend herself, she showed no fear. Though bound and filthy, draped in tartan not her own and dressed more like a lad than a lass, she looked every inch a queen.

In that moment, Asbjørn began to understand why Lady Nuith feared her.

As for Nuith herself, she came towards them, looking from each of their faces to that of the princess' and back. "Sa, Drummond," she murmured in the Danish tongue, "this is what you meant by urgent business in your lands."

Drummond's lips curled up in a cruel smile that made Asbjørn nearly shudder. "I did indeed send fer more men to head to Caerloch. But I also thought perhaps it would be better to steal away something that would more swiftly change this rebellion in our favour."

Lady Nuith returned his sly expression, and Asbjørn could now see the resemblance between them. "For once, I am not angered at your disregarding my command." The smile vanished. "However, I still wish for Asbjørn to lead the army with you as second-in-command."

Drummond bowed his head, his face stern, but in his eyes remained a glimmer of triumph.

Lady Nuith turned her attention to the Scottish princess, the delight in her face vanishing like a winter sunset, morphing into utter loathing. She spoke in the Gàidhlig now, though her Danish accent prevailed. "I knew," she began, "that the Scots were lying when they said you were dead." She stepped closer and seized Fiona's chin in her hands, fingers gripping it so hard that the skin turned white beneath her hold.

Tears sprang to Fiona's eyes, but she hastily blinked them back.

"What do you have to say to that, then, brat? Who shall come to nobly rescue you now? Your harper is dead, and I doubt the Lowlander Chieftains will risk such an expense to free you again." She released her grip on Fiona's face and stepped back, meeting her glare for glare, though Fiona stood a good inch or so above her.

"Does it matter?" Fiona finally said, her voice the whisper of a wind, the sort of whisper that comes before a thunderstorm. Though she trembled now in Asbjørn's hold on her arm, it was not the whisper of defeat. "Kill me, and the flame of hope tha' has e'er burned in my peoples' hearts will rage like an unquenchable fire. Kill me, and ye will hae yet more royal blood on yer hands; it will no' wash out, nae matter how many lies ye tell or bribes ye pay. Kill me"—she tried to step closer to Nuith, but Asbjørn and Drummond jerked her back—"and those loyal to the throne will ne'er stop fighting fer freedom. Burn all the Lowlands, slay all their men, and their ghaists will yet rise up against ye."

As Fiona inhaled sharply before continuing, the wordless pause that filled the air felt all the more empty.

"Nae, they may no' come fer me, but it doesnae matter in the end. Because, in the end, we *will* win." Fiona's voice rose now, her form trembling from passion and not from fear. "And whether it be by my hand or another's, justice will be dealt to ye, Nuith, and all yer kind. Scotland will *no'* remain in bondage forever!"

An ear-splitting *crack* shook the air, and Asbjørn realised that Nuith had struck Fiona. Her hand still hovered in the air, and Fiona's head was turned to the side.

The heir to Scotland's throne straightened and gazed boldly into her enemy's eyes, her cheek reddening from the slap.

"Choose your next words carefully, *princess.*" Nuith fairly spat the word. "Tell us who is aiding the Lowlanders and we will keep you in your old rooms until your execution. Else you can wait those days in the dungeons, without food or drink."

Fiona lifted her head higher—were it possible—her jaw clenched. But she did not answer, and Lady Nuith would not wait forever.

"Put her in the dungeons, Asbjørn. Make sure she is chained and guarded properly. I will not have her escape like that harper did before. Drummond, I wish to speak to you further."

Asbjørn turned, pulling her with him. Fiona followed, stumbling again, but she did not resist.

He risked one look at her face, and he saw that the fire had gone out. Whatever had emboldened her to speak so to Nuith was gone, terror taking its place. After all, one might say anything in such a moment of fear and anguish, not necessarily because one believed it to be true. And yet she did not cry or speak; only her eyes and the paleness of her face—aside from the mark of Nuith's hand—betrayed her.

No wonder the Scots risk so much for her, he thought. *And then, If Drummond truly wishes to make her a puppet queen, I think he will have it none so easy.* But that was not his concern. He knew better than to meddle with Drummond's plans.

Fiona struggled for the thousandth time to free her hands and ankles from the iron manacles that encircled them. It was useless. She was no closer to freeing herself than before, and the skin at her wrists and ankles was chafed raw and bleeding from the constant attempts to thrust her hands and feet through the metal that fit very tight.

Despairing, she raised her fists to her mouth to mute the sobs that helplessly escaped, ashamed lest anyone should hear her breaking. She leaned her head against the damp, grimy wall, her shoulders heaving with a shuddering sigh as tears continued to course down her cheeks. There was no way of escaping. Even if she managed to get loose, there was still the thick iron door that was locked, and then the various guards positioned around the castle.

She had never imagined returning to Caerloch, never dared to think they might win and she rule from her father's old seat. She certainly never expected to return like this, not like...a prisoner. Even Rhiada had not escaped without aid, but she was alone....

The mere word crushed what little hope she had left. Here she was, the last heir to the Scottish throne, captured by the Danes and held as a captive in the dungeon of what had once been her home. She knew her fate, knew what was in store for her, even if it had been discussed while she had been dragged away. In the rare event Lady Nuith did not torture or starve her to death, she would face execution as a traitor to the Danish crown. Eventually her companions and her warriors would be found, caught, and put to death as well for high treason. Because why would they risk everything just to free her? Scotland was what mattered...she gave them courage, but she was not their sole source of it. In that, her words remained true. They would fight until death, and with her as prisoner, Nuith would certainly use her to end this war, or at least attempt to. Everything they had worked for, everything they had suffered for, would come to naught.

All because she had wanted a drink of water.

Closing her eyes, Fiona choked back tears. Even her dreams gave her no peace, for in them she relived the last few days with haunting clarity, over and over and over again: her capture, the ride from Drumdae, and the last few hours in this gloomy cell. The last time she had been in a dungeon, Angus had been with her to comfort her and give her courage. Now she was alone, and the chances of seeing him again were very small. If she would see him again now, it would only be because he had been captured and was soon to face the same fate as she.

And she had never told him how much she cared for him.

Angus' words from before the battle came back to her, and she could hear his voice and see his face in her mind, his piercing blue eyes illuminated by the strange light. *"Donnae be afraid, Fiona. Good always triumphs o'er evil in the end. The sun will shine upon us again."*

"Will it, Angus?" she whispered into the cold dampness of her cell.

Would she see him again?

Or was she doomed to her inescapable execution? She was not Rhiada, and there was no Cameron in this place to free her.

She reached up and fingered the clan pin on her plaid, the plaid which belonged to another, and she thought of her brother. What would Douglas think of her now, trapped and awaiting death yet again in the place they had once called home? What would he think of her attire, of how she had donned another clan's garb only to be captured anyway? Would he have chided her stupidity for entering the forest alone, or would he have commended her courage in facing Lady Nuith? She did not know what he might have said...and somehow, that made her feel all the more hopeless.

Slowly, the sky darkened towards twilight. Fiona watched the slanting shadows gradually work their way across the cell wall from the tiny window somewhere above the stone, out of reach of her sight. The reddish glare of lit torches appeared outside her cell door.

Another day gang, she thought dully, her head throbbing from crying, her courage deserting her. *How many more dawns will I see, or is the next one to be my last?*

"Father, we cannae jist do nothing!" Angus slammed his hands down on the table, his voice breaking despite his struggle to maintain control. The distress and anger that had risen in his chest since the lass he cherished so dearly had been kidnapped a few days ago wore his patience thin, always swelling like a churning ocean but never breaking.

A messenger had arrived only half an hour before from Caerloch Castle, carrying a request for surrender, with the Scots' lives in return for Fiona's. The High Chieftains had not yet been gathered to discuss it, but Angus had overheard the news, and he had run to the tent erected the night before for his father, refusing to believe it was true.

After all they had worked for...had it really come to this? Either way, it would end in death.

"Angus, I ken." Donald paused, looking into his son's eyes. "But wha' can we do? They make impossible demands, aye, but we donnae hae much time to discuss them. We hae but less than three days to choose, and we only arrived here last night, and this no' even our full force! A great part of our army here is Cynfael's men; it would no' be fair to hae them suffer the same fate as us. And how can I choose fer them? Our lives fer tha' of Fiona's? Who's to say they willnae kill her anyway when we are gang? Who is to say she is no' already dead?" His voice shook, and Angus' soul stirred within him.

No, he was not the only one who cared. They would all suffer in some way.

"So we jist abandon her to her fate, then?" His voice was dull, the pain in his chest almost strangling him. If Fiona was gone, then there was nothing left. No reason to claim the throne, no reason to keep on fighting—not for him. Aye, he knew that Scotland mattered too, but they had less of a reason to press on, unless his father or another of the chieftains would take the throne for themselves. The pain within swirled like a windstorm, rising into fury. Did Fiona even matter to them? Or was she merely a figurehead, easily disposed of and hardly missed? "All this care taken to preserve her life," he spat, his words fiercer than he intended, "and we jist abandon her? As if she is nothing to us?"

The look his father gave him both spoke of his grief and also silenced Angus from continuing. "Tha' is something we must discuss wi' the chieftains. But we may hae to risk tha'—fer the present. Scotland is wha' matters, and Fiona kens this too, nae doubt. I donnae wish to make this choice, but it may be tha', in the end. I ken how much ye care fer her, more than any of us, but wha' else can I do?"

"Rescue her," Angus replied bitterly, hating his father's words and yet knowing they were true. "It has been done before, wi' her and wi' Rhiada."

"Perhaps the High Chieftains can decide on a plan, but we donnae hae the time!" Donald replied firmly. "Few of us hae been within those walls, and none in the dungeons except fer our piper, and I will *no'* ask him to risk his life once again. The chance of getting into Caerloch and out again now—let alone wi' Fiona—is very small."

Angus groaned, the ache in his chest warring, threatening to spill over into tears. He wished to stab something, preferably the Danes who had kidnapped her, but he could not. "So we truly do abandon her?"

"Wha' do ye hae in mind?" Donald's voice took on an edge of mockery, which had never happened before when speaking to his son. "Jist show up at the gates, demand entrance, gae down to the dungeons, rescue her, and wave farewell to the guards on yer way out? Donnae be daft! Nae doubt they hae an army amassed there by this time. How do ye expect to slip by tha'? Surely they expect us to try to retake her!"

"Father." The words were whispered, an apology evident in his tone. Angus glanced up, a passionate yet fearful look in his eyes, but his anger had dissipated. "I ken the risk; I ken wha' is at stake. But I cannae jist leave her to her fate, even if I should lose my life in return. Whether fer good or fer ill, our fates are entwined. I will find her or else perish in the attempt. Please, Father, let me free her at my own cost."

Silence hung heavy between them.

"Angus," Donald said after a moment. "I donnae wish to risk losing ye as well as Fiona, yet I suppose this is all beyond our control. I cannae stop ye, but"—his breath caught in his throat—"must I lose yet another son?"

Angus bit his tongue before answering, Sioned and Duncan's dear faces coming before his eyes. "Ye will lose me anyway. In this, at least, I hae a choice in how I die, and I would rather it be fer her than anything else. I swore an oath to protect her, and I would honour tha' oath even if it should cost my life."

"We all swore tha' oath, my son, to protect Scotland as well as Fiona. If the worst should happen, if we cannae free her, then Scotland remains to be freed. Tha' oath still binds us, even without her."

Angus met his father's gaze, blue-eyed and serious as his own. "Fiona is my Scotland. If I lose her, I hae nothing left worth fighting fer. Only an empty and meaningless cause."

Donald sighed, his shoulders drooping. "How do ye plan to free her?"

"I hae an idea. It would only take a very small number of us, but if we all act accordingly, we might succeed. And a chance is better than nothing at all."

The tent flap opened, the High Chieftains and Cynfael stepping inside, shoulders brushing one another in the small space.

Donald spoke to them quickly of the news, all of them remaining grimly silent, except Bryce who growled some choice words in reply.

Angus did not meet their eyes, staring instead at the message before them and reminding himself that this, truly, was the right thing to do. Even if it would end in his death. It had been his choice to leave Fiona's side and fight in her stead because he thought it would thus be best to protect her, and now it was costing them both. He would make it right and serve her as he ought to have done before. And if he failed, he would at least beg her forgiveness ere the end, forgiveness for his inadequacy. He could not save his brothers; he could not but try to save her before it was too late.

"Wha' is the plan?" Cynfael asked when Donald finished, his voice eager and...dangerous.

Angus glanced around, assuring himself that no spies lurked outside the tent, and swallowed hard before answering.

Angus stepped out into the misty light of afternoon, blinking against the moist wind against his face. Breathing in the heavy scent of rain and damp earth, he strode across the camp, his eyes catching sight of the stream running through the centre, two scraggly trees beginning to burst with new leaves. He and Fiona had met here years ago. He had nearly poured out his heart to her here weeks ago. And should Fate smile upon them, perhaps they would stand here together once more.

It was sheer madness, but then, when was hope ever not?

"I promise ye, Fiona," he whispered. "I will see ye again, and I willnae hold myself back any longer."

He tore his gaze away and continued on to where he had left his friends about an hour before, when the messenger had first come.

"Wha' did Father say?" Malcolm asked, meeting his gaze with trepidation. Dafydd and Merwyn also greeted him silently. Perhaps they had all been waiting for his return, speaking little, wondering what the outcome would be.

"He says we can gae. But it will jist be us. He cannae spare more. He would rather ye stay, Malcolm, but he says he willnae keep ye—no' if we still might lose our lives if we donnae try." He caught Malcolm's grey eyes, hoping that this, with his apology from a few days before, would be enough to grant him forgiveness and remove the guilt that hung about his brother's shoulders like a burial shroud.

"Will we be enough?" Dafydd asked, his voice soft and worried. His hazel eyes darkened in thought. "Four against a whole castle? It sounds like a jest."

"Or a tale fit fer legend and song," Angus replied. "I am no' asking any of ye to gae against yer will. But if ye *are* willing, gather yer things, and a harp if someone has one to spare. We ride out now and will rest wi' the sun. If Fate is wi' us, we might succeed. I need ye all to be alert. After the last few days, I ken we are exhausted. But this is the only way we hae a chance." He tightened his sword belt, looking at them all. "And ye, Malcolm and Merwyn, I need ye to become the finest jesters Scotland has ever seen."

~ 20 ~
SCOTLAND'S FINEST JESTERS

THE next day warmed soon after dawn, thin swaths of fog lying low to the ground in the hollows where the sun could not reach. The air was still and sweet, promising a hint of summer by midday.

A small group on horseback rode swiftly across the barren moorland, devoid of human habitation save for a distant tavern far to the northwest. Their hooded cloaks were pulled over their heads, their drawstrings tied to prevent them from flying off in the wind.

They crested another hill dotted with scraggly trees, and there, on the horizon, an immense dark castle loomed against the blue-grey sky, a small village sprawled outside its gates. Beyond, to the north, the shadows of mountains rose into the sky. At the sight of it, the horsemen halted, granting their horses a breathing space. They were now in the Highlands—in enemy territory.

Angus McCladden stared at the castle, having seen it but once before and that as a small child, back when Lady Nuith had wed King Daibhidh and all the chieftains were summoned to the feast. Once it had been the capital of all Scotland, the small village a thriving city; and now the dungeon and future execution place of his beloved—and himself, unless they succeeded.

Cameron MacClaerthun's words came to mind, his instructions as to the layout of the place, especially the dungeons, and how many guards were usually employed. He only prayed that the man's memory would serve them well, that the Danes would not have too many guards, that there would not be a trap waiting for them.

Branwen, his mare, nickered softly beneath him.

Cynfael's farewell echoed in his memory, when Angus had asked if Dafydd and Merwyn were permitted to come with him. His eyes had glinted with a fierceness not unlike his gyrfalcon's gaze. *"I would come wi' ye, if I could. Take them in my stead; they will prove true. Protect the crown and country."* He had smiled then, a sad smile that reminded Angus painfully—eerily—of Rhiada. *"And protect her. Protect yer heart."*

Angus blinked, returning to the present moment. Memories, save that of Cameron's directions, would do him no good now. He spoke softly to the lads beside him, urgency audible in his voice. "Ahead lies Caerloch. Remember yer orders. If they begin to suspect something, run fer the hills and ride back without me. Yer oath lies wi' my father and yer king. If I can, I will rejoin ye. If no', there is nae reason why Donald McCladden must lose two sons today instead of jist one." With that, he rode back down the hill and out of view of Caerloch before dismounting and tying his horse's reins to a small tree.

The others followed silently. They had rehearsed and spoken of this plan all the day before until it had become woven into their dreams.

"May I wish ye well?" Dafydd asked as they prepared to walk towards the village and the castle.

Angus glanced over to his left, and his shoulders, tense with fear, relaxed ever so little. He embraced his friend tightly, whispering a single word in his ear, "*diolch*", but it was enough. Then he stepped back and looked at them all, the gravity of the situation weighing him down. "Death before disloyalty. Death before dishonour."

"Fer Fiona!" the others cried.

Without another word spoken, they set off down the hill, looking more like heroes of legend in that moment than the band of lads they were.

Angus could only pray that their number would not be smaller when they returned.

"Sir, we have visitors at the gate!" the man's voice rang out, hollow-sounding in his steel helmet.

"Who are they?" Drummond growled back, irritated at having

his morning doze interrupted for something most likely beneath his concern.

The guardsman shouted something at the gate, and someone replied back in the airy and harsh tongue of the Scots. The man's voice triggered distant memories—but many had voices like that. All the Scots sounded alike.

The guardsman swore in Danish before answering back in the Gàidhlig tongue. Then he popped his head once more in the door and said, "Scots, sir. They claim to be a troupe of jesters, having come here to join the celebration when Queen Nuith executes the princess."

Drummond lifted his feet off of the herald's desk and rubbed a hand over his eyes. Lady Nuith was not even queen yet, though most took her as such anyway. For Scots to claim her so—that seemed suspicious. Then again, perhaps they were of the sort that did not care who was on the throne as long as there was peace. Most likely they were Highlanders. The Lowlanders would never speak in such terms; the words would probably choke in their throats.

He stepped outside into the humidity of the spring day and squinted against the bright daylight. Down below, before the gates, stood a foursome group of young men, hooded and dressed as if they had been journeying a long time. Mud splattered their clothes, which were not of the finest material either. All in all, they did not look the sort to plan an ambush on the castle, especially since he could see no weapons on them—unless they were well hidden.

"Search them fer weapons. If they possess anything besides a dirk, hold them fer questioning. Otherwise, take them to the kitchens and see that they're fed and out of the way. They can entertain the kitchen staff until the feast tonight. One of the maids can find them a room to stay in if there is none to be had in the village."

The guardsman grunted and gave orders for those below to open the portcullis.

One of the jesters gave a hearty thanks that none of them heeded— for what was a few more to the celebration of the heir's murder?

"So, the man says to his wife, 'Och, I donnae ken who could be a-knocking at the door!' She replies, 'Shame on ye, ye ken very well who it is! 'Tis tha' nasty woman ye hae been seeing!'"

Angus rolled his eyes for perhaps the seventeenth time and stepped towards the kitchen doorway, looking at the courtyard while Malcolm continued to tell terrible riddles to the servants. The lasses especially listened with rapt attention, which he could not understand. The jests were not even that amusing. But any distraction would do. They were supposed to be fools, after all, even if Malcolm seemed to be taking his role a little too seriously.

"Wha' is it?" Dafydd asked softly in Angus' ear, standing by him.

"I dislike the waiting," Angus whispered back. It was still an hour before noon, when the guard would be changed—if Cameron's memories held true. Cameron suspected they might have more guards on duty with the princess being held, but Angus had not expected quite this many. If they had not failed to espy other such guardsmen in the village beyond the gates, Angus would have thought Lady Nuith had gathered all her forces inside the castle. Perhaps she intended to, but they had yet to arrive...

If they came before the lads were well away, it would make rescuing Fiona all the harder.

"The woman gaes to open the door, and wha' does she see but the laird there to demand rent!" Malcolm finished his tale with a squeak, and his audience burst into laughter. Merwyn laughed with them, slapping his knee, and Angus and Dafydd clapped half-heartedly.

Ever since they had been allowed through the gates, Angus' heart had not ceased racing as if he were sprinting across the moors. Drummond was there; he had heard his voice. And while he and Malcolm had grown since they had last seen the Danish traitor, it was not enough to fool him. Malcolm had hidden his face in the shadow of his hood at the gate—they both had—but if they came face-to-face, it would be over. All the more reason to be fled and gone before evening came, when they were supposed to perform. Only Malcolm—and perhaps Merwyn—could dream to pull such a thing off. No, whether or not they had Fiona, they must be long gone from the gates by then. Danger lurked around every corner, and they had not even come close to the dungeon.

"All right, lads, would ye be interested in eating wi' us?" the head cook asked, a plump woman with greying hair, equally grey eyes, and a swift smile that reminded Angus of his grandmother, long since dead.

"Donnae hae to ask me again!" Malcolm replied, grinning. He swung his leg over the bench and eagerly awaited the stew they had smelled cooking all this while. Merwyn sat next to him, likewise licking his lips in ridiculous anticipation.

Angus glanced at Dafydd and jerked his head towards the table. They had to at least pretend, though he doubted he could swallow a bite. Every moment lost meant Fiona was closer to death. If she was even still alive....

Malcolm and Merwyn had no trouble eating their stew, and Malcolm finished off what Angus could not eat, making some jest about it to distract any who might have thought it odd. But the keen look in his eyes told Angus that while he might act the fool, he was on high alert just as much as any of them. Some of the tangled nerves in Angus' stomach untwisted themselves, replaced with a solemn pride. Malcolm was anything but a fool it seemed; perhaps he was the wisest of them all.

Most of the servants left to serve the midday meal in the castle, leaving Malcolm and Merwyn to catch a quick nap against the wall by the door. But their eyes were only partly closed, watching every shadow that moved in the wind.

The door in the tower opposite opened and closed, a guardsman striding to the nearest tower, no doubt to eat his luncheon and exchange places with the new guard.

Glancing at Dafydd, Angus and his friend set off on a leisurely walk across the courtyard, Dafydd talking half nonsense. It was all about the image of the thing. If all the Danes saw was a band of jesters, they would pay no heed to the faces behind the fools. But that "if" grew in size with each passing moment. Angus could hardly breathe, every breath shallow and accompanied by a thundering heart.

The wind billowed their capes and pulled at their hair, blowing it into their eyes, causing the standards above the battlements to crack in the gusts like thunder. Angus was glad when they slipped inside the door, unnoticed.

"Is tha' jist the beginning?" Dafydd whispered, gasping no doubt from the adrenaline.

"I donnae ken. I feel sick," Angus replied, his eyes adjusting to the dimness. If this castle's layout was anything like Caerdun, the entrance to the dungeons should be in this first room as Cameron had said. It would make no sense to have to go up to be brought into the underbelly of this place.

"Keep yerself together, *fy ffrind*," Dafydd murmured, laying a hand on Angus' shoulder as he groped in the dark. "I think I found it," he said a moment later, creaking open a door that led to a small torchlit stair winding below the castle.

Angus stepped up to the entrance, his jaw clenched. So be it.

With one hand on his dirk, he started down the corridor, his ears straining for any sound of danger. Dafydd followed behind him after closing the door, their footsteps as soft as a leaf fluttering to the ground.

Angus remembered the last time he had descended the dungeons back in Caerdun, protecting Fiona against the dark. She was somewhere below them now and utterly alone. He bit his lip, urgency rising in him. She must be terrified. He would do anything to prevent her feeling like that again—anything.

Someone cleared their throat around the bend, and Angus froze, nearly falling backward. A wave of lightheadedness swept over him, and were it not for Dafydd squeezing his shoulder, he might have passed out on the stair.

Whipping out his dirk, he stepped forward and came face-to-face with a guardsman, who looked half asleep. Before the man had even time to sound the alarm, the weapon was buried deep in his neck. He choked on his own lifeblood as he sank to the ground. Quick arms prevented his chainmail from clanging against the walls.

"*Yn gyflym*," Dafydd said, struggling to pull the chainmail off of the dead man at their feet.

"There's nae time to put on his jerkin," Angus whispered back. "I'll jist hae to wear it over my clothes and hope nae one jams into me."

"Risky," Dafydd replied, lifting it over his friend's head and adjusting it over his shoulders.

"Aye, but a bruising willnae harm much in the long run."

Dafydd grunted, handing the guardsman's swordbelt to Angus. "There, ye should be fine now." He hesitated. "I wish ye a good hunting. Be careful. Donnae let yer fear get the better of ye."

Angus nodded, the reply sticking in his throat.

"I need to rejoin the others. If all goes well, I'll see ye at camp." He laid a hand on Angus' shoulder. "Death before dishonour."

"Death before disloyalty. May the wind be wi' ye."

Dafydd flashed a smile. Then he was gone, running up the stairs with the lightness of a deer. The door creaked above and closed, leaving Angus in damp silence, broken only by the sound of dripping water and his hammering heart.

He set off down the corridor, a lump in his throat, threatening to choke him. This was it, now. He could not flee whatever lay before him. He had a princess to save.

Malcolm lay against the hard, stone wall. Sleep had never been further from him in his life. Merwyn snored softly opposite him, but Merwyn was good at feigning such a sound. At least, Malcolm hoped he was not truly asleep.

Angus and Dafydd had left what seemed like an eternity ago, and yet had it been more than ten minutes?

Dafydd burst into the door and threw himself beside Malcolm, closing his eyes as if he had been sleeping all this while. But his chest heaved with heavy breathing, and if one looked closely, one could see blood—fresh blood—staining the sleeves and hem of his tunic.

"Did ye find her?" Malcolm whispered as two servant girls stepped into the kitchen and then left with two jars of Danish ale.

Without opening his eyes, Dafydd whispered back, "Nae. Angus is looking fer her now. Remember, first sign of danger, we must gae."

Malcolm did not reply, his eyes, though half shut, still focused on the entrance to the courtyard.

Outside the door, danger was walking towards them, a familiar tread and dark beard striking terror into his heart.

Malcolm elbowed Dafydd and kicked Merwyn, dashing across the empty kitchen to the far corner, where stood a door leading to the guardsmen's tower.

"Wha's gang on?" Merwyn asked, his voice shaking.

"Drummond MacDougall is headed this way. He might recognise me. We need to leave." Malcolm felt behind him for the door handle and swung it open, the three of them slipping inside.

"Wha' about Angus?" Merwyn asked.

"He said no' to wait fer him," Dafydd replied. "Our own lives matter now."

Without another word spoken, the three of them dashed out of the tower and through the gates, Malcolm weaving in between the alleyways of the village beyond, none of them stopping until they stood at the hill where they had left their horses. Swinging into the saddle, they rode south, hoping against hope that their plan would somehow still succeed.

~ 21 ~

REVENGE IS NOT SO SWEET

SILENCE reigned.

In the depths of the earth below Caerloch, Fiona lay against the wall, her eyes half closed. There was no reason to be alert. Her cell had no torch with which to thrust back the gloom, though a small window high above let in the sun—if the sun shone—and little light came through the grilled window set in the door. Once in a while, she would hear a shuffling from the guard at the end of the corridor, but that was all. Only the water dripping in another cell kept the silence from becoming too heavy.

Her stomach growled, but she ignored it. She was getting used to it by now. One of the guards gave her a little bit of bannock or a small cup of water at times—as if someone meant to keep her somewhat alive—but that was all. Besides, did hunger matter when she was going to die anyway?

She exhaled slightly. Her breaths were shallow, pointless. Breathing no longer mattered either. Die now, and she saved Lady Nuith the trouble and herself the pain of execution—unless they also tortured her first. Yet another reason it was better she die now than at their hands. She had nothing left to live for.

She wondered dully whether the Scots had attempted to rescue her. If they had any sense, they would not. They would lose far more men than they could afford. The dungeons were not heavily guarded, no, but why would they be, when the biggest difficulty would be getting in and out of the gate? That was where the thickest lines of guardsmen were posted.

Nay, the wisest thing was to abandon her to her fate. Perhaps her death would kindle afresh the passion for freedom and thus not be in vain. A martyr's death, like her brother and Rhiada and so many others taken before their natural time.

Still, she would have liked to see Angus one last time. A tear slipped down her face, cold and unfeeling. She had never even had the chance to tell him how much of the brightness in her world he had become, of how, when he was near, this desolation did not seem so dark of a thing. And now it was too late.

She pulled the faded sprigs of heather, pine, and thistle from her clan pin, her brother's pin, and twirled them in her fingers. How bright, how fierce their hope had been only days ago. But like the dried sprigs...it had become nothing in the end—just a memory, a forgotten dream. Like the cut on her palm from the oath-swearing, only a tad sore now, only the scar remaining to prove that she had not imagined it. That firelit night beneath the stars with the crystal blade and thousands of voices swearing allegiance to her—it had been real once. And it still bound them until death set them free, as it would surely do so to her soon. Her eyes closed at the thought.

The door at the top of the dungeon's winding stair creaked open, a faint sound but different from the dripping water. The guardsman at the bottom straightened, his chainmail chiming with the movement. It must be time for the changing of the guard, mayhaps. But no footsteps followed the door's opening, none that she could hear anyway.

Fiona's eyes opened, her pulse beginning to race. Was it time? Had Lady Nuith given the command now?

She heard a scuffling at the end of the corridor and whispered voices, too soft for her to understand what they were saying. More scuffling, the ring of chainmail, and then more whispers.

She sat up, flattening herself against the wall. What was keeping them? Since when did the guards whisper when exchanging places? Why must they delay in taking her if it was time for her reckoning? It would be a mercy to end the agony of waiting now.

The whispers stopped, light footsteps ran up the stair, and the door creaked open and closed again. No, that was no guardsman. None of them ran, and certainly not like that.

What had Lady Nuith in store for her?

Footsteps came hesitantly down the corridor, followed by the ringing of keys. Someone stuck the key in the lock and attempted to turn it but failed. Her heart began to race. The guards knew which key it was, unless they had sent someone new to fetch her.

Two attempts later, the door finally opened, and a man clothed in chainmail and the black wool that all the guardsmen wore entered the cell.

Fiona swallowed hard, her breath catching in her throat. She backed up against the wall, feeling faint. Memories of a ruby ring and lustful eyes came to mind, the burning chill of freezing water nearly drowning her. Had the guard come in to misuse her? Was this how she was to be tortured before her death?

Her question seemed answered when he closed the door behind him and came towards her. The world seemed to spin in fear, and she might have swooned had not he not knelt before her and slipped back his hood.

"Angus?" Fiona gasped weakly. The dimness in the cell became full oblivion, reality slipping away into unconsciousness.

He gripped her shoulders, hard, and whispered in her ear, "Fiona, stay wi' me. I need ye to stay wi' me."

Her vision came rushing back, and she blinked, still unable to wrap her mind around it. "Angus, wha' are ye doing here? This is madness!"

"Shh." He laid a finger on her lips, though she had not spoken louder than a whisper. "We cannae hae them ken ye're gang to escape."

She nodded, tears of disbelief and joy shining in her eyes. Her chest throbbed with emotion, but she could not risk anyone hearing them. Angus—and whoever else was with him—had already risked enough. If this was a dream, she wished it would never end.

Angus smiled that smile so dear to her, his blue eyes sparkling in the haze, and added, "Good. Now, to unlock yer chains." Quickly, he slipped in the key and unlocked the steel bands around her ankles and wrists, making no mistakes this time.

As soon as he finished, he helped her rise to her feet, her legs weak and unsteady. All the same, she leaned forward and threw her arms about his neck, causing Angus to stumble back a step.

"Och, now!" he exclaimed in a hoarse whisper.

She laughed softly and withdrew her embrace. "I am sorry; I didnae mean to nearly keel ye over. I jist...I didnae think ye would come. I was afraid ye had abandoned me fer good." *He shouldnae be here!* a voice cried in her mind. *He should be saving his country, no' me.* Her joy vanished. "Ye shouldnae hae come. If ye are found out, I will no' forgive myself. One sacrifice wouldnae hae mattered much, but two? How many lives are recklessly put in danger by this?"

His lips trembled through his smile, and there looked to be tears in his eyes also. "Nae, Fiona." His voice gently chided her. "I swore an oath to protect ye, nae matter the cost. Ye are worth saving, my princess, always. Besides, I couldnae live wi' the thought of a world without ye." He reached forward and stroked her cheek, brushing away the tears that escaped her eyes at his words. "Fiona McCurragh, my princess," he said, cupping her face in his hands, and whispered gently, as if the words themselves were a sacred thing, "I love ye."

Fiona's world whirled to a standstill. Her heart skipped a beat before she remembered to breathe again, the blood rushing to her face. A sob rose in her throat, and she did not try to stop it. Flinging her arms about his neck once more, she answered, "Och, Angus, I love ye too."

Angus pulled back, his eyes shining. "Truly?" he asked, his voice breathless. "I was so afraid fer so long tha' perhaps ye didnae care, tha' perhaps ye—"

"Nae, Angus McCladden," Fiona replied, shaking her head. "There is nae one like ye, nae one I would trust my life wi', nae one who shares my soul besides ye, no' the way I love ye." The words seemed strange on her lips, but she was glad to say them after so long of holding them back.

He did not answer, but there was an elated smile on his face, the likes of which she had rarely seen before. She had never seen in his deep blue eyes such a pure joy untainted by fear and sorrow. He looked deep into her eyes, no longer hiding his heart from her, before bending slightly to kiss her. And she did not flinch away.

In the cool darkness of the cell, buried beneath the earth, warmth and light flooded through Fiona's veins as their lips met for the first time. Never mind the danger, never mind that they could be killed as soon as they stepped outside of the dungeons. In that moment, their souls, in all their grief and passion, were made one.

Yet without the time to linger, Angus pulled back. They still had to escape, and until they were beyond the reach of Caerloch, their love could easily be destroyed—and then all their fine words would mean nothing.

"Come, my love. We must be gang." He took her hand in his and led her outside the cell, bolting it quietly behind him once more. He hung up the keys outside the door, and then they ran down the corridor, passing the corpse of a guardsman she suspected Angus had killed to gain his armour.

When they had reached the door to the dungeons, however, they halted. Fiona glanced at Angus, and the ecstasy still giving her wings faded away at the sight of worry on his face.

"Wha' is it?" she whispered softly.

"I am no' sure wha' the best way to the gate is. Cameron never mentioned tha', only how to get in from the courtyard. Malcolm's band should hae left by now, so there is nae chance of finding them. I hope they made it out," he added, the courage in his voice failing him a moment.

"Here, let me," she whispered back. "I was born and raised in this castle." She squeezed his hand and they opened the door, relieved that no one waited on the other side for them.

Fiona blinked in the dull torchlight, trying to remember which door led to where. The last thing they needed was to enter the courtyard and be seen by everyone.

She stepped to the side door, hearing the soft *wisht* as Angus unsheathed his dagger. There was no room to use a sword here, not without risking hurt to her.

He gave her a reassuring glance before she opened the door to the gatehouse and met the face of Drummond MacDougall.

Fiona stared in horror at Drummond and clutched Angus' hand so tightly she was afraid of crushing it in two. Her chest seized with sudden fear, and she nearly forgot how to breathe.

"I had thought yer voice was familiar, *Angus McCladden*." Drummond's face twisted into a sickened scoff. "But now ye both must come wi' me." He gave a word of command and the two guards standing beside him stepped forward, ripping them apart and gripping their arms. Neither of them fought for their freedom, unable to move in the steel-like grasp of the guards as Drummond brought them across the blustery courtyard.

Fiona sucked in a breath at the strong hold of her captor, her arm bruising the longer he held onto it. Even if she was not already weakened by lack of proper food and water, she would not have been able to wriggle free.

She did not dare to glance at Angus; she could not bear what she might see in his face. It was her fault they were caught. If she and Angus had not talked in the dungeons, they would have had more time to flee, where they could have revealed their hearts in safety. And if she had not led them through that door, they might have escaped without difficulty, even through the courtyard. But she did not have time to think about it now.

The doors to the all-too-familiar throne room were thrown open, and the pair were led inside. Fiona glanced at the weapons-covered walls and high-arched ceiling, remembering the last time she had set foot in this place, when she had spoken words of fire to Lady Nuith, fire that had dissipated in the gloom of the dungeons.

She looked at Lady Nuith now, sitting proudly on the dais. The last time Fiona had sat on that dais was not on her throne, but at the feet of her enemy while she sang a song of rebellion before escaping, the song whose words Angus had changed to tell her of his love for her. She remembered Rhiada teaching her the harp there and wondered what he would think of their situation, what advice he would give her, had he lived. Now, it seemed, she would follow him beyond the sunset. Strangely...the thought did not terrify her anymore. Knowing Angus loved her drove all her fears away.

Fiona glanced at Angus. If this was the last time she would see him alive, she wanted to memorise his face in every little detail for however brief the rest of her life might be.

He met her gaze a moment, but his eyes were bright and calculating, not the faded despair she had expected. His eyes scanned the room, searching and probing—for a means of escape?

A quiet knot of pride slowed the racing of her heart. Aye, Angus had found his courage even in the face of certain death. She tried to likewise search with her eyes, knowing there was little chance of escape. There was only one entrance, and the windows were too high up; even if armed with weapons from the walls, they were greatly outnumbered. But if Angus had not given up, then neither would she.

At last they stopped walking, the guardsmen on either side coming to a halt. Drummond took his place beside his sister, who sat on the Scottish throne looking at them with an expression of wry, cruel amusement. A bairn played on the floor, perhaps Nuith's son, unaware of the events happening around him. Fiona looked down at the lad and was surprised at a sudden longing to protect the child, the cause of Nuith's passion to see her dead—though what the bairn had to be protected from, she did not yet know.

"So, a noble rescue attempt was made." Lady Nuith's voice caused Fiona's eyes to snap back to her, and she looked the woman straight in the eye. It no longer mattered what the woman thought of her. "A pity it was not successful."

"'Twas indeed successful, though in ways ye will ne'er ken," Angus answered without hesitation, his voice light and almost carefree.

Fiona turned to look at him in surprise, realising a moment later what he meant. She would not die in captivity—she was loved enough to be worth dying for, and she was not abandoned to her fate. Her shoulders relaxed, the tension gone. She gave him the barest hint of a smile, and his eyes smiled in return.

"Guards, leave us—Asbjørn, you as well. I will call you when you are needed. I wish to deal with them in my own way. Oh, and Asbjørn, see that men are placed on the battlements in lieu of attack from the Lowlanders. Send what men you can spare after the others riding north; my army still has yet to arrive."

Asbjørn bowed his head. "It will be done."

Then Lady Nuith turned her attention to the pair before her, no longer held in the grip of Danish men.

Fiona rubbed her arms, trying to get the blood flowing in them again. She bit her lip, resisting the urge to grin in giddiness. Oh, if only Lady Nuith knew.... Escape no longer seemed so impossible.

"Successful, say you?" Nuith mocked, bringing Fiona back to grim reality. "I would hardly call it that," she said, raising an eyebrow. "I need only give an order, and both the heir to the Scottish throne and the now-eldest child of the leader of the Lowlands will be dead. There is no chance for escape now, is there?"

Angus touched Fiona's elbow, jerking his head ever so slightly to the wall bedecked with weapons. He lightly tapped a finger against her arm where Drummond and Nuith could not see, as if cautioning her to wait for a signal.

"I had wished to make a public execution," the Danish leader continued, "but I suppose the mere display of your lifeless bodies will work just as well. It seems you cannot stay imprisoned—even when in chains."

"Nae, Nuith," Angus drawled, his eyes roving the room as if bored, but Fiona could see that his gaze remained alert. "Ye may imprison or even kill our bodies, but our spirits remain free."

Lady Nuith rose to her feet, stepping off the dais, her face colouring with anger a moment before she regained her composure. "Fine words for someone about to die." She looked away from him, disgusted.

Fiona shifted her weight to the balls of her feet, her heart racing in anticipation. Angus' hand had not yet moved from her arm, but she could feel his breath on her neck, the rhythm quickening. He reached up with his other hand and pulled loose the tie of the guardsman's cloak, the black material floating to the ground.

"Drummond, will you allow me the honour?" Lady Nuith asked of her brother, a strange excitement in her voice. Her attention was no longer on the two standing in front of her.

"Gae." With that word, Angus dashed to the side, jumping onto the trestle table and wrenching free from the wall a pair of crossed swords. He tossed one to Fiona before leaping down to engage Drummond, who had noticed the sudden movement and drawn his own blade.

"Henrik!" Nuith cried, stepping down to snatch up her son.

But Fiona was faster, still wearing her garments for battle and therefore not hampered by a lengthy skirt, and warned her back with the tip of her sword. She did not want to kill Nuith in cold blood while Drummond remained a threat in the room, even if it was justified.

Fiona split her gaze between the pair duelling and Lady Nuith, who likewise watched Angus and her half-brother fighting for his life.

Drummond, though older and more experienced, was heavier in build, and wore no protection aside from a leather jerkin. Angus' chainmail glittered in the daylight, and he nimbly ducked and thrust his sword at his attacker, keeping to his feet all the while.

Perhaps there was a purpose to the sword dance after all.

Blades clashed fiercely, the sound echoing up to the high, arched roof.

Drummond dashed forward, and Angus was barely able to block the sudden blow. The Dane's sword slid across Angus' fingers, not enough to cut them off but still leaving a trail of red.

The cry in Fiona's throat died before she ever voiced it.

Angus gasped in pain, the sudden silence deafening.

"Any last words, son of McCladden?" Drummond snarled.

His face white, Angus smirked, a strange light in his eyes. "A fine blow," he said, his voice lilting through clenched teeth. "But unfortunately fer ye, I was always better wi' a blade in my left hand." With lightning-quick motion, Angus switched his sword to his other hand, its hilt stained with blood.

Drummond swore and the fight began again.

Angus all but danced across the floor, his right hand held close to his chest, deep red darkening the silver chainmail. In his left hand, his sword blocked Drummond's movements with a speed unmatched by his right, and the Dane soon found himself pinned up against the wall with no escape.

"Any last words, son of MacDougall?" Angus threw the phrase back into his face, panting heavily, his sword pointed at the man's vulnerable chest.

Drummond looked him square in the face and spat. "Last words? Aye—" He uttered a string of curses.

Angus held the blade steady a moment—as if to be sure of his final stroke—and then the sword met the man's unprotected neck. Angus withdrew the blade shining vermillion, and the heavy body of the black-bearded Dane fell to the ground, shattering the shock that had descended upon the watchers.

Angus stepped up to Fiona and spoke rapidly. "I am gang to see if the courtyard is clear. Do wha' ye must wi' Lady Nuith, but hurry. I will meet ye in the courtyard." He wheeled around, not waiting for a reply, and ran to the doors, exiting the hall.

The moment he was gone, Fiona turned to see Lady Nuith whip out a long knife from somewhere hidden on her person and point it directly at her.

Fiona raised her sword in defence, her heart beating fast in her chest.

"A sad thing that would be," Lady Nuith taunted, though her voice trembled, "if your Angus came back and found you dead, would it not?"

"A sad thing, aye," Fiona snapped, all thoughts of mercy gone. "A sad thing too, if Lord Erland would return and find ye and yer son dead."

"You would not dare!" Nuith snarled.

"Would I no'?" White-hot rage surged up within Fiona, nearly clouding her vision. "Ye didnae hesitate in signing my death sentence—I see it lying beside ye. Ye didnae hesitate in sending yer armies to slaughter those whom I loved best. Ye and yer people were the death of my only brother, Douglas! My father, Daibhidh! My teacher, Rhiada! Ye and yer people destroyed Scotland and her people, and ye would keep on destroying it if ye can. Ye hae caused enough pain in my life. Nae, Nuith. I think I dare indeed."

Nuith side-stepped around Fiona's blade and tried to stab her knife into the princess' side, but Fiona, though exhausted and starving, was faster and better trained. She dodged the blow and plunged the sword deep into Nuith's chest, piercing through fine woollen cloth into flesh and bone.

Lady Nuith struggled to speak, but all that left her lips was a trickle of blood. She sank to the ground, her head slamming against the throne. Her once rigid posture collapsed. Her skirts pooled helplessly in a soft rustle around her.

Fiona staggered back, anger fading away into horror, stomach bile rising in her throat.

Nuith's gaze never left hers even as the life slowly faded from her dark eyes. A crimson stain spread across the woman's violet dress, turning it nearly black.

The silence roared in Fiona's ears.

"Wha' hae I done?" she gasped, falling to her knees. How many times had she dreamed of achieving revenge against Nuith and her half-brother? Yet never had she thought of how hollow and disgusting it might be, how empty it would be, even though she knew they would have had no hesitation to do the same to her.

A frightened whimper broke into her thoughts, and Fiona jumped to her feet. Angus was waiting for her. They were not free yet.

But her eyes landed on the source of the cry and she saw Henrik still sitting on the floor, a small wooden soldier in his chubby hands, his eyes fixed on her in terror. And in that moment, Fiona saw only herself as a child, told the news that her brother was dead. Caged by the unforgiving Danes around her. Played like a pawn.

Something broke within her and, without a second thought, she snatched up the child and ran out of the hall, leaving the two corpses behind her, one sprawled on the ground, the other slain before the very throne she had tried to claim as her own.

Within moments, Fiona burst into the courtyard, but Angus was nowhere to be found. A panicked sob escaped her lips, yet there was no time to calm her fears. She noticed the sudden bustle of activity up on the battlements and knew she had no choice but to run.

Tightening her arms around Henrik, she dashed forward across the cobblestone courtyard and over the bridge that spanned the moat. She hardly knew where she was going, only that she had to get out of the village and beyond the hills before the soldiers on the battlements knew what was happening and fired arrows upon her.

"Fiona!"

She looked up and saw Angus riding towards her through the village, a clumsy bandage tied around his right hand. "Och, Angus!" Her voice broke and she began to cry, the stress of the last few hours becoming too much to bear alone.

He leapt down from his horse. "Come here; we must no' dally any longer. Who kens how soon they'll discover wha' has happened." He lifted her up onto the horse's back before mounting himself. "Tha' is Nuith's child, is it no'?"

"I couldnae leave him," she whimpered, tears falling down her face. The adrenaline of escape was fading away, and extreme weariness took its place. *Wha' hae I done?* She had stolen him; however she might try to excuse it, she had taken him from his rightful father even as the Danes had torn her from her people. But it was too late to go back now. Perhaps the chieftains would know what to do with him once they returned to camp.

The child fussed in her arms but did not try to wriggle away; perhaps he sensed he would fall from quite a height off the mare's back.

"Never mind that now; we can discuss it later once we're safe." Angus held her close, whispering into her ear even as he did so, "I promise ye, Fiona, I will never let ye be taken captive again." Then he kissed her cheek before they rode out, leaving Caerloch behind them in a state of perfect chaos.

~ 22 ~
A CHANGE OF FATE

FIONA opened her eyes, her vision blurred, as the horse she was riding slowed to a halt. She had tried to stay awake as they rode westward from Caerloch, but the exhaustion from the last several hours had won out in the end. Turning her head upward, she saw Angus peering behind them at the barren moors, the grasses bending in the soft wind.

He glanced at her but said nothing, his dark brows drawn together in concentration.

"Is something wrong?" she whispered, afraid to speak louder.

Angus shook his head, a smile appearing on his face for a moment. "Nae, I was merely seeing if we were followed, but I see nae one. Perhaps they hae their hands full enough at Caerloch." He urged his horse on but at a leisurely pace. It was likely he did not want to exhaust Branwen that day, what with all the swift riding that had already happened.

Fiona settled back against Angus as she felt the small bairn shift in her arms, and she watched as the dark-haired lad moved in sleep. He did not utter a sound—for which she was grateful.

His slight movement and sleepy warmth filled her with a maternal urge to care for him, to hold him more closely. But the more rational side of her mind cautioned her against it. Yes, Henrik was a child, but he was still the enemy. It was because of him that Lady Nuith had plotted her death, and it might still cost her dearly. "Do ye think I did wrong by taking him wi' us?" she murmured.

"Nae, I donnae think tha'," he replied after a moment. "I might hae done the same in yer place. And if no', I would be haunted by my choice the rest of my days."

Fiona sighed heavily, her head throbbing slightly from thirst and weariness. "Will the chieftains think the same?"

"I donnae ken. I ken they willnae kill any child, especially in cold blood. He could prove to be a useful hostage, may even turn the tide of the war in our favour, but should he live and grow up, whether among our people or his own, he would ever remain a threat."

She did not say anything to that. She knew it was true, and yet... she would not undo her decision of hours before.

"I didnae ken ye fought wi' a blade left-handed," she said next. "Is tha' why ye swore the oath wi' yer right?"

She felt him chuckle, the sound reverberating through her too, as if warmth could sing. "Aye, though I usually train wi' others wi' my right hand; it makes the fight uneven otherwise. Sioned was also tha' way," he continued wistfully. "He ensured, as young as I was and unable to lift more than a small wooden sword, tha' I could fight wi' both hands. Another man of my father's clan trained me wi' the use of my left once I was older, and I ran through the moves on my own after he went beyond the sunset some years ago. I...I suppose I never thought it might truly save my life, let alone yers," he finished in a whisper.

She laid her hand on top of his for a moment, looking up to kiss his cheek softly. "I am glad, in any case. I had thought us lost when Drummond wounded ye."

He hitched a shoulder in a shrug. "None too terribly. I could hae lost my fingers, but I didnae." He straightened. "Jist a few more leagues, and we'll be back at the camp." He dug his heels into Branwen's flanks, and they flew once more along the ground, this time bending southeast.

Sometime later, as the clouded sun began sinking into the west, they crested a hill and Angus reined Branwen in, the wind gusting about them in welcome. Below in the glen lay the sprawling tents, picket lines, and men of the Scottish and Cymreig war host. From here, she could not see how many men had been lost at the battle of Drumdae, but she hoped it was not many. It still seemed immense, their few thousand.

And yet, despite the multitude of men with their ivory tents covering the bright spring grass, the hills beyond and the stream that flowed through was a place she knew well. As otherworldly and untouchable as the great war host seemed, the familiar landscape grounded her. Amid the aftermath of that day, she almost felt like she was coming home.

"Is this—" she began, awe and something akin to nostalgia piercing through her exhaustion.

"Aye, 'tis the place we met once, long ago," Angus replied, his voice soft. "We won the last battle wi' few losses, since the Danes retreated once ye were stolen. We marched here as soon as we could, and only arrived the other night. Father thought it best to send the worst wounded to An Dùn and retrieve wha' supplies we could from the nearest villages while awaiting news of ye. Besides, this place has a stream that provides water, as well as being close to Caerloch. We jist hae to keep guards on the hills to prevent attack. The High Chieftains wish to strike back at them as soon as may be, I think, but we were held back, afraid tha' they would slay ye should we march on them."

She said nothing to that, sleepiness stealing whatever words she might have said otherwise.

Angus rode Branwen down the hillside, soon greeted by guards who called out the news to others as they approached the camp. At the noise, Henrik awoke and started whimpering, yet he clung to Fiona, as if still afraid of falling off the horse.

A moment later, a familiar red-haired lad bounded into view, his face flushed from exertion. "Fiona, Angus! They said ye were back! Father and Cynfael and all the rest will be so glad!" His face glowed with delight, but Fiona noticed with a heaviness in her heart that his grey eyes remained guarded and sad.

She remembered how he had insisted he come with her, and how she had been equally adamant about him staying. Was he afraid she blamed him for what had happened? It was her fault, not his. Or did he blame himself?

"Hae Dafydd and Merwyn also returned safely?" Angus asked, slowing Branwen to a halt and handing the reins to his brother.

Malcolm nodded, his gaze now drawn to the dark-haired child carried by the princess.

Fiona swung her leg over, Angus keeping her from falling off. Malcolm held out his arms as her feet hit the ground so hard she nearly knocked him over. Henrik wailed at the impact, and she tried in vain to console him.

"Hullo, who is this?" Malcolm said softly, though Fiona supposed by the strange look on his face that he had already guessed.

"Henrik, Lady Nuith's child," she replied, wavering on her feet.

Angus dismounted beside her as Dafydd approached and took Branwen from Malcolm, greeting his friend with a grin and nod of his head. Angus stood behind Fiona and she leaned against him, her legs no longer strong enough to keep her upright.

Malcolm gave a sharp whistle. "However did ye manage to steal him away? Still, a pretend princeling fer a princess—I think tha' is revenge well done." He hesitated from saying more, looking from his brother to Fiona and back, any lightness in his face vanishing away like sudden clouds. "Wha' happened?" he asked softly.

"Drummond and Lady Nuith are dead," Angus answered for them both, his voice taut. "Where is Father? We need to speak to him as soon as may be, and then Fiona needs proper food and plenty of rest."

Malcolm gestured behind him. "I can take ye to him. He's been waiting fer news of ye—they all hae." He set off, Fiona and Angus following him as he led the way through the camp.

Henrik buried his face in Fiona's shoulder and clutched her torn and begrimed shirt, heaving cries shaking his small frame, muffled in her clothes. Around them, warriors called out hearty greetings, relief evident on their faces, followed by confusion quickly masked—no doubt at the strange sight of their dishevelled princess holding a child in the midst of a war camp. Fiona tried to ignore the stares, even if the men and lads remained polite; she did not have any answers for the questions they surely had.

"I see the venture was successful," Alastair McThraedan said, nodding his head at the three as they passed him standing in the queue for supper's rations. "Welcome back, yer royal highness."

"Thank ye," Fiona returned, shifting the heavy weight of the child in her arms whose cries slowly ceased.

Alastair raised his eyebrows at the sight of the bairn, but he said nothing of it, only, "Yer father's waiting, Angus; he has no' called fer a council yet, but I am sure I will hear of it all soon." He bowed his head in farewell, and the three continued walking.

They wound their way to the centre of the camp, where the High Chieftains' tents were erected in a circle, a place made for a fire in the middle. And there, hanging free to fly in the wind, stood the dragon banner: stained and torn by battle but nonetheless alive. Fiona's heart was warmed and encouraged at the sight of it. The Scots had not lost yet; victory might still be theirs.

Malcolm approached the McCladden pavilion and lifted the edge of the tent flap, holding it for his brother and the princess. They ducked beneath it, the linen canvas a welcome shade from the glaring light of the sunset. Malcolm bade them goodbye, perhaps leaving in search of supper or to perform some other duties.

"Fiona, ye hae arrived safely then?" Donald McCladden asked. A burden seemed to lift from his shoulders. He was the only one there; perhaps the rest were all partaking of supper. "When Malcolm and his band returned without Angus, we feared the worst."

"Aye, I hae." She smiled in spite of her exhaustion, nothing seeming quite real anymore. It could be a dream for all she knew.

"Whose is the child?" Donald asked next, bewildered at the small dark head on her shoulder, who was watching everything with sleepy yet wide eyes.

"Lady Nuith's," Angus replied, sitting down on the bench and gesturing for Fiona to do the same.

The ability to sit on a normal bench, as crude as it was, felt a comfort. After being in a saddle for hours and in a seatless cell for days before that...

"Lady Nuith's?" Donald repeated, shock lacing his voice as he sat down in turn.

It was clear he was asking much more than that, but Angus answered his unspoken questions: "Lady Nuith—and Drummond—are both dead. We escaped before anyone else in Caerloch was aware of it, but it was still within an inch of our lives. I tracked westward towards our previous camp at Drumdae to prevent our new encampment from being discovered, hence why we arrived so late."

"How did it happen?" Donald pressed gently.

Fiona shut her eyes a moment, her head pounding from thirst and lack of food. How much longer would it take? She opened her eyes to see Donald looking at her, a tender look in his eyes as if to reassure her, "*Soon*".

Angus told him the full tale, leaving nothing out while Fiona leaned her head on his shoulder, fighting back sleep.

Donald was quiet for several moments when he finished, his brows drawn together and his eyes closed. He rubbed his freckled forehead with one hand, and Fiona could not help but notice how much older he seemed since a few days ago.

Fear chilled her bones. She could not bear to see him like this.

"I applaud ye," he finally said, disrupting her thoughts, "both fer successfully escaping and serving justice to two of our deadliest opponents. However, I fear tha' this will only anger the Danes more. I donnae give blame fer any of this"—he looked at Fiona kindly—"but we shall hae to discuss these events, as well as Henrik's future, wi' the chieftains shortly. We all but lie on Caerloch's doorstep, and they will attack us in retribution—and soon, nae doubt."

"They hae but a small garrison of guards, far smaller than the host we fought against," Angus said.

"Nuith told her captain to send more men north, to look fer her army," Fiona put in, the words like ash on her tongue.

"Lady Nuith is—was—nae fool. The chieftains and I agree tha' this was merely a welcoming party, and her full force has yet to come. Time is short—but I willnae keep ye longer. Ye three need yer rest, and ye, Angus, need to see to tha' hand." His eyes glistened for but a second, softening the stern gravity of his words.

Angus grinned weakly. "'Tis a mere scratch, but aye, it hurts well enough." He stood and offered his unscathed hand to Fiona.

"I will summon ye when 'tis time, but tha' may well be no' until tomorrow's dawn. Rest meanwhile. We are glad to hae ye back, my princess," said Donald.

Fiona smiled despite her weariness and the weight of the child in her arms, and she took Angus' hand. "I am glad to be back, my chieftain."

He bowed his head, and Angus guided her out of the tent.

"Malcolm!" he called once they were out in the warm spring air.

His brother turned away from speaking with his friends nearby and jogged towards them. "Aye, Angus, wha' is it?"

"Take Henrik and feed him some porridge and keep an eye out fer him. See if ye can get him to sleep. If he cries, see if ye can console him, but I would prefer Fiona rest without him keeping her awake."

His brother nodded and took Fiona's charge without a word of complaint like he might have done two years before. He carried the poor child away, who only whimpered at his change of guardian, and Fiona could hear Malcolm talking in a sweet voice to Henrik to calm him, a gentleness she had never seen from him before. Surprised, she watched him go, wondering at this change as she rubbed the feeling back into her arms, which felt light and cold without Henrik, though he had grown quite heavy over the last few hours.

Angus turned to Fiona and laid his hand on her shoulder. "Now, ye must also get some porridge and sleep. Ye need it—badly."

She smiled. "Aye, 'tis truth I am exhausted beyond measure, so much so tha' I would rather sleep than eat now. Yet I doubt I can sleep after all this."

"How so?" he asked, furrowing his brows quizzically. "There are guards all around; ye shall be protected."

She shook her head, her lips still upturned. "My heart's deepest longing has been satisfied, and despite all the fear and happenings of today, the memory of yer kiss yet lingers in my mind. I think I shall no' sleep fer sheer joy."

He returned her smile and caressed her face with his hand, then embraced her fast. When he let go, he murmured, "Then will ye sleep fer me? I donnae wish to see ye so fatigued."

"Aye, I will."

He kissed her forehead and let her go, watching her depart to her tent to repose, guarded by other trusted men. After seeing his hand properly bandaged, he went to his own tent, throwing himself down on the pile of blankets that Malcolm had dumped there, and falling asleep in minutes.

The distant ringing of bells aroused Erland abruptly from sleep. He opened his eyes and rolled over, the pain of a headache returning to him. He coughed, sorry for it a moment later at the rawness of his throat. Sickness was a terrible thing.

He was startled by the sound of knocking on his door. "Enter!" he croaked, hoisting himself up in bed.

A moment later, Asbjørn and several of his guards stood around Erland's bed while Erland stared back at them bewilderedly.

"Lord Erland, I need you to come with me to the throne room. At once."

"Why? Has something happened? Has Nuith decided to interrupt my sleep with news of that lass's execution?" the man responded despite a stuffy nose. He pushed aside the covers and hastily began to dress in more than his underclothes, gesturing away with his hand when one of the guards stepped forward to help him. There was no time to call for a servant, not if it was truly this urgent.

Asbjørn sent the others away with low, murmured commands, and then turned to his lord. "Sir, you had best come with me."

Clueless and irritated, Erland followed the captain of the guard down the tower's stairs and into the main corridor on the ground floor, passing several soldiers scurrying about—which only mystified him further.

Without a word spoken, Asbjørn threw open the door to the throne room and beckoned Erland to enter.

Giving him a puzzled glance, Lord Erland stepped in and halted, staring in shock at the scene before him before rushing forward, his boots slipping through the grotesque puddle of blood on the floor.

Ignoring Drummond's grisly frame, Erland wrenched free the sword still impaling his wife. Then he took in his arms the lifeless form of the bride he had never fully loved.

He did not sob; neither did tears fall down his cheeks. But from his open mouth came indescribable groans from his innermost being as he rocked gently back and forth, holding the bloodied and forever silent body of Lady Nuith.

No, he had never loved her with the love that poets sang of. But he had loved her in an aweful, terrifying way, knowing he would never please her but belonging to her nonetheless. Nothing except death could have ever broken such a bond. Yet her blood soaked into his overclothes. Her fingers were cold. And her unseeing eyes, clouded over, still looked down upon him.

Asbjørn looked away from the spectacle, feeling it not his place to disturb Erland. So he stood there for several minutes until the gut-wrenching moans faded into silence. He turned his gaze to Erland, who now stood looking down at the corpse, blood staining his clothes, his hands clenched at his sides.

"Who has done this?" Erland hissed, his form shaking with inconsolable wrath. "Tell me, who has done this?"

"The Scots, your lordship." Asbjørn stood quietly, knowing better than to provoke Erland's anger further.

"Where is that brat they call their queen? I will end her life myself."

"She is gone, sir. She and another—I believe the eldest son of McCladden, Drummond called him—were the authors of this destruction."

"What?" It was not a shout or a scream, only a quiet, emphatic whisper, and Asbjørn shuddered to hear that tone of voice.

"Lady Nuith and Drummond intended to execute them both, having caught them in an attempt to escape." Yet it had ended in their deaths. Ironic, that.

"Where is my son, then?" His distressed voice rose like a swift spring storm, and Asbjørn winced at the answer he had to give.

"Kidnapped, sir. We believe they took him with them when they fled. One of the guards saw the princess running with something in her arms and we cannot find Henrik anywhere, but I know he was in this room with them at the time."

"And you did nothing to stop them?" Erland stepped closer to the captain and seized him by the shoulders, shaking him like a dog.

"I was not aware of those happenings, sir. Lady Nuith ordered us from the room, and I was in the guard house." Asbjørn struggled to keep his voice steady and unfazed in the sight of pure hatred. "It was only after they had gone through the gates that the guards told me they had escaped. Naturally, I returned here to know the meaning of this and found the bodies."

Erland was too shocked to shake the captain further. "So you did not send a party after them to redeem my son, whom they will most certainly execute?"

"I cannot do anything except by your orders, sir, unless I am expressly given freedom of will in a matter."

Erland let go of Asbjørn, his jaw set. "Then I have orders for you."

"And what are they, sir?" he asked tightly, nearly wishing Nuith and Drummond were still alive to protect him from this strange outburst of the normally calm Erland.

"First, see to the burial of these bodies. Secondly, send word to the Danish host that is supposed to be marching here—including the Highland chiefs, unless the Scots have dealt with them as well—to hasten their march. Leave a garrison here, but prepare horses and rations for us to ride north from where the host is supposed to come, unless Lady Nuith has already ordered so. And tell the messenger as well, if they encounter any village belonging to those Scots, they are commanded to slay every man, woman, and child who does not stand with us. Show no mercy."

"Sir?" Asbjørn asked, stunned. Even Lady Nuith and Drummond had not been so crazed. Were it not for the recent memory of Erland shaking him like a dog only moments before, he might have laughed. For despite the fierce words Erland spoke, his lingering sickness gave his voice a nasally tone, some words almost completely different in the way they were pronounced.

"They showed no mercy to me." Erland glared darkly at Asbjørn. "Therefore, I will show no mercy to them."

"I see, sir," Asbjørn responded, but Erland paid him no heed.

"I will not stay my hand until the two that have taken all that was dear to me swim in their own blood, their country in ruins, their people slaughtered, and all that they love destroyed, *including* each other."

Asbjørn swallowed, his amusement fled. Whatever horrors Nuith had planned for the Scots, it paled in comparison with what was now coming to them.

He almost pitied them.

Almost.

~ 23 ~

RESURGENCE

ONALD McCladden looked across the glen, his gaze roving over the clusters of tents arranged by company, the picket-lines and cooking fires, the warriors rising and preparing for breakfast. The din of humanity, living together in such a small area between the braes around them, seemed to vanish away as he stood at the edge of it all. The brief beauty of being a mere spectator and not a participant was a rare thing.

The wind drowned out all else in its warm, gently gusting breaths. Shadowy clouds dissipated from the eastern horizon, chased away by the daylight, but Donald was not gazing at the remnants of night now. Rather, it was the resplendent glory of the dawn that held his attention, the brilliance of gold, titian, and crimson that enveloped his senses. He shut his eyes against it, feeling still the light searing through his eyelids, but he ignored it.

Though the next few days seemed so uncertain, it was good, in this moment, to remember that hope remained. The sun still rose—and would continue to rise—even if none of them were alive to see it.

He had received a message from Annag the previous evening, saying that she had arrived in An Dùn, wishing to be nearer to him, as she had on war trails long, long ago. Even though some leagues yet lay between them, he could almost hear her voice and feel her warmth beside him in her words. Whatever the next few days brought, he was gladdened to know she was not so far away and that she was in good health. He only prayed it remained so, and that soon he would return to her. Separations were always bitter, and war made a greater danger of it being permanent.

He had written a reply to her during the night, the messenger leaving as soon as there was light to find his way by. And he had sent out scouts to the north, to Caerloch and elsewhere, to look for any sign of the Highlanders or to espy Danish reinforcements arriving against them. Erland surely would not wait long before striking back to avenge the loss of his wife and son, not to mention one of his commanders. If he were anything like Lady Nuith... Then again, Donald had never actually seen him on the field of battle, even in the first war long ago when Sioned had perished. Perhaps Erland would think the cause was not worth fighting—but Donald doubted that. Even if he could forgive what Fiona and Angus had done, there still remained the other Danish leaders.

But that was not the only problem facing them. They were not encamped on defensible ground. This glen gave shelter from the fiercer winds and storms and provided water for all the war host, but it was not fighting earth. And aside from nearby Lowlander villages, food was hard to find—not that there had been much of that at Drumdae either. It was early in the year to begin a war trail, but they had once again not had much of a choice.

Would that the conflict would end in a more decisive victory, Donald mused, whether they reclaimed Caerloch or some other place in the Highlands—or find a better place in which to sustain the host before they starved or were ambushed. Surely after all that had happened, it would not come to that, would it?

If only the Highlands would give an answer to their pleas for aid! But Donald doubted if they would ever rally, let alone in time. They had waited long for them, and no word had come. If they had come to a decision, they would have heard by now, as scattered as those clans were far to the north. It had been weeks.

Sighing heavily, he returned to the camp. There were other decisions to make meanwhile, more immediate concerns. And they could not wait forever for something that might never come.

Fiona stirred as warm fingers gently brushed the curls out of her face. She sighed contentedly and moved her head, desiring to return to the realm of sleep. But against her will, the world around her slowly came into focus, the welcoming depths of unconsciousness slipping swiftly away.

"Fiona, 'tis time to awaken," a dear, familiar voice said.

She opened her eyes and blinked as the beige colour of the tent, illuminated by the rising sun, became visible. Sitting up, she yawned, then looked up and smiled. "Aye, Angus, I am awake now."

"Good. Ye need to eat, and Father wishes to speak wi' the two of us when we're ready. The High Chieftains are wanting to make a decision about Henrik, methinks."

She nodded, weariness still weighing on her eyelids. "Did ye sleep well?"

"Aye," he replied, though his yawn seemed to indicate otherwise. "Much better than the last few nights. And ye?"

Fiona's mouth twitched in amusement. "The same, though I would like to hae slept more. Perhaps after all this is over..." She said nothing for a moment, the mirth fading. She had only escaped yesterday, and Lord Erland would not wait long before striking back, she was sure. Hope was too fragile to trust in. She smoothed out the wrinkles of her kilt and crinkled her nose. "I should probably wash and change first," she said in disgust.

Angus laughed, about to slip out of the tent. "Aye, I will agree wi' ye there. Time in Caerloch's dungeons did nothing good. Jist be quick 'bout it. Henrik needs yer attention as well, I am thinking. Dafydd somehow managed to quiet him, but he's terrified of us. I'll see ye at breakfast." Then he was gone.

She followed him out of the tent, rising to her feet. She was stiff from yesterday, from sitting on Caerloch's dungeon floor to riding for hours, a child in her arms. Unfortunately, she could not wash properly in the stream, with all the war host about her, but washing the outside of her clothes and her hair would be better than nothing.

The sun rose warm and comforting, kissing her skin in the early morning light. Earth and woodsmoke and horse greeted her senses, the world seeming wondrously alive after days in imprisonment. A few soldiers called out to her in greeting, but most were busy concerning themselves with breakfast, seeing to the horses, or still awakening.

She slipped into a less busy part of the stream and let the water soak into her clothes, trying to scrub the dirt and grime of the dungeons out. Then she wet her hair, combing through it with her fingers, undoing the worst of the tangles and getting out the last remnants of the prison.

She waded out of the stream, nearly shivering in the morning air, and walked quickly back to her tent, drying herself off and changing into clean clothes, wearing a proper dress this time instead of a borrowed kilt and shirt. She used a comb in her hair, humming along to herself a strathspey that she could hear Cameron playing on his pipes somewhere in the camp to wake up all the rest for the day. She laid out her clothes to dry as best she could and then went in search of Angus.

Within minutes, she found him sitting near one of the cooking fires close by, speaking to Dafydd, who was holding a shy and easily startled Henrik. Malcolm was nowhere to be seen. She sat down with them and eagerly attacked the bowl of porridge they gave her. After nearly no rations at Caerloch, it tasted almost as good as the sort that Annag made. But not quite.

"Will ye take him now?" Dafydd asked when she had finished. "He is heavy; my arms are numb from holding him long."

"Aye, I will." She reached out her hands and the bairn crawled into her lap, his one hand tightly clenching onto her dress and his other thumb in his mouth as he closed his eyes, his long brown eyelashes delicately contrasting his pale, tear-stained skin. "Has he been fed?"

"Aye," Angus said, swallowing the last of his breakfast. "Hunger won against his fear, but he still is scared of us."

"I cannae blame him," Fiona murmured softly, bitter memories of the day before turning her stomach. "I too would be terrified."

Angus hitched one shoulder. "If I had a mother as cruel as Lady Nuith, I would hae rejoiced she was dead."

Fiona glared at him. "She was supposed to be my mother, and I killed her anyway. I longed to be free of her, but I—I never meant fer it to be like this. All she did against me was fer the sake of this child tha' I'm holding. Even if he is the enemy, I cannae harm a child who has done nae wrong of his own."

Angus met her gaze, pity in his eyes. "I ken, Fiona, I ken. I would hae done the same in yer place. I jist hope the chieftains see it as tha'. 'Twould be cruel to take him from tha' place only to slay him anyway because of his parents. But come, Father is waiting fer us." He rose to his feet and offered her his hand.

Fiona hoisted Henrik up, settling him on her hip as she took Angus' hand and followed him through the camp, leaving Dafydd and others at breakfast.

The chieftains were all gathered around the fire circle in the centre of the camp, sitting on large stones or crudely hewn benches made of tree logs not yet burned. Some murmured to one another in casual conversation, others watching them approach.

Eachann and Cynfael greeted her warmly, and some of her apprehension melted away when their expressions did not change at seeing Henrik. Bryce scowled, but he usually did so; his gaze only softened when he saw her face.

"'Tis good to see ye again, princess," Cynfael murmured, gesturing to a seat beside him. "We were greatly worried fer ye."

Fiona smiled. "Thank ye. I fear, though, tha' my return may no' bring only happy tidings."

His face sobered, gazing at the bairn still in her arms. "Maybe so, but we will be glad fer good news all the same." He laid his hand on her shoulder a moment as Angus took a seat beside her, resting on the ground and leaning back on his hands.

Henrik whimpered and turned his head in her arms, looking around with wide, dark eyes. Fiona glanced down at him and wondered what his fate would be before much time had passed. Would they show mercy? Would mercy be a blessing or a curse? There was always the possibility that Henrik might grow up and turn against the Scots in the end; it had happened before in epics told by the harpers, and it would be no surprise if it occurred again. Yet she could not bear it if he was put to death simply because he *could* be a future threat. It was wrong to murder a child, however right the motives might seem.

Donald cleared his throat before beginning to speak. "As ye all can see, Fiona McCurragh was rescued yesterday from Caerloch, thanks to the work of my sons and King Cynfael's lads. They also brought news tha' two of our worst opponents, Lady Nuith and Drummond MacDougall, are slain."

Bryce inhaled sharply, a whistling sound, but that was all.

Fiona glanced at him and then back at Donald, wishing she felt relief at the thought her worst enemy was no longer a threat, but she felt only dread.

"Ye may guess wha' the consequences of those actions might lead to," Donald continued, "but we'll discuss tha' presently. 'Tis no' wha' concerns us now. Our princess took wi' her the Danish heir as she escaped—" Donald gestured to Henrik in Fiona's arms.

Fiona straightened at this as if to defend herself against hasty judgement, but no one spoke. Perhaps they waited for Donald to finish before saying anything.

"Some might laugh at the irony of one hostage being rescued only to gain another, but this is nae laughing matter. Henrik MacErland, as he would be called were he truly of our people, is of more Danish blood than of Scot. Should we keep him amongst us, perhaps one day he might choose the wrong side—should we be successful and win this war. He might turn traitor and raise an army, slaying us all in revenge. Yet he is also young enough tha' perhaps, should we succeed, he might never ken who his real parents are. But should he live and learn the truth, I think 'tis safe to assume that there'd be nae doubt he would seek revenge.

"He could be worth much to us as a hostage. Perhaps we could force an end to the war wi' this, but should we no', wha' then? If we win and the risk of keeping him alive is too great, wha' would we do?

"There is always the choice of execution—and in most cases tha' would be the unquestionable command. Yet this is a wee bairn, scarcely older than a babe. Murder is always wrong, but when it causes the death of a child, 'tis worse. I ken the Danes would hae nae hesitation, but we cannae be as cruel as the ones we claim are tyrants. Therefore, I hae called ye all to lend wisdom in this matter so tha' we may rightly decide on a unified course of action." He ceased from speaking and sat back as if bracing against a heated reply.

"If he is to be murdered, I will hae nae hand in it," Alastair McThraedan said as soon as there was a pause.

"I hae reason to loathe the Danes more than most, but even I cannae see to this child's death," Bryce MacClydno uttered fiercely, his eyes glittering in the bright sunlight. "I say keep him as a hostage, inform the Danes to surrender at risk of his life. Wha' happens after, we can decide when the time comes. War is a troublesome enough matter without this."

Fiona released the breath she had not known she had been holding; if the two oldest and most respected of the High Chieftains spoke thus, then surely Henrik's life was spared—for the present. And it did not seem they judged her for what she had done...unless that would be revealed later.

Hamish cleared his throat, and all attention landed on him. But he said nothing, his blue eyes flitting from face to face in embarrassment.

"I hae a proposition to make." King Cynfael finally spoke, his words slow and thoughtful.

Fiona turned to look at him, her pulse quickening. What did he have in mind?

"Speak, and we will hear wha' ye hae to say," Eachann voiced for them all.

"Give me the child. Should we survive this war and I return back home, I will raise him as my own. He will be far away from his home country and his own people; he willnae be surrounded by those who ken his true parentage; all he will be told is that he was a child orphaned from the war that I adopted as my son."

"Will yer people object?" Donald asked, his brows furrowed.

"I donnae think they will take kindly to ye bringing in the son of the enemy ye left yer throne to destroy," Bryce drawled, taking a swig from the skin of water beside him.

A smile played on Cynfael's lips. "Nae, they may no', but I am the king. And they would ken that the moment Henrik might turn against us is the moment he is in peril of his life. Likewise, the Danes would think twice before daring to raid our shores at risk of harming one of their own nobility. Besides, it happens often enough in my country and will no' be thought of as strange." He paused, looking away at the ground, though a blush rosied his cheeks a moment. "And I hae nae wife to raise objections."

Fiona opened her mouth slightly, trying to find the courage to speak. *Cynfael's solution may solve the problem I created in the end, but fer now? Wha' will become of Henrik meanwhile?* She struggled to get the words out, but her heart hammered in her throat and the words never passed her lips.

"'Tis seeming to be the only answer to this dilemma," Hamish McLairdun stated before she could say anything. "I am fer Cynfael taking him. Saves us the trouble."

The others murmured in agreement.

"Are we all in consent wi' King Cynfael's plan?" Donald asked.

"I hae a question." Fiona raised her voice at last.

"Aye, wha' is it?" Alastair asked kindly.

"Who will take care of Henrik in the meanwhile? Fer a surety, when the battles come, we must all be fighting, save fer the wounded and those left to tend them."

Donald looked to Cynfael to answer.

"I would ask ye to do it, dear princess," the Cymreig king replied, "since he seems to trust ye more than the rest of us, and I think ye'd be best kept away from the active fighting. But I wouldnae hae him be a burden if he is to be my charge."

"I asked fer this burden, having taken him in the first place," she replied somewhat dryly, glancing down at Henrik in her lap, who watched all the proceedings in silence, his eyes wide and dark. Taking the child for her own after slaying his mother, whom she had hated for so long—now that was a cruel twist of fate.

"That is true," Cynfael consented. "Ye would also ken about these matters more than I, and I would wish fer ye to watch over him when I cannae, at least fer the present."

"'Tis only fitting," Bryce agreed, "since she stole him away. Let her bear the responsibility."

Fiona's face burned hot, but she bit her tongue from snapping back. He spoke the truth.

"I donnae think," Angus said, speaking for the first time, "tha' Fiona meant fer him to be a burden. Wha' happened, happened swiftly. Actions out of pity and horror tha' follow rage and bloodlust are no' the sort we can blame another fer in the time afterwards. Any one of us may hae done the same. I donnae think we can judge her fer it."

"Nae judgement was meant," Bryce retorted, "and young ones, nae matter who they are, should ken better than to correct their elders."

"Peace, Bryce, peace," Donald chided. "Let me deal wi' my own son. He meant nae disrespect."

His father-in-law did not seem to believe Donald's words, but he said no more.

"Aye, I shall care fer Henrik," Fiona finally said, swallowing back the nerves at once again speaking unprompted. Aye, she had scarcely done so before, but she was destined to be their queen—should all go well. If Cynfael could speak to these men as their equal and be respected, and he not of their clans, then certainly she could do likewise, regardless of being a young woman and not an experienced warrior like the rest of them. "I shall care fer him," she repeated, looking at the chieftains intently. "But I wouldnae advise waiting fer the Danes to retaliate. I would suggest we send news to Erland, whether he remains at Caerloch or no'. I will sign it alongside ye; they ken I live now, and perhaps my taking my rightful place would signify tha' we mean this in earnest.

"Our rebellion is no' child's play. And I would tha' we tell Erland to surrender his forces, or his son will forfeit his life." Her voice was cold in her own ears, and her hands trembled even as they embraced her enemy's child. But her tone was firm and steady, and the attentive silence given by the chieftains encouraged her to continue. "I ken Erland cares about Henrik, perhaps more so than fer Nuith. We might hae a chance to end this war now without further bloodshed. But if this willnae force him to yield, then we hae a long struggle ahead of us. I didnae ken him well, but I ken tha' once he sets his mind to something, he will follow it until completion."

Donald bowed his head. "It will be done, yer highness."

A blush warmed Fiona's face, caught off guard by his deference.

"I will sign it as well," Cynfael said, looking at Fiona and Donald in turn. "The Danes might already hae guessed ye hae allies among ye, and having fought and won our first battle, there is nae point fer more secrecy. Perhaps the princess is right; our boldness might help our cause and tell the Danes that we are no' playing games."

"Well said, o king," Donald replied, once more bowing his head. "Unless ye hae more questions," he continued, addressing the rest, "ye are free to return to yer men. We will discuss a further course of action once we hae news."

The chieftains rose to their feet, the older ones grumbling about their aching joints from being out in the weather without proper shelter. But thankfully the sun, which had dried Fiona's hair by now, was warm and pleasant.

"Do ye mind if I leave ye fer a bit?" Angus asked softly.

Fiona shook her head. "No' at all. Jist donnae stay away too long, or else send Malcolm in yer place."

He flashed a quick grin. "Aye, yer highness." He kissed her forehead and then was gone before she could say anything back.

Only Cynfael remained, still seated beside her. "May I hold him?" he asked.

She gave Henrik over to him, struggling to release the toddler's grip on her sleeves. "Shh now," she said to the bairn. "He willnae hurt ye."

Henrik gave her a look of pure betrayal but held his peace.

Cynfael nestled him gently in his arms and showed him the brooch of his cloak, its gold and gems sparkling in the sun.

Henrik's fears fled at the sight, and he held out his chubby hands to take it, turning it this way and that in the light.

"Did I do wrong?" Fiona asked of the king, watching the child play.

"Nae. I would hae done the same unless my duty required otherwise," Cynfael replied. "Ye are no' at fault."

She met his brown-eyed gaze, which sweetened to honey in the sunlight. But still, she was unconvinced. Bryce's bitter words seemed truer than anyone else's.

"We are glad to hae ye back, Fiona. That is all that matters, no' Henrik. Think of that, no' this child, no' wha' the next few days bring. Our hope has been restored. We still hae a chance against them."

"Did ye give me up fer lost?" she asked a moment later, her eyes never leaving him.

A smile crossed his face and he shook his head. "Nae, Fiona, never. I would hae gang wi' them to rescue ye if I could. I feared the worst, aye. But that doesnae matter anymore. Ye hae returned. And as long as ye live and are free, our hope will never die."

Fiona blinked back the tears that suddenly sprang to her eyes at his words. "I pray ye are right."

"I ken I am. But come, methinks someone wants to speak to ye."

She glanced up to see Malcolm walking towards them, his head bent towards the ground. When he reached her, his gaze never quite fully met hers.

"Fiona, may I speak wi' ye a moment?"

She rose to her feet as Cynfael reassured her he could look after Henrik while she was gone, and gestured for Malcolm to follow her. She made her way through the camp, finding a place on the outskirts, out on the hillside, where they could talk without anyone overhearing them.

"Malcolm, is everything all right?" she murmured, concerned by his unusual shyness and having a guess as to what it might be.

He looked towards the camp, his arms clasped awkwardly behind his back. "Yer highness...can—" He cleared his throat and tried again, his voice sounding strained. Her stomach twisted within her, and it was all she could do to hold herself back so he could finish. "Can ye forgive me?" His gaze darted to meet hers, and she could see tears brimming in their grey depths.

Though he was so much taller than her, she pulled him into an embrace and squeezed him hard, burying her face in his shoulder, tears springing to her own eyes. "Aye, Malcolm. There is nothing to forgive. 'Twas my decision to gae to the stream. If ye had been wi' me...ye might be dead—and I couldnae live wi' myself if tha' had happened. We cannae change the past. Donnae blame yerself, please, no' fer my sake." She stepped back and stood on tiptoes to ruffle his hair. "There is nae blame. No' from me."

His freckled face, crinkled in anxiety, softened. "I am glad, princess. I was jist afraid ye might hold it against me because it was my duty to protect ye and I failed at Drumdae. I broke my oath and—"

She laid a finger on his lips. "Nae, Malcolm. Ye regained yer honour by aiding in my rescue. The oath was damaged, aye, but it has been remade. Donnae worry about it anymore."

He bowed his head in submission. "As ye wish, yer highness." But the familiar teasing lilt in his voice was back, and her concern melted away.

"Come now, I am thinking we should return to camp before we're missed." She smiled and offered him her hand.

He offered her his elbow in return and marched jauntily back to camp, laughing with her and ignoring her pleas to be sensible.

But she did not press the matter. It was a good thing to laugh in the midst of war, to remember that the shadows did not last forever.

It was two evenings later when the first of the scouts returned, an evening of clouded skies, the sunlight thinning away into gloom. The air was still, as if waiting, and only the gurgle of the stream remained steadfast beneath everything else.

The company who saw the scout fell silent halfway through eating supper. Fiona's portion of roasted venison nearly stuck in her throat, her heart suddenly hammering in her chest. Angus glanced at her, his brow knit in worry. Only Malcolm carried on as normal, fussing with Henrik as he fed him porridge and scolding him when the child fought against the spoon.

"I ken 'tis no' the greatest thing ye'll ever eat, but at least we are feeding ye. We could be starving ye, and tha'd make ye grateful fer this, would it no'?"

"Malcolm, hush," Angus said, turning his head as he saw his father approach the scout. He rose to his feet along with Fiona and drew near the horseman, as did Cynfael and Bryce, who were nearest.

"Sir!" the scout said, dismounting.

"Wha' news?" Donald asked, his voice tight.

"Any sign of the Highlanders?" Bryce followed.

The scout shook his head. "None tha' I saw, but I didnae head tha' far north, only covered the land east and west after spying out Caerloch. I came to tell ye tha' Erland is nae longer at the castle. I sent my fellow men after him wi' news about his son after we questioned the villagers of it."

"He's deserted Caerloch?" Fiona asked in shock, her voice high. "Why would he—"

"I donnae ken." The scout shrugged. "We asked about tha', and there's the barest guard living there now. Most of them hae withdrawn to the northeast."

Bryce turned to Donald, his face alight in the glow of the setting sun, a frenzied look in his black eyes. "Seize it! This is our chance! We can reclaim the old capital and use it as a defensible place. We hae more than enough men to retake it."

"And wha' if it's a trap?" Fiona asked, Bryce whirling on her as if he had forgotten she was there. "Erland would no' desert tha' place unless he had a very good reason fer doing so. He is a coward—tha's why Nuith married him, because he was pliable and easily bent to her will. Either Asbjørn has persuaded him to do so, or else he had good reason to desert tha' place and seek his people elsewhere."

"Grief and revenge turn cowards into deadly fighters," Angus said quietly beside her.

"I ken, but this?" Fiona asked, meeting his gaze. "He must be meeting the men Lady Nuith summoned, but...I donnae understand why he would set out on the war trail himself. He never has before."

The scout cleared his throat. "There's more, yer highness," he said, addressing Fiona now.

"Pray tell," she replied, though she dreaded to hear it. Based on the scout's expression, it was not good news.

"Erland is wreaking his revenge as he gaes. All the Scots left in the village are dead, and thus he has gang up through the Highlands, leaving none alive."

The silence that followed was like the quiet that comes before the first crack of thunder.

Then Bryce swore, punctuating it by spitting at his feet.

Donald inhaled sharply through his nose, looking towards the northwest, where the last remnants of light still held sway.

Cynfael bowed his head in his hands, murmuring in his tongue what sounded like poetry, perhaps a memorial to the undeserving dead.

Angus stepped closer to Fiona, his arm encircling her waist, the other resting out of habit on his sword hilt. Fiona leaned into him, closing her eyes a moment. Her chest tightened, her heart heavy with all the weight of the world.

Her people—her kin, her flesh and blood in ways the Lowlanders were not. Dead. Slain without cause.

All because of her.

And Henrik yet lived because they had more mercy than Erland. Perhaps the Scots' mercy, always more than the Danes', would be their undoing.

Fiona glanced over her shoulder at the child in Malcolm's arms, her hands clenched at her sides. Loathing blinded her a moment, and she was glad Angus was there to ground her and, if need be, hold her back. Perhaps she should not have taken Henrik, if only it would have prevented this needless slaughter. And yet, she knew that Erland might still have done so because Nuith was dead at her hand—and Henrik's presence among the Scots was the only hope they had to force Erland to halt his annihilation.

"Sir?" the scout asked after no one else spoke or moved. "Wha' be my orders, sir?"

"Rest and eat," Donald said. "Someone will see to yer horse."

The scout nodded, bowing to Fiona and then leading his horse away.

"And now?" Bryce asked.

"Tell the men wha' Erland has done. Tell them we will decide how to act in the morning," Donald said. "And set a double guard tonight in case some sort of treachery befalls us."

"Will we take Caerloch?"

"We will speak of tha' on the morrow," came the response.

"Wha' of the other villages? The ones in the Lowlands?" Fiona asked, her voice weak. Were it not for Angus beside her, she might have stood trembling, but she drew from his strength, and she was not alone.

"Let us pray we keep him from ever reaching them, princess," Donald replied gravely as the sun set the sky in ashes around them, the embers of light dying out into darkness.

"And those they hae massacred?" Cynfael asked, his voice strangled.

"They will be avenged. Lord Erland cannae escape justice forever."

~ 24 ~
RED HORIZON

"DO ye think we will truly regain Caerloch?" Fiona asked Angus as they rolled up blankets and tore down tents, preparing for the road once again.

Half the morning had been spent in council, arguing over the next course of action. Hamish and Alastair wanted to wait for more news, while everyone else wished to reclaim the castle and use it as their next defence. Eachann had no opinion, only that he was content with whatever decision would be reached. But the majority had won out; the risk must surely be worth it, and so they were going to march north, regardless of whether the castle remained vulnerable by the time they reached it or not.

"I think we stand a fair chance," Angus finally replied.

Fiona waited for him to continue as they secured the folded tent with tightly bound ropes.

The warm wind caught and tossed about his dark hair, and he put up his hand to thrust it out of his eyes. "We hae acted on less than tha' before, and we still live and hold the field. In truth, I think it the only choice, but I am less eager to return to tha' place because of wha' happened before." His eyes met hers, and she saw the darkness of uncertainty.

She sighed, her shoulders drooping even as she rose to her feet and hoisted the bundle to her shoulder. "I ken; I hae even more bitter memories of Caerloch, even before wha' happened a few days ago."

He laid his hand on her shoulder a moment before she continued.

"Yet it was the capital once, once a place of pride and power. I think the chieftains mean to make it such a place again, should we win. We may as well regain it now tha' we hae a chance."

"Do *ye* want to live there again?"

She paused, looking at the camp disappearing before her eyes and then to the north, where guards still paced, ever watchful for scouts and messengers. "Do I hae a choice?" she finally said, glancing at him before continuing onward, heading for the picket lines and avoiding soldiers hurrying past on similar errands.

Angus laughed, but not from amusement. "Fiona, ye are the princess!" He spoke softly, but she could still hear the cry in his voice, quiet as it was. "Ye can decide wha' ye wish."

"I donnae think 'tis tha' easy, no' wi' this. 'Twould break years of tradition and history, and our country is weak enough. Besides," she said, walking onward again, "'tis foolish to think about it when we may no' even succeed in reclaiming it, nor even win the war. We might reclaim the castle, aye, but the Danes still hold the Highlands. They might never come to us but rather wait fer us to come to them, weakening us by the long march and endless uncertainty."

They had reached the horses now, and she busied herself laying the bundles of tents and belongings along their backs behind saddles, as others were doing around them.

"But why?" Angus asked when he had finished. He rested one arm against the back of his bay mare and looked at her. "Why would they wait? If I were Erland and my wife had been slain—nae matter how much I feared her—and my child taken, I wouldnae hide away and prepare for the enemy to eventually meet me. I would gather my forces and attack them when I feel they are weakest."

"Do ye think they left Caerloch vulnerable on purpose?"

He shrugged. "Maybe. Or maybe he jist reasoned it would be a good enough loss while he defeated us in other ways. There is more than one way to win a war, and the Danes are kent fer their treachery. Having Henrik as a hostage will help us, but 'tis best to be prepared in case it does no'. This struggle is more than jist a rebellion now. 'Tis a war, and it may be a long and bloody one before the end." He took his arm away and walked back to the camp, Fiona following.

"If it doesnae succeed—the thing wi' Henrik—wha' will they do?"

Angus sighed, squinting against the daylight. "Nae doubt put him somewhere safe. War is nae place fer children."

"I was a child in the last war and fought anyway," Malcolm put in, walking up to them, several bedrolls slung over his shoulder. "I kent I was no' supposed to come, but I still survived!"

Fiona laughed in spite of herself.

"Aye, wee brother, ye looked jist about like an infant in yer over-sized armour," Angus drawled, but he was smiling.

Malcolm scoffed. "Och! I couldnae help it there was nothing small enough. And I daresay the scant rations and freezing cold didnae help me fit into anything either."

Angus playfully punched his brother's shoulder, the sunlight sparkling in his eyes, and Malcolm retaliated in like kind, a grin on his face.

In that moment, Fiona was struck with the irony of it all. To laugh and jest and to simply *live* while war and death lay on the horizon was perhaps the only way they would survive it all. For it was when fear consumed a person, when the good things in life were forgotten, that one truly lost.

Fiona closed her eyes a moment, lost in thought while the sun warmed her hair. She heard Malcolm and Angus laying some of the bedrolls across the horses' saddles and opened her eyes, her brows furrowed. "Where is Henrik?" she asked.

"Back wi' Merwyn. He was making him smile instead of scowl and cry like he usually does, so I thought it was best to leave him and help ye."

"Tha' is kind of ye," Angus replied, surprised.

Malcolm shrugged, looking over his shoulder and then up at the sky, his freckled face scrunched at the brightness. "The sooner we set off, the sooner I can eat. Father's making us hae luncheon while we march again," he explained.

"I should hae kent ye would be working hard fer yer stomach's sake," Angus said, rolling his eyes heavenward.

"I saved some oatcakes fer ye, princess," Malcolm continued as a few soldiers approached him for the bedrolls he had bundled.

Fiona dipped her head. "Thank ye, Malcolm. Jist keep them fer when we march."

The lad raised an eyebrow. "I'll try to restrain myself. But mean-while"—he slipped his hand into his sporran and pulled out some dried remnants of sprigs—"I hae this. I noticed ye lost yers and thought ye might want to be as adorned as the rest of yer army." He stepped up to her and slipped the pine, heather, and thistle bud into her clan pin. "Wouldnae want anyone thinking ye were no' one of us." He winked.

"I highly doubt tha'," Angus commented dryly, but Fiona could see the fond admiration in his eyes, and she could not help but smile back.

"Thank ye, Malcolm."

He dipped his head in a mock bow and threw a grin over his shoulder at his brother as he stepped away. "Always, princess."

Fiona laughed in return. She thought of the many times Angus had said the same to her; to hear his brother say it now—Malcolm was no longer the wee lad he had been. Warmth blossomed in her chest. Oh, how he had grown!

Cynfael watched as the men finished packing up the camp, cooking fires doused completely, tents and weapons and belongings tied up in horses' saddlebags. Gwyn and her small mews and perch were already packed up and ready for the next encampment, though she would no doubt ride on the wrist of the man who helped care for her. Yet she would be hunting again soon, and the fierce look she had given him that morning told him that she could sense it in the air as well as he. The plain with the stream on which they had encamped was left deserted, grass flattened where men had slept, cropped where horses had eaten, and ashen places where fires had burned.

But grass would grow back, the heather would bloom again, and though all who had passed this way could die, the land would remain. Should it be razed and salted, even so, it would not stay damaged forever. It was a comforting thought.

Memory remained long after time erased all else.

Cynfael knelt and cut a small square of earth with his dagger. He filled his hand with the soft, moist dirt beneath it and crumbled it in his hands, staining his palm brown save where the pale ridges of his handprint shone through.

Scotland's ground was just as dark as that of Cymru. Perhaps land was no different from place to place, countries belonging to men only because they staked their name on it. Nay, it was the governance of men and their dreams—the idea of the thing that mattered. And it mattered because the men who named it so believed it did.

Earth was still earth, though hallowed by the blood of those who died defending their land from someone else who wished to claim it.

Cynfael mused on how many of their warband would be lost in the coming days, whether they were strong enough to withstand the flood to come. The price of freedom was ever high; he knew that well. He wondered whether he was worthy to shed his blood for the cause. As he had said to Donald, he had no wife and no one waiting for him back home. Only that fair lass in the Lowlands, to whom he was little more than a kingly stranger. Perhaps, when the war was over... But they would have to win that first, and who knew what the cost would be? He had little to lose but everything to gain. To become a hero of legend to those that survived—that was something worth dying for.

He brushed the dirt off his hands as Donald gave the command to ride out. His hands would remain brown until he washed them, but it did not matter.

Earth was earth, and whether he died on Scotland's ground or Cymru's made no difference. It was the sacrifice that counted, after all.

"Sir, there are two messengers, Scots, and they bear a white banner."

Lord Erland raised his fist, and slowly but surely the immense host ground to a halt. The silence that followed after hours of endless marching by several thousand men and horses was nearly deafening.

He looked at his advanced guardsman with bloodshot eyes. "They wish to surrender? Excellent."

The man looked uncertain. "Sir, they have a message for you. It concerns your son."

Erland stiffened, and the verdant landscape beneath the sun, sinking in the clouded heavens around him, suddenly became clear for the first time in days. "Bring the one carrying the message forth. Watch the other one; it may be a trap."

The guardsman wheeled his horse and rode off.

Erland's nose twitched, sensing the dampness in the air even though the sun shone warm and comforting upon his back. Behind him, he could hear the Danes drinking water or ale from their sheep-skins, murmuring to one another, and the horses nickering in impatience.

Hoofbeats disturbed his thoughts again, and he glanced up to see the guardsman and a Scot on horse approach. The Scot's face was white, but he set his face and shoulders like a man unashamed to die. Erland could respect that, regardless of the news he carried. But all the same, he was a Scot, and a Scot had slain his wife and stolen his child. His respect could only go so far.

"Well?" he asked, his knowledge of Gàidhlig rougher than Nuith's had been.

The man handed the parchment to him without a word, meeting gaze for gaze unflinchingly.

Erland tore away the seal, studying the roughly shaped runes that the Scots had been kind enough to include alongside the round Gàidhlig that he could not read. The words were few but unmistakable. No room for negotiation.

We have your son. He remains unharmed and will continue to remain so should you surrender, withdraw your forces, and return to your native land. Should you fail to comply with these demands, we do not promise to have mercy, and your son's life will be forfeit.
Signed by
Princess Fiona McCurragh of Scotland
High Chieftain Donald McCladden of the Lowlands
High Chieftain Bryce MacClydno of the Lowlands
High Chieftain Alastair McThraedan of the Lowlands
High Chieftain Hamish McLairdun of the Lowlands
High Chieftain Eachann MacDonald of the Lowlands
King Cynfael ap Rhiada of Cymru

Erland swore. They should have known that Rhiada, even dead, had treachery up his sleeve. Of course the Cymry would ally against them. Still, Drummond and Asbjørn had estimated the total number of men they had, and Erland's company far outnumbered them yet. But at the risk of Henrik...

He had come too far and lost too much to stop now. There was more than one way to ensure his son's safety, and it would be easy enough. Even as enemies, the Scots, with their foolish sense of honour, would not harm his son unless he committed severely drastic deeds, even if their threats stated otherwise. He could do much damage before they carried out their plans.

He handed the parchment to the man beside him and nudged his horse forward so that he was alongside the Scot.

The man's eyes widened in alarm, but he remained silent and steadfast.

"Tell yer princess and all her chieftains"—he bent and withdrew a dagger from his boot—"this is my answer." Then he stabbed home in the man's thigh, where he would soon bleed to his death.

The man gasped but still said nothing, meeting Erland's gaze with one of pure hatred. He turned his horse clumsily, his injured leg all but helpless, and rode off to his companion, though he would not last long.

"Was that wise?" the guardsman asked, an eyebrow raised.

A look from Erland silenced him. "March on," he called.

The company began dragging forward once more across the blooming landscape that was now tinged crimson. How fitting, that the land be bathed in bloodlight. The red horizon spilled over his shoulders as they rode south, a herald of what was to come. For it would only be a few days, and then all this struggle would be over.

He smiled. Let the Scots have Caerloch. They would lose far more before this war was won.

~ 25 ~
DEATH BEFORE DISHONOUR

FOG came in at twilight, settling thinly upon the darkening land-scape. The haze hid the remnants of the flaming sunset as the Scots came to a halt on the last hilltop. Caerloch and the village outside its gates spread before them, the distant glow of torches visible even from where the war host had stopped. Only a few lights illuminated the castle walls; from all appearances, it was still theirs for the taking—should they battle in the dawn.

Fiona sat in front of Angus on his horse, holding Henrik in her arms as they waited for further commands. It had been slow going that day, having to wait for those on foot to keep up; it was almost as wearying being on the horse as it would have been to have walked.

She leaned her head back, resting against Angus' neck, as the weariness of the past several days overwhelmed her. She closed her eyes and concentrated on the gentle movements of the horse and the breathing of the sleeping bairn in her arms. Every once in a while, when someone spoke to Angus and he replied, she felt the vibrations of his tenor voice, whose murmuring, sweet timbre lulled her further to sleep. Not even the chieftains' low voices some paces away, discussing whether to encamp for the evening, could keep her awake much longer...

Angus glanced down and saw the warmth of sleep on Fiona's face, her lips parting slightly as her breathing became even, nearly matching that of the child in her arms. She still looked thin after her time in Caerloch's dungeon, and there were dark circles under her eyes. Her face, though relaxed as she rested, did not look as peaceful as it had before her captivity. His arms gently tightened around them. Whatever would happen in the following days, he would do his utmost to protect her, no matter the cost.

"Are they asleep?" Malcolm murmured from somewhere below him.

Angus looked down at his brother standing beside him and nodded. "Aye, they need it."

"So do ye. Ye look awful." He grinned, the words kind.

Angus smiled weakly. "I daresay all of us could use some more sleep. Yet whenever I close my eyes, I worry wha' will happen next. In my dreams, strange and contorted images frighten me, and I wake myself up to prove tha' ye are all still alive and no' dead."

"Ye mean, Fiona is alive and no' dead," Malcolm interrupted, a teasing lilt in his voice. "Merwyn and Dafydd snore loud enough tha' even the ghaists ken they're alive."

"I donnae wish ye to be dead either," Angus retorted.

"But no' as much as ye wish Fiona to be alive." Malcolm threw his head back and laughed softly, his eyes darting to the sleeping lass and bairn. "When she was captured, ye wouldnae sit still even fer one moment. Ye were constantly pacing and arguing wi' Father and the leaders tha' she needed to be rescued. I am surprised they didnae bind ye to a tree to get ye to stop."

Angus scowled. The memory still pained him. "'Twould be a shame if I did anything less. Without her, I donnae think we would hae the courage to keep fighting, especially if the rumours are true tha' Erland is returning wi' a large army."

Malcolm nodded, a sober look on his face. "Aye, true. Anything fer the princess." Then the mischievous twinkle appeared back in his eye, and he grinned up at his brother. "But 'tis clear to everyone tha' ye care fer her a lot more than jist as the princess."

"Och, get on wi' ye," Angus snapped back, but he was laughing too. Even he could not keep the smile off his face as he glanced down at the pair in his grasp.

"Well, I must be getting back," Malcolm sighed, looking around them. "Jist donnae be kissing her while she's sleeping; tha' is jist—"

He broke off, seeming in search of the right word, but then gave up with a shudder. Before Angus could open his mouth, his brother turned and ran back to his companions in the gloom, the conversation clearly ended.

"I willnae make any promises to tha'," Angus whispered when he had gone. Not when the days ahead were so uncertain. Not when the Danes were close. Angus looked down at his princess once more. Not when it might be the last time.

"Donald, someone's riding in," Cynfael said, disturbing the discussion between the chieftains regarding setting camp where they were. "By their dress, 'tis a Scot. Two of them."

Their forms suddenly appeared in the sheer fog, eerily shining in the light of the moon that had arisen overhead.

Donald's breath caught in his throat. The news they brought would shape whatever happened the next few days; while he doubted Erland would surrender, at least they would know the Danes' numbers.

"Hae the messengers returned?" Bryce barked, suddenly interested.

Cynfael did not answer, his expression lost in the mist. "Something is wrong."

But before anyone could reply, the messenger had reached them, leading the other's horse with him. The rider was slumped, only staying on his mount because he had been tied to his saddle. "Sir!" the man cried, his voice hoarse. "I hae bad news."

Chieftain McCladden pulled forward beside the man. "Wha' is it?" he gasped, fearing the answer.

"Erland rejects yer message," the scout replied, still panting from the long ride. "He read it and then stabbed Tàmhas, saying tha' was his answer. He bled to death ere we returned, but I couldnae abandon him without a proper burial."

Donald looked away a moment, numbness seizing his heart. Even in this, the Danes' cruelty could not be matched. To stab someone carrying a white banner on behalf of another... "Do ye ken their numbers and how far away they are?"

"I couldnae count them fer certain; we faced the front of the company. But they are more than equal to our number. I dare no' say twice as much, but certainly more men than us. I'd say they're a day's quick march away, perhaps a wee bit more, but tha's all." The man's voice was thick with pain and exhaustion, but it remained even to the point that it did not sound like it came from a man at all, more like the groan of a wounded animal.

Silence followed his words. Even Bryce forgot to swear and spit on the name of the Danes.

Donald inhaled sharply, anger and frustration welling up in him like a dragon nearly bursting into flame. But he swallowed the fire, though with great difficulty. He would not break before a lower officer in his army, but oh, how he was tempted to! They had known the Danes' army would be great, but more than their number? Where had they found so many men in only a month or so's time? Unless… unless the Highlanders had joined them. In which case, their worst fears had come to pass. Even with Caerloch as a fighting ground, they would be hard pressed to hold the field that day. Yet there was no other option; turning back was foolish, for they would be chased and cut down even as they fled. And where would they go? Erland's men had already begun the destruction in the Highlands, and the only way to stop them was to fight them when the opportunity arose. He could not abandon this war, not while his wife and so many others lay so close and vulnerable to the enemy. He could curse himself for not commanding Annag to remain at Caerdun, but it was too late now.

Sighing heavily, he turned his gaze back on the messenger and replied, "Bury yer friend. I will send out more scouts if I can. Rest meanwhile. We will camp here fer the night."

The messenger nodded. "Thank ye, sir." Then he clicked his tongue and led his horse and that of his dead companion into the ranks behind the chieftains.

The full moon above shone so brightly that the wild landscape was nearly as clear as daytime, save that the plain below this hilltop was thinly blanketed in a cold grey from the fog. And when the sun rose again—if it did—what would it see ere night fell again?

Wheeling his horse around, Donald called out orders that were passed down the ranks. "We are camping here tonight. Picket the horses and set a strong guard. Nae fires. Nae tents. We will sleep on the ground and discuss further movement tomorrow. I want five men, willing and able, to ride out tonight and espy wha' they can. If ye are willing to do so, please come to me."

Within minutes, the soldiers scurried around, fulfilling commands as Donald watched. He did not have the heart to tell them what was coming, though some might already have heard. If they had, it was a good chance their fighting spirit had been quenched within them and he doubted if he could raise it again.

Words could only do so much in the face of fear.

"Donald McCladden," King Cynfael said as the other chieftains left to attend to their men. "Caerloch Castle may still be taken, may it no'?"

Donald did not answer at first, but when he did, his teeth were clenched. "Aye, though tha' may yet change ere morning comes."

"We still hae a chance. We may yet win," Cynfael encouraged.

Donald looked at him, at long last giving in to despair. "How? The Highland chiefs hae sent nae word of their joining us. We will hae to fight against the full forces of Erland's army—let alone if the Highlanders truly march wi' them. They outnumber us greatly if the messenger saw aright. How can we win against tha'? How can the tides suddenly be turned once again in their favour, they who are so evil and cruel to our people?"

"Ye hae won before against tha' army, which was also twice yer size, and lived to fight them again."

"At the cost of many men, one of our chief leaders and supporters, my second son, and yer father. And we even had the advantage of more than a castle. Nae, Cynfael, I ken ye mean well, but 'tis best that ye donnae speak to me at this moment. I need time to think. See tha' my sons and the princess get their rest. I will return." He dug his heels into his horse's flanks, vanishing into the twilight.

Cynfael shook his head, but it was not at Donald. Rather, it was the hopelessness of their situation. Donald McCladden was right— horribly right—and there was nothing they could do about it. Fate had chosen against them yet again, it seemed. If their numbers were equal, it would be hard enough, but if more than that...

Swallowing hard, Cynfael turned his steed and walked it back to the core group of soldiers slowly spreading about on the ground. After seeing to their horses, they simply lay themselves down and slept where they were, few of them even bothering to eat some semblance of supper.

"Cynfael!"

He looked up. "Aye, Angus, wha' is it?"

"Would ye mind helping me?"

Cynfael smiled when he saw the situation and dismounted, letting his gelding's reins hang slack. His horse would not wander off. "Aye, wha' do ye want me to do?"

"Take either Henrik or Fiona while I get down. I donnae want them to awaken."

"Right, how shall I do this?" Cynfael asked more of himself than Angus.

"Take Henrik first. I can hold Fiona meanwhile and then give her to ye. Place them on the ground, unless ye ken of a better place, and I will join them as soon as my horse is picketed."

Cynfael nodded, loosening his cloak and laying it down before taking Henrik. The bairn whimpered in his sleep but did not awaken as he was placed on the man's woollen cloak. Then the Cymreig king took in his arms the sleeping Scottish princess and placed her gently beside the bairn, the cloak protecting her from the chill, dewy ground.

Angus slid off his horse, taking the reins of both his and Cynfael's mounts and earning a thanks from the king. He soon returned, explaining, "Malcolm and Merwyn are seeing to them. Llyf is seeing to Gwyn."

"Aye, that is well. Thank ye," Cynfael said. Then, "Soft now, the princess awakens."

Angus looked down and saw Fiona sit up and look around her bewilderedly. He knelt beside her and helped her to her feet, not saying a word. He did not think she was fully awake, but she followed his movements and was soon standing, though she wavered slightly.

Unpinning his cloak, Angus spread the large, woollen garment on the ground beside Cynfael's.

"I can sleep beside him; let Fiona get her rest," Cynfael offered, lying beside his adopted son, his cloak wrapped around them both.

Angus took Fiona gently into his arms again and laid her down on the other side of the bairn.

"Angus, wha' is gang on?" she questioned, her words slurred with sleep.

"We are camping fer the night. Jist gae to sleep; donnae worry. I will be right beside ye." He spread out the edge of his cloak and lay next to her, listening to the rest of the camp quietly retire for the night. Scraps of conversation lingered in the damp air, but they were soon silenced as all but the guards slept. Cynfael's even breathing with Henrik's quicker breaths could be heard near them, some space away from the princess.

Fiona's warmth of her nearness to him thrust back the cool of evening. Angus turned so he faced her as she slept, his free hand resting on his dirk. If anyone should threaten her, he would see she was protected. He had always been a light sleeper; he would awaken if anyone came near.

He felt someone lie down beside him, but he did not open his weary eyes to see who it was; the rhythm of movement as they settled down to sleep told him it was his brother.

Angus had overheard the words of the messenger, and between that and his father's response, only dread filled his heart concerning the dawn. He remembered feeling this way before in the last war, but they had triumphed and survived then. Surely...surely all this was not for naught? They had a greater chance than ever before; why would it all come to nothing?

He thought of Dafydd, the closest thing to a friend he had had besides Fiona since Sioned had died. He thought of Malcolm's friend, Merwyn. He thought of their allies and all the hosts of the clan. He thought of Rhiada and Duncan and Sioned and all those who had died before. He refused to believe those lives had been in vain.

It seemed a strange thing, to laugh in the face of despair now. But perhaps that was all they could do. And here, lying beside the lass he loved, if only to provide warmth against this chill spring night and so that she was not alone, this was how he helped hold the flame of courage when everything around them seemed bent on snuffing it out.

The sun burned a harsh red.

Grey clouds were swiftly driven away by windless light, and the thick shrouds of fog lying across the ground quickly melted.

Fiona did not want to wake up, but she forced her eyes open and turned her head, taking in the world around her. She saw Cynfael, his face turned towards his child as they slept. Glancing to her other side, she saw Angus lying on his stomach, his head turned away, but his arm was wrapped protectively around her. Next to him was Malcolm, who was beginning to awaken.

Reaching down, she took Angus' arm off her gently so he would not wake. She sat up and ran her fingers through her tangled hair, separating the snarled strands. Not that it mattered, but if they were to reclaim Caerloch today, she wanted to look at least somewhat like a queen returning to claim her own.

At the movement, Angus stirred and raised his face, blinking rapidly and sitting up. "Did ye sleep well?" he mumbled.

"Well enough." She shrugged before continuing, "I am sorry; I didnae mean to wake ye."

"Nae harm done," he replied, shutting his eyes tight for a moment. "'Tis rare I can sleep without something awakening me, nae matter how small."

"I sometimes wish I was back at Caerdun and could sleep all morning," she said by way of an apology.

He smiled. "I do as well." He looked out over the field of men rising to meet the sun. "A red horizon." He spoke softly. "A storm will come ere nightfall."

"Was there news delivered or a decision reached last night?" she asked, her voice level. Emotionless. "I fell asleep, so I missed it."

Angus glanced back at her, his eyes dark. "Aye, news was given. I am sure Donald will speak of it later to the full host. I donnae want to think of it now."

"Is it tha' bad?" Her voice was little more than a whisper.

He leaned forward and kissed her forehead gently. "'Tis grim hearing. But I promise ye, I willnae abandon ye nor Scotland, whatever is decided. I only pray we willnae be among the dead."

Chieftain McCladden returned as the sun rose from the sky with two of the scouts, his face grave. But none approached him, not even his father-in-law, Bryce, and mutual silence filled the space normally taken by conversation. It seemed as if everyone knew—or guessed at—what doom was soon to befall them, even though nothing had been announced.

After a meagre breakfast, of which most ate merely for the sake of the thing rather than to stave off the edge of their hunger, Donald McCladden called all of them to assemble before him.

Gathering together around their leader, the warriors and their higher officers stood quietly, waiting for him to speak. Only the morning breeze, whispering across the land, disturbed the near peaceful silence. Overhead, the sun shone warm from a cloudless sky, splashing the valley that spread below with a dazzling emerald. Even the castle of Caerloch and the distant mountains to the north gleamed in the light. But in spite of the brilliant beauty around them, within each of their hearts lingered a dark terror, a fear of the unknown whispering and pounding in their minds, searing any remnant of courage they had left. Donald could feel it within them.

"Men, warriors, sons, princess, ye ken we planned to take Caerloch Castle and hold it while awaiting the arrival of the Danes," Donald began, trying to assuage the swirling feelings in his own soul. "Doubtless ye questioned each within yer hearts the reason for encamping here last night, why there was nae news given, why a messenger returned wi' his dead companion who now lies buried on the other side of this hill. Perhaps ye even guessed the reason." He paused, looking at each man in turn, at the ranks that stretched far back from him. They had a great war host; but against the Danes, if the scouts' reports were right, they were almost nothing.

"Despite these plans and our attempts to force Lord Erland to surrender, we hae failed. He refused our demands and slew our messenger, Tàmhas MacDonald, while under the flag of truce."

An angered murmur rose at this but soon died away.

"But tha' is no' all. They hae abandoned Caerloch, 'tis true, leaving but a remnant of guardsmen behind. Lord Erland fled to the north to meet up wi' the war host summoned by Lady Nuith, and they will undoubtedly reach this place today. Their numbers, while we yet await the true report, are far more than wha' we hae. The Highlanders remain silent, and we are alone."

The hush that filled this pause was so deep Donald could have drowned in it. Even the birds ceased their morning song.

"Yet we cannae flee. The Danes' attacks on villages and towns are devastating, and great is the damage they hae inflicted. If we flee, they will only push south into the Lowlands, wreaking their destruction there. If we cannae stop them now, then we will never do so again. We hae nae choice but to fight them. We hae nae advantages by which we could possibly hope to win, save perhaps take the castle, but time is short.

"Some might say our cause is lost; some hae already thought it, but it seems to be more true now than it ever was before. We are beyond help." A lump rose in his throat and he forced it down; for once in his life, the desperateness of the situation threatened to overwhelm him. He could not break—not here, not now, not before his men who looked to him for courage.

Despite the brightness of the day, the future was darker than moonless night. Those not executed would no doubt face enslavement, perhaps taken to other Danish kingdoms and made thralls, the Cymry forced to endure the same as their allies. Scotland would certainly be divided among the Danish nobles, the clans eradicated, driven from the lands they had held since before there ever was a king. And Erland...Erland would surely take the throne with Henrik as heir. The Scotland that the Scots had known and loved would be no more.

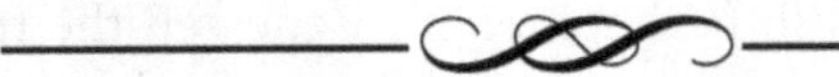

Fiona watched Donald as she held Henrik in her arms, his little hands playing with her curled locks of hair. She watched the leader of the Lowlands seemingly struggle internally. Despair washed over her again, and she glanced beside her as Angus slid his arms across her shoulders, drawing her close. His words came to her, the ones he had spoken before their last battle. *"Good always triumphs o'er evil in the end."*

Memories nearly forgotten came flooding back, and she heard Angus from two years ago: *"The sun will one day rise again fer Scotland, the summer will come again, fer such is the rightful way of things...maybe nae in our time, but it will come."*

And from a further distance, Rhiada's beloved voice: *"Life is full of battles, Fiona; ye cannae escape them. Ye can only prepare to fight them..."*

Tears smarted in her eyes. Who would have thought, after all this time, it would only come to this in the end. Did defeat have purpose? Was there a chance—somehow—for victory? Was it truly too late?

Donald cleared his throat, startling her back to reality. "'Tis the darkest hours of our history tha' remain the brightest, shining amidst a bleak and bitter reality: moments of bravery, and courage, and honour.... Perhaps future Scots will look back and remember this day, the day we didnae fail when freedom called.

"But 'tis more than Scots among us now. We are bound to this cause, body and soul, because it is our fight, our lives, our loyalty, our freedom, our honour, our country, our princess tha' hang in the balance. We hae nae choice but to fight fer her and all she stands fer, or else be shamed as cowards. But we hae allies to whom such a binding doesnae exist, no' in the same way. And it is to them I speak now.

"I donnae ask ye to fight this surely final battle wi' us. I willnae hold it against ye if ye choose to withdraw yer forces. Ye hae proved yerselves faithful and honourable to this cause, and I cannae in good conscience ask ye to stay and die in a land no' yer own, fer a crown and princess no' yer own. Whether ye gae out today is a choice ye hae to make, each man fer himself. If ye fight wi' me, glad I shall be of yer company. If ye choose no' to, I wish ye well on the road ye will travel. I willnae hold it against ye. But I would hae ye ken, all the same, that I would be honoured to die among yer company, those who would choose to stay and fight, even in the face of certain defeat."

The wind answered him, each man thinking for himself, though the choice had been made long ago.

Fiona did not dare to look around her, did not want to remember another man's shame. But though everything yet seemed against them, a remnant of hope burned in her chest. Evil would not triumph forever.

She glanced at Malcolm beside her and he, meeting her gaze with understanding in his eyes, reached out and took Henrik. Then she stepped forward, Donald catching sight of her and stepping back, gesturing for her to speak.

Heart hammering in her throat at the sudden rush of nerves, she opened her mouth. She did not know what to say—nothing that had not already been said in some form—but she knew she should encourage those gathered to fight in her name. Even if it terrified her.

If she did not speak now, she might never get the chance again.

"I am no' a chieftain nor an experienced leader of men," she began, her voice far too soft. At the edges of her vision, she could see some men leaning closer as if to hear her better. "I hae nae skill in speech-making, no' like some," she said, her words growing in volume. "I hae fought among some of ye in the last war, when we faced defeat and yet emerged alive—if scathed. I remember the desperation then, jist as we face now, though the odds were no' quite so stacked against us." She turned to look at those around her, seeing an expectant look on their faces. "I remember the fear my brother, Douglas McCurragh"—she nearly choked on the name—"tried to protect me from when the Danes first landed on our shores. He spoke of Scotland having once been a fighting brotherhood, and how he thought perhaps tha' such days were over. Ye stand here now as proof—Scotland is no' wholly lost. I may be the Highland's princess, but I ken now tha' the Lowlanders, though small in number, hae forged and reforged themselves, again and again, into a sword-bound company tha' ever strikes at the enemy. We hae emerged from the shadows into the daylight, battered and bruised but *alive*—nae matter how many times the Danes push us back.

"My brother never came back home." She broke off, catching sight of Angus—who had stepped around to better see her—and she could not mistake the tears in his eyes. "But I think he would be proud to ken tha' Scotland has no' abandoned her own in their darkest hour." Fiona spoke more quickly now, her voice rising as emotion threatened to win out. "Ye hae ne'er deserted me, nor the cause to free this land at the cost of yer own lives. Whatever is decided here on these fields, before the place tha' was once a home and later a prison to me, I shall no' forget. If ye choose to depart now, I willnae blame ye; I struggle wi' courage also. But if ye stay, I shall hae been glad to ken ye, even if our time together was so brief. If...if we gae down once more into the dusk, the sunset we shall leave behind will be one to remember through the long dark, even if in terror by our enemies. Ye shall no' be forgotten; yer names and deeds shall be honoured as long as the Scots draw breath."

The quiet following her words nearly smothered her. Her face burning, she returned to where she had stood before, taking Henrik back from Malcolm. Perhaps she had said too much, perhaps she had not said enough, but there was little she could do about it now. She saw Angus take his place beside her again, but she did not look up to meet his face.

"Donald McCladden, Princess Fiona." King Cynfael's voice broke the silence. "Some weeks ago, we swore an oath—an unbreakable oath—that we would fight and hold fast together until the end, even if that end meant death. Today, in the face of danger, that oath still holds. We are all afraid of that host out there, marching down upon our ears. But we cannae abandon each other now. We hae waited too long and suffered too much to simply flee. We came kenning the cost. Now that cost must be paid. If we all die today, if we all perish beneath the Danish axe, then let us bring down wi' us such a crimson harvest that our lands will be safe fer many years until another generation rises up to defeat them where we could no.'"

Several cries of agreement rose up at his words, Bryce's voice clearest among the rest. Donald only looked at Cynfael with what looked like tears in his eyes.

Fiona's throat tightened as she glanced up at him, reminded suddenly of Rhiada, reminded so vividly that her eyes stung with unshed tears. She looked down at her hand, at the healing cut that still ached when the weather was damp. She remembered the glass sword, shining beneath the moon, the oath spoken from a thousand voices ringing as one, and she swallowed—with difficulty—the emotion that threatened to break from her.

It had not been in vain. She refused to believe it!

The king continued, "We all hae songs and legends that the harpers sing beside the winter fires, stories of courage, of heroes fighting in the face of utter defeat. Sometimes they are destroyed; sometimes help comes from an unseen source and saves them. Whatever the ending, they live on through song. 'Tis only the cowards and the weak that are forgotten. Should we all fall today, at least those we love will ken that we didnae shrink away from wha' was right, nae matter the cost. Ye say we hae a choice; that choice has already been made. It was made that night we swore the oath. Ye say ye will gae out regardless of if we follow. But I say this: we will be close behind ye. That oath bound us into a fighting brotherhood, and we cannae forget that now. We will fight wi' ye until the end."

If he said anything more, it was lost in the shouts and cheers that followed. And the warriors did not look just at the king, but also at their princess. She heard her name exclaimed with joy and feeling, as if her name alone had *worth*—something worth dying for—not just her, but her country and freedom for her people.

A sob escaped Fiona's lips, but it was that of joy, though perhaps sorrow edged it still.

A few moments later, Donald raised his hand, and gradually they were silenced. "So be it. I will be glad of yer company. But come, we donnae hae much time. Prepare fer battle, and let the leaders of yer bands and companies gather together as we plan this one last attack. Let us bring down wi' us such a great number tha' our dying will no' be in vain!"

"Death before disloyalty!" Eachann cried, recalling the oath sworn long ago that yet bound them.

The reply echoed from the sky to the earth, and Fiona trembled at the sound of it.

"Death before dishonour!"

~ 26 ~
THERE WAS A DREAM

DONALD McCladden gathered the chieftains, king, and princess together for one last war council. Behind them, men robed themselves for battle, the chime of mail, saddling of horses, and last testing of weapons filling the air. Birds twittered their morning song beneath the rising sun that bathed the land in a golden glow, and not a cloud filled the sky. A perfect morning to end all things, and Fiona could not help but feel peace as well as grief at the thought of what was to come.

"So wha' is the plan?" Bryce MacClydno asked as he tightened his sword belt, his face grim and eager. "Shall we try to take the castle?"

"I say aye," Eachann McDonald murmured. "Before, I thought it was a waste of strength, but we could hold out fer some time from within the walls. And should they seek to sweep past us into the Lowlands, we would hae the advantage of attacking them from their rearguard."

Alastair McThraedan nodded. "I second Eachann's words. We donnae ken when the Danes will arrive, but anything to help us is worth it. Especially if they should gain it and hold up against us, picking us off one by one."

"Then so it shall be," Donald replied. "Alastair, prepare a band of horsemen to see tha' we are no' attacked from the village. Bryce, set yer heaviest fighters to demand entrance. They yet hold the drawbridge, but we can retake it. I scouted their defences last night, and they donnae seem willing to fight fer it."

Hamish McLairdun cleared his throat. "Strange, tha'. Why should they no' fight fer it? Methinks 'tis another trap."

Cynfael shook his head. "Nae, I donnae believe so. Why bother holding the castle when the enemy should soon be overrun anyway? 'Tis only a matter of hours."

Bryce grunted his agreement.

"Meanwhile," Donald said, looking at Fiona and Angus beside her, a sad fondness in his eyes, "wha' shall we do about the princess and Henrik?"

"They cannae stay," Eachann and Alastair replied in unison.

"I willnae decide fer Fiona's sake," Cynfael added. "She has been wi' us this long of her own accord, and I willnae force her to leave us now. But Henrik—Henrik must no' stay. If we lose the field today and the Danes retake him, they will still hae claim to the throne, and all this"—he gestured to the peaceful plain before them, soon to become the resting place of the fearless and honourable—"will hae been fer nothing. We agreed no' to kill him in cold blood, and that decision still stands. I say we send him to An Dùn wi' an escort. We must keep him out of Danish hands, even if it should mean he loses his life. 'Tis a cruel thing, I ken, but we cannae risk it. No' after this."

Fiona said nothing, her chest tight at his words. He spoke the truth, there was no doubt about it, but it still chilled her to her bones at the thought. At least...at least he was not forbidding her from staying. She still had a choice. And regardless of what the chieftains said, regardless that she knew she should go, she wanted to stay. She had not come all this way, suffered imprisonment and more than one close brush with death, only to leave when everything might be lost beyond recall.

"I agree," Donald said. "Any objections?"

The High Chieftains shook their heads.

"Then it is settled. Choose men among yer own to guard him, one from each chiefdom. I would ask one of my sons, but I willnae force any man to gae who has set his heart on staying and fighting this last time. Choose, and donnae delay. He must be gang ere we join in battle. If there is nothing more to say, ye may gae."

"Death before disloyalty," Bryce said solemnly, looking at Fiona and bowing at the waist.

The others followed, repeating the oath. "Death before dishonour."

And then they dispersed.

"Give him to me, at least fer awhile. I will see that he is properly sent off," Cynfael said to Fiona, holding out his arms to Henrik, whom she still held. "I think," he added softly, stepping closer and looking at Angus, who remained silent beside her, "ye hae some goodbyes of yer own to attend to."

She surrendered the child without a word, and then followed Angus as he made his way to Branwen and began arming for battle. Her eyes traced his slender—if calloused—hands, still more like a harper's than a swordsman's, even as something grim slithered through her veins like ice. He buckled his belt and sheathed his blade. She likewise reached for her sword, but Angus grabbed her wrist gently, meeting her gaze with a stubborn, cerulean fire burning in his eyes.

"Please, Fiona. I cannae command ye as my princess whether to stay or no', but I...I would hae ye return to An Dùn."

The apprehension within her suddenly knotted itself into anger. "Angus, our men—my men—will be out there fighting fer our freedom, giving their lives fer a cause tha' they believe in. There is little hope they will win, but they hold fast to the cause even in the face of death. Ye will fight wi' them, among them, even wi' yer injured hand. Why can I no' do the same? If all this is lost, then there is nae hope left—there will be nae reason fer me to keep on fighting without them, without ye." The last word came out in a whisper, the fire gone out of her words.

He did not answer at once, only pulling her into an embrace, holding her close, his breath shuddering in her ear. "There was a dream once tha' was Scotland, Fiona. A dream we feared to ever whisper or record wi' a pen lest it remain forgotten in the dark." His arms tightened around her. "Ye were the spark tha' caused tha' dream to flame into life. And every attempt made by the Danes to snuff it out only made it burn brighter. But maybe...maybe this new arisen fury of stormwind—this deluge—will wash it away. It will certainly try to, but we must no' let the light gae out. It must keep burning, even if there is nae one left to see it. Because the day will come"—his shoulders hitched with a sudden sob, and Fiona buried her face in his shoulder, tears running down her face—"the day will come when those tha' are left of us will try again. Because we hae to keep trying. We must no' let the darkness triumph in the end. And we need ye to help us brave the dark when nothing else is left."

She lifted her face, those around her blurred by tears. "But wha' if I cannae see the light? I hae been alone fer so long; if all of ye are dead and I am left in the end, how can I keep fighting?"

"Because ye must, my queen. Because there is nae one else who can." He released her, looking at her with tears brimming in his blue eyes.

She looked down, deepest sorrow overwhelming anything else.

He lifted up her chin with his finger, meeting her gaze, his lips trembling with emotion as he continued, "Promise me, Fiona, promise me tha' whatever happens on the field today, tha' ye willnae let tha' flame burn out. Promise me ye willnae let tha' dream die."

She searched his face, trying to memorise his features. If this was truly the last time she would gaze upon him, seeing the sadness and the bitter fear in his eyes, she accepted her fate. "I promise," she whispered. "I will gae"—grief nearly stole her breath—"and I will do my best to keep tha' vision alive." She bit her lip, unable to say more. Finality swept over her, leaving her heart broken in its wake.

"And so do I promise to never let it die, even should it cost me my life," he responded just as softly, letting her go.

Without a word, she helped him slip on his leather jerkin, tying it, and then the fine coat of mail. She helped him bind the leather bracers around his wrists, sniffling and dashing out of her eyes the tears that still fell.

If this was the last time she would see him—oh, how her heart ached at the thought—she would see him made ready for battle like any hero of old.

She stood back as he buckled his sword tightly around his waist and set his shield on the ground beside him. Then he looked up at her, his jaw clenching. "I must gae," he forced out, his voice barely audible.

"I ken," she said, her voice strangely light. As he stood there, glimmering like a warrior of legend in the morning light, she felt nothing but pride. If he was to die today, if they all were, she was glad to have known him, to have loved him, even if it had all come to nothing in the end. Tears formed in her eyes once again in spite of her smile, and her chest throbbed. She threw her arms around Angus, clinging tightly to him while silent cries shook her frame.

He held her close, and she felt his every quivering breath as he fought in vain to keep back the tears that had dried. "Fiona McCurragh, I love ye."

"Och, Angus, I love ye!" Her fingers gripped the loose folds in his plaid, and she rested her head on his shoulder as if she would never let go.

It seemed forever that they stood so, and yet not long enough. "I must no' keep them waiting," he said, releasing her. He swallowed, still meeting her gaze, asking a wordless question.

She leaned into him, and he kissed her. Not with the joyous passion of the first time, but with the bittersweetness of longing and regret for the time lost that could never be regained. A cruel thing, that the love they had would never blossom to fruition.

War ended more than lives. It ended hopes and dreams and futures.

At last, he pulled back.

"I release ye from being my guard," she said, her voice hoarse and whisper-soft. "Fight fer me instead. And if ye must die, do it well."

He bowed to her, taking her hands and kissing them with his lips and with his tears. And then he turned and followed the others heading out. He did not look back.

But Fiona watched him go, streams coursing their helpless way down her cheeks.

Farewell.

Heart of my heart, farewell.

"Did ye say goodbye?" Malcolm asked his brother softly as they walked forwards, Angus having given his horse to an officer who had lost his in the previous battle. He could not hold Branwen's reins and wield a sword, not with his injured hand.

"Aye, I did." He kept his eyes on the ground. "But I wish 'tis no' forever." Within his heart, though, he was nearly defeated by despair.

"As do we all. Yet 'tis a good chance this is our last goodbye." Malcolm, ever the cheerful one, spoke with joyless voice, and the light that usually danced in his grey eyes was gone.

Angus glanced up at him, wondering if he was thinking of Duncan. "I ken tha'," he replied, "but I still hate it all the same. I feel as if I hae wasted so much time, and now the brief time we did hae is gang forever." His voice cracked at the edges, and it took all his self-control not to break completely. "Did ye say farewell?"

Malcolm shook his head. "I tried. I tried to bring myself to do it, but I cannae. If I do, 'tis like I hae given up on us coming back. And I cannae fight wi' tha' thought burning in the back of my head."

Angus looked at his brother, suddenly reaching out and embracing him as he never had when they were children; now might be the last time, and Malcolm was nearly as tall as himself. Malcolm let out a choked sound, and Angus squeezed him tighter, saying nothing. There was nothing to say, not anymore. Words were meaningless now.

Ahead of them lay the battleground and the uncertain future. Behind them, all that they loved.

Fiona turned away from the departing host, heading back to the small group of men in the saddle, one of them holding Henrik. There was yet a horse kept for her, Cynfael holding the reins.

"I thought Angus would tell ye to gae," he murmured as she approached, no doubt taking in her tear-stained face and swollen eyes.

"Aye. And I ken he's right. Yet it doesnae make it any easier." She hesitated, not yet swinging into the saddle. "So," she said, looking at the green earth beneath their feet, still speaking softly so that the others would not hear. "It comes to this, in the end."

"Who says it is the end?" Cynfael replied, and she glanced up and saw in his face the look of a man who had not yet surrendered to despair.

Fiona struggled to keep her voice level. "Yer father told me...as he lay dying..."—she took a heaving breath—"tha' one day we would win. And he said tha' a dying man's words speak truth."

"My father never lied. Perhaps he saw a glimpse of wha' would come, of wha' we yet cannae see. Donnae surrender, Fiona. This war is no' finished yet." He held out his hand to help her into the saddle and she took it, suddenly throwing her arms around him.

"I am sorry yer people might no' see their king again."

He said nothing at first, only embracing her back. Then he whispered into her ear, "If ye get back to An Dùn, tell Elspeth McBride... tell her I am sorry I didnae get to speak to her after all."

Fiona pulled back suddenly, searching his face, light dawning upon her. "Ye mean..."

A ghost of a smile played on his lips. "I had hoped...if this war was ever over...if she would hae me... Perhaps she wouldnae hae to be lonely forever."

Fiona remembered then a conversation spoken what seemed like ages ago. *Och, Elspeth, must ye come to grief once more?* But she only nodded, looking away as her eyes began smarting again. "Aye, I will tell her tha." She gave him one last glance, kissing his cheek before swinging into the saddle and taking the reins into her hands.

"Ride hard and donnae look back," Cynfael called.

They rode off south as the sun rose ever higher in the sky.

And Fiona McCurragh did not look back.

The Scots waited on the outskirts of the village outside Caerloch, waiting for news that the drawbridge and gates had been secured while Bryce and Eachann's men battled for it. It was the pettiest of skirmishes as those things went, the guardsmen upon the walls having little desire to fight, but the Scots would give them no peace.

Then a couple of the scouts returned from the north, dismounting and talking hurriedly to Donald, soon joined by another riding in from the northwest.

Angus could not hear what they said, for what little wind there was that day blew the words away from them, but whatever it was had those at the front quite animated. Cynfael nearly threw his hands into the air before he remembered that Gwyn was still perched on his wrist. Angus saw him lift and then pull down very quickly, no doubt realising such a thing usually signalled for Gwyn to take flight.

He turned away, swallowing hard against the sour taste in his throat, nearly choking him when he thought of what lay before them. Of Fiona now riding south to his mother and to what safety remained this day, though it surely would not last long. He glanced up at the castle and the enemy soon to be upon them, pushing away the memory of Fiona. He could not think of her now, not when he needed his head to be ruling him instead of his heart. He must concentrate on survival, even if they perished. They were beyond hope. The familiar feeling of fear rose within him, and his grip on the pommel of his sword became slick with cold sweat.

"If anything happens," he murmured to Dafydd beside him, "will ye—"

"Aye," his friend replied, knowing what he was to say. "I will take care of her. But best ye keep yerself alive. I ken how danger seeks after ye, yet ye are much better suited fer her than me."

Angus only answered with a faint smile.

"Wha' are we waiting fer?" Dafydd whispered beside him after several more moments had passed.

"Whoever shall break through the gates. Or perhaps whatever news the scouts hae brought. Nae doubt word of the Danes' arrival, and all this retaking of Caerloch will be fer nothing."

Angus felt a nudge. "Nae, nae, I donnae think 'tis bad news," Dafydd said.

His brows creased as he looked up to see what was going on, for indeed something was happening. Resounding cheers hailed from the front, though his view of the castle was limited, and the cries echoed down the line, though scarcely anyone knew what they were cheering at this far back.

"Wha'..." Angus began, but no one could answer.

A moment later, Donald rode down the line, crying out the news followed by commands to separate in bands by leaders and follow their orders.

His words had scarcely landed on Angus' ears before he covered his mouth with his hand, tears suddenly springing to his eyes.

No, no one was ever truly beyond hope.

"Wha' did he say? 'Twas so fast I couldnae follow it," Dafydd asked, turning to him and nearly shaking him.

Angus turned to Dafydd, a grin on his face, though tears rolled freely down his cheeks. "The Highland chiefs hae finally come. They're joining forces wi' us. Father wants us to get into position, head around the castle, and attack the Danes as directed. We hae a chance!"

With hope burning brighter than the sun in the heavens, they swiftly formed into companies and marched nearly at a run outside the village and around the castle's moat. Light-hearted and over-joyed, they headed towards the Highlanders. Their kilts rippled in the breeze, yet the distant glimmer of mail to the north signified the arriving Danes.

"Sir, the Scots are in sight," Asbjørn said as the land spread before them, a vast green plain with Caerloch Castle in the distance. Even from here, they could see the Scots getting into position, seeming quite an army from this distance, though Erland knew of a certainty they had nearly twice their numbers.

"Get the men into position," Erland said. "And send out that escort of horsemen to the south. I doubt they are fools enough to keep that princess and my son out in front. They must be at their camp or hidden away somewhere. Find them, take my son, and slay the Scottish brat."

"Aye sir, it shall be done."

There was no time to think. The din of battle crashed into Angus' ears and drowned out all but the constant whisper in his mind to survive, to somehow make it through to the other side. He fought with a ferocity that he had seldom felt before.

"Angus!"

Angus whirled around and blocked a sword thrust from a Dane before plunging his own blade into the man's exposed neck. The man toppled to the ground, and Angus nodded at Dafydd.

"Keep yerself alive, ye maniac." Dafydd laughed before turning to the next threat.

"Aye, yerself!" Angus called back, glad to know, even for a brief moment, that his friend was with him. To death or to long glory, to fight alongside his sword-brother was a sweet thing.

They might live to see the storm's ending after all.

Fiona reined in her horse as the escort crested the hill, leading them to the glen where the army had encamped only a day before. The warm sun shone upon her hair, and sweat beaded on her brow as her horse halted. She spurred it on, entering the glen at a trot as they all came to a rest by the stream, allowing their mounts to stop and drink.

She looked around her, seeing the familiar hills, trees, and streambed where she had fought years before, practising with only the memory of her brother to guide her. Meeting Angus here for the first time, speaking of war and her escape from Caerloch. Meeting Angus there again two years later. The misunderstanding and awkwardness that befell their friendship. Then Angus leading her back after her second escape from Caerloch, where they had stayed for a few days before marching on the castle itself.

Her breath caught in her throat as she wondered once again how it had come to this. Panic seized in her chest and she glanced behind her at the way they had come, at the sun sliding westward past noon. She thought of the leagues they had yet to ride. She thought of entering An Dùn as the sun set, not being able to tell Annag whether her husband and sons were alive, telling Elspeth of Cynfael's words, and then waiting in agony to learn whether it had been all in vain or not.

And she could not bear the thought.

She turned her horse slightly and cleared her throat. She looked at the horsemen, the fivesome, one of whom carried Henrik, and met the eyes of them all.

"Continue on without me. Ride to An Dùn; see tha' Henrik is kept safe. I cannae gae wi' ye any further."

One of them opened his mouth to speak, his brows furrowed. "And wha' will I tell Annag McCladden?"

"Tell her all tha' has happened. She will understand."

The man worked his jaw, seeming unconvinced. "As ye wish, yer highness. But I would hae one of us ride back wi' ye, so tha' we may no' be accused of abandoning ye."

Fiona nodded. "Aye, tha' is well. But the rest of ye must ride on."

The man bowed his head. Then he cried to his company and they rode off south, soon becoming a distant speck on the horizon and then nothing.

Fiona clicked her tongue and wheeled her horse around, her guard following. She dug her heels into the mare's flanks and sped back the way she had come, northward bound, to where her heart and the future of Scotland lay.

Cynfael had told her not to look back, but she found she could not keep herself from doing so. Looking back was all she could do.

It seemed an eternity before Fiona came in sight of the last hill before Caerloch. She rode over it, seeing nothing between her and the village, which appeared from this distance to be deserted. The sun sank further to the west, golden light spilling over the land, and there, glimmering on the battlements, she saw a few men in mail hoisting down the Danish flag, the banner of a crimson raven upon a field of ebony.

"Hae we won?" she asked of no one. She pushed her steed further, her guard following, as she rode around the castle and finally came upon the field of battle.

The plain before her was covered with the bodies of men and horses, most of them dead, and others that still lived and moaned in agony. Yet the clash and clamour of battle could not be heard; either they had passed on that far into the north or it was over.

Bewildered beyond words, Fiona dismounted and quickened her weary pace on foot, ignoring hunger pains from having skipped the noonday meal. She could not pause now, except to turn over the bodies of those who looked familiar, to see if it was a face she knew. The battle had been brutal, the wounds of the dead—and some of the living—sickening her.

Heaps of slain men lay everywhere, the ground drenched with blood. On the outskirts were many of Eachann's men, their crimson and teal plaid stained in death, and warriors who could only be Cynfael's company. Farther in, she recognized the violet and emerald of Jamie McBride's clan, now governed by Hamish, and among them the black armour of the Danes, and others wearing tartans she did not remember ever seeing among the Lowlanders. And torn and bloodied in their midst was the shredded remnants of the banner she and Annag had spent so many months weaving. The emerald dragon was slain, trampled into the ground.

She clenched her eyes shut a moment. Had the Highlands come and fought against them in the end? How then was the Danish flag being torn down from Caerloch castle?

She glanced up, seeing many walking around the field, tending the wounded and counting the dead. She assumed they were Scots and Cymru, for Danes did not wear armour nor tartan like that. In the far distance, she saw armoured men running for their lives. And there, upon the battlements of Caerloch, rose a banner with a blue field and silver cross, the symbol of an ancient hero once beloved by the Highlanders and Lowlanders alike—a flag she never thought to see fly upon those walls again.

We hae won? Her breath caught in her throat. Surely she was dreaming! They had been so greatly outnumbered!

She took a few more steps into the open and one of those standing nearby ran to her.

"Fiona! We hae won! The Highland chiefs hae joined our side; they're busy chasing the Danes away wi' Bryce and Eachann!" The words spilled out of Malcolm's mouth like a sudden flood in the mountains. He embraced her tightly, swinging her off the ground.

Stunned, she could only stare at him as he pulled back. The Highlanders! Her people—her clans had finally answered the call! After so many years of separation, the clans of Scotland had finally united under one banner to defeat the Danes once and for all.... Could it even be true?

Tears slipped down her face for the second time that day as she fumbled for a response to the news she could hardly dare believe. *Douglas...Rhiada...we did it!* But then a thought came to mind that drove away the joy with the cold finger of fear. "Where's Angus?"

Malcolm's face fell. "I donnae ken. He was in another company wi' Dafydd. I hae no' seen either of them yet since midway in the battle; they were both still alive then. He might be wi' the Highlanders running down the last of the Danes. Father wants to make sure they donnae return and attack us in the night, and the rest of us will follow them in pursuit once we hae rested."

Fiona continued to stare at him as all possible scenarios rushed unbidden to her mind. Without thinking, she pushed past him and stumbled across the bloodied ground. All around her was silence, her pounding heart and harsh breathing the only sound in her mind.

She made her way through the field, searching the face of every dark-haired lad clothed in the McCladden weave lying upon the ground, fighting the terror choking her throat.

She soon reached the centre of the plain where the carnage was the worst. She had seen so many dead faces, but none that she knew and loved. Yet she did not dare to hope, not until she knew with utter certainty that Angus was alive.

Her hands were stained dark with blood and her hair stuck to her face, but she cared not. She was too occupied with overturning bodies, frantically searching faces, many of which were marred beyond recognition. It was a near hopeless task, and the sun began sinking further and further into the west; and still she had not found him nor heard him call out her name.

She stood up, squinting against the sunset, and wavered on her feet. So much cruelty and violence...it was sickening. Her stomach twisted within her.

"Fiona! Hae ye—" Malcolm stopped, the blood rushing from his face.

Fiona glanced at what he was looking at, and her heart leaped into her throat. Running forwards, she fell to her knees besides two bodies, the end of a spear jutting out of one lying atop the other.

"Nae, nae, nae—" The words came in sobs, and her hands shook so badly she could hardly turn the first one over.

Malcolm was beside her the next instant, his face tight as if biting back panic.

It was Dafydd, his hazel eyes glassy and lifeless. Yet unlike so many she had seen that day, there was no fear or regret. Only acceptance, as if it was meant to be this way all along. The spear had passed clean through him, the tip protruding from his chest, his shirt stained with his blood.

Bile rose in her throat, and she choked, trying to swallow it down.

But then she looked at the other lad, the lad that had been beneath him, the lad he had tried to save.

And the world suddenly spun out of sunset into darkness, and all became as still as death.

~ EPILOGUE ~
WHEN THE MOORS FELL SILENT

THE sun shone from a cloudless sky, illuminating every blade of grass and blooming flower with a radiant intensity that nearly dazzled one's eyes. The air was warm and humid, little clouds of miniscule insects hovering in odd places, seemingly suspended above the ground by the heat.

Annag McCladden stood alone, looking northward across the glens outside the gates of An Dùn, shielding her eyes against the bright spring sunshine. In her mind's eye, she sped across the distance to her husband.

But no one was there.

When the morning had dawned a strange red, she knew in her heart that this was the day they had been dreading. She wished she knew what the outcome would be, whether her husband and sons would survive, whether the princess was safe, whether they would all come home again. She longed to be beside them, but as she could not, she kept them close in her thoughts.

She had received Donald's letter only a day or two ago, and its words still burned fresh in her mind. Words speaking of his longing for her, of the happenings of the war. Their despair when Fiona had been captured; their joy when she had been regained. The hope between Donald and herself now realised. That Angus, ever their quiet child who had buried so much pain within him, had found love; that healing for their country did not seem so far off. Donald had spoken of the silence from the Highlanders, the threat of Erland's revenge, his fears of the future and the next battle....

Overhead, the sun reached its noontime peak and began to sink slowly westward, yet still she stayed. Standing for so long did not weary her, for her concerns were not on herself but rather those she loved.

The monotone buzzing of insects was the only sound to be heard, for the wind had died away and no birds sang in the afternoon heat.

Then the earth itself hushed, the humming clouds of gnats silenced. The air grew still, as if holding its breath.

A sudden chill rushed over Annag, and her soul filled with dread.

She turned sharply and picked up her skirts, running back to An Dùn as she had not run in years. She gave no explanation to the guards, who called to her as she hurried through the gates. Annag did not stop until she reached Elspeth in the McCladden croft, flinging the door open and not closing it behind her in her haste.

"Annag, wha' is wrong? Ye look as if ye had seen a ghaist!" Elspeth exclaimed. She rose from her place beside her two children and took Annag's trembling hands in her own.

"I need to gae to my husband and sons."

Elspeth stared at her. "Annag, are ye mad?"

"I ken where they are. I cannae wait fer news."

"Suppose ye get attacked on the way? Suppose the Danes find ye?" Elspeth tried in vain to persuade her.

"'Twill no' matter to me. If my sons and husband are dead, I hae nothing else. Will ye come wi' me?"

"I—" Elspeth looked at her children even as Cynfael's face flooded to memory. "If I can find someone to watch them, I will gae."

Annag smiled grimly. "Can ye leave within the hour?"

Elspeth looked at her as if her eyes were wild and mad. "Aye, I think so. I ken a woman who would be honoured to watch the bairns. It willnae take me long to find her."

Annag said nothing, only embraced Elspeth and kissed her on both cheeks. Then she was gone.

Scarcely an hour later, she and Elspeth rode out of the gates with only the barest provisions and other necessary supplies, riding north. A couple guards accompanied them, but that was all. The leagues flew beneath the horses' hooves as they sped north. But it could not be fast enough to calm Annag's anxieties about what lay in the distance.

Despite her desire to keep her fear contained, tears spilled down her cheeks as dread filled her heart. What would she find when she arrived there?

It seemed that even the ground beneath her feet trembled in apprehension of what might be. As the sun sank towards the west, a distant wailing of wind bent the tall grasses.

The storm had broken across the land.

And the moors were no longer silent.

GLOSSARY

Bannocks - a variety of flat or any large, round article baked or cooked from grain. Also known as oat cakes, barley cakes, etc.

Bairn - child

'Bout - about

Brae - hillside

Burn - stream

Cannae - cannot, can't

Couldnae - couldn't, could not

Cymraeg - Welsh word for the Welsh language

Cymreig - Welsh word for something pertaining to Wales, i.e. Welsh harper

Cymru - Welsh word for Wales

Cymry - Welsh word for the Welsh people

Didnae - did not, didn't

Diolch - Welsh for "thank you"

Donnae - do not, don't

Fer - for

Fy ffrind a brawd - Welsh for "my friend and brother"

Gae - go

Gang - going, gone

Ghaist - ghost

Glen - valley

Hae - have

Isnae - is not, isn't
Jist - just
Ken - know
Kenning - knowing
Kens - knows
Kent - knew
Mae'n ddrwg iawn gen i / mae'n ddrwg gennyf - Welsh for "I'm very sorry" and "I'm sorry"
Mae hi'n merch hyfryd iawn - Welsh for "she is a very lovely lass"
Mae'r tywysoges yr Alban yn brydferth - Welsh for "The princess of Scotland is beautiful"
Mo mhac - Scottish Gàidhlig for "my son"
Nae - no, not
No' - not
Och - oh
Seanair - Scottish Gàidhlig for "grandfather"
Shouldnae - shouldn't, should not
Sut mae'r tywysoges - Welsh for "How is the princess"
Tha' - that
Teulu - Welsh word for "bodyguard"; can also mean family
Urram - honour
Verra weel - very well
Wee - little
Wha' - what
Willnae - won't, will not
Wi' - with
Wouldnae - wouldn't, would not
Ye - you
Yer - your
Ye're - you are, you're
Yerself - yourself
Yerselves - yourselves
Yn gyflym - Welsh for "quickly"

ACKNOWLEDGEMENTS

IT is a well known saying in the writing community that you write initially for yourself. And in a way, that is true. Every story is written as a form of personal creativity, but sometimes it's more. Sometimes it's to fill a void or to explore a concept just as much as it's a process of creation or an artistic endeavour.

But I have noticed that every book I've worked on, while initially created for one of those reasons stated above, always becomes something more. It becomes a lesson (or many lessons) that God uses to teach me, whether about others, myself, or even about Him. *Dìlseachd ~ A Stolen Crown* taught me about loneliness and friendship and the beauty of hope. *Urram ~ Rekindled Hope* taught me about relationships and courage, but most of all, what it means to write with God as well as unto Him. I cannot begin to count the times where I would be stuck during the many rounds of edits on this book, and breakthroughs would only happen *after* spending time praying and inviting God into the process, seeking His wisdom. Because, after all, He is the master storyteller, and each of us are supporting characters in the grand tale that He is penning of all creation.

So, first and foremost, I thank my heavenly Father for His faithfulness in sustaining me through the years it has taken to write and publish these stories. For the memories and experiences He has used to teach me, many of which became the inspiration for scenes in this tale. And above all, for His goodness, mercy, and patience with me in my many shortcomings. Thank you for giving me the pen to tell this story. It is as much Yours as it has been mine.

As I said before, with the previous book, it took an entire clan to publish *Dìlseachd ~ A Stolen Crown*, a clan that has only grown since.

To all who have come after, thank you so much for your encouragement and support. I could not have gotten this far without you all:

To Victoria Smith, a.k.a. Sary, for not just being one of the first to read through these books in their rough draft state, but also for coining "Fiangus" and being one of my biggest supporters from the beginning. Thank you for all your enthusiasm and also your ideas about the book titles. *Princess of the Highlands* would look very different without you.

To Ver and Bri, my loyal duo, for reading this book ages ago on Wattpad.com, and for all your continued encouragement and ideas. Thank you for all the late night chats, moments spent analysing, and for sharing and reading each other's stories. I am so glad to have you both in my life.

To my alpha readers: Grace S., Hannah W., and Ethan W., for all your feedback and catching of typos. Thank you for being champions of this tale even in its rough-hewn form.

To my beta readers: Thane Merrick, Alexus Wiebe, Morgan, Ellie Sivils, Anne Elizabeth, Hannah Yu (now Myers), Amanda Smith, Ella Meyer, and Rachel Rowbottom, for all your wonderful feedback, both critical and encouraging. (Also, for those of you who formed a fan club for Cynfael, I think he'd be both embarrassed and impressed. King Cy for the win!)

To my sweet bunny, Evyn, for his patience with the many hours spent working on edits instead of cuddling his royal fluffiness. I have many fond memories of working on this book with you sprawled nearby, waiting for me to finish and snuggle with you on the floor.

To the Nerdworms and my fellow admins for Write for Life: for being the best co-hosts of numerous writing challenges during which much of this book was edited. Thank you especially to Erin, Kirsten, Katie, Naomi, Hannah, Rachel, and Sarah, for all your support and friendship. I don't understand how I lived life so long without you all!

To Brianna De Man (yes, I must mention you twice) for being the best editor I could ever ask for. There is no one else I would rather trust with my words. Thank you for helping me make my stories what I've always envisioned them to be. Here's to many more!

To my copyeditor, Deborah O'Carroll, for all the fangirling, and also catching all the mistakes that had survived thus far.

To all of you who have read the first book and left such lovely reviews. I often go back and reread them as an encouragement and a reminder as to why I began writing in the first place. Thank you for your kind words: Katja, Jennie, Brooke, Morgan M., Amelia, Chloe, and so, so many others.

To everyone in the Instagram community, for all your endless support and friendship. I especially want to thank Tabby, Nathaniel, Bri, Ver, Penny, Morgan, Arianna, Ruby, among many more.

To my OPC gang, who I met and forged friendships with during 2018 when this first draft was written, and to those of us who came back for our final year in 2021, when I once again began to tackle this story and turn the rough draft into something decent. In memory of those days of church camp and youth rallies, I think J.R.R. Tolkien put it best: "Here free unfaded is the flower of time, that men shall remember through the mist of years, as a golden summer in a grey winter." I have tried to capture a fleeting remnant of those golden days within these pages, since it was your friendships that inspired much of this book. Thank you for being my shining company, even if only for a little while. The road now leads onward, and while we do not know where, the path has been brightened for a time by knowing you all. Thanks for everything.

And lastly, to you dear reader, for coming this far with me on this journey. I hope you are not too upset by the ending. (If you are, remember the postscript in the author's note). At any rate, I hope that the next book will more than make up for it.

To everyone who has been a part of this tale, whether friend or stranger, thank you for giving my stories a chance.

Soli Deo Gloria!

THIS STORY WILL BE
CONTINUED IN

BOOK 3

OF THE

PRINCESS OF THE HIGHLANDS
TRILOGY

about the author

Cheyenne van Langevelde is a young author and musician whose greatest passion is weaving tales through story and song. When not struggling to attempt the most metaphorical prose, she enjoys composing and recording soundtrack pieces for books, practicing calligraphy and Irish dance, and studying the Welsh language. She occasionally emerges into the real world to restock her chocolate supply, of which she hoards like a dragon would his gold.

You can follow her on her website and social sites listed below:

Website: https://www.thedancingbardess.com
Instagram: @thedancingbardess
Twitter: @dancing_bardess
Goodreads: Cheyenne van Langevelde

www.ingramcontent.com/pod-product-compliance
Lightning Source LLC
Chambersburg PA
CBHW051437190726
48289CB00001B/221